the pretender

saving luke

by

Steven Long Mitchell
&
Craig W Van Sickle

TELEMACHUS PRESS

Cover design by Brightspark
https://thebampotpress.wordpress.com

Published by Telemachus Press, LLC
http://www.telemachuspress.com

Visit the author website:
http://www.thepretenderlives.com

ISBN: 978-1-940745-91-6 (eBook)
ISBN: 978-1-940745-92-3 (paperback)

Version 2015.10.15

Printed in the United States of America

10 9 8 7 6 5 4 3 2 1

Table of Contents

Personal Message
From
Mitchell & Van Sickle

We love The Pretender and it's our life's passion to continue Jarod's story for all of the faithful fans and for the new ones just joining in.

We write for thinkers, creators, innovators and the curious who love to unravel a tale and enjoy the odd and unexpected, people who, like Jarod, know that 'life is a gift.'

If you are reading this, you are one of them—one of us—and we are truly thankful you came along to join us.

*Writing for you is an honor and it would be an even bigger honor if you would write to us. If you like what we are doing with **The Pretender** it would mean a lot to us if you'd send a short email to us at centreinsider@thepretenderlives.com to introduce yourself and say hi. We always personally respond to our readers.*

*We'd also love to add you on our mailing list so you can receive notifications about future books, updates, contests and other information about all things **The Pretender**.*

*You can find us at **www.thepretenderlives.com**. We hope you follow this link and say hello so we can personally thank you for your readership and loyalty.*

What readers and fans around the world are saying about
The Pretender—Saving Luke

SAVANNAH MAE for Say What? Savannah Mae (5/14)—*"'The Pretender—Saving Luke' is action packed and a super fast paced page turner that, once again, I was not able to put down ... it is filled with elements of fear, rage, guilt, emotion, lies, deceit, cover-ups and of course the very colorful characters all come together perfectly for an edge-of-your-seat read. 'Saving Luke' has the depth and quality required to make it as a best seller."*

NATHALIE: *Paris, France—"After reading Rebirth, all I wanted was to get my hands on Saving Luke, and let me tell you, I wasn't disappointed. If you loved Rebirth, you'll enjoy Saving Luke just as much ... if not more."*

JACCI: *Sydney, Australia—"Saving Luke is exciting and intriguing right until the very last page. New insights allow for a deeper, richer understanding and connection to the characters. This just keeps getting better."*

ANDRE: *Chicago, Illinois—Damn! Saving Luke is a thriller from start to finish— one of the best books I ever read. Bring on the next one!*

DANI: *Pepperell, Massachusetts—A Pretender fan since the beginning, I was psyched for the novels, which are getting better and better. Reading Saving Luke, I was on the edge of my seat repeatedly, found numerous great Easter eggs aimed at fans of the series, and am falling in love with more than one of the new characters.*

R.M. ESPARZA: *Durango, Mexico: Saving Luke is an intellectual adventure true to the core dynamics of the TV series complete with twists and turns, as well as ANSWERS and new questions that will satisfy old and news fans alike!*

VANIA: *Lisbon, Portugal With fast paced storytelling, Saving Luke tells the extraordinary adventure of Jarod, a genius that will do anything it takes to save a kidnapped little boy. The second Pretender novel is the perfect companion to Rebirth—if you enjoyed reading the first novel, you can't miss the follow up.*

LINDA: *Perth, Western Australia—The Pretender creators are pushing their skills—and Jarod's—to the limit, to bring us amusing, dramatic, thrilling and touching fare on which to feast and savor. Rebirth is a delightful little amuse bouche. Saving Luke is an astonishingly impressive hors d'oeuvre. Bring on the next course!*

MALLORY: *Washington D.C.—Saving Luke is a captivating combination of elements—mystery, suspense, intrigue, and, of course, love—that make the second Pretender novel a true page-turner.*

JACOB: *Dubai, UAE—Saving Luke is ten times as good as Rebirth and I loved Rebirth! The story is thrill ride, the Pretends incredible, the revelations about the characters—especially Miss Parker—are fantastic—and the surprises at the end are worth the entire read. I want more Pretender and I want it now!*

KYLIE: *Omeo, Australia—Saving Luke is a fast paced, thrilling novel that keeps you on the edge of your seat. Combining elements of danger, romance and humor, the next installment in the Pretender series is a must read.*

Dedicated to:

Craig: For Martha, whose love and spirit will always guide me.

Steve: For Lupe, my partner, my friend, my guide, my incredible wife.

A Special Thank You ...

To some very special people whose help with notes, thoughts, proof reading and the editing of Saving Luke was invaluable.

Danielle Littig, Linda Johnson, Jacci Olson, Mallory Johnson, Vania Araújo, Ruthanne Esparza, Mark Dodson, Katie Mitchell and Wendy Van Sickle.

If it weren't for you guys, it would look like we coudnt spel and was kompletely inliterate.

saving luke

Prologue

There are Pretenders among us,
geniuses with the ability to
become anyone they want to be.
In 1983, a corporation known as the Centre
isolated a young Pretender named Jarod
and exploited his genius for their research.
Then, one day, their Pretender ran away ...

Chapter 1

JAROD WASN'T SURE how old he was.

For the near decade he'd lived in captivity, he had kept count of the days and by his calculations thought he was roughly thirteen.

All that time his living space had been a sterile, Plexiglas dome biochamber. Located in the middle of the cavernous, warehouse sized, concrete walled room, the dome glowed like an island in a sea of black and was reminiscent of a zoo exhibit—with one disturbing distinction: the dome was surrounded by surveillance cameras recording everything that happened within.

Everything.

As the cameras constantly swept the dome, their glowing red lights indicated they were on and watching.

They were always on.

They were always watching.

For each of the 3,587 days he'd lived in the Centre, Jarod watched the camera's *red eyes,* as he thought of them, watching him. After years of calculating their exact angles and timing of their sweeps, he had found blind spots where he could not be seen, that he could escape into and relish precious moments of privacy.

To anyone monitoring the images on this night, it appeared Jarod was the lump asleep in bed, but the young Pretender was not asleep. Nor was he the lump.

While executing a germ-warfare simulation days earlier, Jarod had secretly pocketed two dozen latex gloves. Tonight he inflated and arranged them beneath his blanket to resemble the human form, then slipped unseen into one of his areas of refuge.

Many times Jarod hid under his bed and on those occasions, he'd press his face to the floor's air grate. Eyes closed, concentration intense, he'd focus on the sounds that echoed through the vent and imagine the world it connected to. The world beyond. The world he longed to explore for real. The one he was only allowed to experience through the simulation experiments his masters forced him to do.

The world *out there*.

From an early age, Jarod would make up stories to accompany both the laughter and turmoil from far off corners of the Centre—people enjoying their lives and more often, those who were not. Distant shrieks of anguish from the numerous incarceration areas, desperate pleas from the T-Board sector and even disembodied moans Jarod imagined to be spirits haunting the place. Clearly, both joy and agony were components of the life *out there*.

Yet, it wasn't through his sense of sound that Jarod found his greatest escape. It was smell. In the warm updrafts, he detected an array of scents: spices he dreamt of tasting, colognes and perfumes, the musky tang of test chimpanzees quarantined on Sub-Level 17. In springtime, he noted the hint of something that made him sneeze but he didn't mind. He liked the thought that it was pollen from flowers and trees living free *out there*.

But Jarod didn't have time to daydream about that now. Tonight, he was on a *mission*.

Jarod maneuvered under the bed and looked up at the observation window on the outer room's concrete wall. The window, made of a two-way glass, was slightly open, as it often was. It meant Sydney was still in his office, but unlike Jarod, he wasn't awake. He was snoring lightly in his recliner, listening to the same Spanish song he always fell asleep to, on the nights he could sleep. *Piel Canela* was a stirring melody about the connective power of true love and the nickname Sydney had given the love of his life on the day they first met.

When Sydney had locked Jarod in for the evening, the young man had caught sight of the Benrus wristwatch Sydney's father had bought during the war and given to his son on his deathbed. That was at 11:34. Jarod calculated it was now 1:17.

One minute left to determine if his plan was a go. One minute left to reflect on having spent over three-quarters of his life inside this chamber. Sixty seconds to anxiously contemplate his strategy and what it would cost him if it failed.

Jarod slipped his shirt off and his gaze fell upon a hook-shaped scar on his chest. He had others on his young body, including the large one, mid-back, he got in a near-death fall during a botched Sim when he thought he was about nine. Yet it was the one on his chest that made him wonder. Though still a mystery, it was the only scar that caused him pain—more mental than physical. As he touched it and wondered how it ended up above his heart, the world changed.

Shuuummmmm!

The lights suddenly died in his bio-chamber, the lab, and in Sydney's office. Air stopped blowing from the vent. All power in the Centre had stopped.

As had Jarod's heart. His breath caught in his chest as he was plunged into perfect stillness. Even the piercing red eyes of the cameras could no longer *see*.

That's what he'd been waiting for. It was a signal from his accomplice.

It was time for Jarod to escape.

Chapter 2

YOUNG JAROD'S LIVING space was on SL-19, 218 feet below the Centre's main building. But to escape the prison he'd been locked in, he wouldn't go up.

He would go down.

Feeling his way confidently through the darkness, he made it to the door of his bio-chamber. With the electricity off, the door's magnetic locks were disengaged and quietly swung open. Jarod was certain the designers would soon be paying for that oversight.

Getting out of his transparent cell was easy, but finding the exact spot he needed to get to on the lab wall would be more challenging. Standing in utter darkness, Jarod pinpointed his exact position in the room and constructed a mental topographical map. At times he'd been allowed out of the chamber to perform simulations in other sections of Sydney's lab and had burned the measured steps he'd taken into his memory—every single one.

Three steps left, turn right, cross over the drainage trough and then fourteen and a half paces forward. Reaching out, he found the cinder block wall and the hairline crack there. His fingers explored up the crack to the spot where the grout had flaked away. This fissure was a perfect finger hold as were the series of others above it. Despite no rock climbing experience, Jarod spidered his way up with natural ease, his muscular but nimble body his most under-utilized asset. Passing Sydney's window he heard his mentor's quiet breathing and Eydie Gorme's lilting voice as she sang *Piel Canela*. Jarod peeked through the window. In the faint glow from Syd's battery powered cassette player, he could just make out the framed photo in Sydney's hands of the young wife and newborn son taken from him so long ago. Even asleep, Sydney held it tenderly, the same way he had held Jarod when the young Pretender's fears or sadness had overwhelmed him. Sydney had always taken care of and protected Jarod, especially in those times when other Centre powers wanted him for more dangerous assignments.

Jarod wondered how long it would take the psychiatrist to find a flash-light and come down to look in on him. He then imagined the despair that the Belgian would feel when he found him gone. The thought caused a wave of anxiety to wash over Jarod. Sydney was, after all, the only person he could remember that he knew loved him. Jarod would *miss* Sydney, and worse, feared he would *need* him. Yet, in his heart, Jarod was confident his destiny lay outside these walls.

Banishing these thoughts, Jarod kept climbing until he made contact with the grate to the air intake vent. With an awkward tug, it hinged upward and Jarod wriggled inside.

It had been three minutes since the power had been sabotaged by his accomplice. In only nine more, the backup generators would be fired up and electricity restored. Only 540 seconds to reach his objective.

Sweat trickled down Jarod's nose and dripped onto the ductwork he crawled through. The sub-levels were so far underground that without constant heating, the temperature was a brisk 54 degrees F.

Jarod knew the ventilation infrastructure served as more than just a respiratory system for the Centre. Occasionally, the labyrinth of tubes acted as a secret subway that Jarod was not the first to travel through. The Pretender had been in captivity for a year when he'd first felt the other child's eyes peering down from the vents. Two more would pass before they actually exchanged words.

Now, seven years later, Jarod slid on his belly with a handmade Braille compass to navigate the twists and turns to a different tunnel far, far below.

Chapter 3

DELAWARE'S SECRET GROTTOS were known to exist by only a select few. None were more secretive than the one deep inside the bluffs overlooking Blue Cove, the discovery of which led Grandfather Parker to make it the home of the Centre.

Later, the environmental movement made pumping sewage into Blue Cove a major infraction. To keep government snoops from testing the pristine waters and subsequently wondering what went on inside the structure above, the Centre installed a water treatment plant in the cavern adjacent to SL-27.

All effluents and *other human waste* from the 33 floors above were collected in massive sedimentation tanks where thicker sewage settled out of the wastewater. That liquid was then treated to a purity that would make Al Gore proud. The remaining sludge was stored in an enormous vat until pumped out and trucked to landfills. Since the process was prohibitively expensive, the bean counters at the Centre devised a way around it. On nights when the automated system detected sufficient rainfall to disperse it, the sludge wasn't processed. Instead, at precisely 1:30 am, it was pressure extruded directly into those same pristine waters of Blue Cove.

Crawling onward, Jarod replayed what his accomplice had whispered to him earlier. *"A storm blew in this morning. It's supposed to rain for 24 hours. Tonight is the night."*

Jarod dead-ended against a vent grate, and then sniffed. The air beyond wasn't laced with cologne or spices, but was heavy with the rotten egg smell of hydrogen sulfide. Jarod smiled. Not only was he exactly where he was supposed to be, but as the lights began coming back on, he knew he was right on schedule. It was 1:29, and he had exactly 60 seconds to escape.

Or die trying.

Jarod kicked open the grate and dropped to the floor of the industrialized cavern. The instant he hit the ground, the massive pump next to him whirred to life. Jarod rushed through the maze of pipes connecting the enormous storage containers, twisting over and around each other like snakes. The treatment facility was coming back online and he only had 45 seconds to reach the far side of the cavern. Jarod dashed past aerating pools bubbling with disgusting gases, leapt over the scum skimmers, took a left at the digestive vats and made it to the ladder of the auxiliary air compressing tank. He was half way up when it began shaking under the pressurizing force within. He scurried up, then vaulted out onto the metal roof of the sludge vessel itself.

By his mental clock, he'd arrived with 20 seconds to spare, but was met by an obstacle he hadn't counted on: a watertight, crank wheel service door.

But the wheel wouldn't turn.

Jarod's eyes bulged—less than fifteen seconds before he would be discovered. A new wave of fear washed over him as he strained to crank the wheel with all his strength, but it was frozen.

He frantically scanned for something to pry it loose. Wasting precious seconds searching, his eyes landed on a metal bar. He gripped it like a baseball bat and swung away. After four bone-jarring bangs, the wheel finally gave, but each swing had cost valuable time and created a cacophony of unplanned noise. With only seven seconds left, he flung the door open and was consumed by the foulest stench imaginable—far worse than his mental simulations had contemplated, so much so that it nearly brought him to his knees.

The auxiliary tank began to rumble, maximum pressure about to peak. It was now or never. Jarod filled his lungs, tightened his abdomen to fortify himself from retching, then plunged into the foul stew.

The instant his head went under, the compressed air released and, like a giant pressure-flush toilet, blew the sludge out of the evacuation pipe.

Jarod shot like a torpedo through the darkness within the 48-inch-wide tunnel on a death-defying ride. Moving at over 60 miles per hour, the turbulent buffeting was exactly as he had prepared for. Night after night he spent hours holding his breath for increasingly longer periods of time, always taking it to the edge of passing out.

There was one thing he *hadn't* anticipated: the two 135-degree turns in the pipe at the halfway point. Suddenly Jarod was slammed violently against the pipe wall, knocking the wind from his lungs. Before he could comprehend what had happened, his head viciously smashed against the second turn. The pain exploded in his skull as his mind slowly began shutting down.

As he plunged along like a broken doll, Jarod fought to remain conscious. He knew if he fainted, his involuntary muscles would take over, expand his diaphragm and fill his lungs with a liquid death he wouldn't wish on his worst enemy.

Barely hanging on, Jarod separated his mind from what his body was experiencing by concentrating on the fading single memory of his parents: a diffused image of a woman with red hair rocking him in her arms while a man's voice gently sang a nonsense nursery rhyme, '*Kri Kraw Toads Foot, Geese Walk, Bare Foot.*'

Desperately clinging onto this memory, his limp body began spinning like an out of control top. Jarod realized he was losing his battle. His last thought was *Where are my Mom and Dad?*

Then all was silent.

Chapter 4

WITH A BELCHING, pressure release thrust, young Jarod was jetti-soned out of the extrusion pipe, launching him 30 yards to a hard splash-down into Delphine Creek, a frigid stream bordering the Centre. The land-ing shocked him into full consciousness. Gasping desperately for air, he found himself swallowing water. *White* water.

The storm had resulted in the brook swelling into raging rapids that tumbled him against rocks, tree stumps and blinding whirls of madness that sucked him under. Jarod did not know how to swim and yet deliverance from the hell he'd just been in, felt far greater than any sense of panic. He'd never been in water before, but remembering all he had read, he paddled, kicked and fought his way to what he hoped was upward.

Finally breaking the surface, he filled his lungs with desperately needed air. It tasted cold. It tasted fresh.

It tasted *free*.

Just as quickly as his ride began, it was over. The water calmed as it emptied into the placid beauty of Blue Cove.

Pacing uneasily in the drizzle on the shadowy shoreline, Jarod's ac-complice awaited. Even from a distance, Jarod noticed the figure cut an impressive form. And yet, through the darkness, he could sense the im-mense anxiety from his savior; an emotional weight of uncertainty and fear over their conspiratorial endeavor. Even years later, it was a feeling Jarod would never forget.

She held soap and clean clothes in one hand and the reins of two white stallions in the other. One of the horses belonged to her.

The other to her daughter.

Upon meeting eyes with Jarod, Catherine Parker's expression went from concern to joy—the waves of her concern ebbing. Her plan—*their* plan, had worked. But Catherine's relief was quickly supplanted again by fear. The Centre, looming on the cliffs above, made this beach a dangerous place to be for very long. She checked his abrasions, found them only superficial, then instructed him to quickly wash and change.

Jarod disrobed and scrubbed until reflections on the water captured his attention. He looked upward. The rain had stopped and the parting storm clouds revealed a sky full of shimmering stars and a hypnotic full moon. The radiant glow lit a smile on his face, but not on Catherine's. "Jarod, we have to hurry."

So transfixed by the real life wonder of the heavenly objects, the young Pretender didn't hear her. The universe seemed as infinite as the possibilities Jarod now felt his future held.

Catherine, however, was persistent. She pulled the horses alongside and held a stirrup out for him. "There'll be time for the beauty of the world later. We have a long way to go." Catherine turned to him, but he hadn't moved. He was staring at her through welling tears. He tried to speak, but his throat constricted and wouldn't let him. So instead, he threw his arms around her and hugged tightly, finally whispering, "Thank you."

Knowing Jarod had been locked behind Plexiglas for most of his life, Catherine had feared how he would adapt to interaction in the outside world. The fact that at the first opportunity for human contact, Jarod had reached out for it instinctively, told her all she needed to know. Her eyes glistening, she returned his embrace with more love than she had for any other child, but one.

Hooves thundered across the white sands of the isolated, pristine beach.

Jarod had never been on a horse before, had never seen one in real life, but Miss Parker's stallion proved the perfect beast for his first experience. Following Catherine's mount up the cliff trail, he marveled at the animal's strength and agility. When they burst onto the rolling fields behind the Centre, Jarod was amazed to feel the stallion accelerate. Wind whipping through his hair as they made the long dash toward the Ceon Forest, Jarod felt an indescribable excitement until sirens rang out behind them and searchlights began scanning the fields.

Out of nowhere, Dobermans, sleek, fast, and deadly, were on their tails. Behind them, headlights of chase Jeeps appeared. Hearing the distant but unmistakable *whop-whop-whop* of a Centre chopper lifting off, Catherine's gut clenched. The Centre couldn't have discovered their Pretender was gone this quickly unless someone had suspected what she was up to and been waiting for the escape to expose her. She gave her steed more reins. The dogs were beginning to tire, but she and Jarod had to get into the forest trails before the Jeeps caught up. "Jarod. Follow me!"

Jarod lay in behind her. Their horses sprung forward, devouring the turf toward the forest. Jarod looked down and behind and saw the exhausted Dobermans were dropping back: but 400 yards behind, the headlights were gaining.

A man stood in the lead Jeep securing a rifle to his shoulder. Jarod leaned down to his stallion's neck when the rifle fired. A bullet whizzed by Jarod's ear, shattering the foreleg of Catherine's mount. Horse and rider cartwheeled, coming to rest with the broken stallion atop Catherine's leg.

Jarod pulled up. Catherine, trapped, shot him an urgent look. "Jarod! Go!"

"I'm not leaving." Jarod cried, twirling his frenzied stallion in a circle. "They'll get you!"

Catherine looked at the onrushing Jeep then back to the frightened boy. "It's not me they *want*. It's not me they *need*." She spoke calmly. "Get to the trestle, hop the train. She'll be waiting for you in Dover at the station."

"Who is she?" Jarod pleaded.

"Someone who loves you, Jarod." Catherine's eyes glistened. "There's no time to tell you everything but remember, if you don't see me again— find my diary. It has secrets you'll need. Now go!"

The headlights of the chase Jeeps illuminated the indecision on Jarod's face. Jarod looked from them to the pleading in Catherine's eyes. His eyes filled with tears. Then, reluctantly, Jarod twirled his reins, spurred his stallion and disappeared down the narrow forest trail.

The vehicles screeched to a halt, forming a semicircle around Catherine. A menacing man wearing leather riding boots got out. He stood above her. Grimacing, she looked up. Back lit by the moon's glow, Catherine couldn't see his face, but his voice she recognized immediately, and except for when they were once estranged, it was a voice she heard daily.

"I'm so disappointed in you," he drawled self-righteously.

"You're also too late," she said defiantly—"The Jeeps are too big for the trail and your dogs are played out."

He turned and opened a cage on the Jeep's rear. "I brought fresh ones." Catherine's heart sunk as two growling Rottweilers leapt out and tore off into to the trees after Jarod.

Galloping through the forest, Jarod was more terrified than he'd ever been. Rainwater dripped from the trees like tears falling from the shadows. To calm himself, Jarod closed his eyes and again focused on his mother's hair and his father's rhyme, 'Kri Kraw, Toads Foot, Geese Walk, Bare Foot.'

Then he heard it. A train whistle up ahead. It was right on time and so was he. Jarod emerged from the woods on a riverbank, where up a steep rock embankment to his right, there was a wooden trestle. Jarod dismounted, appreciatively patted his exhausted stallion and bolted up the incline.

The train appeared on the far side and was headed toward him. Jarod scrambled over the loose limestone and arrived up top just as the 80,000 tons of thundering steel began to pass. Jarod was surprised when he felt the radiant heat from the engine and the cars themselves. It was something he hadn't expected. He smiled to himself wondering about the millions of other discoveries he'd make in the outside world, but also knew he had to get aboard the train before he could have them.

Running alongside it, he kept his eyes over his shoulder and spotted an approaching boxcar with a low ladder on the side. It was just like the one he had practiced leaping onto in his mind.

Sprinting faster, Jarod moved in closer to the train. There was only one safe way to jump aboard: two hands and one foot landing on their rungs *at the exact same time*. If either missed their target, it was certain his body would be sucked under the monstrous train wheels. With no time to spare or ponder failure, he timed it out in his mind and then leapt.

Jarod sailed through the air, his hands gripping onto the fifth rung as his left foot made contact with the bottom rung.

Realizing he'd made it, he breathed a sigh of relief, until out of the corner of his eye he saw the blur.

A black blur.

In that nanosecond he sifted through his grey matter to identify what he'd seen, the snarling Rottweiler sunk his fangs into Jarod's dangling leg. The beast had struck just below the knee, clamping bone-crushing jaws around the boy's calf.

Pain *exploded*. Still, Jarod held on for dear life, but the violently squirming dog not only tore at Jarod's skin, Jarod's hands were losing their grip on the damp rungs.

The young Pretender watched helplessly as his hands slipped from the cold steel and he crashed onto the train bed below.

Lying against the raw rock in the wake of the train's sound wash, Jarod's physical agony paled against the anguish in his soul.

Chapter 5

HIS HEART POUNDING, eyes darting around the darkness, Jarod awoke wondering if he had screamed.

The dream seemed so real, yet he knew it *wasn't* a dream. It was a nightmare he'd lived long ago that had haunted him since. As always, he caught himself massaging the scars on his right calf. Every time he relived this memory, he felt the same pain.

The ache wasn't just in his leg. Those wounds had healed long ago, unlike the gash in his heart. His torment wasn't caused by a Rottweiler's bite, but by a lifetime of crushing uncertainty. *Who am I? Did the Centre adopt me? Was I bought? Was I stolen? And where are my Mom and Dad?*

Two decades of not knowing the identity of the woman waiting for him in Dover the night of his escape tortured Jarod's heart. How many times had he imagined himself meeting her at the station had he not been pulled off?

A woman he was told, *loved* him.

As he grew into manhood, Jarod feared he might never know whom the woman really was. The only person he knew was certain of her identity had died less than 24 hours after the Rottweiler left him scarred.

Whenever he thought of either of those women, Jarod felt guilt and regret, and terribly alone.

But he wasn't alone now.

Oscar the Harlem rat sniffed the air as he peered from the upper loft into the darkness below. The man in the recliner had finally stirred.

Knowing what that meant, Oscar took a running leap toward the chain of the lamp hanging from a ceiling beam. With a perfect four-paw grab, he descended tail first down to the copper shade, free-fell to the floor, scampered across the hardwood, up Jarod's leg and plopped onto his lap.

The Pretender was happy to see the small creature. Given his highly controlled upbringing, Jarod was strongly opposed to the concept of 'pets,' feeling that no living creature had the right to own or control another. Oscar was Jarod's friend and roommate, and he was comforted by his presence.

Jarod sat up in the black leather La-Z-Boy he'd taken to sleeping in, reached down and scratched Oscar behind the ears. The recliner was just like the one Sydney slept in every night and Jarod didn't want to admit to himself why he had begun doing the same. Despite the fact that Sydney had held him in captivity, Jarod was intrinsically connected to his mentor and knew deep down he always would be. The one big difference now was that Jarod was *free*.

The apartment was just as it had been when he'd left the morning before. The water stains on the brick walls were as rusty as ever, the cracks in the chicken wired windows were just as filthy, the beams holding up the ceiling were as saggy, and soiled furniture was as moldy.

Jarod loved every square inch of it.

It was the nicest home he'd ever lived in—because it was *his*. Though after the events of the previous day he no longer felt as comfortable in it. Jarod went over them in his head for the hundredth time.

Thirty minutes after he walked out of the loft he had entered Guardian General Hospital in the persona of a hotshot surgeon, only to transform himself into an albino orderly planning to kidnap a comatose patient hidden in the psych annex there.

The patient's name was Kaj, a notorious one-eyed Libyan terrorist who had kidnapped a ten-year-old boy. The boy was the reason Jarod came to New York. A boy whose parents were heartbroken by their son's disappearance. A boy that, if Jarod didn't find within the next seven days, would be dead along with hundreds of other innocent people.

A boy named Luke.

Unfortunately, Jarod had been too late, someone else had absconded with Kaj—a man named O'Quinn who was also trying to find Luke. Now, Jarod still had no idea where the boy was, nor what the planned event to kill so many entailed. All he knew was that his only hope of saving Luke rested with two people.

One was a doctor named Bilson; the other was a young woman who had touched Jarod's heart.

A woman with violet eyes.

Chapter 6

FOREVER CAPTURED IN time on canvas with oil, Catherine Parker's portrait looked down on Mr. Parker. The man who ran the Centre was sitting at his imposing mahogany office desk, fighting a rage that threatened to burst forth and ruin his Brooks Brothers suit. "We cannot allow Jarod to get a foothold in society!" he said. "Because if he does—we are screwed!" Mr. Parker's lips then almost formed a smile. It was the same *almost* smile that he often had right before he smashed something.

Although she thought he'd never hurt her, his daughter wasn't absolutely sure. Like she had so many times when she was a little girl, Miss Parker again found herself seated in the hard-backed chair in his office apologizing for her failures. "I know that, Daddy, but …"

Mr. Parker pounded his desk. "Then why in hell is he still out there?!"

"I was close …"

"*We* were close." Sydney corrected, as he sat on a stool at Mr. Parker's bar in the corner, the handmade bar that served one thing and one thing only, Maker's Mark.

Mr. Parker stood, disgusted with both of them. "*Close* only counts in tiddlywinks and thermonuclear war—which is exactly what those crazy Zulus at the Triumvirate will rain down on our sorry asses if we don't bring Jarod back."

"*Alive.*" Sydney firmly interjected.

Mr. Parker shot Sydney a questioning look. "What's that supposed to mean?"

The Belgian bolted to his feet. "Your progeny is being reckless with a major asset."

Miss Parker spun and unleashed. "In about three seconds, this progeny is gonna be reckless with a saggy handful of what could be your progeny!"

Sydney walked toward the desk holding in his anger. "Threaten me all you want, Miss Parker, but if you continue to push Jarod, he will disappear forever."

"Enough!" Mr. Parker's frustration silenced the room. "First the hotel, then the hospital. Maybe Zane was right. Maybe I do have the wrong people trying to bring Jarod in."

"Daddy!" Miss Parker turned back to her father, a childlike pleading in her voice. "We would have nailed Jarod while he was playing doctor, but we walked into a total shit storm—other players and agendas in the mix we couldn't have anticipated."

"So you're saying that catching Jarod just got *more* complicated?"

Miss Parker, now biting incessantly on her lip, then answered. "Yes—and no, Daddy." Mr. Parker glared. She knew that look, knew she had little time to explain before he'd explode again. "We're not playing exclusively by Jarod's rules anymore. Which actually gives us an advantage."

Mr. Parker cocked his head, dubious. "What advantage is that?"

"A mystery that, when solved, will lead us right to him." Miss Parker hoped her answer would pacify her father, or at the least pique his curiosity for the 30 seconds it would take to explain herself. She quickly removed a stack of photos from her Polyvore carbon-fiber briefcase hacked from the security cameras at Guardian General Hospital. His attention span already waning, she fanned them out on the desk before her father. The first was taken on the hospital rooftop helipad, where a bald man was eyeing a Middle-Eastern man on a stretcher. "We need to determine three things. First, who the towel-head on the gurney is that Jarod is after, as well as the men who took him."

Mr. Parker looked closer, which she took as a good sign. Even Sydney was impressed with her psychological manipulation of her father. She tapped on a picture of the bald man with the eye patch. "Especially Mr. Clean here. He was in charge."

Her father leaned in, studying the three images of Jarod in particular. In the first, Jarod was in a doctor's coat; in the second he was exiting an operating room in scrubs; and the third showed him stealing quietly through the Annex late at night dressed in black.

"These were taken three days before we found him." She said.

Mr. Parker looked up and, as was his nature, began his interruptions. "Any idea what in Goddamn-hell Jarod was doing at that hospital?"

Miss Parker smiled—inwardly. Only 15 seconds and her father just had to regain control, or least, he thought he had. She'd actually employed a bit of reverse psychology that she'd learned from her mother, one that allowed him to feel in charge while she still very much led the discussion.

"That's question number two. At the offshore wind farm where he did his first pretend after his escape, Jarod was targeting the owners. Maybe he was doing the same at the hospital, but I suspect it's more."

This time, before he could speak, she'd answered his question. "Don't worry, Daddy. We'll find out who owns the hospital, what they're about, chapter and verse, and we'll find out *exactly* what Jarod's motivation was for being there."

Mr. Parker raised the last picture up for a better look. It was Jarod outside the ER with a young woman in his arms. "I assume the girl is question number three?"

Miss Parker glowed inside. "Precisely."

"Do we know why he's kidnapping her?" Mr. Parker asked tersely.

Sydney chimed in fervently. "Jarod would *not* kidnap someone."

Miss Parker took the photo from her father and Frisbeed it smugly to Sydney. "Well, it doesn't look like he was taking her out for a double dip, now does it, Syd?"

Sydney studied the picture, well aware that, moments before it had been taken, this same woman had knocked Miss Parker unconscious, aiding in Jarod's escape. The photo could be perceived as if Jarod was forcibly removing her from the hospital, so Sydney decided to allow Mr. Parker his interpretation by asserting, "There's another explanation for this. There just has to be."

"Well, whatever it is—whatever *all* this is—we'll find out," Miss Parker assured her father. She pointed to the photos. "I.D. Sleeping Beauty and the bald man, find the answers to the questions surrounding the hospital, and that's how we'll find your Pretender."

Mr. Parker slowly nodded. He liked what he was hearing and his rare show of approval, however hesitant, made Miss Parker's muscles untense.

However, as quickly as he gave her a glimmer of outward approval, his smile faded and, he snatched it away. "It's been 24 hours and *all* you've got is this? Unanswered questions?"

Miss Parker summoned every muscle in her face to cover the tension growing in all of her others. "Yes, but ... I have Cornelius and his team working round the clock. I wouldn't let them leave."

Mr. Parker's disapproval didn't budge. "You trust that carnie reject with the caterpillar on his forehead?"

"Well—yes, Daddy. I—Cornelius may be a little freak, but he's an intelligent little freak ..." Miss Parker stammered into silence, hating to defend him.

Mr. Parker tossed a hard stare at the Belgian. "What about you, Sydney? You have a psychiatric perspective on this whole thing?"

"I don't trust Cornelius." Sydney walked over to the massive desk. "I told you that years ago in my psychological evaluation of him, and my assessment hasn't changed." Sydney then looked past Mr. Parker and into the soft eyes of the portrait of Catherine Parker. "Unfortunately, few people around here take my counsel any longer," he said mostly to himself.

"I'm not talking about that deformed clown," Mr. Parker barked. "I'm asking about Jarod."

Sydney looked directly into Mr. Parker's eyes as the headman of the Centre continued. "Why exactly is your boy playing with us?"

"Jarod isn't mine and he isn't a boy. He's a Pretender, a genius who can become anyone he wants to be. And he's not playing 'with us,'" corrected Sydney. "He is *playing* us." Sydney cannily looked at Miss Parker, "At least *some* of us."

Before she could release her fury, Sydney explained to her father the theory he'd laid out to her earlier. "Jarod is in extreme bio-psychosocial distress triggered by his perception of himself as a victim of *betrayal trauma*."

"What the hell does that mean?" Mr. Parker asked Sydney.

"*Betrayal trauma* is a condition caused by a violation of a psychological contract by persons upon which the victim relies for some aspect of his holistic well-being."

Mr. Parker wasn't buying what Sydney was selling. In fact, what Sydney was saying about the Pretender only pissed him off more. "Jarod feels betrayed? For what?"

"For *what?*" Sydney was astonished. He had thought Miss Parker arrogant, but Mr. Parker's conceit and disassociation bordered on sociopathic. So Sydney stated the obvious—"Jarod's sense of betrayal is tied to what he was doing at the Centre, the work we had him doing here—and how he got here in the first place."

Mr. Parker gritted his teeth with boiling contempt. "We gave that boy—*I* gave that boy, that *orphaned* boy, a great life. And this is how he repays me?"

Sydney tried to read Mr. Parker for any sign of reason. *Could he possibly be serious? Had Mr. Parker never listened to any of his late wife's warnings before she'd …?*

Sydney didn't dare go there about Catherine or Jarod. Sydney had stuck his head in the sand on both of those 'classified' issues, but Mr. Parker hadn't survived in the executive suite for four decades by being oblivious to reality. Sydney also knew Mr. Parker was a consummate poker player, who never revealed any card in his hand to an opponent, especially not to Sydney. So, as he often did when met with confrontation he couldn't deal with, Sydney retreated into his shell.

Mr. Parker did what he always did when he smelled fear in another— he attacked. "You know what I wonder, Sydney? I wonder if the person Jarod is *playing* is you. I wonder if that clever son-of-a-bitch you raised is a master at manipulation and is working you with just enough guilt so you won't be able to dispassionately use your emotional connection to track him down." He glowered at Sydney, "Most importantly, I wonder if you've forgotten where your loyalties lie." He let the question hang in the air.

Sydney did not lose control of his emotions often, but when he did it was explosive. "My fidelity to the Centre hasn't been questioned for the 33 years of my service and I damn well won't have it questioned now!"

Mr. Parker froze.

So did Miss Parker.

No one raised their voice to her father. Certainly no one expecting to survive very long. She expected something terrible to happen to Sydney, in fact was relishing it. But was stunned when instead on unleashing his legendary anger, her father slumped his shoulders and eyed the Belgian with tenderness. "I'm sorry, Sydney. Catherine always believed in you, and I do as well. I'm just—monumentally frustrated." He then clasped Sydney on the arm. "You know Jarod better than anyone. Please find a way to get him back."

Sydney was shocked by this show of—what was it—affection? Confused, he was unsure of how to react. If it wasn't for Mr. Parker's support, Sydney would never have had the intellectual opportunity to work with Jarod.

On the other hand, he also would never have been in a position to hurt Jarod. He wondered then if just maybe, Mr. Parker was right. Perhaps Jarod had been manipulating him. *Simulating him.*

Sydney did not know the truth behind Mr. Parker's assertion, but it was unnerving. His inner conflict was eating away at him, and the only thing Sydney was sure of was that he had to get out of that office. "If I'm needed, I'll be in my lab trying to do just that." With a quiet look to the dumbfounded Miss Parker, Sydney turned and left.

After the heavy door closed, every ounce of the warmth Mr. Parker had just expressed to Sydney vanished.

"I'll never know what your mother saw in that man."

"Me neither, Daddy." Miss Parker looked up to the portrait of her mother. She really didn't know why, but her mother had always been fond of Sydney. She'd said that, deep down, he was a good person, despite his flaws, which was *all* Miss Parker could see. Mr. Parker looked up at the portrait as well. There was turmoil in his eyes—the kind Miss Parker couldn't define.

He stared at his wife's image for a few moments—moments Miss Parker found uncomfortable—then said, "I'll never know why she left us like that. Just the two of us." He kept staring. "That's what we are now. Just the two of us."

Miss Parker moved to get closer to her father—she felt an urge to touch him.

"I like it this way, Daddy. As for Jarod, don't worry. I won't let you down."

He turned, just as she reached out to embrace him, stopping in her tracks when she saw the coldness in his face. "Make damn sure you don't! I won't stand for anymore excuses."

"Yes, Daddy, of course, but ..."

"Good and keep an eye on Sydney—that Belgian is the key to this whole thing. There are two degrees of separation between the Centre and Jarod—and Sydney is one of them. His emotional ties will lead us to the boy, even if you can't."

As the slap of Mr. Parker's words stung his daughter's sensibilities, his desk phone buzzed. He didn't snap his fingers this time, nor did he have to. Miss Parker had already stopped speaking—her words caught in her throat.

He snatched the receiver and barked into it, "What?—Zane is *here*? Oh for God's sake!"

He pinched the bridge of his nose as he listened. "What do you think, Mrs. Gazp? Of course I don't want to see him ..." And as those words left his lips, the door to the office burst open and, after a long pause, in came Mr. Zane.

Chapter 7

MR. ZANE LIMPED in on an ivory cane. Everything was limp about this odious creature, especially his wrist.

Zane was the exact same age as Mr. Parker, yet looked old enough to be his father, a phenomenon Miss Parker had never understood. That, or why she had always been told to call the disturbing man 'Uncle'. When she was a child, Miss Parker had once heard someone being described as 'death eating a cracker.' She did not understand what that meant until she laid eyes on Zane.

He was older now, and wasn't gumming a saltine, but "Uncle Z" looked overdue for his date with the embalmer. The detestable man had always been sickly and, except for the purplish-pink lips that he wetted with his grey tongue, the rest of his being was pale.

The only physical features Zane possessed that weren't frail were his, heterochromatic eyes—one green, one blue—that darted back and forth, taking in everything as if seeking a target. Once detected, they locked on with such magnetism, his victims were sucked right into them. Into *him*. In this way, Zane reminded her of the hypnotic serpent from *The Jungle Book*—a hundred years old and still in his prime. She'd always been afraid to look into Uncle Zane's eyes and she had always been afraid of *him*.

Zane twisted his head until his neck let out a sickening crack, then with a relieved grin drawled to Mr. Parker, "It's *so* good to see you again."

Mr. Parker jumped up from his desk, bounded across the room, flashing his thousand-watt smile and said, "Where've you been, you old son of a whore?" He shook Zane's hand like he was his most loved sibling instead of his most loathed step-brother. As they shook, Mr. Parker glowed to his daughter. "You remember my Angel?"

Zane's gaze raked over Miss Parker as if surprised to find her in the room.

"Remember her? How could I forget?" Zane's eyes painted Miss Parker's body with lascivious strokes—then looked up to Catherine's portrait, eyeing it in the same unseemly way. "She looks more and more like her lovely mother every day."

The thought that this loathsome being knew *her*, had no doubt gazed at *her* in the same sordid manner—made Miss Parker want to vomit bile, blood, or both.

"I'll never forget the last time I set eyes on her exquisite face," said Zane as he gazed back to Miss Parker. "God bless her soul." As those words hit her ears, she felt his pull, but it wasn't just the menacing gleam in his eyes that made cold sweat form on her neck. To Miss Parker, Zane was a harbinger of evil. Uncle Zane's arrivals had always been a prelude to something horrible. On one day in particular, many years ago, his sudden appearance had foreshadowed horror itself.

As he stared deeper into her eyes, she realized he hadn't blinked since he'd entered the room. "It was not long after your fifteenth birthday."

"I turned *twelve* that year." Miss Parker said icily.

"Ahh—and you *matured* oh so rapidly."

Miss Parker broke the stare and looked at her father.

Reading the revulsion in her eyes, Mr. Parker switched gears. "What brings you to your old hunting grounds, Zane?"

"Not back, just yet. I'm passing through. Our friends on the Dark Continent are getting anxious—especially that former machete-wielding assassin himself. He summoned me for a 'private consultation'."

"Consultation? About what?"

Zane lashed out with a strike as swift as a rattlesnake. "You know damn well about *what*!" A deafening silence echoed in the room.

Miss Parker shot daggers at Zane. For decades, the duplicitous bastard had schemed numerous times to make her father's position at the Centre his own. He smelled her daddy's blood in the water and was on his way to stir that proverbial pot of malaria.

With a wide disbelieving grin, Mr. Parker broke the silence. "Jarod? Aw for God-sakes—that panicky Rwandan—hasn't a thing to be concerned about."

Zane sized up the candor in his step-brother's eyes as he put his arm around his daughter. "Why, we were just discussing how she and her team virtually have Jarod in the bag. Don't you, Angel?" His smile was *almost* genuine.

She wished her own confidence was as strong. "Of course we do, Daddy."

As she brushed past her reptilian uncle to exit, Miss Parker could feel a renewed sense of pressure to catch Jarod on her shoulders. She was hoping, even *praying* that her mother's eyes were watching *her* back.

Chapter 8

JAROD PUT OSCAR on his shoulder and walked to the far corner of the loft, where he had set up a hospital bed surrounded by vitals monitors connected to a patient lying under the sheets.

The woman with the violet eyes was sleeping, but she was far from restful. *Very* far. Skylar's breathing was labored, and her face and body had begun to spasm. Jarod examined her EEG and EKG readouts and understood why; the electrical activity in her mind was off the charts, her heartbeat was erratic, and she was sweating profusely.

As Jarod bent to wet a compress in a bowl of water, Oscar jumped off of his shoulder, landing next to Skylar's pillow. Oscar stared at her face, twisted in agony, then looked up to Jarod. Even a rat could tell something was terribly wrong with her. Fortunately, Jarod knew exactly what it was.

Skylar had been under the 'care' of Dr. Bilson in a pharmaceutical test of anti-schizophrenic drugs—but Skylar wasn't schizophrenic. Nor were the other people that had been 'involuntarily committed' to participate in the trials. Unfortunately, the meds the test subjects had been given had caused the exact symptoms they were designed to prevent.

Jarod was weaning her off the drugs and she was in the early stages of withdrawal. The effects were disturbing and would get worse. *Much* worse. Skylar moaned as her brain chemistry fought to rebalance itself. The delirium tremens would begin soon.

In a medical setting, a supervised detox could minimize this pain and reduce risk of dangerous complications. Regrettably, Jarod did not have the time for that and neither did Luke.

To save the boy, Jarod had hard decisions to make. Starting with Skylar. Though wracked with guilt, Jarod would not only let nature take its course, but he would speed it up. And nature's course would be ugly.

Skylar let out her first whimper and clenched her teeth. Over the next two days she would get worse before she got better. *Much* worse. During that time, the woman he was attracted to in more ways than he understood would face nightmarish hallucinations and terrifying DTs.

Jarod reached into his pocket, produced a 'Nilla wafer and gave it to Oscar as the door to the loft opened. Strolling in with two grocery bags was a woman in an old-fashioned white nurse's uniform, but she wasn't a nurse. Nor was she a woman, at least not in the traditional understanding of gender that Jarod had known before they'd become acquainted.

While walking through Harlem one night snacking on a stalk of celery, Jarod heard the words, "Baby, I gots something you can chomp on dat's tastier than that rabbit food." He turned to the sound of heels clacking concrete as a thick, tall Puerto Rican Creole, stutter-stepped on platform f-me pumps to catch up. "What's a big strong man like you in such a hurry for?"

"I'm on my way home," he had replied innocently.

Chaz, who was wearing a huge, blonde Beyoncé wig and exaggerated, winged out silver glitter eye shadow, ruffled her new friend's hair. "You's a funny little 'Nilla wafer—ain't cha? You ever think about dunkin' yourse'f in some chocolate milk?"

Jarod soon realized two things: first, that Chaz was a prostitute, something Jarod had heard of, but never experienced. The second was something he'd neither heard of *nor* experienced, but felt compelled to ask about.

"You are a man, wearing women's clothing, correct?" A confused Jarod asked.

"No, honey-boy. I'm a woman trapped in a man's body, wearing clothing of the gender that identifies my true me."

Chaz explained it as something called gender dysphoria—a disconnection between his assigned and perceived gender. Jarod smiled at this. For a man who was searching for his own identity, Jarod had nothing but respect for someone strong enough to be *himself*—even if he was being *himself* as a *her.*

In little more than a week Chaz and Jarod had become friends.

Chaz loved and was accepting of all of God's creatures except for the one eating the 'Nilla wafer crumbs she was now scowling at. "I can tolerate me lots of things—but filthy-ass rats ain't one of 'um. You feel me on that?"

Oscar looked at Chaz, seemed to snicker, then hopped down and skittered away.

Jarod looked into the grocery bags. "Did you find what I needed?"

"Yeah, but I had to traipse all over Chinatown looking and my dogs are howling." Jarod wasn't sure what dogs Chaz was talking about, but he put two and two together when she flopped in the La-Z-Boy, tossed off her big white shoes and began massaging her even bigger black feet.

Jarod removed various herbs and roots from the bag. He put several into his mortar, added water and began grinding them with his pestle.

Chaz looked over at Skylar shivering in the bed.

"Mm, mm, mm. Looks like you got'chu a mess on your hands now, 'Nilla man. Think a 9-1-1 to Chaz is gonna save the day for you, huh?"

Focused on his herbal concoction, Jarod didn't answer.

Unaccustomed to being ignored, Chaz cracked her toes and stood. "It's not like I mind you calling in the middle of the night, asking me to come play Florence Nightingale for the bargain basement rate of only $250 an hour, Mr. Genius Man," Chaz pointed at Skylar. "But that little girl's ass belong in rehab for'sho."

Jarod knew rehab was where Skylar belonged, but he couldn't put her there. He desperately needed information she had overheard about where O'Quinn had sent the terrorist he'd kidnapped *and* he feared that if O'Quinn knew that Skylar had that information, he would be watching rehab clinics to silence her. For her own safety, Jarod would detox Skylar himself.

The Pretender transferred the greenish liquid into a glass and brought it to the bed. Jarod gently touched Skylar's face. What he was about to do would propel her into a living hell, but he had no other choice. The time for saving Luke was running out.

Jarod poured the fluid into her mouth and waited.

The nightmare would soon begin.

Chapter 9

LUKE DREADED SUNDOWN. For the last four consecutive
nights he had experienced a recurring nightmare.

He stood on the edge of his cot, peeking out at the sinking sun
through the small narrow crack in the painted over basement window. All
was quiet upstairs where his captor, Adidas Man, was and the stillness filled
Luke with angst filled thoughts. *The silent enemy is he who sneaks up on you.*

Slowly enveloped by the growing shadows, Luke wished he had his
Hulk PEZ with him, his favorite superhero, to bolster his courage. He
knew that was impossible though. *Maybe,* he thought, *maybe if I think about
the nightmare while there's still some light in here, I won't have it tonight.*

Scooting back on the cot so his head could rest against the block wall
where he once drew the face of The Hulk, he closed his eyes.

*Luke entered through the front door of his house. It was dark inside, the light switch was
dead and the only illumination was the ominous glow from his father's neon bar light.
His eyes strained in the darkness—his dad sitting on a stool, rigid, silhouetted in the
blue light, staring without expression.*

"Dad?" His father remained frozen, silent.

*Fear seeping in, Luke's voice cracked, "Mom?" He wondered why his mother
wasn't there to greet him, especially since every other Halloween she was always passing
out candy to the neighbor kids. Especially since she was happy he dressed as Nick Fury
from The Avengers instead of The Hulk.*

"Luuuuuuuuuuuuuuuuuuke," a whispering voice beckoned inside his room. Luke turned toward it, his trick or treat bag slipping from his fingers, candy scattering at his feet when it hit the floor.

"Luuuuuuuuuuuuuuuuuuke."

His heart raced as he crept toward his bedroom door at the end of the hall—a hall that seemed darker and longer than he remembered it.

He stopped in the doorway and looked in. There his mother sat in a still rocking chair, a bowl of candy on her lap, a blank expression on her face, staring at Luke's bed.

"Mom?" But like his dad, she too could not hear him.

"Luuuuuuuuuuuuuuuuuuke." The whispering voice was coming from the form of a body lying under his bed covers.

"Mom? What's going on? Mom!" His mother stood and floated out right past him.

He eyed the bed now—gulped in a deep breath, aghast at his discovery …

The form under his bed covers began to stir.

The body slowly began to sit up—Luke edged back—the covers began sliding down—a voice from below whispered "Luuuuuuuuuuuuuuuuuuke …"

The covers fell revealing the body was Luke, his face and skin, dead and rotting— gums oozing puss, teeth putrid as he smiled at his living terrified self. "Trick or treeeeeeeeat."

Luke's eyes shot open. He winced and clutched his stomach, then scrambled up and ran to the nearly full chemical toilet, and vomited.

Adidas Man thought he heard the kid puking but wasn't sure. He stood, staring at his nude reflection in the mirror. The last light of dusk filtered through the blinds casting prison bar shadows across his hefty frame. He also wasn't sure how long he'd been standing there, but knew it was long enough for his bloodshot-eyes to follow a drip of sweat from his forehead down to his puffy belly.

He wasn't sure of much of anything anymore. How long had he been overseer to the boy in the basement—two weeks? A month? Five months? A year? Wasn't time itself little more than a mirage now masquerading as a glorious but unreachable destination? In truth, wasn't he just as much a prisoner as Luke?

The drip of sweat drifted through the last thicket of hair around his pasty navel and trickled over the final roll of belly fat, landing onto the back of his hand gripping his cell phone.

The same phone he was long ago promised would ring in *'a day or two tops'*, courtesy of Kaj, with Luke's delivery instructions to their bald client who would then pay them an enormous sum. The same cell that Kaj had ordered him never use, *especially* if it didn't ring as planned.

Which it hadn't.

Something was wrong, *very* wrong with Kaj, and the plan. He'd worked for the Libyan on plenty of kidnappings and bombings and nothing like this had ever happened. Not even his boss could argue that this radio silence didn't change things—altered the very ground rules by which Kaj hired him in the first place, right?

In many ways it seemed like yesterday that Kaj picked him up from the rehab facility and gave him a second chance to leave his troubles with alcohol and crack behind.

And yet, that was then, this was now, and damn if these walls weren't closing in on him big time.

Chapter 10

THE GLOW FROM the submerged light in the Hearns' algae-coated swimming pool illuminated the silhouetted man as he slipped over the fence. He carefully edged around in the shadowy perimeter toward the kitchen door.

The lock was no challenge and the man crept in. The table in the dark kitchen was littered with fast food bags and drained scotch bottles, the dishes in the sink smelled of preoccupation and apprehension.

The figure found Roger Hearns' charging cell phone, right where he knew a man in Roger's current state of mind would leave it: on the neon-lit bar in the den. The figure gazed into the framed mirror etched with a picture of a beer can, the logo of which was a smiling man yelling, *Hey Mabel— another Black Label!*

The figure was Jarod.

The Pretender silenced the ringer on the cell and did a check of recent calls, texts and emails, but found nothing of relevance. He removed the phone's casing, delved into its circuitry, and after a few adjustments, synced it to his own smartphone. Jarod could now monitor Roger Hearns' calls.

A noise from the hallway ambushed Jarod's attention. Returning the phone to its exact former position, Jarod slipped out the back from whence he came.

Cassandra Hearns stirred in bed, awoken by a low droning sound from somewhere in the house. She reached her arm over to her husband's side. She could still feel his residual warmth on the sheets, but he was not there.

Concerned, she climbed out of bed and followed the mysterious sound toward Luke's room. Before she got there, she recognized it as her son's model train.

Her mind raced. She let herself hope until she stopped at the threshold of his bedroom.

The figure sitting on the floor was not her son. It was Roger. His empty gaze glued on the train as it went around and around him in circles—never ending circles.

Cassie knelt beside him, watching as tears streamed down his cheeks. "I miss him too," she whispered, caressing his shoulders. Roger pulled away, her touch feeling like an intrusion. He shut the train off, stood, and vanished into the darkness of their crippled home.

Still on her knees, Cassandra leaned her face forward onto her son's carpet—and cried.

Outside, through Luke's bedroom window, Jarod watched. Cassandra, experiencing the ultimate pain of the loss of her child, ignited his own feelings of loss and unanswered questions within him. Wondering if this was the same kind of anguish his parents went through when he had been taken from them carved an ache in his soul. As a natural defense to escape his own emotional trauma, Jarod had long ago learned how to compartmentalize his feelings, and did so now. The emotions underlying his life's mysteries would wait for another day. Tonight he had to focus on the Hearns family.

Jarod felt certain that Cassandra and Roger's heartache for their son was genuine, but he knew Luke's father was harboring secrets about Luke's disappearance, if not flat out lies. Secrets and lies were topics about which Jarod knew a great deal; his life, and the life of everyone he'd grown up around at the Centre were full of them. Something told Jarod that the lies that surrounded Luke's kidnapping felt different, *benevolent* rather than *malicious*. The bridge accident that had been concocted to cover up the truth of Luke's vanishing was the last resort of a man trying to protect his son, the only way he could. Now, Jarod could see that those secrets were tearing both the man and his marriage apart.

At that moment, Jarod fought the tide of feelings washing over him about all the lost souls in his immediate world, wondering how one man who didn't know who he himself was, could help them find themselves.

Chapter 11

THE IMAGE OF the attractive brunette was lying atop the steel and glass desk in O'Quinn's efficient office. While it showed her on the hospital rooftop, firing her Smith & Wesson at the Life Flight helicopter, the photograph was not in focus. Nor were the other photos of the man hanging onto the chopper's skid, the man who had been impersonating a doctor at Guardian General. At least O'Quinn didn't think they were.

He leaned closer, squinted his good eye, but it was strained from working overtime since he'd lost the use of the other and was now losing clarity as well.

Well, isn't that just fucking perfect?

The aggravation felt by the man with the eye patch and ramrod straight spine was not strictly fuelled by the recent events at the hospital his corporation used as a clandestine facility for their special patients. Nor was it because he was running out of time to find the kidnapped boy, Luke Hearns. His upset was amplified by his exhaustion. O'Quinn hadn't had a good night's sleep since the Libyan had snuffed out a Marlboro in his eye while escaping his interrogative captivity. Since then, O'Quinn's chronic irritation was caused by a seared cornea that had healed poorly and felt like a thousand red ants stinging the inside of his eyelid. It hadn't gone away, as he'd hoped, it had gotten worse, weeping intermittently—and not just tears.

His eye had started to die and his surgeons had suggested he have it replaced with an ocular prosthesis—but the idea of a marble in his head was one O'Quinn's vanity couldn't abide. Besides, he didn't have time to be out of the game right now and that was what was really behind his frustration.

O'Quinn sat back and peered at the man whose face looked like a butcher's dog's.

"So you're saying this guy's after what we're after and Miss Tight Body is after *him*?"

"That's my 20/20," Dog growled, adjusting the cast on his broken paw.

"You figured out who these people are?"

"Neither raise flags on any database we're wired into—and we're into them *all*." O'Quinn tossed the pictures on the desk and massaged his temples. People who could erase themselves from meta-databases were trained adversaries just like he and his group, and O'Quinn *hated* a fair fight.

He pointed at the picture of the sexy brunette and then to the man who was dressed as a doctor. "So the hot chick is after the fake doc and the fake doc is after what we're after—the location of the boy."

"All the news ain't negative," Dog added. "Fake doc may have given us a way to get it out of Kaj's head."

O'Quinn looked up, hopeful.

Dog opened the door and Dr. Dojame, the swarthy Indian who was dressed as an EMT when he had removed Kaj from the hospital with O'Quinn, walked in.

Dog angled his paw. "Tell the boss what you told me."

Dojame unlatched a small case and poured out broken glass, large needles and plastic plungers.

O'Quinn studied it. "Broken syringes?"

"With remnants of nanoparticles on them, identical to traces I found in Kaj's blood before he was sent to *recuperate*."

O'Quinn raised an inquisitive eyebrow to Dojame, who tried to explain Jarod's experimental drug until O'Quinn stood, a surge of adrenaline replacing his exhaustion. "You got my juices flowing, Doc, even though I haven't a clue what you're saying."

"In theory, this nano-drug excites the synapse responses to shock-awaken coma patients, allowing their memories to be accessed. It's quite ingenious, as must be the man who created it. I'm certain it was used to *'awaken'* Kaj the night before we moved him."

O'Quinn's wheels started turning. "Reverse engineer this nano, whatever it is, so we can get it into Kaj ASAP." He pointed at the photos of the fake doctor, and the leggy brunette. "I have to find the boy before they do."

Chapter 12

THE LOOK ON Miss Parker's face was as primal, animated, and as angry as the actions of her body. She looked down at the meaningless Adonis she was grinding on, finding him staring back up at her obsequiously. He was the same chiseled, god-like ornament she'd used—*when was it?—a few days?—a week ago?* She couldn't remember, nor did she give a damn. All that mattered was that he had not forgotten her instructions and had faithfully maintained eye contact this time. *Good boy,* she thought as she began bucking, approaching the summit she was climbing for. She wondered, *Now what was his name again?* Then she answered her own question— *Who gives a damn?*

Life had become more complicated since the last time Miss Parker's submissive was splayed on her four-poster bed. Before then, she'd been able to lose herself on him during at least a dozen other 'dates,' but that was before the night her phone rang with the wake-up call that changed *everything.*

Trying to regain her sexual focus, she reached over to the bedside table and grabbed a cigarette and her lighter.

His eyes widened in disbelief. "Seriously?"

She stared back and snapped, "Just keep moving!" While riding him harder, she put flame to cigarette, took a deep drag, and hoped that the nicotine would give her at least a momentary wave of relaxation that could take the edge off long enough to get her over the edge. But it didn't help. Nothing could quiet her internal storm.

Before that call, she'd been able to keep things locked in places where they could not affect her. Yet when she caught sight of the Etch A Sketch on the chair with Jarod's sketch of herself as an anguished little girl staring back at who she was now, those emotional compartments crumbled and she lost all interest in her current activities. Frustrated beyond the point of no return, she surrendered to the fact that she wouldn't be able to achieve even momentary refuge in her desires of the flesh tonight. "Damn it!"

She dropped the cigarette into Adonis' Red Bull and dismounted, "Your work here is done."

"But—but I didn't finish. *Again.*" He pouted.

She shot him an cutting look. "I didn't think that mattered to you people."

Dejected, her lover skulked away without bothering to meet her frigid eyes. They were busy with other things and hadn't looked his way since she had moved on to the closet. He was a disposable chew toy she cared nothing for, and hell, he would probably get off on that too.

As the bedroom door closed behind him, Miss Parker caught sight of herself in the full length mirror. She was wearing her black Lorna ensemble. The scalloped edges, satin bows and tiny lilac bud at the center seam on her bra accented Miss Parker's beguiling power. Combined with the matching garter belt and stockings painted on her magical body below, she went from a simple sexual treat to a provocative siren.

Miss Parker loved her lingerie—which she wore only to please herself—and which was purchased exclusively from Fleur of England or Agent Provocateur. In them she felt sexy, strong and powerful. Unfortunately, she wasn't feeling any of those things tonight.

She wrapped herself in her old terry cloth robe in which she liked to think.

A few seconds later, she was at her minibar, dropping three rocks into a tumbler. She cracked the red wax seal on a fresh bottle of Maker's Mark and poured herself four fingers of courage.

She took a long pull of the bourbon, enjoying the oaky-caramel aspects as it slid down the back of her throat. But even that momentary pleasure was washed away as she lowered the glass and, again, caught sight of the Etch A Sketch. The image of her younger self with a tear about to drip from her eye uncorked a flood of sorrow and put a sour taste back in her mouth.

It was the same sadness she'd felt so long ago—sadness from a terrible dream on her twelfth birthday about the events of the previous day.

She and her mother were horseback riding on the Parker family's luxurious, horse farm through a field of flowing heather, the focal point of which was a majestic old-growth hardwood young Miss Parker called the Grumpy Old Man. She felt secure in the huge creaking arms of the ancient oak and she loved him as much as any human being— except her mother.

Miss Parker adored her mother and wanted to be just like her in every way. She'd even secretly wished her first name had been Catherine, but her mother explained that only boys were 'juniors' and that she had a beautiful name in her own right, which was okay with young Miss Parker. Besides, the secret nickname only her mother called her, "Little Miss," made her feel special.

Hours before, Catherine had awoken her with butterfly kisses on her cheek and reminded her about their upcoming trip to France, a trip just the two of them were going to make. 'A time to be ladies together.'

She was so happy thinking about that, she didn't notice the storm blow in until it was upon them. The first thunderbolt ripped through the sky and filled Little Miss's heart with fear. Even at a full gallop, she knew they were too far to make it safely home.

With her horse rearing up and whinnying, Miss Parker began to panic until her mother reached out and put her hand onto Miss Parker's steed and calmed the frightened beast. She then looked into her Little Miss's eyes and said, "No matter what happens, stay with me. I'll never let anything bad happen to you, Little Miss."

They began to ride and, as they did, a second lightning bolt erupted behind them, splitting the Grumpy Old Man in two.

Young Miss Parker awakened from her nightmare finding her mother in her bedroom at the crack of dawn. Catherine opened the curtains and sunbeams shot inward and touched the face of Little Miss. Pretending not to be frightened, which was something she often had to do, she opened her sleepy eyes and saw that the stormy night was over and it was a beautiful new day. Her eyes went wide with the sudden realization of what day it was! With a sparkle of excitement she turned to the pillow next to her, atop which rested a present wrapped in lavender paper with the royal purple bow.

Miss Parker beamed at her mother, who nodded, and then with boundless joy, she ripped open the paper and pulled out the gift from inside.

It was the exact present she'd asked for. A gleaming square of bright red plastic, framing a grey screen with two white knobs below that you twisted and turned to create a drawing. But the delight on her young face didn't last as she looked up and saw her mother's lip was quivering.

Catherine sat, took Miss Parker's hand and announced that their trip to France, their 'time to be ladies together', would have to wait. Someone else needed her help.

Little Miss had never seen such pain in her mother's eyes—heard such distress in her voice and it frightened her. She wrapped her small hand around her mother's large one—the one on which she wore the square shaped platinum ring—and told her mother that it was okay. That she understood.

Even though she really didn't.

The truth was, she was fighting back her tears—again. Just as her father had always instructed her to. She was being brave, or trying to, despite not feeling that way at all.

Her mother then pulled out an old book. It was the diary in which Miss Parker had seen her mother write 'And under the hand of God, ye little children shall never be lost.' The day Miss Parker had seen her pen those words, her mother had been more full of sorrow than Little Miss had ever witnessed, until this very moment. Mother looked at daughter, and said, "If anything ever happens to me, find this book—this diary—it has everything you'll need to know."

Pressing her lips onto Little Miss's forehead, her mother then stood and left the room without looking back.

As she clung onto her new Etch A Sketch, Little Miss didn't know that before her mother's favorite daffodils would bloom in the spring, her mother would be dead.

Miss Parker was still staring at the Etch A Sketch, her adult eyes welling with tears identical to those in the image of her younger self. She downed the rest of her bourbon, remembering the anguish she'd felt that long ago morning, the utter despair that soon after engulfed her life and the one person she had shared it all with.

Thirteen-year-old Jarod stood traumatized in the living room of a shitty one-bedroom apartment, fighting to keep from going into shock. He was standing face to face with, and staring into, the dead eyes of serial killer Jeffrey Dahmer.

"Feeling what he feels scares me, Sydney," Jarod whispered timidly, "and—it smells like rotting meat."

"To be a master Pretender, you must emotionally disassociate yourself, Jarod," Sydney said firmly.

"I can't!" Jarod cried, looking away from Dahmer's eyes focusing on the killer's hands. They were long and bony and he thought he could detect blood under his fingernails. "He lured them into his home, Sydney and—and then murdered them." Jarod looked back at the killer, who cracked an unsettling smile. Jarod whispered in horror. "He ate parts of their bodies—and did even worse things. Please, Sydney, make him go away. I don't want to be inside him!" Jarod pleaded, shaking with fear.

Seeing his suffering, Sydney pushed a red button on the wall next to where he was standing. "Okay, Jarod." Sydney said gently.

The serial killer and his virtual reality house of horrors disappeared and the two were alone in Jarod's living dome.

"Write a red notebook report and that will be all for today."

Jarod sighed, but his relief was short lived when raised voices erupted in the hallway. A woman then screamed—followed by what sounded like a gunshot!

Sydney and his panicked protégé swung their heads toward the door to the lab from beyond which the sounds had come. Jarod shot a look to his mentor. "Sydney! What is it?"

"I don't know." Sydney frowned and rushed toward the door. Shouts and running footsteps could be heard out in the hallway, followed by the shriek of a young girl. "Sydney, she's in trouble! Help her!"

"Momma, no! Momma! No!!!"

Jarod pushed his face into the Plexiglas wall that separated him from humanity as the door to the lab flew open and a Sweeper entered holding a screaming twelve-year-old Miss Parker fighting to be freed. "No! Let me go to my mother! Let me go!"

Sydney stared out into the hallway and all the blood drained from his face. "Oh my god." He turned and yelled to the Sweeper. "Keep her in here!" Sydney rushed into the hallway, slamming the door behind him.

The Sweeper let Miss Parker go, then stood in front of the door. "I'm sorry, Miss. You have to stay in here."

Little Miss was in a daze—she spun around, spotted Jarod and then stumbled over to the Plexiglas chamber. Her eyes, filling with tears.

Feeling her pain, Jarod's eyes began to fill as well. "What happened?" he asked, not understanding the dread that had descended upon him.

Her words came out in whimpers. "My mother—she's in the elevator—there was a gun—blood." Little Miss looked into his eyes. "She wasn't moving." As Jarod stared back, her tears overflowed and trickled down the tip of her nose.

With the Etch A Sketch trembling in her hand, Miss Parker fought to hold her adult tears inside, the whole time wondering *why? Why* had Jarod picked *that* moment to freeze frame and give back to her? It was the most painful snapshot of her life and he was tossing it in her face. The long dormant volcano of her grief and fury erupted. She flung the Etch A Sketch against the wall. The plastic fractured and a large crack appeared across the disappearing face of Little Miss inside it.

Miss Parker released a deep, emotional lament but the relief from torment it afforded her was short as she again watched the picture on the Etch A Sketch restore itself. Tilting her head, she stared at it in an uncomprehending way. Unless her mind was playing tricks on her, something even stranger was happening.

The tear, about to drip from the eye on the face of the Little Miss drawing, began *moving*. It was slowly falling, slipping through her lashes. The drawing point of the toy was somehow spontaneously continuing the etching process—causing the teardrop to slide down the side of her nose.

Exactly as it had happened on that day long ago.

Miss Parker sat back, astonished, but that was only the beginning. The screen cleared and then something else began appearing on it. Letters etched one at a time, until they spelled out, *I know the truth about what makes you sad.*

As if punched in the gut, all of the air rushed from her lungs.

Furious, she ripped off the back of the Etch A Sketch and clawed through the controlling orthogonal rails and fine aluminum powder until she found an electronic motherboard and gears that had been guiding the drawing stylus. It was an ingenious engineering marvel, created by Jarod— *but why?* Miss Parker was determined to find out.

"You son of a bitch."

Chapter 13

JAROD STOOD AT the bathroom door watching Skylar's sweat-soaked body convulsing and moaning next to the toilet. He'd learned that with any addict going through withdrawal, the worst symptoms struck on the third day. Skylar's trek would be no exception.

Today was her day three.

Jarod knew that time was afoot in his quest to save Luke and to stop O'Quinn. He was also aware that Skylar's life was in the balance and even though the crossing of their paths was still brief, he couldn't deny she had found her way into his soul.

Jarod didn't know exactly what was going on in her tortured body, but he could sense her pain in ways that made him feel guilt for his choice to keep her in the loft.

Skylar's knees quivered on the tile as she heaved bile for the umpteenth time. *It was messed up*, she thought—that the jackhammers banging in her head made simple addition a forgotten memory, but regardless of how hard she tried, she couldn't silence the acidic decades-old words that spewed from her predatory foster father's booze hole.

"Open the door, you little bitch, it's my time again." Young Skylar pushed all hundred pounds of her fifteen-year-old body against the door, pressing her bare feet onto the face of the bathroom vanity on the opposite wall to create a human barricade. The door thumped

and thumped, cracking and buckling under the force of the ramrodding monster. "Open the door, you bitch!"

Skylar swiped spittle from her dried, splitting lips as her head lolled and her eyes rolled. Then, she hocked up a nice thick one and spit it into the commode. "*Life's* the bitch, you asshole." Jarod knew she was talking to herself, a disconnected dialogue with an unseen devil.

Flushing the toilet with a spent smile, she watched with detached fascination, as if seeing her foster daddy being sucked down the drain in the swirl of her puke, but it was Skylar who was swirling back down.

Skylar stiffened her shoulder against the splintering door and pressed her feet harder against the vanity. Her body was at an odd angle but she knew if she could reach up to the deadbolt above her, it might buy her the precious moments to grab what she'd hidden in the toilet tank. "Open up, you little slut!"

She stretched her arm up and back, feeling the tendons in her shoulder straining as her hand pawed urgently at the deadbolt's base, trying to grip the throw. Her fingers grappled, again and again until finally the deadbolt latched. Skylar collapsed to the floor. The door kept buckling. She climbed up, slipping on the small puddle of her own nervous urine, then yanked off the toilet tank cover, looked inside; it was still there, right where she'd put it for the next fucked up moment like this one.

Skylar screamed as the shower rained carpenter nails onto her skin. Naked, she found herself on the floor of the tub like a punch-drunk fighter being pummeled in the corner, praying for the bell. Despite the incessant ringing in her ears, there was no *ding*, and no scantily clad girls circling the ring with cards announcing the next round. If she was lucky, God would be merciful, and take her sooner, but there was fat chance of that. God was too busy with the famished and the frail, the diseased and the demented to worry about her insignificant little withdrawals. Because of the alternating chills and sweats, she couldn't tell if the shard-like droplets of water raining down were hot or cold. And at that moment she didn't care. She just needed to stop the mad man's onslaught pulsating in her mind.

His fist came through first, dislodging a door panel. Her mind flashed to the Shining, expecting her repugnant predator to poke his head through with a maniacal, "Here's Johnny!" His hairy knuckled mitt wrestled with the deadbolt muttering, "Little cunt." She plunged her arm into the toilet water tank, maneuvering around the plumbing guts, trying to grab the handle of the butcher knife. Her heart beating faster and faster, she tugged and tugged—but it was caught on something. As she yanked with all her might, the deadbolt released.

The door kicked open and he paused. The monster grinned at his possession, his sexy little prize, his demented fantasy, and as he swaggered into the bathroom to have his way with her, the moment unfurled like a twisted ballet.

Now back in bed, it was the termites eating her legs that woke Skylar from her fitful rest. They started inside the balls of her feet and in a flash scurried up her calves to her thighs, gnawing from the inside out. Thrashing, Skylar tumbled from the bed, but Jarod was there to catch her before she hit the floor. Disoriented, she scratched and clawed at the insects' resilient march on the cold turkey Appomattox that was her body. With primal grunts she reached for the pitcher Jarod held, grabbed it and doused herself with the cool water. Slowly, painfully the termites burrowed into her memory, becoming strange bedfellows with her tumultuous past.

C'mon c'mon! The knife's edge then pulled free from under the floatation bulb. Skylar had, in that split second, a moment of utter clarity. As her fist tightened around the butcher knife, she knew in her heart that a rebirth was in the offing. Hers. Her attacker, her guardian by writ of the blind and deaf foster care system, lurched as she spun.

The knife entering flesh caused a sound like she'd never before heard, a silky thud followed by a groan. Foster daddy's eyes widened in shock, mouth agape, his body rigid with surprise at her ultimate 'no'. Her hand remained on the hilt, even when it would go in no further. Finally letting go of it she fell backward onto the toilet seat. He crumbled to his knees, still incredulous over his foster daughter's little surprise—staring wide-eyed at her like a puppet without strings.

There was no panic on her part. In fact, fifteen-year-old Skylar was consumed with a pride of ownership and accomplishment she'd never felt before. This reckoning was her Girl Scout Gold Award, she thought, the straight 'A's' she never received, the Debutante Ball she'd been denied, all in one. Or balls, plural in this case, she thought to herself, given that the knife landed into her foster father's scrotum and travelled in an upward motion, all but severing his 'goods.' Feeling his blood on her bare toes caused the briefest moment of guilt about what she had just done, but it passed and never resurfaced. The truth was that she had slayed a dragon, an incomprehensible monster that deserved every lost drop of blood.

Rebirth.

And as she stood over him, she showed her ultimate humanity by fishing his phone out of his pocket, dialing 911, then tossing it onto the floor on her way out of this hell hole for good.

Skylar reflected later, long after she'd awoken in the basement of a nearby church, her body crusted with his dried blood, that she was pleased he didn't die; solaced that he'd have to live the rest of his pathetic life as less than the man he never was.

Jarod was brewing Skylar a pot of dandelion root tea when he heard her cries. He hurried to her bedside and placing his hands on her temples, chased away her demons employing a technique used to calm night terrors. With a cool cloth across her forehead and a dollop of honey on her tongue, she settled down.

Skylar's eyes, calmer for the first time in days, gazed up at Jarod with relief and gratitude. Her hand crept from under the covers and slid itself into Jarod's. Her touch both excited and frightened him, conflicting emotions that he was not sure how to reconcile. His first thought was to call and ask Sydney about them. He was the person Jarod had always depended upon to help him understand complexities within emotions and human feelings. Today though, he decided to trust his instincts.

Jarod applied balm to Skylar's cracked lips. Her eyes closed for much needed rest. He smoothed her hair and re-covered her with the blanket. After days of bathing, feeding, soothing, and serving as her defender against pain, rays of light were beginning to filter through the haze in Skylar's utter darkness.

For Jarod's search of Luke, however, there was yet no light. He still needed to know who O'Quinn worked for and where he had sent Kaj after kidnapping him. There were only two people he knew that could have those answers. Skylar, whose mind he feared may take more time to heal than he had, and another whose mind was so arrogant Jarod would have to crawl into the darkest corners of his own tortured soul to retrieve them.

Chapter 14

THE CONCEITED DOCTOR gazed at his reflection in the cloakroom mirror of the L'Endroit de L'Homme Club, the barest hint of a smile flitting across his lips.

In his clothes, as in every other aspect of his life, Bilson prided himself in his attention to details, so the fact that he'd missed the ones that would have told him Dr. Jarod Russell had been an imposter, made him furious. O'Quinn was livid that he had been duped, but in reality it wasn't his fault. He had been doing O'Quinn a favor by attempting to restore the cognitive abilities of the bald man's captive. He wasn't the one who'd scrambled the Libyan's brain. O'Quinn and his one armed cowboy had done that.

As Bilson thought about this, a sense of relief overcame him. Now that Kaj was gone from his hospital, as well as Jarod, whomever the hell he really was, Bilson had dodged a bullet—literally atop the hospital's roof and figuratively as the shootings had been swept under the press rug by O'Quinn's bosses.

Things had now returned to normal; in fact, they were better than ever. The pharmaceutical trials he was running would now go on without interruption.

Counting in his mind the millions he would make, he exited from the exclusive club and into the Manhattan evening. He walked toward the rear of the one cab in the taxi stand, banging on its side.

The cabbie fired up the engine, and watched through his rear view as Bilson got into the backseat, "What can I do fer ya this foine evenin' me foine sur?"

Perfect, thought Bilson, 40,000 *cab drivers in New York and I get Dick Van Dyke from Mary Poppins.* "You can keep your inane chatter to yourself and head toward Midtown."

Bilson watched the gregarious spark die in the cabbie's eyes in the rear view—he'd gotten the message. As the taxi pulled into traffic, the doctor reached into his pocket and pulled out a Gurkha Black Dragon, which, at $1,150 was one of the most expensive cigars in the world. *Attention to details.* He was clipping off its tip as the cabbie shot him a look via the rear view. "Don't mean to be too *inane,* Sir, but, uh …" The driver knocked on a 'No Smoking' sticker on the separation window. It was a detail the doctor had overlooked and a rule he had no intention of following.

"Crack your window and take me to 81st and 8th—and don't try to screw me by going south around the park. I'm not a tourist."

Punctuating his pomposity, Bilson made a brazen show of sparking his lighter, then twirled the cigar in his fingers and sucked the flame into its ligero. When the cabbie took a left turn, heading south, the doctor's pretentious grin faded. "I told you not to go around the park."

When the cabbie spoke into the rear view, the once upbeat quality of his voice was replaced by a flat monotone. "That's the difference between people. Some *tell* and some *ask.* I *asked* you not to smoke in my cab and you *told* me not to go around the park." Staring with cold intensity at the doctor's reflection, the cabbie continued. "I guess some people are so arrogant they're determined to have things their way, regardless of what happens to others around them."

With that, the cabbie held up a key fob with two electronic switches on it. He flicked the first one theatrically. Bilson heard the *thump—thump,* as the rear doors locks engaged. He reached for the door handle to escape only to find they had been removed. Adrenaline flooded his system and then he heard another *thump—thump* this time coming from his chest. Panicked, he looked up as the driver put on an oxygen mask then flicked the second switch on the fob. This time the *thump—thump* was a *Pssss—Pssss* as a mist began spewing out from under the seat. Immediately disoriented,

Bilson began to lose consciousness. As he slipped away, he caught a glimpse of the driver's eyes in the rear view and realized another detail he'd overlooked.

He knew those eyes. They belonged to the imposter that made his way into the hospital.

Then, his world went black.

Chapter 15

STAINED WITH BLOOD and ripped where the knife had stabbed through it, the white blouse was laid out on the testing table right next to a cracked coffee mug.

The little girl's fingers touched the mug first. Sitting at the table, she caressed the side of the drinking vessel where the blue glazing was still shiny. She brought it to her face so she could get a good look at it—a good *feel* of it.

Reflected on its surface, the girl staring back looked like Cindy-Loo Who's twisted black-haired sister. It was a reflection of the young empath Dara.

On her head was a B Net EEG cap with multiple electrodes that read every electronic signal passing through her brain. They were translated as animated cerebral imagery and wirelessly projected on the flat screen strategically placed behind where Dara was doing the psychoscopy *reading*.

It wasn't her own reflection Dara was *interpreting;* she was *intuitively sensing* the emotional resonance left behind on the mug by its last user. "She saw her killer's reflection in the shiny stuff on the mug, as he came in through the back door of the farmhouse and walked up behind her but seeing him didn't make her scared. That would come later."

As she received and related the feelings and memories of the woman who had last held the mug, the anatomic imagery on the flat screen display showed that three areas of Dara's brain were hyper-stimulated.

Her amygdala, the region that processes emotion, was pulsating red. The caudate, the section where memories are stored, was glowing blue but it was her parahippocampal gyrus that stood out. The electrical activity of the area of her brain associated with clairvoyant, intuitive ability was white hot.

Sitting at the table across from her, Sydney was supposed to be watching all of this. They were in his lab after all, and he was conducting this Empathic Ability Comprehension Analysis. Sydney, though, was lost in thought in the parts of his own brain that were associated with emotions, memories and empathy, so much so that he didn't hear Dara as she picked up the blouse and went on.

"The old woman didn't feel the knife as it entered her back and ruptured her heart. She died too quickly. Her last thoughts were of her cats. Her *13* cats." A sadness flitted across Dara's face as she received the distant energy from the blouse. "Who would feed them? Who would care for them? Would anyone find them? No one ever visited her. No one loved her anymore."

A weighty silence filled the room.

Dara came out of her receptive mode and looked over to Sydney, who was trapped in his own ruminative retrospection. "Do you want me to go on? Sydney?"

Sydney remained silent. He was lost in his own mind, reliving a nightmare that had happened to him in real life.

The memory played out as if he were watching a movie in his head. It was the night Jarod had come to him pretending to be a fireman.

Standing in the hallway of the Fountain Grove Hotel in New York City, a distraught Jarod looked Sydney in his eyes. "I want the truth."

Sydney was frozen in Jarod's unrelenting gaze. "About what?"

"Who I really am. Did the Centre adopt me? Was I bought? Was I stolen? And where are my Mom and Dad?"

Sydney felt a pang of empathy, for Jarod's anguish. "I've told you a thousand times—your parents died in a plane crash in Cincinnati."

"I know what you told me!" Jarod flared, *"You seared that story into my brain for years, Sydney, but the first thing I did when I got out was to check every detail. Joe and Evelyn grew up on farms outside Cincinnati just as you said. They are buried overlooking the Ohio River just where you said. Everything, every little detail is just as you said! Except for one. Me."*

It was Sydney's turned to be confused. *"You?"*

"I did a DNA profile of me and my so-called parents and guess what? Evelyn and Joe had RNA factors in their chromosomes that aren't in me. It's impossible that I'm their son."

Sydney was stunned. *"I don't understand, there must be some mistake."*

"My only mistake was in trusting you."

These words stung the Belgian's heart. *"I would never have knowingly lied to you, Jarod, you must believe me."*

Jarod turned back to his mentor. *"I can be a doctor, a lawyer, an electrical engineer."*

"And so much more, Jarod."

"Yes, you taught me I can become anyone I want to be—except me. I don't know who I am." Tears welled in Jarod's eyes. *"Please tell me who I am."*

"I'm sorry, Jarod. But I—I don't know."

Jarod spun Sydney up against the wall. *"Now you may not know the truth, but the secret to who I am has to be in the Centre's mainframe archives. I can't get in—but you can."*

"Jarod—only people with Miss Parker's security clearance have access to that. And even if I did—if the Centre found out they'd crucify me."

Jarod pressed Sydney harder against the wall. *"I did everything you asked of me for the last 30 years; now I'm asking you to do one thing for me."*

"Sydney?"

Startled, Sydney looked up and saw Dara's perturbed expression. His gaze shifted to the screen where the five-year-old girl's brain imagery had returned to its sedate norm. Sydney became stern. "You're not concentrating, young lady."

"Me?" Dara looked indignant. "You're the one whose head is scattered. I can *feel* it from here."

She was right, of course. A downward vortex was consuming him. At first, he'd tried to convince himself that Jarod's escape would not affect his work, but, as the days dragged on, he found himself increasingly unprepared for the hole in his soul that Jarod's absence had created.

"I'm sorry, Dara, my mind is elsewhere."

Dara stared at him and cocked her head left. "It's not your mind, Sydney." On the flat screen, her parahippocampal gyrus began glowing burning white again. Dara was feeling something else as she looked into her teacher's troubled eyes. "It's your *heart*. It's not in what *we're* doing."

Not wanting to give the little clairvoyant an opening to read inside him further, Sydney decided to curtail their session. But before he could utter the words' Let's take a break,' Dara flashed a shrewd smile.

"Does that mean I can go ride my trike now?" She asked.

Relieved, Sydney nodded. "Yes. We'll work again later."

Dara immediately transformed into a carefree five-year-old. She darted towards the door and was opening it as Sydney, always the caregiver, called after her. "Take off your headgear, young lady."

But it was too late to stop her momentum. Dara flung open the door and ran straight into Miss Parker, who was about to enter. The collision caused Miss Parker to drop her Polyvore briefcase.

Dara's eyes popped wide in terror but the young empath was more shocked with what Miss Parker did next, an action her perceptive mind never expected.

Miss Parker looked at the pale-skinned girl and actually—smiled. "Good morning, Dara. How are you today?"

Dara deadpanned back at Miss Parker and then over to Sydney. The little intuitive wondered if their bodies had both been taken over by parasitic intruders—it had to be something like that because neither one was acting like themselves today. Dara shrugged, "I don't know."

Dara then reached down to pick up Miss Parker's briefcase and in the very instant she touched it the imagery of her brain stimulation on the screen began exploding like fireworks on the 4th of July. Dara let out a sharp breath as the emotional resonance she *felt* coming from the briefcase—from *within* the briefcase—overwhelmed her with sadness. It was the same unhappiness Miss Parker always felt. A sorrow fuelled by the unresolved grief she tried desperately to contain every day.

As Miss Parker took the case from Dara, the little psychic peered into her cheerless eyes and fake smile. As Dara half-heartedly grinned back, she decided she'd had more than enough for one morning. She pulled off her EEG cap, tossed it to Sydney and ran off.

Miss Parker turned and smiled at Sydney. "Cornelius is about to give an update briefing. I thought you might like to tag along."

Assessing her demeanor left Sydney confused. *Was she really being nice to him?* Genuine or not, he was too concerned about Jarod to take time for his suspicions. He wanted to know what Cornelius had discovered. "Yes, I would."

He grabbed his tweed jacket and passed her at the door on his way out. Miss Parker looked after him as he did, lit a cigarette and shook her head. Her father had taught her to play both sides against the middle and that's what she was going to do—for as long as she could stand it.

Or Sydney.

Chapter 16

BLACK ON EACH end and white in the middle, the single brow above Cornelius' left eye undulated. The man without another follicle on his body was nervously moving around the tech theatre ensuring that all 37 computer screens were dark—but ready. The hairless cretin had something up his sleeve.

As instructed, Daphne was putting out bagels and cream cheese on the hospitality table for Miss Parker. Why? The blonde in the Wicked Wendy Cat Eye glasses had no idea. Few had been the times she'd seen Miss Parker in the Centre cafeteria and *never* had she seen the beautiful creature as much as look at a carb. Still, her job was to do what she was told by the creepy Cornmeister—*at least for now.*

While opening the tub of Philly, she felt the one-browed pervert breathing down her neck.

Literally.

He had snuck up behind her and was looking over her shoulder—into her cleavage. His left nostril whistled as he said, "Those look tasty." Trying to hold her breakfast down, she squirmed out from under his chin and made her way to her computer station.

He smirked.

Blondie had responded to his touch and his clever come-on line as he'd intended her to do; even if she'd been too turned on to realize it, she would soon enough. In short order they'd all realize it was futile to fight his seductive charms. For now, however, he had to get down to other business.

The business at hand.

Cornelius wasn't prepared for the dog and pony show he was about to put on, but Miss Parker had insisted. He was smarter than her—more intelligent than Sydney—and far brighter than Blondie, so he was confident he could put lipstick on the pig of what little he'd learned and still look brilliant in their dull eyes. He'd been the one to discover the hospital Jarod was in and, if the mini-skirted warrior had allowed him to go, was sure he'd have captured the elusive one himself. While he didn't have all the answers yet, he had found out more than mere mortals could have discovered. So all in all, he was pimped, pumped and primed. Good to go. A lean, mean, thinking machine!

That was, until Miss Parker walked in with Sydney in tow and he felt a wave of insecurity descend upon him like a dark cloud. He covered his anxiety with a head bow, raised the bagel tray to her and spoke a greeting in incorrect French. "*Bonjour*, Miss Parker. Would you like *un petit pain*?"

Miss Parker snuffed her cigarette out in the cream cheese. "No."

For once, Sydney approved of Miss Parker's crudeness, though he didn't show it. Daphne, on the other hand, couldn't stifle her smile, as she looked out of the corner of her eye at the stunned Corndog.

The clammy one looked as if his favorite pet had just been drowned. Fighting to keep his composure, he cleared his throat, "Let there be light." This was Blondie's cue. At the same moment he waved his hand, she hit a computer key and as if triggered by magic coming from his fingertips, every computer screen lit up and the theatre came to life.

As he did this, Miss Parker, Sydney, and Daphne were all thinking some variation of *what a douche.*

On the screens appeared different images from the surveillance footage Cornelius had acquired from Guardian General of Jarod, the shaved-headed man with the eye patch, a young woman and a Middle-Eastern man being pushed on a gurney.

Atop each, a software program over-laid a shifting laser graph that took measurements of distinguishing facial features.

Cornelius explained. "When I was a mere lad of 13 or 14, my sophomore year at University, I devised a face recognition app that was so advanced that my professors were bewildered trying to grasp its ramifications.

Fast forward to now, and well, let's just say I'd love to see their 'facial recognition' if they witnessed what I'd discovered utilizing it today."

The vein on Daphne's left temple began to pulsate. She was the one who'd been busting her ass here doing all the work for the last 36 hours and yet, the hairless weasel was taking all the credit.

Some things never changed—but they were about to.

"I'll try my best to describe, in a manner that all can comprehend, what my findings have been up to ..." he checked his Tag Heuer, "90 seconds ago."

Miss Parker cut him off. "Shove the PowerPoint. We know the questions, what are the answers?"

This time, both Daphne and Sydney caught each other's eyes and couldn't hold back their grins.

Cornelius swallowed the dryness in his mouth and loosened his tie. "I'm afraid I don't have as many of those as I'd hoped to by now." He felt Miss Parker's negative energy shift and overcompensated. "But more than most could have expected, I assure you."

Tired of dinking around, Miss Parker pointed to the picture. "Then *assure* me with the name of the guy with the eye patch."

Cornelius snickered. "Funny you should ask about the bald man first. He's a blank slate. A spectre. No database in the world has any record of his face. Which means he was never caught on camera at any time or any place on the globe, all of those images have been destroyed, or he's some kind of clandestine spook."

Miss Parker pondered this. "If he does what we do, then we might have mutual friends who can help us out here."

Cornelius froze the image of O'Quinn as he continued. "My guess is he is former military, Blackwater, covert ops type."

Miss Parker raised an eyebrow, "Then we *definitely* go to the same cocktail parties." The tall brunette leaned down and put her hand on Blondie's shoulder. "Send me his picture now, I'll blast it out."

Feeling Miss Parker's warmth on her skin, Daphne felt as if live wires were sparking all over her body. She looked at Miss Parker's strong but delicate left hand—the one with the square shaped platinum ring on her forefinger—then looked up at her face. Daphne loved Miss Parker's face and the way she enhanced the delicate features and sharp angles with her impeccable makeup. Miss Parker's look was of course designed to draw others in. Not a lot of eye makeup. Just liner, some mascara, a hint of brown powder and enough shadow to highlight the glistening magic of her bottomless azure eyes. That's where Miss Parker wanted the focus and that's where Daphne's was as she answered in a near breathless whisper. "Anything you want, Miss Parker."

Sydney had a different focus on Miss Parker. He was watching her open her briefcase and remove her laptop. As she turned it on, he noticed she was also carrying the Etch A Sketch in her attaché, the one Jarod left for her at the hotel. He realized it must have been what triggered Dara's clairvoyant responses. The young empath had felt something powerful in the emotional resonance left behind on the Etch A Sketch by Miss Parker. Or by Jarod.

Or perhaps by both.

Sydney recognized that Jarod's drawing of Miss Parker's younger self conveyed a personal message. Sydney could only wonder what emotional connection the act of keeping it with her signified. This notion was pushed out of Sydney's head as Miss Parker wirelessly linked her computer into the Centre mainframe. He stared as she waited for the prompt to ask for her access code, the code that would allow him to access any computer in the Centre—one that would allow him to find Jarod's answers.

Recognizing this was a chance to get it, he focused on her fingers. As a child Jarod had told Sydney that shutting down all other parts of his brain except for his concentration allowed him to chisel information he wanted to possess into his mind forever.

Sydney washed every other thought out of his mind and focused on nothing but retaining Miss Parker's every keystroke. The access code prompt appeared on-screen. Her right forefinger was above the '7' key where he knew it would be and she struck it first, followed by a capital 'V', and Sydney thought *this just might work*. But her fingers began typing light-ning fast and everything turned to a blur. As quickly as her fingers started, they stopped.

Miss Parker pointed to the screen and the picture of the Libyan terrorist being whisked away by O'Quinn's men. "What about Haji?"

Cornelius sighed. "Unfortunately—we haven't had any luck finding
out anything about him. At all."

Miss Parker jerked around to face Cornelius and was deciding whether
to shoot him in the head or the heart when she heard a timid voice peep
from behind her.

"Actually, we have."

Miss Parker swiveled. Daphne parted a grin. "Well, at least *I* have."

Parker had never thought Blondie was capable of much of anything; in
fact, she'd never thought about Blondie at all. "You found out who he is?"

"Yes ma'am."

"Don't call me 'ma'am'."

"Yes, Miss Parker."

Cornelius laughed though he knew this development wasn't funny.
"And why didn't you inform me?"

"I tried, but you told me to shut up and lay out the bagels."

Miss Parker put an end to this. "What did you find?"

Daphne cleared her throat, "I hacked into the NSA and discovered the
Middle Eastern man is an unscrupulous Libyan named Kaj Rahamzada."

Cornelius interrupted Daphne, wanting—*needing* attention. "I believe
that's an oxymoron."

"So are you." Miss Parker didn't bother looking at him. "Go on,
Blondie."

Daphne plunged ahead. "During the insurgency, Rahamzada worked
as an interpreter for the Allies by day and as an operative who planted IEDs
to kill them by night. He made a fortune looting government arms caches
and selling the contents. He was one of the guys behind the consulate attack that supposedly wasn't 'terrorism' in his hometown of Benghazi.
Kidnappings, car bombings, murder for hire, he's been on the wrong side
of the law since before puberty." Daphne handed Miss Parker a paper file.
"I've printed all of this up for you."

Miss Parker was impressed. Sensing that, Daphne continued on.
"Rahamzada has dodged death many times, but lost his eye when a Mossad

agent stuck a bomb on his car. Since then, he's been an international free-lancer, working for the highest bidders."

Miss Parker shot disdain at Cornelius while addressing Daphne. "You did all this—on your own?"

Blondie beamed, "Yes, me, totally."

Cornelius cracked his neck and quavered, "Well, I have taken her under my wing."

"What was Jarod's interest in this terrorist?" Interjected Sydney. "That's the key to finding Jarod."

Daphne shrugged. "That's where the mystery starts. The Libyan's hospital records vanished along with him the day he was moved. I was able to discover something quite interesting, though. Kaj Rahamzada was in the room right next to the woman Jarod carried out of the hospital."

Trying to remain relevant, Cornelius almost shouted out, "All we have on her is a name: Skylar Cohasset. Her background is a dry hole at this point." Then fearing he was about to get bitch slapped again, he gazed at Daphne. "Right?"

Daphne just shrugged.

Miss Parker looked at the screens featuring Skylar. "The one he kidnapped?"

Sydney shook his head. "Miss Parker, how many times do I have to tell you? Jarod would not kidnap anyone."

While Miss Parker was thinking how tired she was of Sydney being a pain in her ass, she felt one in her foot. She looked down to see Daphne's heel on her toe, realizing the tech was trying to get her attention *clandestinely*.

With a short head toss, Daphne indicated for Miss Parker to check out the main screen, on which was an image of Jarod outside the ER helping Skylar into the Town Car. Daphne zoomed in on something specific— Jarod's gentle touch on Skylar's back as he placed her inside.

Miss Parker's eyes narrowed. "Looks like you're right, Sydney. Boy genius *wasn't* kidnapping her. It looks like he's found a treat he likes better than ice cream."

Sydney regarded the photograph and was both surprised and pleased to see Jarod enjoying physical contact with another human being.

Miss Parker grabbed her briefcase and was halfway out when she yelled at Cornelius. "Shake the trees and find out who she is or I'll have someone prune *you* down to a stump."

Cornelius felt the slap of her words, his single eyebrow now undulating in fear.

Chapter 17

THIRTY SECONDS LATER Miss Parker was rounding a corner when someone called her name. It was Daphne who'd been chasing after her down the hallway.

The blonde was out of breath, "I'm not sure if Cornelius can find her. I mean, the Cohasset woman, Skylar ..."

"But?" Miss Parker prompted, with a delicately raised eyebrow.

Daphne regained her composure and stared into Miss Parker's eyes. "I know how to find women."

Miss Parker took Daphne in. All the way. "What's your name, Blondie?"

"It's Daphne, ma'am—I mean Miss."

"*Daphne*, huh? Nice handle." Daphne grinned. Miss Parker reached into her bra and pulled out a business card—her personal one with her private cell number. Daphne accepted it. "Tell you what, Daphne *who knows how to find women,* find Skylar for me and I'll make your dreams come true."

Parker turned and walked away. Daphne studied every step, her eyes ogling Parker's sculpted legs and the curves above, absorbing her every lithe movement. To Daphne, Miss Parker moved with a sinuous grace. Daphne closed her eyes and listened to the fading echo of Parker's Jimmy Choos as she breathed in Parker's unique scent on the business card. The essence caused a smile to form on the young blonde's face, one that curved up sinfully at the corners.

Chapter 18

ALONE AND FEELING isolated, Cornelius tossed his surprise hospitality tray into the trash. He even threw out the Philly cheese's plastic container. *Screw the 'Centre is Green' recycling campaign.* He was pissed. That ponytailed bitch had just embarrassed him. Just *betrayed* him—and after all he'd done for her.

How the hell did she find out what he had failed to? His facial recognition program was flawless—except for all the defects he *didn't know about.*

What the hell's wrong with you Cornman!? You were a child prodigy! As recorded by Mensa, Cornelius was the *third* smartest person born in 1987. A fact he disputed and was tormented by; convinced he deserved the silver medal and arguably the gold. Yet somehow, he'd still been bested by the bitch that had only gone to community college.

He'd already had to suffer through a life as a bronze medal winner in the IQ bowl and would be damned if he'd slip off the awards podium.

If Blondie wants a war, he fumed, *she'll get one.*

Chapter 19

SKYLAR STIRRED FROM her 24 hour sleep. There were no more sweats, nausea, or pounding thuds behind her eyes. Her wicked Nor-Easter of detox had finally moved offshore.

As her eyes fluttered open she thought one last hallucination was still overstaying its welcome; sitting at the foot of her bed was Chaz in a sleek throwback sequined cocktail dress. Skylar gave up a giggle mixed with a throaty cough as the man in the wavy wig threw a beautiful smile right back.

"First a brilliant surgeon, now the queen of pop. What's your next trick, Jarod?" Skylar chuckled.

Chaz laughed heartily. "Ain't no Beyoncé but thank you girl for the props—and J-Rod's good, but he ain't *this* good. Name's Chaz, baby, and rest easy, this be a friendly room."

Skylar slowly sat up and shook Chaz's silky hand. She swung her feet to the floor and stood. All good. She made it to the window and basked in the warmth of the sunlight. For the first time in recent memory she felt free—free from the overlords of Guardian General, free from the desperate strains of living on the streets. Free, and it felt wonderful.

Skylar looked around for Jarod. Chaz noticed her disappointment in his not being there.

"All good, girl. Just temp subbin' for Jarod who's off doing who knows what." Chaz chuckled. Chaz's laugh eased Skylar, who understood. Before long they were chatting it up together like old friends about everything from politics to the most lucrative Manhattan street corners to panhandle from. Jarod's loft had become the land of misfit toys and three was good company.

"I gots myself a real job interview this morning, baby. Massage parlor—a legit one over on Eighth needs one them street corner sign holders whose *milkshake brings all the boys to the yard*. Looks like you gonna be alone for a while, that okay?"

"I've been alone most of my life. I'll be fine." Skylar shrugged, not the least perturbed by that notion.

Chaz left Skylar a tray full of Harlem home cooking and her cell number, then sashayed out, sequins and all.

After a glorious shower and a fresh set of clothes from Jarod, Skylar moved to the main room and found a chubby rodent sniffing under a closet door. From her years on the streets, she was comfortable with all of God's creatures.

"Big Boy smells a treat?" She tugged open the door with a yank and sure enough, there was an open bag of beef jerky tucked just inside of Jarod's backpack on the floor. She brought it to the table for a more thorough examination.

Oscar followed her, nibbling as she scattered bits of the tangy shreds for him. It was what was under the jerky bag that caught her attention: dozens of cell phones, exquisitely made fake I.D.s, a couple of modified Etch A Sketches, some odd-looking data discs and an intriguing high-tech device the likes of which she'd never seen before—Jarod's DSA player.

At first, she tried to ignore it, push down the feelings of an overactive curiosity that had been her greatest ally and her worst enemy. It was the same curiosity that had at times enlightened and at others, unnerved her. *The Lady or the Tiger?* But Skylar had always been a risk taker—it had made her stronger. No risk, no reward, taking chances had helped her survive out there.

As she eyed the player, she considered what hidden truths or secrets potentially lurked in there about this man she found herself caring for. The risk/reward of her choice in that moment seemed greater somehow.

Did she have any right to even open this Pandora's box? She felt a twinge of guilt about violating his privacy and while her gut told her she could trust Jarod, the scars left by men in her past brought her back to self-protection. Knowing the truth about people was a necessity going forward. She vowed to never be victimized again.

With that, she raised the screen and activated the POWER button on the DSA device.

The first sound was that of a nonsense nursery rhyme, '*Kri Kraw, Toads Foot, Geese Walk, Bare Foot.*' Skylar was taken by the image of the beautiful four-year-old boy who was singing. She knew it was Jarod as a boy. Then the words appeared on screen: *JAROD 2/4/83, PSYCHOGENIC STUDIES, FOR OFFICIAL CENTRE USE ONLY.*

Entranced, as if gazing into a wizard's crystal, Skylar sat, her eyes never leaving the screen from the moment the cameras took in the boy's amazing re-creation of the Manhattan skyline to his words into the camera—'*Where are my Mom and Dad?*'

With a random flick of her charcoal grey fingernail to the touch screen, a new image appeared.

Young Jarod, around age seven, shivering and unkempt, was slouched over a small homemade bomb he was building. Superimposed words came up on the screen: JAROD 1/10/86, PSYCHOGENIC STUDIES FOR CLIENT: FEDERAL BUREAU OF INVESTIGATION—CASE 3555467—UNABOM (UNIversity & Airline BOMBer)—FOR CENTRE USE ONLY.

Skylar realized this had something to do with the infamous Unabomber, Ted Kaczynski. Even at his callow young age, there was a thousand yard stare in Jarod's eyes and a troubling edge in his voice.

"That summer, there were too many people around my cabin, so I decided I needed some peace. After two days of hiking, I arrived at my favorite place at the waterfall, but when I climbed up onto the plateau I found they had put a road right through the middle of it. I can understand the pure anger that moment presented inside of me."

Jarod continued tinkering with his homemade bomb, wiring the detonator into place, his body relaxed though his shirt was drenched with sweat.

"I know what I have to do—revenge on the system, violent revenge on America's industrial complex, is my only practical recourse to spark the people into rebellion."

There was silence for several seconds and then young Jarod's body sagged and the youthful clarity in his eyes returned. He was a boy again. "He has to be stopped, Sydney, or this monster is going to kill a lot of innocent people."

Jarod pivoted around, searching for Sydney, but instead caught his own reflection in the bomb's polished steel casing. He stared at himself in that moment, his words not only prophetic about the man he was trying to decipher from within, but very personal as well. "He's trapped inside his own brilliant mind, Sydney—feeling lost."

The disquiet in young Jarod unnerved Skylar, and she quickly tapped another icon on the touch screen. Non-stop explosions and gunfire echoed from the DSA player as a new video appeared. She watched, horrified and yet absorbed.

Jarod, now a very different young man, tall, handsome, maturing into his teen years, stood in a swirl of residual cordite smoke moving through an interactive Sim world of a high school—in the midst of a killing rampage. In his left hand was a 12 gauge Stevens 311D double barreled sawed-off shotgun and in his right was a Hi-Point 995 Carbine 9 millimeter semi-auto assault rifle.

"Darkness. Light. God. The Devil. Heaven. Hell. The fight between good and evil becomes endless, but the morons think it's a fight they can win. Morons. I am a God compared to those idiot zombies."

Out of the corner of teen Jarod's eye, three terrified students rushed out of a classroom to escape—a spinning Jarod peppering a spurt of bullets, cutting them down in their tracks amid screams and moans. Possessed now, he kicked open the door to the boy's room, finding two more teens. With an eerie calm he raised the sawed-off at them and blasted a series of double rounds, leaving his victims in a bloody, smoking heap.

Hearing voices, teen Jarod moved back out into the hallway in time to mow down two escaping teachers, then reloaded a new clip into his automatic, pondering aloud. "Everything is connected, yet I remain separated. Unable to break through into their world—break through in their normal way. So I shatter the din. It's the ultimate cry of my voice they now have no choice but to hear—and the cries of the disenfranchised voices that echo behind me."

A riveted Skylar watched as Jarod's face began to tighten and his body tensed like a coil in pre-release that had snapped.

Jarod spun, raised the shotgun and the semi-auto assault rifle, unloading both in a rage-filled coda sending glass and wood splinters showering around him. Shedding his weapons, kicking them away, he smashed his fists through the last remaining panes while unleashing a loud, unhuman, anguished cry.

Finally spent, he slid down the wall with emotionless futility. He pulled a TEC-9 from his waistband and began tickling his temple with it—fighting the tears welling in his eyes. "Isolation equals madness, Sydney—and we won't soon see the end of it. He just wants to be like the others." The gun spilled from teen Jarod's hand. "Why can't I be like the others too, Sydney? Why am I trapped—and how can I get out?"

Skylar froze the image. She stared into the silent space of the loft, her heart breaking for Jarod's vulnerability, for the secrets of his past that he kept from her to shield her from this pain and in turn, shield himself. She could only wonder about the man who had been so tender and loving to her after having endured so much madness.

She looked over at Oscar, who'd crawled inside and become trapped in the jerky bag, only to find him in a clawing frenzy trying to dig his way out.

Madness indeed.

Chapter 20

ADIDAS MAN AWOKE with the sweats again. They paid their first visit just a few days ago—out of the blue, like a devil at the door—and had returned every day since.

At first, a cold shower washed them away, but with each passing hour of uncertainty over Kaj's fate, and his own, the sweats were becoming the guest who wouldn't leave.

How could a sip of Cuervo hurt?

Shit, he deserved it, having to keep watch on that kid—feed him, keep him quiet—hell, the little runt even attacked him one time. The way he saw it, he deserved several shots of the golden agave. Hell, he *earned* it.

So he snuck out and bought a bottle—Kaj wasn't around, right?

On his second run, he even zip-tied the kid to his cot to be sure he'd stay put, while he went and grabbed three more.

Still the sweats got worse. The dementia of doubt opened wider and wider like a black hole he felt sure was swallowing him.

Before long, he found a shank of PVC in the dusty garage, sheared a piece of aluminum from the drooping gutter and fashioned himself a good ol' DIY crack pipe.

Then, he used the cell phone he promised Kaj he wouldn't, called his former supplier Slick Ray and placed an order for a Venti sized *to-go* rock of the crystal messiah.

Meanwhile, Luke had had an epiphany the day before about the power of his imagination as he had once again awoken from his recurring body-under-the-covers nightmare. It was a sudden realization he'd never expected. It seemed the more he had the nightmare, the more he recognized it was actually helping him *not* be as afraid of what was happening to him in his *awake* life.

He knew nightmares weren't real, that they were just products of his imagination and as scary as his was, it did distract him. So Luke figured that if he could just twist his brain a little so he could turn that nightmare into something cool and more hopeful, maybe, just maybe those new mind games might help him keep calm.

So he started devising new endings to the dream and before long, whole new stories centering on a lone hero taking on bad guys who were hurting someone weaker than themselves. Like him. Kind of like Luke's very own lone hero coming out of the night to save him.

His mind spent hours on these fantasies, but before long these tales began losing their power of escape. The deep gouges on his wrists from the zip-ties served as a constant reminder that the line between fact and fantasy was a fine one, and that here he still was.

Adidas Man peeped through the blinds and, squinting into the sun, spotted the rooster tail from Slick Ray's Torino as it wound its way up the long gravel driveway.

Adidas Man licked the drop of sweat beaded on the tip of his nose with his snake-like tongue. Slick Ray always was as automatic as a hard-on in a whorehouse. A giggle of glee bubbled up in the fat man's chest. His long wait was almost over.

It would only be minutes now. The rock would help him get his head on straight, stay on top of the bad *sitch,* be more chill with the brat in the basement—until bad turned good and wrong met right. A hit or two of glory and he'd be back in the game with stamina that wouldn't quit on him. Hell, wouldn't that make Kaj proud of him? Wouldn't Kaj be pumped that there was something that could keep him from going absolutely stark raving mad?

Chapter 21

HE COULD JUST feel the gentle gust of warm, humid air that blew onto his cheeks. It stopped then started again. Stopped then started. The cycle slowly coaxed him out of a heavy slumber. His eyes flickered open and the darkness Dr. Bilson found himself in was blacker than any he'd ever experienced. The gust stopped then started, stopped then started.

He tried to move but couldn't. His body wasn't awake and his mind was a muddled mess. Though barely conscious, the arrogant M.D. had already decided to sue *L'Endroit de L'Homme*. This was the worst hangover he'd ever had and it was their fault. *The Boston Brahman* made it a point to never drink cheap libations and theorized the management must be switching the cut-rate stuff into good bottles. *It's disgusting what people will do for the almighty dollar.*

Head exploding, throat Death Valley dry, stomach queasy, Bilson was falling away again when the next gust of warm air brought with it a familiar smell. *Mildew? No. It's sour, like the wet tip of a cigar, like my pillowcase the morning after a night at the club.*

The humid warmth stopped then started, stopped then started. *But why is it blowing into my face?* Bilson's eyes widened. He couldn't see in the dark but he could in his mind. *Every time I exhale the air blows over me. It's my breath—my cigar breath—ricocheting off something blowing back onto my face.*

His heart began to race as adrenaline flooded his system. *My head's in a fucking sack! No, it's not a sack. It's a hood! Like the ones terrorists use on their victims. Oh shit! I'm a victim ... But of what?*

He tried to search through snapshots in his mind. Tried to dredge some memory, any memory of where he'd been. What he had been doing last.

The cabbie!

He flashed to the door with no handle and the look of the cabbie's eyes in the rearview and the gas.

Oh my fucking god! I know that cabbie. It was that doctor. It was Jarod.

Gasping for air caused Bilson to gag. There was a foreign object in the back of his throat beyond the soft palate where his nasal and oral cavities met. Something long and slender was coming up through his throat and out his nose. When he swallowed, whatever it was pulled on his cheek! It was taped to his face in the exact manner as the feeding tubes he used on his comatose patients.

A second jolt of adrenaline surged through his body. His body now totally awake, he tried to sit up but couldn't. *Holy fucking shit! There's something across my chest. Around my wrist and ankles—and cutting into my skin. Am I naked?* Except there was something he felt around his waist digging into his love handles and bunching between his butt cheeks. It was like a fluffy Speedo and it was very damp.

Oh dear God.

He heard a door open, then footsteps coming his way until they stopped next to him. A hand grabbed his upper wrist. He flailed and tried to jerk away, until he heard an emotionless voice say, "If you move, this will hurt."

Bilson felt the puncture on the back of his hand, followed by a prickling sensation in his right dorsal metacarpal vein—just like his patients felt when he introduced a drip I.V. into their bodies. Whatever he'd been given was pulling him back under.

He opened his mouth to scream for help, but nothing came out except for a gentle gust of warm, humid air that blew onto his face.

Chapter 22

THOUGH HIS EYES were crazed and he was frothing from near exhaustion, Miss Parker would not ease up on her white Arabian as it thundered through the field of heather. With the command of her crop, she demanded the last bit of his strength, as she urged him onward toward the old abandoned church. Not until he cleared the fallen wall that faced the Parker family gravesite, did she give him the command to stop.

Miss Parker rarely rode up to the old church anymore. She didn't want to be tempted to look at her mother's headstone. She'd purposefully only set eyes on it once in her life and today would not be the second. Instead, as her steed whinnied, fighting to regain its wind, she gazed across the field and stared at an old friend. On the rise above the heather, the huge oak tree, the Grumpy Old Man still lay broken and lifeless where it had fallen after the lightning bolt struck it so many years ago.

Her father told Miss Parker that, one day, a sapling would grow up from the heart root of the majestic old growth oak, take hold and be an even stronger tree than the one before. Miss Parker had always felt she was that sapling—that she had grown out of the tragic death of, and was stronger than the one whose headstone she could not bring herself to look at.

However, Miss Parker did not feel strong today.

The truth was that no sapling had grown from the broken heart of the Grumpy Old Man, nor had one sprouted from within hers. She was angry and had been taking that anger out on her horse, a beautiful white gelding

who did any and everything she asked of him with just a touch of her hand
or boot.

You couldn't buy that kind of loyalty from a human being, certainly
not from Sydney. Of course Miss Parker had not only been there the day
the stallion had been turned to a gelding—she was wielding the red-hot
knife. Since that moment he would respond to any and all of her
commands.

She thought maybe she'd do the same to Sydney one day.

Or better yet, Jarod.

His Etch A Sketch torment was still on her mind. His, *I know the truth
about what makes you sad*, eating away at her. Yet it was really something else
altogether that had her so emotionally volatile: the image of Jarod gently
touching the woman from the hospital. Jarod's hand on the soft curve of
Skylar's back had replayed over and over in Miss Parker's mind all the previous night and had awoken her this morning. She had told herself that her
mind was rewinding it only because it was in that clue that she would find
the bastard.

It was more than that, though. More than just an intellectual deduction
by a trained investigative mind, it was an unwelcome pang of something
else. Something she thought was akin to jealousy, or jealousy itself, a jealousy tied to the memory of a sapling that had broken through the soil and
reached for the sunlight long ago.

*Teenage Miss Parker quietly opened the door to Sydney's lab. Throwing a covert look
over her shoulder, she scanned the hallway behind her. Assured that she had not been
seen, she slipped inside and caught sight of the target of her clandestine adventure—a
shirtless young Jarod in his living dome, chiseling a replica of Rodin's Thinker out of
marble. With one hand, Miss Parker unconsciously began to twirl her hair as she stared
at him—painting his body with her calculating eyes. Though only mid teens, she could see
Jarod's lean and muscular frame was already becoming that of a man.*

And Miss Parker was interested in men.

*As she took in his broadening chest, watched sweat beads form on his developing
biceps and abs as he worked, traced the muscles in his thighs as he moved, a desirous look
began to form on her nubile face, the look a hungry cat might get, as it stared at a mouse*

across the room, a mouse it planned to toy with before devouring. Thinking of this, Little Miss leaned back against the door, and locked it. The sound of the mechanism engaging caught Jarod's attention and that was when he looked over and saw her.

As Jarod stood from his work and faced her, the same inquisitive look he had been chiseling into the Thinker's eyes began to form in his own.

Young Miss Parker had spent most of the previous year growing out of her white button-down and plaid skirt uniform. Her body had developed earlier than the other girls and, as it did, she liked the way the boys were drawn more and more to her, and only to her.

She liked that a lot.

At first she was surprised with the sudden change in the behavior of boys. How when interacting with them, no matter what she was saying, their attention would fall onto her blouse. It was a curious phenomenon that seemed to increase in frequency in direct proportion to the increasing strain on her buttons. It was a powerful phenomenon.

She liked that a lot too.

She had discovered something amazing over the last few months that would change her forever. The unforeseen power of her blossoming femininity.

She had decided weeks ago while staring down at him from Sydney's office to use that mystique with Jarod. Miss Parker displayed a slow captivating saunter as she walked toward him, rocking her hips ever so slowly, her enticing, voluptuous lips pursed.

She could see how his eyes became bigger and his breath more shallow with every one of her delicate steps. As she stopped outside the glass door to his chamber, still twirling her hair, she knew from his stare she had him in her spell. He swallowed, long and dry. "You're not supposed to be in here."

Miss Parker stopped twirling, a devilish smile parting her lips. "I'm Miss Parker—I can go anywhere I want in the Centre." Never losing eye contact, she played with a St. Christopher's medal dangling around her neck. "And this is where I want to be."

Jarod's eyes were drawn to her hand's movement, exhaling as he glimpsed, something silky and delicate under her blouse. His heart began beating much faster. She pulled an electronic card key out and brought it toward the slide lock on his door.

As he stared at it, Jarod's voice only came out in whisper. "Sydney is . . ."

"Gone for the night." She said meeting his eyes again. "I saw his crappy Volvo puttering out of the lot."

She slid the magnetic strip through the card reader, typed in some numbers on the keypad and, after a tense second, the door unlocked. She stared through the glass.

Jarod's anxiety rose to a new level, and to deflect his nervousness, his natural won-der took over. He looked at the keypad, "How did you know the codes?"

"I stole them when they weren't looking." Then the young temptress, of single-minded purpose, pushed open the door and walked in. As she approached, Jarod re-treated. "You stole?"

Miss Parker traced her hand over The Thinker's head as she continued to pursue him. "If you want something bad enough, sometimes you just have to take it."

Jarod's back hit the wall and he had no escape. Miss Parker could feel the fear and the desire her presence, her newfound power, had over him.

She leaned in very close to his face, ran her hand through his hair, and whispered. "Do you want something, genius boy?"

Jarod nodded.

She then puckered her lips and touched them to Jarod's.

Seated in her saddle, subconsciously twirling her hair, Miss Parker was pulled out of the memory by the shrill ring of her cell phone. "What?"

On the other end was Daphne, who said five words that made Miss Parker smile. "I have what you want."

Chapter 23

MEEEAAA—MEEEAAA—MEEEAAA.

Bilson snapped his head up, down, left, right, eyes searching the darkness. The voices were back. Again. It seemed he'd been hearing them for hours. For days.

Forever.

They were approaching from every direction and the nearer they got the more incessant the chatter. Laughing, mocking, spiteful, a lifetime of echoes of how worthless, pathetic, loathed he was.

The closer he listened, the louder they got, and the closer he listened, the louder they got, *and the closer he listened, the louder they got!*

Then just as suddenly they were gone.

Just as Bilson realized he was still hooded and restrained, the silence of his reality was shattered by a click, then a mechanical hum.

The pump that controlled the tubes had turned back on. *Oh shit!* He concentrated to determine if it was one that fed him through his nose or the one that *oh no! Oh, please, no!* He felt the warmth spreading through the back of his hand.

Meeeaaa—Meeeaaa—Meeeaaa.

NO. NO. PLEASE NOT AGAIN!

The nausea would soon be churning, his heart palpitating—then the visions. "I don't want to see the bad things!"

Dr. Bilson wasn't sure he could survive another round. Wasn't sure if he was screaming out loud or internally. He wasn't sure of anything.

Except for the hand that was suddenly on his head!

In one motion the hood was ripped off! Light screamed through his dilated pupils, bullet trained down his optic nerves and then the supernova exploded in his mind.

He gritted his teeth, fighting the pain. Tears flowed out the sides of his eyes, dripping into his ears until ever so slowly, they began to adjust to the light. He could finally see. The sun was streaming in through a window with cracked glass. It illuminated the room which was—what? Clinical. Tiled walls. Could be a hospital. *Yes. That's what it is. I'm in a hospital, but not the one I practice in. Is it? No. No. Those walls were sterile, these were, were—what's on these walls?* The unscrupulous doctor fought to focus. *These walls are covered in grime and coats of—what are those—colors? It's graffiti—years of it.*

He noticed near empty I.V. bags hanging from a stand beside his bed. One had a tube that led to his hand, the other into his nose.

A long *Pssssssssssssss* sounded from behind his head. He caught a whiff of something chemical. Panicked, he craned his head back and caught a glimpse of a man in surgical scrubs, latex gloves who was shaking a can of—*spray paint?*

Jarod smiled cheerfully. "Doc-a-doodle-do! What's up with you?"

"Me? What the … What the hell are you doing?" Bilson crackled.

"Treating you for your illness, of course." Jarod put the paint can down on a rusty cart piled high with I.V. bags and wheeled it up next to the bed. "In fact it's time to up your dosage."

Confusion flashed across Bilson's face as he watched Jarod trade out full I.V.s for the empties.

"What—what are you talking about?" Bilson said in a panicky voice. "There's nothing wrong with me."

"Of course there is, Jonah, and denying the indications are, in fact, one of the symptoms of your condition."

"What condition?"

Jarod grabbed the medical chart at the foot of the bed and tapped the diagnosis line. "Schizophrenia."

"Schizo—are you out of your mind?"

"I don't think so, but according to this—*you are.*" Jarod pulled out his smartphone. "Hey, but let's double check with Google to be sure." The

Pretender searched 'symptoms of schizophrenia,' then read from the results. "Now, and this is from Wikipedia, so we know it's medically correct … 'A person diagnosed with schizophrenia may experience hallucinations.'" Jarod looked at Bilson. "That'd be check, right?" Jarod made a mark on the medical chart. "Hearing voices?"

"I do not hear voices," Bilson protested.

"Then who have you been yelling 'I don't want to see the bad things' to for the last few days?" Bilson didn't know what he was talking about. Jarod gave him a 'hmph'. "Don't remember, huh? Well, trust me, that's a check too." Jarod made that notation and, in mock seriousness, read on. "Are you suffering from delusions?"

Bilson snapped. "Listen to me, goddamnit! You let me out of here! I'm a doctor for God sakes! And an important one!"

Jarod threw him an *uh-oh* look. "Not only delusions, but of *grandeur*." Jarod flicked his pen on the chart. "Check-a-roonie on that one." Jarod continued. "Let's see. 'Social withdrawal,' well you *are* here all alone. 'Sloppiness of dress, forgetful of personal grooming and hygiene.'" Jarod curled a lip. "Just look at that diaper."

Bilson simmered. "Who are you?"

Jarod shot him a dubious look, then found this topic on the chart. "'Difficulties with long term memory'—well, you beat me to that one."

Bilson exploded. "I am not schizophrenic!"

"Then why are you on anti-psychotic meds?"

Jarod adjusted the gage of the infusion pump that controlled the drip flow into Bilson's hand. Initially set to deliver 25mL/hour, Jarod doubled the dosage to 50.

Bilson struggled against his restraints like a snared animal.

Jarod leaned down, patting his chest comfortingly.

"Shhhh. Shhhh. Relax. There's nothing to worry about, these are the same meds you were testing on your patients. And you'd never give *them* anything you wouldn't take *yourself*, would you?"

Bilson barely found his voice. "That—that's not what we were using. Ours was in pill form."

Jarod began hanging several more I.V. bags. "I thought I'd make a super concentrate and speed up the results." Jarod began linking bags together, the exit tube from one connected to the entrance tube of the next, creating a daisy chain that would eventually deliver every drop of the psychotropic cocktail into Bilson's body.

The chemicals swirling again, Bilson snapped. "You can't do this! Overexposure to psychotropics can …"

Jarod finished his terrified thought. "Permanently alter brain patterns *causing* the very symptoms they were designed to treat?" He reached over for more bags and continued. "Don't worry about that, Jonah. I took a hypocritical oath—to do no harm."

"It's not 'hypocritical'—it's 'Hippocratic.'"

"Hmmm." Jarod shrugged. "I guess sometimes guys like you can't tell the difference."

Jarod began linking the new bags into a chain connected to the feeding tube. Realizing there was enough nourishment in those I.V.s for several weeks—and enough psychotropics in the others for several lifetimes caused Bilson's heart to pound uncontrollably. "Who the hell are you?"

Jarod looked up. "Let's just say I'm someone who'd never destroy another person's brain function for fun and profit." Jarod's fury erupted. "But *you* did, Bilson. Didn't you!?"

Didn't you—didn't you—didn't you?—echoed three times off the tile.

Jarod paced, in a losing attempt to contain his rage. "How many people did you leave trapped in a nightmare in their own minds? How many lives were ruined because of what you did?"

Bilson pleaded, "These weren't real people, they—they were outcasts—homeless. The nobodies. The ones that don't belong!"

Jarod stopped and shot a look of cold fury. "Like Skylar Cohasset?"

"That lunatic?"

"She's not a lunatic and she's not a *nobody*!" Jarod grabbed and raised Bilson by the scruff of his neck. "She's a human being!"

The arrogant MD was genuinely confused. "*This*—is about *her*?"

Jarod's stare drilled into Bilson's very soul. "Among other things you are going to tell me *all* about."

"I'm sorry! I'm sorrrrryyyyy," Bilson whined.

Jarod flung him back onto the sheets. "Apology—*not* accepted." He then reached over and cranked up the dosage on the pump gauge.

"No!" His diaper getting warm, Bilson came unglued. "Please turn it off and I'll tell you anything you want. Just please, no more!"

The Pretender lifted his fingers and shifted his gaze to the dirty doc. "First tell me about O'Quinn."

Bilson's eyes filled with fear. "O'Quinn?"

"You remember him, your partner in crime, the one who kidnapped Kaj from your hospital."

"He's some big player at the corporation that owns the corporation that owns the company that owns us."

"What's their name?"

Letting out an abrupt sigh, Bilson countered, "If—if I told you that he'd kill me."

Jarod cranked the drip up higher. "He can't, if there's nothing of you left."

Before Bilson could say more he felt something was moving on his body. He looked down and saw a cockroach crawl out from his diaper.

Meeeaaa—Meeeaaa—Meeeaaa.

"You give me your word, as a doctor. If I tell you, you'll stop?"

"I'm going to count to *one.*"

A second, then a third and a forth roach followed the first one—all running right up his pasty belly.

Meeeaaa—Meeeaaa—Meeeaaa.

Bilson jerked his head toward the infusion pump. "Please turn it off, please."

"What's the name of O'Quinn's corporation?"

Jarod cranked the juice up higher.

Bilson's breath escaped him as he saw scores—then hundreds—then thousands of cockroaches spewing forth from his Depends in all directions and climbing all over his skin. He knew they weren't real—but he could feel their tiny feet. Thousands and thousands of tiny roach feet everywhere!

Meeaaa—meeaaa—meeaaa. "It's Emtrex. They're powerful bastards, like Halliburton on steroids—who do evil things for the highest bidder!"

"But you don't care, because you make tons of money and in return, all you have to do is handle a patient or two of theirs with no questions asked."

"I told you *I was sorry*! Now Please. That's all I know. I swear. Please—please turn it oooooooffffffffff!"

Jarod looked down at him and frowned. "I'm afraid I can't do that."

"But what about the Hippocratic oath?" His voice had risen to a hysterical scream. "You promised me—as a fellow physician!"

Jarod leaned down close. "The oath doesn't apply to me. You see, I'm not really a doctor." Jarod reached over and turned the pump to the max. "And you're not going anywhere." With an *oh well* shrug, Jarod slammed the hood down over his head.

Meeeaaa—Meeeaaa—Meeeaaa!

Chapter 24

THE 1920S BUILDING Roger Hearns worked in was one of the most non-descript in lower Manhattan. Off a little-known side street near the Battery, it seemed to blend in with everything around it, like a phantom or a chameleon. Much like the company he worked for: NNC.

NNC was something of an enigma. Under significant time constraints, Jarod was not able to discover anything more than a vague conceptualization of the company; its assets were well protected, likely in some offshore account, and it was privately held, with the only information available being a self-description as *specialists in industrial technology.*

What meager information Jarod could dredge up on NNC did nothing to solve the current predicament Roger Hearns was in. Jarod, however, discovered that NNC had been incorporated in Delaware, the only place in the U.S. that offered substantive corporate tax shelters. It was for that reason many companies that did not want to be found picked the small state as their on-paper headquarters. Jarod had firsthand knowledge of that fact; the Centre just so happened to be one such corporation.

Roger Hearns emerged from the building, just as he had for weeks at the same appointed time, pacing back and forth with the phone glued to his ear.

That day, like most every other day, Roger was too preoccupied with his call to notice the man across the street wearing a New York Giants football jersey and backward Yankees cap, happily serving hot dogs to the hungry homeless who migrated to him from alleys and parks upon word of free food.

The back of the vendor's jersey said *Manning,* but the smiling server was of course, Jarod.

Long fascinated by the delectable and juicy New York tube steak tradition known as the *dirty water dog,* Jarod was pleased that he could kill three birds with one stone: feed the less fortunate, immerse in the discovery of his new favorite food and create a pretend that would seamlessly blend in to the vicinity of the NNC building across from him.

Through his Bluetooth earbud, Jarod listened in to the call between Roger and O'Quinn, just as he had been since cloning Roger's cell. Just like all the previous calls, the conversation lasted less than 30 seconds.

"Checking in," O'Quinn said *gruffly. "You on schedule?"*

Roger fought to keep the panic from his voice. "I want to talk to Luke."

O'Quinn laughed, knowing that Roger was in no position to make demands. "Keep asking and it will never be an option. There's not much time now to our deadline. My people need assurances."

Roger stuttered, frustrated with the man on the other end of the call. "You promised me—"

"No!" O'Quinn cut him *off. "You promised me that everything would be ready for the day. Is that still the case?"*

There was a long pause before Roger answered. "Yes," he admitted with a sigh.

"Then have a spectacular rest of your day," O'Quinn mocked, before ending the call.

Jarod recognized that the lack of hard information exchanged in these calls was the work of prudent professionals, at least on O'Quinn's part. Jarod had stopped expecting any usable knowledge from these calls, but he still held out hope that there would be the need for O'Quinn to divulge real details to Roger.

Jarod concentrated on the pacing man across the street. With each passing day, he observed Roger's physicality changing; his steps became shorter and more clipped, his shoulders sagged a bit more, and the sleepless bags under his eyes grew more pronounced. Most telling of all, though, were the changes Jarod perceived in Roger's voice. Its pitch and timber rose and his words were swallowed and mumbled, tell-tale signs of pressure mounting from the inside out.

Even if Roger was able to fulfill O'Quinn's logistical demands, Jarod feared the man was likely to crack under the intense heat of the situation. If Roger crashed and burned before the appointed hour, Jarod had no doubt that O'Quinn would kill Luke and slip back into the shadows from which he had appeared.

Chapter 25

THE AVANT-GARDE WAS a new club in North Blue Cove, located between the fashion district and the College. Miss Parker pulled into the parking lot of the old Victorian and a smoking hot, tatted-up Suicide Girl wearing a valet jacket over black fishnets opened the door to her Porsche. She had barely climbed out when the sexy vixen slid in purring, "Me like."

Miss Parker dropped the keys into the valet's open palm, an unmistakable threat in her voice. "Scratch it—I scratch you."

As usual, Miss Parker's entrance silenced the buzz in the club as every head turned her way. Using her usual captivating, man-melting stride, she made her way through the patrons. She was so preoccupied with the anticipation of what Daphne had discovered about the girl with Jarod that she had already ordered her usual 'Maker's, three rocks, four fingers' before it dawned on her something here was unusual. She hadn't felt her usual *man-melting* stride having its usual *man-melting* effect on those in this room. As she stared into the mirror behind the bar, she realized why.

There wasn't a man here to melt.

What there was were women, all of whom came in two distinct flavors: Alpha females and frailer little Betas circling them in orbit, hoping they would choose to bestow their gravity on them. Early on in the boys club of the Centre, Miss Parker had learned to use her sexuality as a powerful weapon, and in this *girls* club, it was having the same effect—*on steroids. She* was the ultimate alpha female and her gravity appeared to have a strong pull on them all.

None stared at Miss Parker more than a nude temptress in a glass box suspended above the dance floor. With her arms behind her at a 45 degree angle, her back arched, Barbie boobs standing at attention and her outstretched legs raised up at the knees, she reminded Miss Parker of a famous silhouette she'd seen on the back of many 18 wheelers.

Miss Parker had never been with a woman, well, not *completely*. If the unexpected ever happened and a beautiful creature she found amusing or enticing one day crossed her path, as long as they kept eye contact and realized who was in charge, well, you never knew. As she scanned the room, she didn't see *that* woman here tonight. She didn't see the person she was there to meet either.

Just when she was thought Blondie had stood her up, she realized why she'd overlooked her, even though she was only one stool down. Blondie wasn't blonde tonight; her signature golden ponytail had been replaced by long brown strands. For a split second, Miss Parker thought she was looking into a mirror of herself from years earlier when she was still experimenting with her style during her training days in the CIT in France, the time before she'd evolved into the unique persona she had become.

Daphne was wearing a Spandex catsuit with high-heeled boots and had done her makeup in the same manner Miss Parker wore hers. The chick in the glass box peered down at the carbon copies and smiled. Parker noticed, then looked to Daphne. "Who's the slutty-mud-flaps-girl?"

Daphne replied coyly, "An admirer."

Miss Parker gazed around. "Interesting place."

"I thought it best to meet off the beaten path—avoid the over the shoulder prying eyes of the Centre."

Miss Parker had to acknowledge she had a point. She sat on the stool next to her. "What do you have for me?"

Daphne produced a thick file. "Skylar Cohasset. Twenty-six, the only child of an unwed mother who died in a car wreck when Skylar was 10. After that, she bounced through the foster system, where she had more than her share of abuse. One of her 'dads' was a real piece of work."

Parker took the file and thumbed through it. Without looking up she asked, "Any idea where she lives?"

"*Lives*—no. *Lived*—yes." Daphne studied Miss Parker's hands, losing herself in the way her delicate fingers moved as they flipped through the pages.

"You did good, Blondie." Miss Parker stopped herself and looked into her doppelganger's eyes. "What's your real name again?"

"Daphne."

"*Daphne,* right. I like that name."

As Parker again studied the file, Daphne could feel her cheeks warming. "Speaking of names, I know it's none of my business, but there's a pretty significant bet around the Centre about your first one."

Miss Parker asked casually, "Is that right?"

"Most people, including Nathalie, you know, the shooting range manager in SL-14, thinks your first name is either Catherine, like your mother, or something starting with an 'M.' Dai from the London Annex and Annie T from the San Diego Street Team agree that it starts with an 'M,' but their guess is Margaux because they dug up some old record of your mother's friend from Labenne-Océan, but my research told me that wasn't true. And then there is Mallory, the Centre Counsel, who thinks your first name is 'Mallory' for her own egotistical reasons."

A glint of a smile flashed across Miss Parker's face as she returned her focus to the file.

"But I told them your name would be *much* more unique than that—as distinctive and beautiful as you are." Miss Parker held up a hand to silence her. Daphne noticed Miss Parker's eyes narrow in triumph as she zeroed in on something on the page that listed Skylar's childhood address. It was something Daphne knew would put her idol hot on the trail to finding Jarod.

Miss Parker gazed into Daphne's baby blues and held the look. "You were right when you started."

Daphne began to glow. "Your first name starts with an 'M'?"

"No. My first name is *none of your business.*"

Miss Parker stood, ready to leave, noting that all eyes in the bar gravitated back to her, especially Daphne's. They contained a twinge of hurt caused by Miss Parker's parting shot.

Oh good God, Parker thought. *Young girls and their sensitivity.* Since she was going to need this girl she decided to throw her a bone, make it up to her. "Daphne, you're much more attractive than you let on at work. But I have a tip." Parker moved so that she was standing directly in front of Daphne on her stool. "Your eyes are striking but your shadow is rough and flat. The key is blending and you can't do that with both hands at once."

Daphne grinned, realizing Miss Parker knew her ambidextrous secret, had noticed that about her, had noticed *anything* about her.

Miss Parker leaned in close to Daphne's face. The blonde in the brunette wig had to remind herself to breathe as she watched Miss Parker touch her finger to the tip of her tongue, and then bring it towards her eyelid.

"Close your eyes," Miss Parker commanded gently.

Daphne did as she was told. The instant Miss Parker's finger touched her eyelid Daphne felt her entire body shudder. After a few seconds of Miss Parker moving her finger back and forth, Daphne was once again able to comprehend the words Miss Parker was saying. "When you blend, you need to take your time and rub it with care."

Parker leaned back and smiled, and not the fake or predatory one that so often appeared on her face, but a genuine one. "You look perfect now. Beautiful."

Daphne had never seen a smile like that from Miss Parker and knew in her heart it would enslave her forever, her voice was now soft as a dove. "Thank you, Miss Parker."

She gazed at Daphne in a way that left the blonde wondering if there was a hint of tease in her smoky blue eyes. "No, thank you," she raised Skylar's file. "I owe you one."

As Parker floated away, Daphne stared, her heart beating out of her chest.

She'd never felt so alive.

Chapter 26

LOCATED NEAR EL PASO between the southern end of the Franklin Mountains and the Rio Grande rift stood a multi-story modern glass and steel structure, known as Emtrex. The ultramodern architectural creation was built in a way to allow in the maximum amount of light but with light came shadows and the ones on the 13th floor hid the truth of what happened within its walls.

Security was nearly impenetrable. No one got on or off the elevator, past the armed guards there, unless they had the high security clearances expected of a trained operative.

There were only two such operatives in the building that night. Both had special access badges, so the armed guard did not blink when he noticed them exiting an executive office suite down the hall. Other guards in other buildings might have been surprised to see that one of the men had a cast on his arm and looked like a junkyard dog and that the other was sporting an eye patch. At Emtrex though, men who looked like they'd been in recent fire-fights were hardly an unusual sight.

Especially on the 13th floor.

O'Quinn was angry and it wasn't just because the surgeons had been pressing him to remove his dying eye. Nor was it the headaches caused by the increased swelling. He was heated because of what his number two was telling him.

"How do I know why? Dojame just said the nano-drug isn't ready yet."

O'Quinn despised uncertainty. "I'm sick of excuses, yours, the ones from those idiots at the hospital, and from that Indian quack downstairs," O'Quinn fumed. "Goddamnit, I'm running out of sunrises!"

Knowing better than to meet his master's gaze, Dog looked down and kept his mouth shut. Through his good eye, O'Quinn saw the message had been delivered. As he turned to lock the office door, though, he noticed the white marble floor at his feet was glistening and wet.

Scowling, he spun his head and spotted the culprit, a janitor slinging a mop down the hall. O'Quinn's anger kicked up a notch. Not because he feared the old black man would splash his new non-iron chinos, but because it reminded him of his failings. He couldn't tell if the janitor was 20 paces down the hall or 30.

Goddamn depth perception! Goddamn Kaj!

O'Quinn led Dog toward the elevator, counting his steps the whole way. He passed the janitor at 25 paces, which only pissed him off more. He glared at the old man sliding the mop. "Don't you know you're supposed to do that shit at night?"

The janitor didn't know that. This was his first day on the job and half of it was spent getting his various biometric data, pin and chip badges that would allow him access to this floor, *so I can mop up after assholes like this bald bastard and his pussy-assed puppy*, he thought to himself, then kept his head down and mumbled, "Sorry, sir."

O'Quinn continued to walk his Dog down the hall, past the guards and into the elevator. As he did, the janitor appeared shocked that the important men had even paid him mind. No one was as invisible as the man with the mop, and that was just how the man with the mop liked it.

As the elevator doors closed, the old black man looked and caught a glance at himself in a mirror. With his white hair and clean-shaven face, some would say he looked like that classic blues guitarist Johnny Boy Creed. But as he gazed into his own eyes, he knew behind the mirage of make-believe he looked just like himself, whomever that might be, just like the Pretender he was.

Jarod leaned the mop against the wall next to O'Quinn's door and in less than 15 seconds, picked the lock and entered the bald man's office.

Chapter 27

EVEN THOUGH IT was late, Skylar honored her mother's memory by cleaning Jarod's bedroom. To Sal, the phrase *cleanliness is next to Godliness* was true. Skylar's childhood home had been small and their possessions meager, but always spotless, a fact she had never forgotten.

The sound of the door opening startled her. She hadn't expected Jarod back this soon and had not yet put his things away.

She rushed in, but it was too late. The Etch A Sketches were still out, the backpack was open and Jarod was staring at the DSA screen where she'd frozen it.

"Jarod, I …" His look stopped her.

"It's okay …" his voice hitched before he continued. "I'm glad you saw it."

She joined him, slid her hand atop his, which was still resting on the player. In this shared silent moment between two disparate people, her mind rewound to life after her mother had died, to the loneliest, most painful times and the thought of what she'd always needed and never received: a hug.

Skylar pulled Jarod into her embrace and soon enough he was holding her in return. A mutual unspoken comfort, that both knew the other had rarely, if ever, received. They broke, she smiled. "Guess now we've both seen each other naked." Her giggle brought a blush from Jarod. She slipped around him toward the sink and began making coffee.

"I'm ... sorry about your mother," Jarod returned gently. He saw the look of confusion cross her face. "You spoke quite a bit during your withdrawals."

"Oh. Not even cold turkey shut me up, huh?"

"Or cold showers." Jarod grinned, "They made you talk even more. Faster."

Skylar's laugh brought on a full smile from Jarod.

"You seemed to have done a lot of things in your life." Jarod commented.

"After my mother ...," She thought reflectively. "Well, I had to *become* a lot of things to a lot of people, too. The tomboy in one foster family, a princess in another, chambermaid, drug runner, sibling punching bag, you name it. I played the game until my little voice finally grew up and screamed in my ear *screw this, any place is better than this*."

"How long have you been on your own?"

"Since the day there was someone else's blood on my hands, right after I turned 15."

"You did the right thing," Jarod said intently.

Skylar looked at him in worry, "I told you about that one too?"

He nodded, then closed the lid on the DSA player with an extra firm snap. "There never seems to be a shortage of people waiting to take advantage of someone, does there?"

"Is that who Sydney is to you?" she queried.

"If I could answer that with certainty, I would. He's been mentor and manipulator, confidante and conspirator, papa and prison guard." Jarod looked up at her, "The Centre I'm sure about, but Sydney's a moving target."

"I wish I could tell you the outside world was so different, but it's not. Least, I haven't seen many of the good parts in the last few years. I was a mess, no money, no hope. Believe it or not, I thought Guardian General was my saving grace."

"I've seen homeless people. Life out there couldn't have been easy," Jarod said.

"A lot of the others were from the city shelter, but I lied about how Bilson found me." She shifted away from Jarod, pouring two cups.

It had been such a long time since she had trusted anyone. She felt a pull toward Jarod, the need to see and be seen by someone, to care about and be cared about. She suddenly realized she hadn't felt this calm or this comfortable with someone since her mom had died. "Truth is, I found myself standing on a street corner in the Bowery ready to start my next chapter. It was just sex, right? But my mother's voice whispered in my head the whole time—*Baby girl, always respect and protect what God gave you. You lose your dignity, you've lost it all.*" Skylar sighed. "So I'm not sure what to do when this limo pulls up. The back window comes down and I'm thinking it's decision time. Turns out the guy inside doesn't want sex, he's looking for research participants for a pharmaceutical trial."

"Dr. Bilson," Jarod said with a knowing tone.

Skylar nodded. "He promised a clean room, dry roof and three meals a day. The moment felt like I'd just been rescued from a burning building. Within the hour, I was scarfing the first hot food I'd had in months and signing papers that may as well have been written in Esperanto. Within two hours, I was so drugged out of my mind I could've *read* Esperanto. They kept me like that the whole time ... hell, you saw me." Her laugh was forced, full of pain. "In hindsight, I'd have been better off just screwing him that night when I was still free."

Jarod eyed her, processing, then gave a nod of support. "Thank you for your truth."

Skylar handed him his coffee. Silence hung in the air until she forced a nervous grin. "Pretty stupid, huh?"

"No. You were the perfect recruit for Bilson; anonymous, no family, no loved ones to miss you. He was trying to steal your life."

Skylar glanced at the DSA player. "Like *they* stole yours."

"Guess we're quite a pair, aren't we?"

Skylar's gaze dropped to her steaming mug. "At least I grew up in a place that brought me joy, a place I can always go to smile again." She took Jarod's hand. "I want to take you there."

Their eyes locked. Skylar then leaned in and kissed him. He held it for a moment, but it triggered many mixed and complicated emotions so he pulled back and stared at her.

"I'd never forgive myself if something happened to you." Jarod placed his fingers on her cheek with a sense of longing he didn't fully understand.

"I'm pretty tough," she said with conviction, leaning into his touch.

"And so are the people I'm up against, especially the ones who took Kaj."

She looked up into his eyes. "You discovered who they are?"

"Yes. I went to where they work." Concern appeared on his brow. "But I came up empty. They have a huge global presence and where inside of it they have Kaj hidden, I couldn't discover."

"There must be another way."

"At Guardian General you said you overheard their conversation about taking Kaj to a 'safer place.' I need you to think back, to remember everything they said. A boy's life is at stake."

Skylar stepped back, pensively sipped her coffee. Her face tightened as she struggled to grasp a memory whirling around in her head. "He looked like a pirate."

"Yes. The man with the eye patch who took Kaj? His name is O'Quinn," Jarod filled in encouragingly. "He could be the key to saving Luke."

"Somewhere, somewhere, taking him somewhere safer," she whispered.

"Where, Sky, where was this *safer* place?" Jarod prodded gently.

Her mind reeling, she closed her eyes. "A man with an arm cast. O'Quinn told him to make a call, someone, I wanna say to someone or some place they worked for."

"Emtrex?"

"Yeah—I think that was the name."

"Think, Skylar. What else did they say?"

Skylar closed her eyes again, concentrating, wanting so to please Jarod. "The pirate wanted Arm Cast to have them prep a room—that they needed to transfer Kaj."

Jarod placed his hand over hers.

"Somewhere. My mind is telling me it was *Iceland Rangoon*—but I know that's wrong ..." She shook her head for what seemed to be a minute, then looked back up at Jarod—"I'm sorry, it's not coming to me."

Sensing it was time to give Skylar's tattered memory a break, Jarod stood.

She then glanced at the red iPad like something else was on her mind, but wasn't sure whether to broach the subject or not. "I saw your notes about Luke," she confessed. "It seems pretty obvious he's not coming back."

"He's *missing*." Jarod could see that Skylar was confused. Jarod pondered, then started his iPad and played her the black and white video of Luke's kidnapping.

"Luke," was all she said. Skylar put her cup on the table, concern etched on her face. "What do they want with him?"

"I don't know—*yet*." Jarod set his coffee cup down next to Skylar's, the force of the movement indicative of his building frustration.

"What about the police?"

"This is way beyond the police." He interrupted.

"Why are you doing this, Jarod?"

He replied flatly. "Because no one else will."

Skylar eyed him, amazed at the idea of someone risking everything for someone he didn't even know. Yet she felt it was more than that. Surely it was not that simple, maybe Jarod himself didn't understand why and neither did she, but she was determined to help. "I'll remember what you need to know. I promise."

Jarod hoped so. Without that information, he was very much at a dead end.

A short smile grew on her face from some silent epiphany. "I want to take you somewhere in the morning, a magical place where memories are made—and hopefully restored."

Chapter 28

ALL THAT COULD be heard was the Centre's cooling system humming its relentless theme song of emptiness.

There were no bagels or cream cheese today. There were no grandiose, pie-in-the-sky, bullshit presentations brewing in Cornelius's hollow heart. No romantic fantasies bubbling up from Daphne's libido. Not even any tired justifications from Sydney for his weak-willed failures with Jarod or protestations of his supposed allegiance to the Centre.

No, those all required one essential ingredient missing from this meeting: Miss Parker.

For the last hour, all the impotent trio could muster were empty, and sometimes resentful, stares across the table. They passed the time with compulsive checks of their smartphones and the clock.

"Missing her own update meeting isn't like Parker," Sydney said, breaking the monotony with the obvious.

"You don't think she could be hurt, do you?" Daphne feared.

Cornelius snorted a raspy snicker. "The bitch is up to something." He stopped Daphne's weak protest of his word choice with a glare and wave of his hand. Then it dawned on him. He moved to his computer console and tried to type as fast as his blazing mind reeled. Sydney and Daphne shared a curious gaze, then both joined him.

"Care to share with the rest of the class?" Sydney demanded, in an unconscious imitation of Miss Parker.

Cornelius stopped typing, stared at the screen and muttered, "Son of a bitch."

He defiantly pushed his roller chair away from his keyboard and, at the exact same moment, Sydney insolently stopped it with a firm foot on the wheel. "Talk to me."

Cornelius looked up, surprised by the Parker-like incarnation that suddenly possessed the mild-mannered Sydney. "I found an encrypted requisition Miss Parker implemented last night for a round-the-clock Sweeper stakeout. Ten Sweepers, *minimum*." Sydney glared impatiently. "Brooklyn, Coney Island, someplace called Astroland," Cornelius announced.

Noticing Daphne dart her eyes away, a wrathful wave swept over Cornelius … *Has this bitch betrayed me again?* Wisely, Cornelius chose not to push the point. Sydney also noted Daphne's demeanor switch as she jumped up and gathered the untouched agenda sheets she had assembled at Miss Parker's vacant place.

"What's an Astroland?" Daphne asked awkwardly.

Sydney turned his worn brown loafers toward the exit.

"I'm coming with," Cornelius said, struggling to his feet.

Sydney spun, "*We're* not going anywhere—and that's an order! If Parker is insisting on wielding her sword by herself, then she must also be prepared to fall on it alone."

With that, Sydney left Daphne and Cornelius holding their proverbial private parts, leaving them to work out whose would be violated, when, how hard and by whom.

Sydney shut the door behind him. It echoed in the expanse of the Centre's sublevels. Out of sight of any prying eyes, he did something very uncharacteristic. He dashed down the corridor, like a man with his own plan.

Chapter 29

SKYLAR BEAMED AS she pointed to the upper right window of a four story, paint-chipped quadruplex on West 10th Street on Coney Island. Jarod read the mix of melancholy and joy in her expression as she shared memories of the home in which she grew up.

She took Jarod by the hand and led him to a stairway next to the building, which took them down to below street level.

The passage, once part of a planned subway line, was now dark and damp, with only a few dim lights illuminating the 'T' intersection at which they stood.

She pointed to her left. "If you go that way it dumps you out on Surf Street—to the right is 9th."

Jarod grinned, imagining what it must have been like for her as a child. "Your mother let you come down here by yourself?"

"Never but some nights I'd sneak out after she was asleep, other times she and I would use it together as a shortcut to my happy place."

As they walked, Jarod's attention turned to the dim passage. "And where does this tunnel take you?"

"To my happy place." Giggling like a child, she ran off into the darkness with hopes of Jarod chasing after her. Which he did, laughing at her laughter, curious about where this adventure might lead. It took him to another stairwell going up, but no Skylar.

"Skylar?" he called, the slightest tinge of worry in his voice.

"Up here!"

Jarod climbed the steps to emerge back into the daylight of Brooklyn—right on the doorstep of Skylar's *happy place*.

He followed her gaze to a sight the likes of which he'd never seen before: a one square block amusement park full of color and laughter. His eyes opened wide as he gasped in wonder, trying to take in everything at once. High above them was a sign, one that was even more grand than The Apollo Theatre's marquee in his mind. It had blinking multi-colored flashing lights, a bright red border and vibrant yellow letters: *Astroland*.

She turned his body around, guiding him with her hands until they were now just across 10th Street from her childhood home. Skylar beamed. "How many kids get to grow up across the street from their *happy place?* Hurry, c'mon."

And with that she rushed toward the main entrance to Astroland with Jarod, to get in line to buy their tickets to *happy*.

Chapter 30

PINK'S *FUCKIN' PERFECT* blasted from the Burmester sound system in Miss Parker's smoke-filled Porsche ...

While she'd never stoop to singing to herself in the car, the pounding anthem did fuel a self satisfied smirk as she ground out another Pall Mall.

She'd driven this route from home to the Centre so many times she could do it in her sleep. What she realized in this moment was that it was always dark outside when she did it. Morning or night, her toil always beat daylight.

When she awoke this morning she'd just thought, *fuck it,* and laid in bed puffing Pall Malls. She didn't give a shit about missing the meeting she'd called with the *Freak, the Geek* and the suddenly not so *Meek*—Cornelius, Sydney and the increasingly interesting blonde. Thanks to her *tête-à-tête* with Daphne and burning her usual midnight oil, Miss Parker was now way ahead of her Stooges, rendering said meeting as nothing more than a somnambular boondoggle.

No, in this moment, she found herself *in the moment.* Going the speed limit for a change, she took the tight winding curves of Blue Cove's coastal road without squealing her tires and caught herself actually looking out the window.

For the first time in memory, she was seeing what she'd seen before but never really saw. American White Pelicans dive bombing into the azure blue waters, snaring their prey, which brought another smile to her face. The purple-striped, all-seeing Blue Cove lighthouse guiding idiots lost in their own wake, even a fleeting glance at a Red-bellied Water Snake slither-ing out from the weeds.

For a split second, she wondered if this unexpected mood of hers was an epiphany of sunlight, if the nocturnal world she normally found herself in was a cloaking device for reality, maybe there were other discoveries she'd missed that were dwelling right under her nose all along. She dis-missed the thought as quickly as it came. For one, there was this Skylar to be dealt with and, of course, the most pressing *Damocles* was Jarod.

As she backhanded the power button, silencing Pink, her hands-free Bluetooth caught the call she'd once again been waiting for.

The suited man behind the wheel of the black Town Car parked in the shadows, held the binoculars to his eyes and his cell to his ear. His field glasses were trained on Jarod, who stepped into view with Skylar, both headed to the ticket booth at the entrance to Coney Island's Astroland,—a colorful amusement park landmark.

"Miss Parker, it's Sam. I just got a visual on Jarod and the girl. We've got him."

Parker's grin grew again, but her eyes went steely with resolve at the news. "Keep him in your sights, I'm on my way."

"Would you like me to inform your team?" Sam asked.

"No. I've seen their work. Just secure me a chopper for take off from the Centre in 20 minutes."

With that she clicked off the call, gunned her engine and turned *Fuckin' Perfect* back on.

Chapter 31

LESS THAN AN hour outside of Brooklyn, Sydney pushed his vintage Volvo up I-295 for all it was worth, and then some. His loyal four-wheeled Swede had seen him to his honeymoon with his wife, to the hospital for the birth of their son and to his convalescence after *the incident* took them both away from him. Sydney knew better than most that, in life, even loyalty had its limits.

He'd tried to talk his way into requisitioning the Centre jet, a helicopter, even a Town Car, but the Centre's transport captain made it clear they were spoken for; Mr. Parker the jet; Miss Parker the chopper; Sweepers the Town Car fleet.

So he drove. It gave him a chance to think things through anyway. Yes, he was taking a leap of faith with the trip, but while there was a lot he doubted about Miss Parker, he never doubted the accuracy of her intel, especially when it came to her pursuit of Jarod. No, he had no idea when Jarod might show himself at Astroland, if ever, but then again, neither did Parker. There was solace in the fact that if and when Jarod did go there, he would at least be on the doorstep, instead of twiddling his thumbs with the likes of Cornelius and Daphne in Blue Cove.

He often wondered if Miss Parker would actually hurt Jarod, bouncing back and forth between sensing her hidden feelings lingering from their childhood and the strong pull to please her father at all costs. Being at the Centre as long as he had, Sydney had seen more than his share of desperate people in desperate moments, and Parker was no exception.

One thing was certain in Sydney's mind. He had made regrettable decisions, ones that had lasting consequences on the life of another. He owed Jarod, and as recompense for his destructive actions, he vowed to do everything in his power to protect his surrogate son.

The Volvo shook like a paint mixer as Sydney pushed the speedometer past 85. The urgency he was demanding from the car had nothing on the thoughts racing in his mind, thoughts of what he would say to Jarod if he could just get to him first. If he was able to, would Jarod even listen?

Chapter 32

AS THE CYCLONE rollercoaster climbed toward a weathered 'Remain Seated' sign above them, Jarod's eyes grew wide with anticipation of what lay beyond.

In the moment their coaster car reached the peak, he shared a look of childlike glee with Skylar, and when they began to bullet downward, a scream of pure rapture bellowed out of him. For the next minute and 50 seconds it only got more exciting. When it was done he said he had to do it again.

Jarod was so overjoyed by this looping, lolling, lunging contraption of rails and wood that he bought out the entire roller coaster for any child who wanted to ride free.

Later, Skylar clutched a stuffed mouse that had the words, *I Survived The Cyclone,* as they strolled through the sideshow. "It may sound strange, but if it wasn't for this place, I don't know where I'd be. As a girl, the glow of the neon, the music and laughter were my nightlight and lullabies. On nights she stayed up with me, my mom and I would sit by my bedroom window and gaze across the street and watch the people on the coaster. I'll never forget what she said—*that Cyclone is just like life itself, highs and lows, moments of joy and fear, of security and helplessness. But one thing's for sure—if you are feeling down, The Cyclone will always help you to forget.*"

Skylar paused, "I rode The Cyclone the day she died. For her. And she was right. For that incredible two minutes, she was still there next to me."

As they walked on, Skylar told Jarod how, regardless of where she was in her life, the park had always been a refuge she could return to, where she could clear her mind of all her troubles and to—"Get back in touch with the child inside of me."

All of a sudden the child inside of Jarod wanted to hold Skylar's hand, so he offered her his. When she smiled and took it he felt a deep connection in their mingling warmth, the exact likes of which he'd never experienced before. He felt safer than he ever had with her and although he didn't understand most of it, he was desirous for more.

Jarod then cocked his head at something, "May I ask you a question?"

"Anything."

"What is this pink item that looks like a hairball on a stick that I see so many children eating?"

Skylar tilted her head realizing the ramification of this. "Oh my God. You've never had cotton candy?"

"I was never allowed sugary substances—certainly not ones merged with clothing materials."

Skylar pouted her bottom lip. "Poor baby, you're in for a treat! Wait here." She dashed off, vanishing around the corner and into the crowd.

Jarod stood basking in how alive he felt, by the sweet and sour smells in the humid air. He spun in a slowly circle taking in, the dazzling colors, the panoply of human interactions and even the glorious grime this little corner of the word offered. The Power Surge, the Top Spin 2, the Gyro Tower, and then something curious that caught his eye. It was an old arcade machine with a giant red heart and the words: *Test the Power of Your Love. 50 Cents.* The machine featured a bronze hand onto which the examinee placed their own hand to measure their amorous strengths. Inside, lights flickered next to words like *Cuddlesome, Kissable, Passionate, Naughty But Nice, Shy, and Hot Stuff.* Though he doubted the veracity of any scientific method it might claim to employ, Jarod nonetheless grinned, fished in his pocket for some change, and couldn't drop the quarters in fast enough. He pressed his palm down on the hand plate and watched, dazzled as the lights swirled around to the various levels of love, until a bell sounded and a light flashed next to Jarod's love level. His answer though, came from a source he didn't expect.

"Well, ring a ding ding, *Hot Stuff.*"

Turning toward the speaker, his smile vanished. It was Miss Parker.

Joy vanishing from his soul, Jarod scanned the scene. In every possible escape direction, there seemed to be Sweepers. In a world of tank tops and flip-flops, the Centre's suited warriors stood out like mold on bread.

Realizing in that instant that it had happened. He'd lost sight of the prize, taken his eye off the ball, been swept toward the land of freedom and fun. This exploitable lapse in judgment had caught up to him; his only relief was that Skylar was not here at the moment.

His mind raced with potential escape options, weighing the outcomes that would keep Skylar as safe as possible. He of course played it as calm and cool as possible with Miss Parker. "How did you find me?"

"A lady knows to go for a man's weak spot—his heart. Or your little friend Skylar's anyway." Miss Parker allowed herself a victorious smirk.

He eyed her firmly, "She's got nothing to do with this."

Parker glanced at the love machine, "Hate to be a buzzkill, but this contraption's missing the most important level: *Love's a Bitch*. But then you're handy with kiddie toys, I'm sure you can Sim-up a fix for that."

Parker's passive-aggressive slight didn't go unnoticed. "Glad you enjoyed the Etch A Sketch," Jarod replied. "It's really more an educational toy than one for kids, but I figured you'd appreciate it anyway."

Parker gave a nonchalant half-shrug. "Found it a little on the nose, frankly."

"That was the point," Jarod shot back. "Exactly on the nose, the place none of us can see." With that, Jarod stuck out his wrists indicating his surrender to the handcuffs, which he knew they would never use so publicly. Parker gave a nod and four of her Sweepers started escorting Jarod away.

"Jarod?" The Pretender turned to find Skylar holding a ball of pink cotton candy and a Sweeper holding on to her arm.

"Hello, Skylar," Miss Parker purred with her teeth showing.

"Jarod, I'm sorry I brought you here." Skylar shot Miss Parker a look with her violets eyes. "What? My clipboard across your sorry ass face too subtle for you?"

"There is *nothing* subtle about you, sweetie." Parker eyed her up and down. "How's that angel tat workin' for you now?"

Sam touched his ear bud. "Miss Parker. Transport's in position."

Miss Parker turned to Jarod. "Now you get to show *your girl* the carnival *you* grew up in."

Emerging from Astroland, the Sweepers, with Miss Parker at the helm, led Jarod and Skylar to a windowless van idling between two Centre Town Cars. Sam opened the rear door. Miss Parker turned to the Pretender. "Consider your wings clipped, *Onyssius*—we'll do the flying back to your coop."

Jarod gazed at Skylar, then to Miss Parker. "You don't have any use for her, you've got what you came for."

Miss Parker saw the painful conviction in his eyes, the same eyes that once drew her into his sheltered dome so many, many years ago. She was now feeling *something* she couldn't quite put her finger on.

Jarod reached over and gently touched Parker's hand. "Please, Miss Parker."

It stopped her. She eyed him. "Don't," she warned. "Don't try and make sense of the world when there's none allowed." So much hurt, so much damage between them in that singular touch; the emotional barbed wire that had always kept them apart, yet on these rare occasions offered a fleeting mutual promise for escape. It was even in their eyes, locked onto each other now.

What devastated the moment, neither of them saw coming—first the screeching of tires, then the ear-shattering crunch of steel on steel. By the time they turned toward the sound, the air was already filled with the pressurized explosion of the sheared-off fire hydrant shooting water in every direction, and their reactions were almost too late.

An out of control Volvo with Sydney driving was now headed straight for them. At the last minute, Sydney jerked the wheel, scattering a half dozen Sweepers as he ploughed into the rear side panel of the transport van. The crunching of the Volvo's front end and its rear end careening left no time for anything but instinctual flight from its path of destruction.

Glass shattered. A chunk sliced into Jarod's upper back as he wrapped his arms around Skylar and shoved her away. Sam was bounced over the

Volvo's hood, while another sweeper, clipped by the spinning rear bumper, went flying.

Miss Parker dove away.

Jarod turned to the rear Town Car, spotted Pedro's hands raised to block flying shrapnel. Before the bug-eyed sweeper could respond, Jarod grabbed him by the ear and slammed his head into the open door of the Town Car. Before Pedro's body hit the ground Jarod was tossing Skylar across the front seat and sliding behind the wheel.

Miss Parker peeled herself off the pavement only to have to dive away again as Jarod 180'd the black Lincoln and roared away.

So consumed with outrage, Miss Parker did not notice Sydney as he staggered from the Volvo with blood dripping down his face from a gash on his forehead. The truth was that she didn't give a shit about Sydney's condition, or his incoherent mumblings about his car's failed brakes, or the fact that she was sure he was lying about it just to save his precious skin once again. Over the sound of shocked screams from bystanders, water spraying everywhere, and approaching police sirens, Miss Parker knew that even before she barked to every Sweeper within earshot to "Find Jarod!" that they would not.

The human chameleon had escaped again.

Chapter 33

THE GLOW OF the moon shone through the skylight onto Jarod's bare back. There, a thin, shallow, raspberry streak of abraded skin ran across his scapula and climbed like a crimson rollercoaster up to the top of his shoulder.

Skylar, cradling a pan of warm soapy water, sat on the edge of the sofa next to him, and cleansed the wound with a soft towel. Jarod found her gentle touch soothing.

When she saw that the injury was not serious, she started to giggle. Jarod looked askance at Skylar, which made her chuckle. "Kinda funny that the nurse who isn't a nurse is healing the doctor who isn't a doctor," she said.

Jarod laughed, then grimaced as she pressed a bit too hard. "Ahhhh ..." He composed himself and smiled. "Healing is yet to be determined."

Skylar winced. "Sorry, almost done, then I'll dress it."

"It'll be fine just like that."

Skylar grinned and playfully punched his arm. "Don't be such a baby."

Jarod was entranced by her confident hands as she dried and dressed the wound with gauze and medical tape. Jarod had rarely been touched as he grew up and had ached to be held. To know he was cared for, to bond in the most basic of ways. For as long as he could remember, he had craved human connection, and now that warmth and caring he felt through Skylar's hands stirred something deep inside.

"I thought your friend Helen Wheels was gonna single-handedly bring the shooting gallery back to Astroland."

"*Friend* isn't the exact word I would use for Miss Parker. A childhood acquaintance, maybe," Jarod corrected, now snapped out of his reverie back to reality.

It wasn't jealousy, but rather *curiosity* that propelled Skylar's questions. "She must've made quite an impression to rate your Etch A Sketch Michelangelo's."

"Meteors make impressions too, but you never want to see one coming at you," Jarod said wryly, Miss Parker the last thing he wanted to be thinking about right now. "How about we talk about something more pleasant, like road kill or acid rain?"

The more he thought about Miss Parker, the more Skylar felt his tension mount. When he started to sit up, she stopped him. "Not so fast. You are one big knot. Now lay back down, take three deep breaths and leave the bulldozing to me, okay?"

Jarod stared at her, not knowing what to say.

Skylar placed her hand on his chest. "Living tied up is no way to live." She could feel his heart beating. She smiled. "Trust me," she said quietly, and when he relented, she eased him back down.

Within seconds, he felt the glorious bounty of her knowing hands, and the tension melted away, the sensuousness of her massage stirring his soul. But this incredible relief gave rebirth to another sensation deep inside, one that was intimate. A sensation that brought with it the reminder of a primal calling he'd first felt as a teenager.

Skylar lost herself in her task. Her feelings for Jarod had developed quickly, a man unlike any she'd ever encountered before. Without thought or hesitation, she lowered her face down to his back until her lips touched his skin. She felt the pleasure rippling through him, and rising in her. In the moment, she found her lips caressing his neck.

Jarod rolled over and drew her into his arms. He kissed her lightly, almost timidly and reluctantly separated. The kiss lingered on his lips, his body reacting to these warm stirrings, his heart feeling that he could lose himself in her violet eyes now alive with love and joy. In her eyes was freedom itself.

He pulled her back to him, yearning for more of that touch, that connection. Their kisses deepened until they were adrift in each other. When they broke, Skylar stood, offering her hand in invitation. Without hesitation, he took it.

As they headed for the bedroom, a new sensation grew in Jarod. It wasn't fear but it had a kinship with it, one he found exciting. Their eyes met as their hands folded into each other's, electricity surging inside them—anticipation. Skylar slipped her arm around Jarod's bare waist as she lead him in with a smile, then closed the door behind them with an unspoken promise of taking him to a place he would remember for the rest of his life.

Their bodies entwined under the covers, and she burrowed into him, their kisses intensified, passion building with the ultimate warmth of their flesh upon each other. The world around them was now gone and their possibilities seemed endless.

Skylar shuddered with pleasure, her purring urging Jarod on beyond the realm, her escalating sighs swelling in his soul, crescendoing in a fitful unison of ecstasy.

Jarod took her into his arms as she nuzzled against him, her head on his chest as they found sleep together, this timeless moment, theirs forever.

Fresh from an all-night Pre-Halloween party, Chaz came up on the freight elevator and stepped into Jarod's warehouse loft, decked out in a sexy French maid number—fishnets, a black lace hemmed skirt and a snug shirt and jumper that clung to all the right places as only Chaz could pull it off. It didn't have to be Halloween season for her to deck it in such a look, but there was plenty of one-upmanship in her circle when it came to actual costume parties this time of year.

Chaz had come early to show Jarod her gratitude by cleaning the place, but noticed it was already spotless. She grinned to herself, surmising who'd beaten her to it—Skylar.

She also noticed how quiet it was, not a creature was stirring, not even a mouse, unless one included Oscar, that is. Jarod's bedroom door was also closed, something she had never seen in her various times in the loft.

Feeling nosy, Chaz put her ear to the bedroom door and as she did, it crept open revealing a naked Jarod sleeping on his stomach with his arm draped across a sleeping and also naked Skylar next to him.

Jarod opened one eye to see the grinning Chaz, who shared a knowing smile with him, as a waking Skylar stirred.

"Beats the hell outta 'Nilla Wafers, don't it, J-Rod?" Jarod and Skylar both smiled coyly. Chaz cackled, her laugh fading as she closed the door, leaving them alone.

Jarod leaned over to Skylar. He stroked her hair and kissed her.

For the next two hours they talked, in the safety of each other's arms: Jarod, about the parents he could barely remember, and his uncertainty about how he ended up at the Centre. He spoke of his odd life and how, until only later as he matured, never felt it was odd. It was all he had ever known and, believing his parents were dead, never questioned the life that had been chosen for him.

Skylar opened up about the father she never knew, how it had been her mother's choice, not his, to take Skylar away. She didn't know anything else about him except that they both shared the same violet colored eyes. His identity was, and remained, the only secret her mother ever kept from her until the day she was killed. Skylar confessed to Jarod that she knew in her heart one day she would find him, assuming he was still out there, or if he didn't find her first. In her heart she had always sensed he was a good man.

After they had shared some of the deepest parts of themselves, these two kindred spirits made love again. A cavalry of two, struggling to find their place in a world that had rarely shown them its smile. For now, for this short little place in time, they each took comfort in knowing they had each other. For the moment, it was enough.

Jarod felt Skylar's sudden silence and could tell something was on her mind. "Was it something I did?" he asked tentatively.

"No, baby, you were perfect," she reassured him as her smile faded.

"What's wrong then?" Jarod ask with a tilt of his head.

"I had a dream, but it wasn't," she said with a frown, knowing that made little sense. "It was about my last night in the Annex at the hospital, the bald pirate."

Pulse racing, Jarod eyed her inquisitively, this was what he had been hoping for. "O'Quinn."

"Yes, and O'Quinn told the guy with the arm cast to call Emtrex. That he wanted to transfer Kaj somewhere safer …"

Jarod hugged her, this was promising news, but when he looked into her eyes she was troubled. "What?"

She took his hand, "I can't shake the feeling that now you're going to go away from here," she confessed. "From me."

He lifted her chin up and her eyes followed to his. "Doesn't mean I won't be coming back, Sky, I promise. Now tell me where they sent Kaj?"

She wrapped her arms around his neck and held him tighter than she ever had any man. "A place called Isla Raton."

Jarod felt all of her love and for the first time in a while, sensed he finally had a real shot again at finding Kaj and saving Luke.

Chapter 34

SYDNEY HELD THE stairwell door open just enough to not be seen, but enough so that he could keep his eyes on the elevator bank down the corridor on the top floor of the Centre's North Tower.

Five minutes prior he'd been dismissed from his latest flogging at the hands, or rather, the acid tongue of one Mr. Parker, who had voiced his irrational opinions about everything from his disgust of Volvos—'Ga-dam Swedes couldn't engineer a piss in a brewery,' psychiatry as a profession 'Nut jobs stroking nut jobs,' Sydney's handling of Jarod, 'You screwed him up, then stripped the screw' and amusement parks in general, 'nothing but staging areas for unemployable inbreds.' It was a classic, but not unexpected Mr. Parker dressdown, and it rolled off Sydney's tweed-covered back the minute he was booted from the room. Somehow, he managed to all but escape the most indicting discussion of all: Did Sydney crash into that transport van on purpose or by accident? The psychiatrist also knew it didn't matter to Miss Parker or her father, because they would always assume he did it to save Jarod. And maybe he had. He, himself, was evading his *own* motivations on that one, truth be told. With each passing day, Sydney found himself relying more and more on pure impulse, living moment by moment, second by second. In many ways, he was surprised he hadn't found himself in on the wrong end of a T-Board inquiry, or the incinerator on SL-26.

As tempestuous as Mr. Parker's verbal beatdown was, especially when he pulled the Mr. Zane threat card on Miss Parker, the odd highlight for

Sydney was catching her stifling a grin at Daddy's *unemployable inbreds* line. But he was certain she wouldn't be smiling after emerging from Daddy's one on one nuclear rant on her and Sydney was right.

He perked up spotting Miss Parker trudging into view at the elevator bank. His instant assessment of her was that she looked like she needed a drink, or several. When she vanished in her own haze into the lift, Sydney eyed the numbers on the wall read-out; she'd gone all the way to the ground floor, figuratively and literally, post-Daddy tirade.

He also understood that meant she was done for the day, and that was all Sydney really cared about.

Sydney slipped into Miss Parker's office on the second highest floor of the Centre's North Tower. Her office was directly under that of her father's, and one he hadn't seen the inside of for three years. Checking to make sure no one had seen him enter, Sydney closed the door, turned and took in the entire room.

Tastefully appointed, it was quiet, cold and spotless, in an almost sterile fashion. There was a place for everything and everything was in its place. Not just in a way that Sydney would classify as 'tidy' but, using Freudian analysis, one that reflected Type A, anal-retentive personality. Sydney knew it hadn't always been that way. The last time Sydney had been within these walls, the mood had been raucous and celebratory. He had even been served a piece of King Cake that Mr. Parker had had specially flown in from his favorite New Orleans bakery. It was the one where he had met Catherine in when she was a pastry chef working her way through Tulane. It wasn't as good as the ones Catherine used to bake at home, but nonetheless, to commemorate his daughter's promotion from Centre Field Operative to the executive ranks, it seemed appropriate. Miss Parker had grabbed the next rung on the ladder that one day would land her in the office her father now occupied, the penultimate position at the Centre that was destined to be hers.

On that happy day, as he'd eaten the delicious cinnamon roll-like confection with its purple, green and gold icing, Sydney had to acknowledge that, despite what it had cost her personally, Miss Parker had more than earned her new job. Over the years she had worked her way up from Cleaner, those responsible for making the distasteful remnants of collateral damage, 'disappear.' Later she became one of the secret Operatives the Cleaners cleaned up after. From Hong Kong to São Paulo, Dubai to Detroit, carrying out the wishes of her father or those of the African Triumvirate that controlled the Centre itself.

As he moved across the room, Sydney noticed that Miss Parker had set up a bar in the corner—and not just any bar, but one that was identical to the ones in Mr. Parker's office at work and at home.

The psychiatrist thought about what the presence of the matching bars said about Miss Parker's psyche and her dysfunctional relationship with her father, the domineering, duplicitous, semi-benevolent tyrant who ran the Centre and her life with an iron fist in a velvet glove.

Sydney could only imagine what her life must have been like as a child, growing up alone and isolated on the horse farm with that man, after her mother had left this world.

Sydney missed Catherine Parker.

Theirs had been a special relationship, one he wished he could share with her daughter. Certain promises had been made though and he was determined to keep his word to Catherine in death as he had in life. It was a special loyalty they had shared and ironically one that, by searching through her daughter's office, he was actually being true to Catherine, though he doubted Miss Parker would see things quite that way.

His search didn't take long.

Sydney knew very well that Miss Parker was a creature of habit and always kept her Polyvore briefcase in the exact same place next to her desk on the right side where she'd placed it on that celebratory day three years ago.

The attaché case had been a gift from her father at the celebration and now it contained what Sydney wanted, what he *needed* to help Jarod. He opened the case and there it was.

Miss Parker's laptop.

Chapter 35

LUKE STARED AT the dangling light bulb glowing down on him in his cot.

He was still the corpse under the covers of his nightmare.

He was still without that lone hero from his imagination.

He still missed his mom and dad.

And he was rapidly losing hope.

Thankfully Adidas Man's temperament, while more hyper than he had ever seen him before, had also been more upbeat, almost kind of goofy at times. Whatever hopeful dream Adidas Man was suddenly riding on, Luke prayed would last. Yet he knew now from experience that, with each passing day, anything could spin his captor's mood 180 degrees back into a darker place.

As he gazed back up at the light bulb, feeling tired, he knew it was time for a new tale. Before the wheels of his imagination could begin to spin, the bulb went out, plunging him into blackness.

Adidas Man was slouched at the kitchen table in mid swig of the final drops residing in his last bottle of Cuervo, when the world went dark. Given his drunken blur, he didn't react right away, just sort of tilted and bobbed his head around the suddenly lightless room. Staggering up, he tried the light switch. Nothing.

With sodden mind and body, he lit his Zippo and shuffled into the dusty garage in search of the breaker panel. Stumbling through, he tripped over a hay bale, a rusty trike, a rake, but eventually found it. He threw the main down and back up again to reset, but the silent darkness remained.

He had a bad feeling about this and in fact was beginning to feel the beads of sweat starting to form on his hands.

Without warning, the delightful lull of Diablo's nectar went sour as if feeling the tines of Satan's pitchfork beginning to press against his soul. The paranoia of reality was starting to break the skin. His mind rewound with both clarity and confusion. He vaguely recalled Kaj bitching about having to secure this place longer than they were ever going to need it and with that came a realization: The Gods of New Jersey Light and Power had cut them off.

Tripping over the same rake on his way back into the house, Adidas Man snatched his cell phone off the kitchen table—then froze. Who was he going to call? Not Kaj and certainly not New Jersey Light and Power— *Hello? I'm a kidnapping son of a bitch who's holding a young boy captive in the base-ment and I'd appreciate you sending someone out to turn my lights back on.*

He set the phone back on the table, its glow shining on his three empty tequila bottles and the unfolded and barren patch of foil that was once crammed full of crack. To kill the buzz even further, his eyes spotted the battery-power bar on the phone that showed less green than a month old bag of lettuce. *Seems like I just charged the damn thing,* he thought to himself. *Then again, the 30 or so calls to that prick Slick Ray, who never answers his fucking phone any more, just when I need a refill the most, might have something to do with the lack of juice.*

His hands were trembling, as they raked through his hair. Within the hour, if he was lucky, his days-long high would be but a memory, his last tether to the outside world would be deader than snot and he would be lit-tle more than a jonesing pawn with a target on his back, freezing his ass off in the dark.

Chapter 36

MISS PARKER ENTERED her penthouse with one thing and one thing only in mind. She made a beeline to the bar stocked with one thing and one thing only—Maker's Mark.

The *clank,* as she placed a tumbler on the bar top, was followed by the opening of the freezer door and the *clink, clink, clink* of three ice cubes dropping into the glass—always three—never more, never less. The end of the routine, the *gurgle, gurgle, gurgle* of the bourbon and the cubes crackling as they were covered with the honey-brown liquid, was music to her ears.

She drank down the smoky nectar, then poured another quad, hoping against hope they would give her momentary refuge from her self-torment. *But then, wherever you go, there you are,* an unpleasant thought she chased away.

She drained the second glass and slammed the tumbler down with enough force to crack the lead crystal. Jarod had gotten away—*again!* As Miss Parker poured a third belt, she wondered what the hell had happened at Coney Island. What she had *allowed* to happen?

Sydney was an idiot, but not a total fool. He had figured out that she tracked Jarod to the amusement park and the Belgian Geppetto had bumbled his way in, causing a disturbance large enough for his Pinocchio to escape.

She took another long pull that included one of the pieces of ice. As she crushed it between her molars she felt a new pang of unease, a growing sense of trepidation that her father was losing confidence in her. Who could blame him? She understood the Triumvirate, fuelled by Uncle Zane's evil whispers, was breathing down Daddy's neck.

She was pissed that Zane had called in the middle of her meeting with her father, and even more peeved that Daddy not only took the call but that he put it on speaker. Zane had always been a foul storm cloud in her life and she certain that he would do anything to slide a knife into her father's back—or *hers*. Neither of which she was willing to let happen.

Even worse was Zane's comment about the African's suggestion to bring Alejandra into the hunt for Jarod. The mere mention of the smoldering beauty's name incensed Miss Parker and the words she stifled in front of her father—"Brazilian Whore," came out now as she poured another Maker's.

This one she guzzled, her mind awhirl over the very thought of Alejandra Ferreira coming back to Blue Cove. The woman had been like a festering cold sore to Miss Parker ever since they were young women together in CIT fighting over both who would be number one with the men in their midst and number one in their class. They would be fighting over who would be number one at the Centre before their careers ended. No, she had worked too hard and sacrificed too damn much for her long-term goals at the Centre to have them screwed up by the men in Africa, or *Zane and Alejandra.*

She looked out at the lights of downtown Blue Cove through angry, pointed eyes, lights that normally soothed her soul, but tonight seemed only to be mocking her. *How pathetic have I become? Have I been out of the field too long? Have I gotten soft?* The hard-as-nails part of her brain scolded the sentimentality. *It's more than that and you know it. Jarod? Hasn't he always been the key to my problems, as a child, as a teenager, as an adult?*

There was no doubt that there was more to their relationship than what was at the surface. She knew the roots to her tormenting moment earlier ran far deeper and were far more confronting. With her bourbon barricade weakening by the second, she knew she couldn't push the distressing thoughts away or close the blinds on the truth. The lightning from the storm Jarod was stirring in her wasn't one she'd ever be able to quell with a gun or handcuffs.

It was *emotional*.

And that the shattered pieces within her that she was now trying to mend were not just in her psyche, they were in her *heart*. The *one* place her CIT mentor taught her to be master of—the *one* place she'd always held her true edge against the world—and the *only* place she could ever lose that edge forever.

Miss Parker finished off her third drink, deciding it was her last. A fourth would cloud her mind and that would be unacceptable if she was ever going to catch and lock that son of a bitch back up. She was fighting for the mastery of herself, that which made her free and that he now threatened. What she needed to do more than ever, was focus on the heart of the matter.

She saw it out of the corner of her eye, this *heart of the matter* she needed to concentrate on, the one thing that had been screaming out to her since the day she had brought it home. She stared at the broken Etch A Sketch still resting against the wall where she'd left it after ripping its back off. On the screen beneath the face of her younger self were the nine words Jarod had written on it that had been haunting her since they first appeared.

I know the truth about what makes you sad.

Who the hell did Jarod think he was?

She sat on the floor, picked up the toy, and stared into her younger face, the face of the sad little girl she still was inside. The Etch A Sketch exchange she'd had with Jarod at Astroland came ringing back in her ears, until a light bulb went off in her head. Actually, it exploded. A scowl formed on her face as she flipped the Etch A Sketch over—dug into its inner contents of fine aluminum powder surrounding orthogonal rails, upon which was a drawing stylus that was touching the tip of the nose of Little Miss.

"On the nose, indeed," she growled with a sense of irony.

Miss Parker ripped the stylus off, stood and took it over to her desk, where she had a magnifying glass in the pencil holder. She held the convex lens above the stylus and studied the tip. Looking at it closely, she could make out what appeared to be a grain of sand, just like the ones she had found when searching Jarod's living dome with Sydney. Miss Parker smiled with grudging respect, as she realized this wasn't a grain of sand at all. It was a nano origami in the shape of Onyssius, the Greek God of retribution that Jarod had made and left for her to find.

Miss Parker grabbed her cell and speed dialed. After a beat she barked, "Where are you?"

Daphne groggily sat up in bed feeling around for her glasses, as she spoke into her phone. "In bed."

"Did I wake you?" Parker asked, unconcerned.

"No. I was just laying here, thinking of you."

Miss Parker wasn't sure what this meant or if she *wanted* to know, but she ignored it, told Daphne a place and time to meet her and promptly hung up.

"I'm on my way." Daphne replied even though Parker was already gone. She then looked to her right. Laying next to her, *au naturel*, was the slutty Mud Flaps Girl. She was more tempting than when she was in the suspended glass box at the Avant-Garde, but nonetheless, Daphne looked and said two very simple words no one had ever said to the sultry temptress before.

"Get out."

Chapter 37

THERE WERE THREE things in life that Dara loved: The first was the freedom she was allowed to ride her tricycle in the hallways of the Centre, the second was the satisfaction she received eating grape Blow Pops with the double gum interior, and the third was the sense of floating in nothingness that overcame her when drawing on her sketchpad.

The young intuitive's room off Corridor 15, in SL-26 was a sparse little space more appropriate for a cloistered nun than a five-year-old child. It was furnished with a cot, a stool and a chrome table upon which her sketchpad and pencils were always laid out. Her walls were covered with hundreds of sketches, all of which had come through her hand, none of which she had a memory of having drawn.

She could remember picking up her pencil—and had total recall of opening her sketchpad, but the moment the point touched paper, she disassociated. Seconds, minutes, sometimes even hours later, she would realize that she was finished and afterwards she would look at what she had created as if seeing it for the first time.

Sydney told her she was psychically channeling things from deep inside, though he was unsure of whether they were things she *felt* or things she *received*. However, she had *felt* a great deal of late, and her hand hurt from all that had poured through her onto paper.

Dara felt lots of things, including *his* presence outside her door even before she heard approaching footsteps. She rose from her tiny cot and was speaking as she opened the door.

"What do you want, Sydney?" she asked curiously. Standing next to her tricycle parked outside in the hallway, the startled Sydney was in mid-knock, his knuckles missing the door—and rapping air. Her anticipatory insight caught him off guard and fueled his paranoia. Covering, he raised the leather valise reminiscent of his position as a psychiatrist. "I brought you something." Sydney reached inside the bag and pulled out a Blow Pop. He offered the candy to the little girl. She looked up from it and into Sydney's eyes, leery of his intentions.

He forced a generous smile. "It's grape. Your favorite."

Dara didn't take the sucker. "It's 3 a.m., Sydney, what do you want?"

"I want you to do me a favor," Sydney stated, unfazed by her abruptness.

"Want? Or *need?*" she asked, narrowing her eyes.

"Need and it's a private favor."

Dara was compelled to look at Sydney's valise, sensing something inside of it, something she didn't like. With a bit of apprehension, Dara looked to a corner of her room where there were dozens of sketches of Miss Parker. She then jerked her head back to face the Belgian. "You stole—*from her?*" she asked, although it wasn't really a question, her eyes growing round with surprise.

Sydney wasn't sure if Dara was picking up on what was in his bag or in his heart. Either way, Sydney was unsettled by the odd little girl's perceptive talents. Still, her gift was the reason he was there, so he plunged ahead. "I didn't steal, I borrowed it," he clarified, wondering why he felt the need to justify himself to her.

Dara studied him for a long beat, finally backing away. Exhaling, Sydney nervously checked the hallway before entering, and closed the door behind him.

Reaching into his bag, the psychiatrist pulled out Miss Parker's laptop. He opened and placed it on the table. "Miss Parker types the same string of numbers and letters into this every day."

Dara was already deciphering the *energy* emanating from the computer. "Numbers that open ... a lock?"

"Yes, something like that. I need to know what they are." Sydney spun the computer around, so the keyboard was facing the young empath.

Dara stared at the keyboard and was drawn to it. She gazed up into Sydney's eyes. "I want *five* suckers, Sydney."

"I'll give you ten." Sydney had to work hard to contain his smile.

Dara weighed his sincerity, found it to be true, then sat and faced the computer. The intuitive opened her sketchpad, and with her left hand, picked up a pencil and held it above the paper, her right hand resting above the keyboard. Her right began to tingle and vibrate as she connected with the energy remnants Miss Parker had left behind on the plastic keys.

Sydney watched Dara's eyes begin to quiver and roll down into her head. Her right hand began to move as if possessed by some outside force. Sydney couldn't tell what was really happening, but the experience reminded him of when his mother used to get out the Ouija board and ask questions from her deceased relatives. Sydney had always considered his mother's preoccupation with the metaphysical world to be a coping mechanism for her survivor's guilt, a tragic response to her own desires to say goodbye to those that she had been unable to save during the dark time.

He had not believed things of this nature were possible until he first met Dara as an infant, watched her hold her hand over a pile of 103 photos of different women, and then, as if pulled by an unseen force, pick out the picture of her mysteriously murdered mother.

The same unseen force seemed to be moving her hand now, guiding her right forefinger above the 7 key. With her left hand she wrote down 7. Next her hand was drawn toward the letter V—a capital version of which she wrote next to the 7. Her hand then was compelled to the number '1'. As she wrote this down in sequence, Sydney realized it was working.

The code he needed to find the truth about Jarod was going to be his.

Chapter 38

DAPHNE HAD NEVER been on Sub-Level 19 and the ominous hallways that gave so many pause had her bubbling with excitement. The Centre was an enigmatic world full of hidden truths Daphne wanted to discover—secrets concealed behind every heavy carbon fiber door she passed.

She stopped next to three electronic card key readers, a photo-volvic palm scanner and a video keyboard that required a special access code. Without a clearance level Daphne did not have, this door was impossible to open, so she did the second best thing to using a blast of C-4 to open it.

She knocked.

After a moment, it electronically unlatched from inside and the door opened.

Courtesy of Miss Parker.

Unable to hide the amazement on her face, Daphne followed Miss Parker inside ... Of course, she could not have known what to expect from the space where the Pretender had been raised. She'd heard much speculation but hardly anyone had ever been inside his *space*.

In the middle of this dark cavern of a room glowed the sterile, Plexiglas dome, bio-chamber.

Inside, the dome was divided, by clear glass walls, into three distinct areas. Reminiscent of a prison cell, the rear section contained a small bed, toilet and shower. A section to the right was a work area complete with desk, computers, an electron microscope and a viewing screen. The third section was completely empty.

Everything in the dome was white.

Except one thing in section three, a six-inch circular touchpad on the wall.

It was red.

This room was Jarod's Simulation Theatre where with the push of the pad, the room transformed into any environment imaginable, from a crashing 747, to the 95th floor of World Trade Center Tower One on 9/11, to the mass shooting hallways of Columbine High School. Conceived to be a totally immersive virtual environment, the theatre came complete with cutting edge holographic images, pristine surround sound, as well as temperature, smell and taste variances to engage all of Jarod's senses at once.

Mesmerized, Daphne voiced how she'd heard rumors about this place and had always wanted to see how it worked.

"Keep pulling rabbits out of the hat for me and I'll bring you back down here some other time and let you really experience it." Miss Parker replied, "But right now I need your help."

Parker fired up the electron microscope where she had placed the nano-origami she'd found on the Etch A Sketch stylus. "Jarod left this for me—I'm assuming as some kind of a message."

Daphne examined the winged figure on the screen as Miss Parker continued. "Sydney said Jarod folded hundreds of these 'angels' as relaxation before he escaped. But he didn't know why. Truth is …"

"They're not angels," Daphne finished Miss Parker's thought as she turned to face her. "The wings are bent. That's Onyssius, the Greek God of Retribution. He defends the weak and abused."

Miss Parker was impressed by Daphne's recognition of Onyssius, as she had said those *exact* same words to Sydney not two weeks earlier. "You're a lot smarter than your hairstyle suggests. Now, fire up some of that grey matter and help me decipher what Jarod is trying say with this thing."

Daphne smiled wide on the *inside,* but on the *outside* she played it professionally. "A Pretender is not just a genius with an eidetic memory, but someone blessed with the use of their brain well beyond even the most gifted among us, permitting him to see and experience the world from a unique perspective. The question is, what would he see differently about Onyssius?"

Miss Parker could tell an idea was forming in the back of Daphne's mind. "What's stirring in your bonnet, Miss Blondie?"

Daphne felt an electric prickling on her skin. She liked when Miss Parker referred to her as *Blondie*—but that she added a 'Miss' before it made her, well—elated.

Daphne smiled, this time on the outside. "In the deeper levels of the Onyssian lore, the God of Retribution realized that a person's true identity was embedded in their heart." Daphne brought the microscopic Onyssius into sharper focus. "While I could never dream of really thinking like a Pretender, if I were asked to try and Sim how he might, I'd guess he'd have left a message in the heart of this."

Daphne slid an electronic device into place over the lens.

"What's that?"

"Molecular tweezers."

"And of course you know how to use them."

Daphne grinned coyly and placed her fingers onto the guidance mechanisms. "Bear with me, this will take a minute." Like she had done it a thousand times before, Daphne began the painstaking microsurgery-like work of using the molecular tools to manipulate the nano-origami.

Miss Parker was more than fascinated now. "Take as long as you need. Just keep whatever we find here a secret."

"Don't worry, Miss Parker," Daphne said flatly. "I'm almost as good at keeping secrets as you."

"What's that supposed to mean?"

"Well, not around here; your job is clandestine. I'm talking about the personal ones. Like your first name." Daphne repositioned Onyssius with the tweezers and began to unfold his paper wings.

"Are we back to that again?" Miss Parker curved an eyebrow.

"Some of us never left." Daphne concentrated on not tearing the delicate paper as she continued. "I have a theory—would you like to hear it?"

"Why not?" she said, amused by this.

"Your mother grew up in France and it's fondly remembered by the old timers around here how much she loved her adopted country. I'm guessing that she named her daughter something French, tying her two great loves together."

Before Miss Parker could respond, Daphne opened the last origami fold and revealed that in the exact spot where the heart of Onyssius would be, there was a heart drawn on the nano-paper. Inside was written an elaborate set of 16 numerals, letters and symbols.

Miss Parker's head tilted to the right. "What the hell is that?"

Daphne studied the screen. "Jarod loves cryptology. My guess is it's a *secret of the heart* in some kind of code."

"How is it that you know so much about Jarod?"

"I study the things in the Centre that fascinate me." Something dawned on Daphne and she turned to Miss Parker. "It's not a code, it's a game. An unsolvable equation like the Hodge conjecture, or Gromov's Knot Distortion, the kinds we played at math camp."

Miss Parker gave Daphne a look. "I occupied my summers with *other* activities."

"Luckily, I didn't. We solved these things all the time. This one's almost identical to the *Happy Endings* problem."

"Then, maybe I *can* figure it out."

Daphne blushed. "Not that kind of happy, Miss Parker. Think Euclidean geometry, specifically the Ramsey theory, so named because it led to the marriage of George Szekeres and Esther Klein—the mathematicians who solved it. The H.E. is based around the postulation that every set of five points in a general position in space contains the vertices of a convex quadrilateral or a polygon with four edges and corners."

Miss Parker's look was, *say what?*

Daphne simplified. "Think of it as a sheet of paper suspended in space that is bent and twisted."

"What's that have to do with Jarod?"

Daphne wrote an equation, as she explained. "S and K's theorem stated that for any positive integer N, any finite set of points in the plane has a subset of points forming the vertices of a convex polygon. Where $f(N)$ denotes the minimum M for which any set of M points contain a convex N-gon. But instead of N and M—Jarod's problem uses N and W and he's tossed in variables where f(N) >6."

Miss Parker's eyes were glazing over as Daphne stood back and gazed appreciatively at the formula. "It's pretty ingenious."

Parker was wondering just how ingenious Blondie was but didn't have time to delve into that right now. "So the human chameleon's given me a twisted *happy ending* in the form of an unsolvable problem to solve."

"Exactly—only different."

"How poetic." Miss Parker looked from the screen to Daphne. "Can you pretend you're back in camp and come up with an answer?"

"No, but the supercomputer in SL-18 can. It'll take at least 48 hours."

"You have *24*."

Miss Parker's cell rang. She pulled it out and barked. "You better not be calling empty handed, Cornelius."

The Cornmeister was in his tech theatre and feeling feisty. The Blonde terrorist had somehow sabotaged his face rec program and fucked him over, but two could play at that game and he now felt he was back in charge. "My fists are full with the five words you most want to hear."

"You're going to shoot yourself?" She asked hopefully.

"No, I have what you want." He smiled at his computer screens where pictures of the familiar eye-patched bald man appeared. "His name is O'Quinn. Former military. Black ops type. Now works for a company called Emtrex."

Parker frowned. "Don't know them."

"Think Halliburton, Booz Allen Hamilton, Blackwater. Basically, us with a newer building. I'm texting you the address as we converse."

"And to think I was just about to fire you, you bought yourself another life, Corn-cat. Better hope it's a long one."

Before he could respond, Miss Parker hung up and turned to Daphne. "Solve the unsolvable and I'll owe you more than one."

A smile danced over Daphne's face. "Consider it done, Miss Parker."

Without another word, Miss Parker walked away. Daphne's eyes painted her body. She blushed when Miss Parker turned abruptly, expecting to be called to task for ogling, but all Miss Parker said was, "By the way, you're on the right pathway—I *was* named for something in France. Something to do with my mother's childhood."

After Miss Parker left, Daphne found herself resolved to two things: that she wouldn't rest until she'd solved the unsolvable math problem and that she would discover the first name of the woman of her dreams.

She planned to whisper it into her ear one day, or even better, one *night*.

Thirty seconds later, Miss Parker's stilettos echoed on the marble floor as she walked down the hallway. She was glowing inside—Daphne was solving one mystery for her and the idiot deviant had, amazingly, just solved another.

As she reached the elevators, she thought about calling Sydney to gloat. Once the lift arrived, though, she changed her mind. *The old bat's probably at home asleep in his chair. I'll tell him tomorrow. Or not.*

The doors closed and she was gone, though the hallway was not empty as she had presumed. Stepping out of the shadows was a man who was not at home asleep in his chair.

Sydney was in the bowels of the Centre and he was on a mission.

Chapter 39

TEARS ROLLED DOWN Chaz's cheeks. She could not hold the pain back any longer. Years of self torment had burst forth like water through a dam, and that was the only word she could say. "Damn."

With her left hand, she grabbed a tissue from the box in her lap and blew her nose. Without looking, she reached over to the TV tray with her right. As if reading Braille, her fingers knew exactly where to find what she was craving, one of her last three Double Stuffed Oreos.

She took it from the little saucer, dunked it in a glass of milk, then transferred it to her mouth. Nabisco goodness exploded on her tongue. She knew that, while the calories may not soothe the pain inside, they damn sure tasted good.

Black on the outside and white on the in, her cookie was just as sweet as the troubled young lady that Chaz was watching on MTV's Catfish, a show about people who used fake online identities to attract a love interest.

Filling the TV's screen was Chantrel, a confused, mixed-race teen peering out the peephole of her front door, too terrified to open it. On the other side was the man with whom she had been conducting an internet romance. Edgar, a 20-something MMA fighter, was holding a bouquet of flowers for the woman he believed was an Asian beauty queen, instead of the 280lb couch potato Chantrel really was.

Chaz felt a jolt of pride and sat up in the La-Z-Boy. "Answer it, girl! Embrace who you really is." She blindly reached for the second to last cookie, gave it a milk bath and was in the midst of her blissful munching when Chantrel cracked the door and explained, that she was not who she had claimed to be. She feared no one would love her as who she really was, but knew it was time to face the music.

"That's right, girl. Preach it! Ain't nobody better than the true you!" Chaz was so pleased to see that, unlike most of the people who'd been played on Catfish, Edgar didn't care. He was attracted to the real Chantrel, bringing a lump to Chaz's throat. True love wasn't just on the surface and she hoped that maybe, one day, she would find it too.

As she groped for her last Oreo, Chaz was shedding tears of joy. She loved a happy ending.

In that moment, Chaz didn't find a happy ending for herself. Instead of grabbing Double Stuff, her hand grabbed *rat*. She flinched. This time, screaming, "Damn!" Turning her head, she came face to face with Oscar. One of the biggest rodents in Harlem was on Chaz's plate, whiskers deep in white cream frosting. He looked up from his meal to the man dressed as a woman and sniffed disdainfully.

Chaz shot a look over her shoulder to where Jarod was sitting at the kitchen dinette, facing the opposite direction. The Pretender was busy at work removing what looked like white and green bricks from a duffle bag and stacking them on the table in front of him.

"Hey, 'Nilla man! That foul ass ghetto gopher done just committed a mortal sin, so you may as well start preparing the eulogy!"

Jarod didn't look up from his task. "I thought you two were friends."

"With friends like this, you don't need no enemies!" she shot back, keeping her eyes on the rat.

Oscar looked up from Chaz's cookie and seemed to snicker.

"Oh, vile-ass vermin think that's funny, huh? Well, laugh at this!" She flung the Kleenex box at Oscar. The rotund rodent ducked, leapt off the TV tray, and bolted away.

Chaz grabbed a broom and was smacking the floor behind, aside and almost on top of Oscar. He dodged, darted and scurried for his life. She was right on him, with the broom raised high, as Oscar slipped past the metal legs of the dinette chair. Chaz changed her aim mid-swing but missed the rat; in fact, she even missed the floor, the broom crashing down on the kitchen table.

The cash it landed on exploded into the air.

The realization of this stopped Chaz in her tracks. She saw everything in slow motion; piles of thousands of hundred-dollar bills on the table and at least 200 grand snowflaking down all around her.

Jarod, who'd been counting and stacking, looked up at Chaz, amused at the antics. "I told you two not to play in the house."

"Baby, in my days as a stripper I've seen't it rain, but this'a damn monsoon!" She caught a falling bill and smelled it. "Ummm mmmmm baby. Screw the sign spinnin'—dis is what Momma's talkin'bout." She pulled out a chair and straddled it backwards, her eyes never leaving the money. "Is that what I think it is?"

"It is, if you think its ten million dollars in cash." Jarod smiled.

"You wanna tell a hardworking girl what chew doin' with all them Benjamins?"

Jarod tucked several bundles into a satchel. "Going shopping. Want to come?"

Chapter 40

WITH EVERY STEP through the shadowed hallways of SL-13, Sydney found it harder to breathe. Acute stress had his sympathetic nervous system dumping copious amounts of adrenaline, noradrenaline, and dopamine into his bloodstream. The medical community called this condition a Catecholamine Hormonal Episode.

In layman's terms, it was known as *freaking out*.

Sydney was only seven the first time he thought he was having a heart attack. On that day, his mother, Greta, a trailblazing psychiatrist from Brussels, shook him by the shoulders and said, "This is not death, Männchen, but hyperventilation syndrome."

Later, Sydney discovered that panic induced hyperventilation was related to a specific fear like heights or claustrophobia. In Sydney's current situation, the dread was being tortured and killed if he got caught.

His breathing even more frenzied, he reached the end of the corridor and the ominous black doors of the Centre Archives. When physically losing control like this, his mother would make him breathe into a brown paper bag. As Sydney typed a password into the security screen keyboard he wished he'd had one with him. It was not *his* password; it belonged to the curator of the items stored behind the doors.

Part librarian, part cyber genius, Kris Russell was the attractive and mysterious Centre Archivist. A fellow Belgian, Sydney had a standing Thursday lunch date with her in the Sub-Level South Commissary. Their friendship had started in the soup and salad line one afternoon when they were both fighting over the last bowl of new Chef Phillipe Van der Mussa's Paling in 't Groen, a traditional dish of their homeland made of eels and herbs. After a bout of Flemish bickering, they decided to share the *fish-mongers'* delight. Over the meal and reminisces of the old country, they discovered much in common and became fast acquaintances. At least that's what they were in Sydney's mind; he feared that, in hers, their relationship was more.

Kris was also a kindred spirit in another way: She, too, was a chronic insomniac. Sydney would often stop by and converse with her after hours, as they both so often found themselves in the bowels of the silent Centre when the other staff had gone home, home to wives and husbands and children, the kind of family neither had waiting for them.

On those nights, they would sit in a hidden spot halfway down the main aisle of archives. There, Kris would smoke her disgusting non-filter, Polish cigarettes while they shared childhood stories about their homeland.

Tonight though, Sydney was hoping, *praying*, that she was home in her tiny cabin on Brice Islet. The doors unlocked with a loud click, startling Sydney and sending another jolt of adrenaline surging through his body.

Chapter 41

THE WORLD SYDNEY entered was green. Determined to accomplish his mission under the cover of darkness, he wore the same night vision goggles Jarod had used while designing a search and destroy operation inside a mockup of an infamous three-story house in Abbottabad, Pakistan.

If the space Sydney was in now were to become common knowledge, it too would be equally as infamous. The vast storeroom reminded Sydney of the warehouse at the end of *Raiders of the Lost Ark* where the crated up Ark of the Covenant was stowed. Little did George Lucas know how close his vision was to the real thing.

Sydney often imagined what truths were hidden away in here. One day he hoped to return and explore them, but tonight, the target of his inquiry wasn't in any of the boxes or crates. What he was after was housed in the middle of the enormous room, where the towering stacks gave way to a 40 foot wide, 40 foot long, 40 foot tall ultra-modern glass-walled structure known as the Ice Cube.

The day he first set eyes on it, Mr. Parker christened the vessel with the nickname he claimed came to him not because the building looked like the custom made ice his custom ice maker made for his custom made bars, but because it was damn near glacial inside.

The sealed environment was kept at a constant one degree above freezing. No more. No less. As Jacci, the notorious Australian tech nerd who ran the Centre's website, was known to say, 'You gotta keep those babies cool or the circuits'll fry.' And the Centre could not let that happen.

The electronics she referred to were multi-story banks of massive servers that stored 11 thousand terabytes of highly sensitive data from the 88 major Centre Annexes around the globe. Somewhere within it all were the secrets Jarod needed to discover his true identity.

As Sydney approached the glowing Cube, another Catecholamine episode kicked into high gear. Something was wrong. *Terribly* wrong. The glow emanating from the cube was *pulsating*. The closer Sydney got to it, the faster it pulsated, it seemed to expand and contract. Sydney was turning to run when he realized the strobe of the light was in the exact rhythm to the pounding in his chest. The blood pressure in his eyes was causing the photoreceptors behind his retinas to flare with each heartbeat.

He slipped the night vision goggles up onto his forehead and the sensations ceased.

He was not going to fail, he hoped. *He prayed.*

Sydney focused on the Ice Cube. He did not see movement on any of the levels inside, but was not sure of Kris's whereabouts. She worked in the Cube *alone*. For the last seven years, since *the intrusion*, no one but Kris had entered the Cube. *No one.* Sydney knew of only four other people who had access clearance high enough to get in: Miss Parker; Mr. Parker; his repugnant half brother, Zane and a Centre bottom feeder with a chronic case of emphysema.

Sydney himself had only been inside once. Thirty years earlier, Mr. Parker and the unnerving Mr. Zane had brought him there to perform a secret evaluation on a three-year-old child brought in from the Argentina Annex. The old time rivals were split on whether or not the boy was to be the first child in the Pretender Program and wanted Sydney's expert opinion to settle the matter.

Sydney's memory no longer had clarity on the boy's given name but recalled his surname was *Bookman* or *Borman* or *something like that*. What Sydney could remember clearly and to his dying day would never forget, was the young boy's eyes and the chill that went through his body as he looked into them. Although they were in the face of a seemingly joyful child, when Sydney stared deeply, he saw through the glistening façade and into the developing mind of a cold-blooded psychopath. In that moment Sydney felt he had glimpsed into the soul of an agent of intelligent evil.

Knowing those were the exact qualities Zane wanted in Pretenders, Sydney argued against the child's inclusion into the program. He refused to have the boy interact with any of the others out of fear of the negative influence the child would have upon them. These words of warning had a pleasing effect on Mr. Parker, but they'd left nothing but simmering resentment on the scowl of Mr. Zane. On that day, Sydney had made a life-long enemy.

The man from Brazil was the least of his worries now. Leaving the shadows, Sydney crossed to the entrance and began typing in the security code Dara had read from Miss Parker's laptop. He closed his eyes as he keyed in the last digit.

A vacuum *whoosh* sounded as the door unlocked.

Chapter 42

JAROD DIDN'T HAVE to knock on the door; he was shoved through it by Doo-Rag. The 19 year-old enforcer and his gangsta posse had grabbed Jarod and Chaz as they entered the hallway of the Wagner Houses on corner of East 124th Street and FDR Drive. The housing project served as both the home and the hangout of the notorious Harlem gang, the Thrill Cru Boyz, the place from which Jarod had stolen their BMW less than a week earlier.

T-Dope, the cunning leader of this pack, looked up from the leather couch on which he was sandwiched by two ladies destined to be dancing stars in a future rap video. Doo-Rag tossed Jarod to the floor in front of him. The Pretender banged his head on the coffee table, disrupting a large pile of white powder.

T-Dope looked at Jarod without any sympathy, then to his crew. "White boy either done gone Forrest Gump or got him some big ass stones coming back up in here after stealing my ride."

The Thrill Cru Boyz gave authoritative nods to one another and the ladies smiled as they rubbed their nails on T-Dope's pecs. He stood and looked down upon Jarod with an air of superiority. "Got any final words, Forrest, before I send you and Bubba Gump for a dip in the East River?"

Chaz, wearing a full length blue sequined dress and a flowing mid-back curly black wig, stepped forward indignantly. "Who you callin' Bubba, bitch?"

"*You*, you Nikki Minaj-looking drag-ass-queen, dat's who." One of the Thrill Cru Boyz grabbed Chaz from the back. "Hey, don't be trying to undo my bra like I'm some easy ass ho. I ain't yo momma!"

Some of the Boyz made faces like 'whoa' while others said things like 'You got served!' It was quickly turning into gangbanger chaos until T-Dope regained control. "Shut the fuck up!"

"Chill your jets, homeboy." Chaz put a defiant hand on her hip. "We here to make a deal."

T-Dope turned his focus on Jarod, who sat up and rubbed his head. "How much for the pile on the table?" Jarod nodded toward the cocaine.

An astonished grin escaped T-Dope's face. "What? Mista Roger's Breaking Bad now?"

T-Dope looked at Doo-Rag and tossed his head toward the door.

Doo-Rag reached out to grab Jarod, but in a lightning fast move, the Pretender grabbed his hand and twisted it behind his back, then spoke calmly. "Before your ulna breaks, ask your boss again how much money he wants for the pile on the table."

Doo-Rag turned his head to T-Dope, but was in too much pain to speak. He was flapping his lips helplessly, high-pitched notes seeping out.

T-Dope gave in. "100 K, you cracker ass cracker."

As quickly as Jarod had grabbed Doo-Rag, T-Dope produced a Glock and had it aimed at Chaz. "And I don't take American Express."

The vibe in the room was suddenly very tense. Everyone felt the jolt— except Chaz. "Hund'ed K my sweet black ass! You must be trippin'. My man look like a chump to you, pay a 100 for a double cut baby laxative like dat?"

"Look, Bitch, dis ain't some ghetto ass Bodega where you haggle to buy yo' triple XL pantyhose. The price be the price."

"Triple XL—huh …?" Chaz's head started bobbing, but Jarod didn't so much as flinch.

"I've got a better deal," Jarod said calmly.

Jarod let go of Doo-Rag and moved his hand as if reaching into his inside jacket pocket. Before his hand was within 6 inches of the lapel, a dozen other guns appeared, all aimed at the Pretender. Jarod paused. He showed his palms and then with his left hand pulled back his jacket and with his right reached in and out slowly. He tossed several big stacks of hundreds onto the table.

"Give me twice as much and I'll give you 500 thousand and the toy outside."

The vibe switched to stunned, none more so than T-Dope. He stared at Jarod suspiciously, then pulled the curtain away from the window and took a peek out. A sparkling new Cherry Red BMW 640i coupe, identical to the one Jarod had stolen from him was parked under the streetlight. T-Dope turned back to Jarod and flashed his glinting diamond grills.

Twelve minutes later, Doo-Rag was playing chauffeur, driving Jarod and Chaz back to their more-loft-than-apartment.

The latter pulled off her wig and gave her head a good scratching, while shooting Jarod a disapproving look. "I ain't no coupon cutter baby, but I coulda saved you some scratch."

They turned off 7th and headed down 125th. Jarod's attention was fixated, as it always was, on the marquee announcing *The Apollo Theater* and gave a big smile, remembering his early escape days with Johnny Boy Creed.

"There's a lot more money where that came from."

"Well, look 'Nilla Man, long as we talkin' scratch—the caretaker job with Miss Skylar is coming to an end, and I have a list of expenses and unexpected surcharges and whatnot that have accumulated during my employment."

"Just make me a list and I'll reimburse you." Jarod assured her. Truth was she didn't even need to make a list of her expenses. Jarod didn't care about money and was sure he never would, given all of life's more important discoveries. He figured out early on that living in the real world and providing for others was the currency of his heart.

Doo Rag pulled a turn at 8th, leaving the lights behind. As they moved into a less hospitable section of Harlem, Jarod turned to Chaz. "I've got another job for you, if you're interested."

"Depend on how much it pay?" She said, playing it cool.

Jarod pointed to the satchel on the floor. "How about whatever's left in that bag down there?"

Chaz opened the bag, looked in, and almost fainted. "I ain't got to kill you again, do I?"

Jarod deadpanned. "Not all the way."

Chapter 43

THE LIGHTS IN the Ice Cube were on, but Sydney didn't know if anyone was home. Standing frozen at the open door, the voice in the back of his mind was pleading with him to turn and run. That this was his last chance to return to his lab and the secure life he had led for so many years, to do the sensible thing. That if he did, no one would ever find out about him being down here tonight. However, if he got caught entering the Cube, the cocoon of security he'd hidden away inside of would unravel, exposing him to a harsh reality he didn't even wish to imagine.

Sydney moved forward into the Cube. It was much louder inside than he anticipated. The hundreds—*or was it thousands?*—of servers were alive with a grating white noise. The sound was more disturbing; a deep vibrating resonance that he could feel in his chest. He imagined it was what killer bees sounded like in the hive when hundreds of them were dancing atop the honeycombs sharing thousands of communications. It was as though an alternating current of a million secrets were being whispered back and forth with intermittent chuckles for those in the know of the truth. Sydney listened and could pick out one annoying thrum in a lower octave than the others. It was coming from down the hallway, where he knew Kris's workstation to be.

He stared long and hard at the doorway and detected no signs of life coming from within. Satisfied, he then took in the entirety of the space with a 360-degree scan. The only movement inside the Ice Cube was his own frosty breath and the only clue of note he detected was a parka hanging by the door that Kris wore religiously when working inside.

The fact that it was here calmed Sydney's nerves. He was alone. Or, at least, he thought he was, until he caught sight of a man moving right outside the Cube.

His spine went ridged at the same time as did the other man's—both sharing identical shock at seeing the other. Key word: identical. Sydney let out a sigh realizing he was staring at his own reflection and found himself thinking how ridiculous he appeared, the quad-lens night vision goggles looking like he was wearing a high-tech tiara.

Steadying himself with a deep breath Sydney tasted a coppery and acrid flavor he assumed had something to do with the millions of waves pulsing through his body were doing to the buds on his tongue. The annoying, low level thrum had again seeped into his consciousness when a pungent odor awakened his olfactory senses. The fragrance was one that did not fit in the Ice Cube. He sniffed, recognizing the scent from his youth.

It was Waterzooi, a rich stew of fish, cream and eggs, from the town of Ghent. Sydney was puzzled. *Why would that aroma be in here?* He then recalled reading in the Centre Employees Newsletter that Waterzooi was to be Chef Phillipe's special in the cafeteria. He surmised that since he had been too preoccupied to meet Kris for their scheduled lunch date earlier, she must have taken hers back to the Cube. *Calm down, focus and do what you came to do.*

Sydney hastened down the hall of servers to Kris's workstation but was surprised by what he found.

In the middle of the multi-thousand square feet of technological wonderland, Kris's cubby sized office was not what he'd expected at all. Her desk looked like something out of a decades old IKEA catalog, which, in fact it was. It teetered on a broken leg that was duct-taped to a wooden board for stability and strained under the weight of the stacks of memos and search orders overflowing from the 'in' and 'out' trays atop. Partially obscured by all the disarray was a 20-year-old dented computer tower and an aged tube monitor that looked like something Steve Wozniac had soldered together in the late 1970's. And she didn't have a chair, she had a big exercise ball.

He sat, teetering his large frame on the ball and went to work. Bringing the antique computer to life was simple. It actually had a switch that denoted both 'on' and 'off'. What looked like a dinosaur of a machine was surprisingly fast. On the screen three words appeared: *Hello, Kris Russell,* followed by four letters, *CA-BC,* which stood for *Centre Archives-Blue Cove.* This was both good and bad, Sydney surmised. If discovered, the powers-that-be would think it was *Kris* who had accessed Jarod's information, not Sydney. He typed 'The Pretender Project' into the search window and within less than a second, the first name on that list appeared.

Jarod.

Sydney plugged in an external hard drive he swiped from the Centre's tech supply room, hoping the memory capacity would be enough. He knew Jarod's file was enormous. Sydney placed the cursor over the 'download' icon, took in a deep breath, then clicked. Light bars jumped from the file onto the EHD icon. For the first time since entering the Ice Cube, Sydney breathed a sigh of relief.

If it hadn't been for the fact he was hungry and freezing, Sydney thought he might be able to relax. He'd missed lunch and dinner and the Waterzooi essence in the air was making his stomach growl. Blowing warmth onto his freezing hands and thinking about beer cheese soup, he suddenly noticed something strange on the monitor. The transferring light bars of the downloading Jarod files stopped.

Sydney raised a confused eyebrow, placed his fingers on the ice-cold keys and hit a few strokes to restart the process. Nothing happened. The cursor just blinked.

Then, much to his astonishment, the bars then reversed themselves. Slowly at first, then faster and faster. The information he was stealing was now being stolen back from him.

Chapter 44

AS HIS BLOODSTREAM flooded with adrenaline, Sydney's
heartbeat erupted. As he began typing to reverse this, the screen exploded
with lines of scrolling code. Words he knew were from Jarod's intake file:
'Candidate Identified By …'—'Obtained on …'—'Assigned to Sydney'—
'*JAROD 2/4/83*'—'Parents: Unaware'—'Charles and Margaret'—'Flyer'—
'Red File # …' zoomed past.

The faster the text flew by, the quicker the light bars were being vac-
uumed out of the EHD icon.

"No!" Sydney screamed. He hit the requisite keys to determine who
was responsible. An ID icon appeared: MARTA—SA-RDJCA. Sydney felt
a trapdoor release beneath him. He was in free fall. A Security Analyst from
the Brazilian Centre Annex, Rio—the annex Mr. Zane oversaw—was over-
riding his download.

The low-grade thrum now began screaming in his ears, its accom-
panying headache detonating in his skull. To salvage what he could, he tried
to unplug the USB, but it wouldn't disengage. It was somehow locked in
place. His mind was screaming at him, as he frantically tugged at it. *Get out,
Sydney! Get out now!* But Sydney didn't want to get out—he typed furiously to
save his information. The more he fought, the faster the information was
sucked away. The vicious cycle repeated itself over and over until the Jarod
file icon onscreen was destroyed and pixelating into electronic dust, all cli-
maxing with a loud *Ding!*

Ding?

Sydney froze. He was in utter shock, fighting an oncoming hyper-ventilation episode as it dawned on him that the noise had coincided with one other thing—*the low level thrum was no longer present.*

Sydney realized he had broken the cardinal rule he'd hammered into Jarod about assessing each environment he walked into. He twirled around on the ball, taking in the room with all of his senses at once, and then he saw it.

On one of the cluttered bookshelves, not 18 inches from where he was sitting, was the lowest tech piece of equipment in the room, in the entire Ice Cube.

A microwave oven.

Sydney reached over and opened the door. Inside was a piping hot bowl of Waterzooi.

Sydney lost his balance and fell off the ball. Heart pounding out of his chest, he scrambled to his feet. Why hadn't he seen that? He'd smelled it! Of course it wasn't frozen! It was the exhaust from the microwave as Kris reheated her frozen lunch/leftovers for a late night snack.

That could mean only one thing—that she was here, *somewhere.* Sydney's mind raced. How long would it take to reheat soup, even if it had been frozen solid? 3–5 minutes? *She must be out smoking,* he surmised. How long did she smoke? 3–5 minutes? He dashed to the entrance and hid behind the parka. He reached his hand into the coat. The lining was still warm. Sydney peeked out from behind it staring out into the vast darkness of the warehouse to the spot in the archives where he would sit with Kris while she smoked.

Unable to see anything in the dark, he slipped the night-vision goggles back down over his eyes. The eruption of light from inside the cube exploded in his head. As his sight returned, it revealed the sign of life that would one day cause her death: the glowing ember of Kris's cigarette. Sydney caught a glimpse of her face as she took a long pull of the cancer stick. She then dropped it to the floor, put it out with her sensible shoe, and began walking toward him. Acid refluxed in the back of his throat as his stomach contracted for a second time. *Open the door and get out right now,* the voice in his mind shrieked.

He reached for the door, when he remembered the external hard drive. He turned to run back down the hall and slammed his right thigh painfully into the sharp corner of a server shelf. Most of the air escaped his lungs, and he would've let out a cry, had he been in a different situation. Instead, he gritted his teeth, and limped as fast as he could back to her work cubby. Even over the hive hum, he thought he could hear Kris typing her code into the door lock. Sydney grabbed and yanked on the EHD and it now came out effortlessly, nearly causing him to overbalance. He pocketed the drive, pushed the papers back the way he thought she left them and was looking around, certain that he had forgotten/overlooked something, when he heard the door to the Ice Cube open.

Kris entered, grabbed her parka and slipped back into the comfort of its warmth, but as she walked toward her workstation, she suddenly felt something that did not feel comfortable, did not feel *safe*. She stopped, reached under her shirt and wrapped her fingers around the snub-nosed .38 in her concealed carry holster. She removed it, slipped off the safety and cocked it all in one smooth motion, just as Nathalie had taught her to at the gun range. Connecting all her senses, Kris twirled around to determine what was triggering her unease. She took in every nook and cranny in the Cube, sensing something was amiss. The humming was the same. She barely heard it anymore. Everything was the same, except the smell.

Was it the Wazooi? No, it was something else Belgian. She stopped. It was the scent she had missed today at lunch—*Sydney's cologne*. Was that possible? Or was her exhausted mind playing tricks on her?

Sydney lay hiding behind the second row of servers not ten feet from her, peering through the gap between the rack and the floor. He closed his eyes, fighting the rising fear. What would he say if she caught him? He got to one knee, snuck a peek around the stacks and saw she had a gun. *Oh my God!* he thought. He was terrified, not only of being shot, but of what he might be forced to do to protect the secret of his incursion. His failure of Jarod was horrendous, so he vowed that if he had to hurt someone he cared about to protect someone he loved, he would. Even with that thought, he wasn't sure what he was capable of anymore, and then he heard it.

Kris had twirled around when she heard the ding of the microwave. She stopped and looked at her watch. She'd thought for sure she'd set the microwave for 5 minutes, but must have set it for 6. Her late night snack should be nice and warm now.

Kris holstered her weapon and breathed a sigh of relief. It had been nothing but the thrum of the microwave. The instant she entered her cubicle, Sydney was out the door and sprinting through the archive warehouse. He ran like he hadn't in years, faster even than when he was chased by bullies at boarding school. Not even those tormentors would have caught him after that escapade.

Sixteen seconds later he was back, moving swiftly through the dark shadows of the SL-13 hallways. Sydney abruptly stopped in a corner alcove and threw up.

Chapter 45

AFTER HE PUKED for a second time, Luke felt his way in the darkness from his chemical toilet back to his cot. He wasn't exactly sure how long they'd been without power, but he was sure it'd been long enough that it was never coming back on.

He lay silent and scared on his cot in the dark, flinching at the crashing and thrashing sounds happening above him. Smashing glass, anguished furious cries of frustration and tables being flipped over skewered his senses. Luke feared that whatever dream had been carrying Adidas Man for the last few days had just had a head-on collision with a nasty nightmare.

He was certain that life would get much darker before there was ever to be light again.

Chapter 46

OSCAR STOOD ON the table, rubbing his ears in disbelief. His crazy-ass roommate was playing *that jazzy music* again, and, as Oscar had learned, *that jazzy music* meant the human was plotting something. The rat peered at the glowing silk curtain on the second floor, behind which a jazzy beat emanated.

The rat bebopped up the stairs toward the glowing divider, wondering just what he might find inside. He had seen his friend doing strange things behind that cloth before: practicing surgery, both from the point of view of the doctor and the patient. He'd also seen Jarod watching a video experiencing a joyful Christmas morning with a young family and later sharing their grief through news reports of their son's disappearance.

As Oscar sniffed the air, he realized something new was happening. He detected a metallic tang, the hint of electricity and another mysterious odor, something similar to burning leather. Shrugging, the former dumpster diver slid under the curtain to discover what it was.

Oscar barely had time to duck before a white metal box with a glass door sailed over his furry head and smashed into a pile of seven identical appliances. He had no time to discern what they were before a barrage of incoming wires and other electronic parts began showering down all around. Oscar scrambled to find a safe refuge from whatever was happening, but the floor he rushed around was different from when he last visited.

His roommate was a meticulous animal, but Jarod's simulation room was a cluttered mess with dozens of empty shopping bags with the words

'Shack' and 'Radio' printed on them scattered on the floor surrounding a tall stack of empty cardboard boxes.

Oscar ascended the Jenga-like tower to get a better look at what Jarod was up to. During the precarious climb he noticed the smaller boxes had photographs of police cars with their blue lights flashing, as they chased cars driving too fast and the larger ones had human letters printed on them: M-i-c-r-o-w-a-v-e and O-v-e-n. Reaching the top, Oscar caught his first glimpse of the Pretender.

With his head bobbing in rhythm to the beat, Jarod was again working at the operating room table. He didn't look like any doctor Oscar had ever seen. The Pretender was soaking wet and nude, a combination that had Oscar's mind again asking, *What the hell is he doing?* Water dripped from Jarod's chiseled body onto a rolling tray of tools of some kind—used to rip the circuitry out of the last microwave—before the naked man tossed the remaining shell onto the pile of the other carcasses. Jarod then reached over to the tray and picked up a mystery tool and went to work on the guts he had harvested. Jarod's back was obscuring the table itself, which only added to Oscar's desire to know what was going on.

Oscar leapt from the cardboard tower toward Jarod's tool tray to get a better view.

From this vantage point, Oscar could see Dr. Naked's operation. Instead of a scalpel, Jarod grabbed a soldering iron and leaning over his patient—an amalgam of electronics—touched its hot tip to the end strand of the silvery metal. A curl of smoke rose from where it melted, dripped onto and solidified as it cooled connecting the harvested components together.

The Pretender picked up the creation and studied it.

It looked to Oscar like a cross between an electronic octopus and the light ball that dropped in Times Square once a year at midnight. While its design and purpose were known only to Jarod, a few things in Oscar's math still weren't adding up. The soldering iron accounted for the smell of melting metal, but not the electric tang, nor the burning leather. Oscar didn't realize what was causing the foul odor, until he saw a figure emerge from the shadows and sneak up behind Jarod.

It was Chaz. Dressed in dominatrix leathers, she held a strange device that seemed to have blue lightning bolts sparking at the end of it that she plunged right into Jarod's spine.

Oscar's little eyes bulged out as Jarod screamed through clenched teeth while 50,000 volts surged through his body. Chaz pulled the wand away and smiled broadly until Jarod looked at her with displeasure on his face.

"First, I heard you coming and second, you have to hold it on me longer or this won't work."

Chaz made an *I don't think so* face. "Any longer and you gonna crinkle like a dirty water dog tossed on a hot griddle."

"That's the idea." Jarod agreed.

"Whatever you say, Boss." Chaz shrugged, and grabbed the bucket. "I'll get a refill." Jarod went back to work, unaware, as Chaz spun on her heels and zapped Jarod right in the back of the neck.

This time, Chaz left the nodes in place a good spell before yanking them away. The smell of electronic tang mixed with burning leather filled the room. Jarod caught his breath. "That was a good one."

Chaz smiled. Turning to leave, she ran into Skylar, who was just walking in. Skylar took in the bizarre happenings, then shot a curious glance toward Chaz. "What's he doing?"

Chaz shrugged. "Hell if I know, but it's the easiest money I ever made for making a grown man cry." Skylar looked at the rodent. Oscar shook his head and rubbed his little rat ears in disbelief.

And the jazz played on.

Chapter 47

IT WAS AN old-school, classic rock morning and Miss Parker was blasting Heart. She was beaming ear to ear. She may have only had three hours of sleep, but she was happy, so happy she found herself breaking her own in-car rule by singing at the top of her lungs along with Nancy Wilson.

Miss Parker had always felt a kindred spirit with Barracuda. She floored the Porsche and pounded the steering wheel along with the epic driving beat. This barracuda, hot on the scent of her prey, had the upper hand now.

Miss V., known as Vania to her friends, was looking out from her little office with the big window atop the Centre hangar. The office served as a control tower for the airstrip below where the Centre's new black Gulfstream G650 jet was roaring down the runway.

The most advanced business aircraft in the sky, its two powerful Rolls-Royce BR725 engines could reach a speed of Mach 0.999 and if conditions were right a little more. It came standard with advanced safety features and next-gen technology designed to improve pilot situational awareness, an EVS II Enhanced Vision System, Heads Up Display, the Synthetic Vision-Primary Flight Display package, a Triplex Flight Management System, Automatic Emergency Descent Mode, 3-D weather radar and Advanced Flight Controls.

None of which Vania gave a damn about. The Portuguese beauty was *extremely* frustrated. Miss V. was a recent bride, and as such, had expected the status to come with the physical fringe benefits newlyweds throughout time had *always* enjoyed. Ones she had planned out and scheduled meticulously. Maddeningly, this wasn't the reality in her case. She voiced her exasperation and spoke into her laptop, video chatting with a friend.

"What good is it to have a husband to come home to if he's never there?"

On screen was Vania's childhood friend who had grown up in the miracle prone Portuguese village of Fátima. Miss Bougainvillea was a mysterious woman with a voice that demanded you listen when she spoke.

"Hot Pedro? Senhor. Testosterona doesn't come home to his new wife? Porquê?"

"'Cause he works for *her* now!" Vania spat out.

Miss Bougainvillea's hazel eyes with the gold flecks shot wide open. "*Her* her?"

Vania nodded solemnly. "Since he was promoted to Miss Parker's team, I hardly ever see him."

Though Miss B worked in the Image Analysis and Decoding department, it didn't take a codebreaker to read between the lines. "There's a *reason* they call her a slave driver in a miniskirt."

"Tell me about it!" Vania let out a sigh of vexation. "Pedro got 19 stitches on his scalp from a set-to with Jarod in New York and the Ice Princess wouldn't even give him a day off!"

"It's all starting to make sense now." Miss B. mused.

"What?" Vania asked, with piqued curiosity.

"I've been doing some photographic research into her family history and came across a female's first name that may be Miss Parker's—*Eva*."

Vania gave an ironic smile. "If her middle name is *Peron*—that would certainly fit."

The shared giggling obscured the footsteps that came up behind Miss V. It did not, however, mask the feel of the hand that grabbed her shoulder and spun her around. Vania came face to face with an unsmiling face—Miss Parker's. "Holy shit!"

"That's not my first name either, but maybe I should change it. Everyone seems to say that when they see me."

Mortified, Vania stumbled to her feet. "Well, I, ah—I only said it because—I *shouldn't* be seeing you, Miss Parker."

"And why's that?"

Vania gaped in disbelief. "Well, because *you're on the jet* that just took off."

It was Miss Parker's turn to be mortified. "Holy shit."

Twenty three seconds later, they rushed into the Centre hangar and found the Centre pilot, bound and gagged, the jet's transponder in his lap. Miss Parker stared down at the young man with disgust. She could never remember if his name was Bradley Christian or Christian Bradley, but for some reason she recalled he was from outside Dallas somewhere. Either way, it didn't matter. To her, he was the chimp who'd worked his way up from the Centre mailroom and always would be. The little monkey man looked up at Miss Parker with pleading eyes and shrugged.

Vania shrugged as well. "I don't get it. If the pilot is here, then who's flying the jet?"

Miss Parker realized she was no longer the barracuda. Once again, she was chum in the water, courtesy of the Pretender. With a growl, she answered humorlessly, "Who do you think?"

Chapter 48

TWO MINUTES BEFORE the window rattling explosion nearly ruptured his eardrums, Wang had been at his boring desk, staring at boring blips on his boring radar screen, hating on stuff. And, as that's what members of the 'H8rs' club do, Wang was writing out his daily top *8 to hate* list.

In reverse order: Today he was really hating him some iced coffee. It was too hot on this ass-crack island to drink java at the optimum temp of 180°F, as Howard Schultz taught the world. No, he had to take his caffeine in a glass full of cubes.

Next was spending his days trapped in his Drone Command Trailer that was little more than a shithole cargo container with a piss-ant wall air conditioning unit that had no chance of keeping his computer processors cool enough to fly his pilotless birds with efficiency.

As on every list, his 5 and 6 slots were reserved for his dislike of his parents—Mom for the ridicule-inducing giant nose she genetically passed him, and Dad for giving him the last name Wang, *when they weren't even Asian!*

In 4th place was his Groundhog Day existence staring at radar for flight schedules that never changed. Even his recon drones flew the same loops taking dirty pictures of banana republic dictators to be used as blackmail by governments around the world. Number 3 with a bullet was reserved for the people he worked for on his side of the island that he hated with a passion, and number 2 was for the people his employers were partnered with on the other side, whom he despised even more.

Wang wiped his forehead with the glass of cool joe, but found little relief. The air was as hot as gorilla piss and twice as humid. He loathed how it caused him to sweat through his new Tommy Bahama wardrobe. Hell, Wang even hated Tommy Bahama and he wasn't sure if Tommy was even real.

What *was* real was the permanent number 1 on his top *8 to hate*. The U.S. Air Force. In Kandahar, Wang had been in charge of a drone squadron that he had taken upon himself to modify with specialized weaponry and turning standard recon platforms into unmanned fighter jets. Wang was convinced he would have been promoted to the Pentagon had it not been for a malfunction that resulted in his bots shooting down one of the RAF's 30 million-pound Harriers.

Though his military career was shattered and he was stuck in the middle of nowhere, in his spare time he had been mastering his plan and would soon prove to the whole world what he was all about.

Then, they could hate on him for a change.

He was savoring this thought when the manmade thunderclap shattered his glass, sending its ice-cold French roast onto the crotch of his new chinos.

Two minutes and 10 seconds before the same window rattling explosion and three hours and 26 minutes after he'd taken off from Blue Cove, Jarod had Isla Raton in his sights.

That he'd made it without problems was amazing even to Jarod, considering he'd been reading from the *Complete Idiots Guide To Flying* the whole way.

The book, resting on his lap, had several sections marked with paper clips, just like the one he was flicking between his teeth. It was open to a page regarding the techniques of *treetop* aerodynamics that he was adapting to *wave top* flying. The jet he was piloting was only 50 feet above the Gulf of Mexico.

Jarod pushed the G650 toward its maximum speed. He was on a mission and running out of time. If the plan worked, all would be good; if not, a boy would die, along with thousands of other people. Jarod felt he'd harmed too many people from the things he had been forced to do at the

Centre. He couldn't fix the past, but he was determined to do something about the future.

He would save Luke or die trying.

During the flight, Jarod had surmised that the Pretend he was about to execute had an eight percent chance of success. Not great odds, but Jarod had faced worse. Besides, 8 was his favorite number, and he had two other things in his favor: he was about to get a recon look at the topography of the island dead ahead, and would without a doubt gain tactical advantage over those below by providing a wake-up call no one could miss.

Two flies, one swatter.

He turboed the engines with fuel. The afterburners kicked in, propelling him toward the speed of sound.

Skimming across the island at treetop level, Jarod caught a glimpse of a massive 20-room Spanish-style, walled villa that looked like the secret compound of an international narcotics trafficker, because that is exactly what it was. The hard bodies by the sparkling pool fawning over a middle-aged, swarthy man were startled by the reverberations from above. So were numerous bodyguards who were fumbling for their guns, as Jarod's wake rattled the windows.

Three-tenths of a second later, Jarod zoomed perpendicular across the runway that bisected the island and over a completely different world. This one consisted of a dozen small Quonset hut-shaped aircraft hangars and an ominous three-story black brick building surrounded by barbed wire. It looked like a secret off-the-books drone base and a black site rendition facility designed to interrogate and instigate the secret surveillance of bad guys, because that's *exactly* what it was. Jarod's focus was on the black brick building in which he suspected was where the Libyan terrorist Kaj was being held.

The Pretender had a plan to get to him and hoped like hell it would work, but after seeing one thing he hadn't anticipated, he recalculated his odds of success. Jarod watched a vapor cloud form as he nosed through Mach 1, and the sound barrier itself.

It was in the instant when the sound waves collapsed upon themselves, resulting in an enormous sonic boom which rattled the world below, that he realized his odds were now down to seven percent.

Chapter 49

ON HIS TRIP, Jarod had discovered he enjoyed the true freedom of flight. He'd worked simulators before, but next to the real thing, there was no comparison. Flying came naturally to him, as if it were in his blood. If he survived, maybe one day he'd pretend to be an airline pilot and go see the world.

First he had to manoeuver a landing on the ridiculously short runway, which at first sight he was sure was even shorter than his specs had indicated.

As he made his final approach to Isla Raton, he continued to flick the paper clip between his teeth in a rhythm that seemed to relax him.

The truth was that Jarod was not only flying by the seat of his pants in the cockpit, but in this entire endeavor. He was normally the master of his environment with each and every possible contingency prepared for, studied and researched; in this case he was underprepared with his pretend backstory. He hoped it would last long enough to get to Kaj and retrieve the secret he needed to save Luke, but he knew he hadn't had time to thoroughly reason out every angle. He'd cross those bridges later. If he got to them. There was still a better than even chance that he would crash.

Jarod looked down and flipped the page over to another chapter, an important one he had only skimmed once: *Landing Instructions*. Following them one by one, he looked to the flight attitude indicator, the gauge with the miniature wings and artificial horizon. Seeing he needed to correct his pitch and bank, Jarod pulled the yoke and rotated it left, raising the nose and turning the plane in that direction. As the mini wings found perfect level within their glass sphere, Jarod was surprised to find images dancing in his mind of the flight simulator game he had played in the sideshow section of Astroland, Skylar's beautiful smile when he won her the stuffed mouse, the mixture of happiness and sadness he saw in her violet eyes as he gave her the simple gift—a look he'd only once before seen in the eyes of another female. A beautiful young girl he had once given a handmade infinity bracelet to long, long ago.

Focus, Jarod! Sydney's voice in his head brought Jarod back to the moment. He bit down on the paper clip as he realized he'd gotten lost in his thoughts at a time when he was supposed to be of absolute single-mindedness. For years he had trained his mind not to wander and had scars to show when he had failed. It hadn't happened to this extent for years, but then he'd never been challenged by the distractions of the real world either, a new factor he would have to register in his brain.

Jarod lined the jet up to the runway. He pulled back the throttle and noticed a strange clicking noise. He checked the landing gear lever, but it was still in place. Jarod's brow furrowed. Was it an alarm? A warning of some kind? Jarod scanned all of the instruments, realizing he was coming in too fast and descending too quickly.

The G650's landing gear scorched rubber as it slammed down hard. *Really* hard. The second it did, Jarod noticed the clicking had intensified. He wasn't sure if he'd severely damaged the plane and, if he had, he had no idea how he would escape this island. But that was the least of his worries.

Jarod was still moving too fast and was heading toward a fuel tanker at the end of the runway. He jammed both feet down atop the jet's braking system, but quickly calculating distance and velocity, concluded they would never stop him in time. The clicking noise was deafening, as if the plane was coming apart at the seams, as he reached down and reversed his thrusters and poured on power.

The Centre's jet came to a halt 8 feet from the tanker. Lucky 8, indeed. Now the clicking sound was out of control. Jarod made a final sweep of his controls and warning lights, trying to determine the source of it—before realizing *it was him.*

He had been anxiously working the paper clip back and forth between his tongue and teeth like a jackhammer.

This was a new phenomenon for Jarod. He'd never before felt nervous going into a pretend, but the stakes on this one were high, and the subset of unknowns and the unexpected were even higher. Even though he was no longer in the air, he was still flying blind.

After shutting down the jet's engines, Jarod began the immediate task of *becoming* another person. He instantly became one with his current outer-skin, an ensemble best described as *Mercenary Casual,* right out of the Blackwater catalogue. He resembled one of the warriors from *Zero-Dark Thirty* before they suited up for their fateful mission, one that Jarod recalled he'd secretly provided tactical moves on with a Sim a few years back. Just like those men, he found his spine straightening, felt a certain swagger and increase in situational awareness that defined the men and women who continually put themselves in harm's way, in some cases for honor, in others, for profit. Jarod was playing both roles and it was finally show time.

When he popped the exit door of the G650, he felt the blast of Isla Raton's tropical heat hit him in the face. Yet, it wasn't the local climate that demanded his attention in that moment, it was the local citizenry. Jarod and the jet were surrounded by dozens of uniformed men aiming assault weapons at him.

These men were not happy, which was good. They were scared and surprised and both of those feelings added up to them being unpredictable in their actions and reactions.

Which is exactly what Jarod was counting on.

There was only one thing left to do before he alighted the plane and faced the music.

Jarod smiled smugly to his welcoming party—then swallowed the paper clip.

Chapter 50

AS WANG RUSHED down the landing strip, he wished he hadn't put so much sugar in his coffee. His wet crotch was sticky, and he feared chafing his inner thighs, what the locals referred to as *swamp ass*.

Normally, the hater would have been incensed by this possibility, but at this particular moment the he didn't care. Sure, he'd take a bucket of shit from all the beaners carrying AK's, but what had just occurred was astounding. He hated that he didn't know how it had been done, but was determined to discover how the hell someone had managed to fool *his* radar defences.

For the first time in three months, something had stimulated his mind and that was the one thing the hater *loved*. He spent 24 hours a day, 365 days a year surrounded by morons, so as he dashed toward an idling jet, he found solace in the assumption that the pilot had to be someone with an intelligence nearly as ingenious as his own.

Jarod descended the steps with a duffle on his shoulder, a smile on his face and a southern drawl on his tongue. "Damn, boys, I thought it was muggy in Georgia, but this is like skinny-dipping in Momma's chicken gravy." Jarod looked at the two men who appeared to be in charge. Minaya, a man without the capacity to smile, was the brains of the detail. Next to him was Ramirez, a bucktoothed Neanderthal with a permanent grin and twitchy trigger finger on his SR-15, was all brawn.

Before either could respond, a Range Rover roared up almost hitting the arriving Wang and the swarthy man who had been by the pool of the mansion climbed out. By the reverence given him by his men, it was clear to Jarod that he was the ringmaster, and the circus was about to begin.

Chapter 51

"GOOD. YOU MUST be the Jefe." Jarod plopped his duffle down and smiled. "Now before we get down'ta business, can you have one'a your boys here fill my bird with hi-test? I want her good to go when *I'm* good to go." Jarod smiled.

The man didn't. He grabbed Ramirez's SR-15 and slammed it into Jarod's gut. The Pretender collapsed on one knee. Struggling to suck air back into his lungs as he stood, Jarod noticed a man stop next to El Jefe wearing short Zanzibar chinos with a Starbucks stained crotch.

Jefe took note of the wet spot, then raised his menacing eyes to Wang's. "How did this gringo get on my island undetected?"

Wang stepped past Jarod and unlocked the transponder compartment under the jet's nose. "Somehow, he stealthed this thing. Must have acquired a state of the art radar jammer from the U.S. Navy or the Israeli Air Force or ..." Taken aback by what he found, Wang turned to Jarod. "*Radio Shack?*"

The H8r removed the device Jarod had been soldering in the Harlem loft. Jefe tossed an inquisitive glare his way. "What is it?"

Wang scratched his head. "It looks like he took the microwave oven magnetrons, boosted their outputs through police radar jammers and re-directed their lasers to cloak incoming audio waves." He looked up to the dull faces of the surrounding idiots and then to Jarod with admiration. "The gringo made a world class anti-radar device."

El Jefe shifted his gaze onto the Pretender. Jarod shrugged. "What? You boys ain't never watched Bill Nye the Science Guy?"

El Jefe slammed the SR-15 into Jarod's gut for the second time. He landed on all fours at Jefe's feet. "You don't appear so intelligent to me."

The soldiers snickered, at their leader's machismo as Jarod, spitting out blood, labored to stand. He stared at the big man, but he was no longer smiling nor speaking in a southern drawl. "I'm smart enough to find one of the most elusive drug lords in the world, and to know *why* no one else can. Señor Montoya."

Jefe let fly a third blow for that, but this time, Jarod caught the butt of the rifle, twisted it from Montoya's hands and quickly had its barrel under the swarthy man's chin. The armed men's fingers were twitching on their triggers.

It was a Mexican standoff.

Jarod glared at him. "Me considera un tonto que vine aquí sin saber lo que estaba haciendo?" *You think me a fool who came here not knowing what I was doing?*

Some of the armed men shared confused glances.

"Perhaps you are smarter than you appear," he conceded.

Jarod explained he was smart enough to know two truths: that while D.C. 'officially' banned the use of *enhanced interrogation* 'privately,' they hired subcontractors to off-shore this minor inconvenience to the truth and they do the same thing with secret drone surveillance. "You provide them a way to slice two mangos with one machete. A secret air base and a mini version of Abu Gharib, all for the bargain basement price of making sure the DEA and its satellites look the other way." Jarod could read in Montoya's eyes that he had become fearful. Wanting more of this reaction, the Pretender continued. "Of course the PTB's never leave fingerprints on deals like yours. They outsource these kinds of places to the Emtrexes of the world."

Jarod saw something flash in Montoya's eye. "You are a smart man. For a Merc."

"I'm not a mercenary, *per say* and I'm not that smart but I'm working on it." Jarod removed the gun from under Montoya's chin. "See, I used to play for the team that built compounds like this, until I got tired of them making all of the money. Now I'm self-employed, and looking to make a deal with a man like you."

Montoya was dubious. "You expect me to buy that?"

"You got all of this being a brilliant businessman. I'm here to do business." Jarod looked at Minaja and indicated his duffle. "Reach in there and grab what's on top, *por favor.*"

Minaja looked to his boss. Montoya nodded. He reached in and retrieved a bag of white powder. Minaja tasted T-Dope's coke, made a face and spat it out.

"Exactly. Harlem's finest is shit. I want pure. I'll undercut the street price with a higher grade. Once I own the market, well, who knows, maybe I'll go on eBay and buy me an island like this one."

Montoya reappraised Jarod. "Why would I believe you?"

Jarod tossed the SR to Ramirez, then dumped the duffle onto the tarmac. Bundles of Benjamins kicked up clouds of dust. "Because of this ten million and the hundred I have behind it."

Montoya looked at the money, then evenly to the Pretender. He slammed the SR-15 into his gut for a final time, leaving Jarod rolling on the ground, eyes squeezed shut in agony. "If you are who you say you are, perhaps we can make a deal. If not. Well ..." he trailed off in warning. Montoya nodded with authority to Ramirez and Minaya. "Find out the truth."

Chapter 52

ALONE IN THE Emtrex elevator, O'Quinn's status was *having a bad day*. Seventy-two hours until the biggest operation of his career and he still hadn't found the little boy who was the key to its success. That sword over his neck was causing as much stress as the pressure in his decaying eye. Something had to give, in both instances.

The elevator doors opened and O'Quinn flashed his ID to the guard as he dragged his tired body out. Midway down the hall he dug in his pockets for the keys. When he pulled them out, they snagged on a thread of his silk-cotton slacks and tumbled onto the tile. *Great.* If this day wasn't bad enough, his new pants had one of those annoying thread pulls with a knot in the middle. Adding insult to injury, as he bent to pick up the keys, he misjudged his one eye's spatial relations and slammed his head on the doorknob.

Rubbing the dancing stars out of his good eye, he revised his status to *having a shitty day.* As he entered his office, it got worse. Inside, a smoking-hot woman with a smoking-hot body was bending over his credenza, smoking. He slowly took all of her in. Starting at the toes of her knee-high, black leather boots, he let his eye slide up the eight inches of enticing skin showing off her silk stockings, past to her miniskirt and, as she stood and turned toward him, her skin tight angora, finally landing on the stunning face of Miss Parker.

She glanced at him with staid emotions. "If you're trying to look stupid, you're doing a bang-up job."

O'Quinn was as taken by her beauty as he was put off by her smart mouth, neither of which were welcome. "You're the bitch who was on the hospital roof."

"And to think, with a sharp mind and a smooth tongue like that you have trouble with the ladies." Miss Parker smiled sarcastically.

"Who the hell *are* you?"

"I'm the bad thing that happens to good people." Miss Parker stared, emotionless. "But seeing as you're not one of them, you don't have *that* to worry about."

"You didn't answer my question." He spat in annoyance.

Miss Parker fired right back. "That's cause you're not Alex Trebek and this ain't Final fucking Jeopardy!" Miss Parker turned back to the credenza and examined the framed photos he had atop it. "Relax your prostate, Patch. All you really need to know is I was able to get past all your so-called 'security' and into your office without being seen."

"Lady, are you telling me you got in here wearing *that,* without being seen?" He demanded incredulously.

"It's amazing what a woman can do if she puts her mind to it and the name's not *lady*, it's Parker. Miss Parker. Not *Ms.*, and damn sure not *Mrs.*"

While he stood there, sizing up the challenge before him, she turned back to the credenza and picked up a portrait of the smiling O'Quinn clan: pre-eye patch daddy, wifey with a dated 'do, and a teen in her 'awkward' years. "This nuclear family real?" She turned and raised an arched eyebrow. "I mean, you never know who anyone really is anymore. Least not with people who do what 'we' do."

"My wife and daughter," he said blankly.

"Nice." Miss Parker actually felt that it was. "The girl's a bit of a chunker though."

"You should see her mother from the neck down," he replied truthfully.

Miss Parker gave him an ironic smile. "Still, looks like a happy little life." There was a slight wistfulness in that admission that surprised Parker for half an instant.

O'Quinn used that time and studied her. "But you're not here to talk family are you, *Miss* Parker?"

"No, Blackbeard." She put down the portrait. "This is strictly business."

O'Quinn thought about that as he crossed to his desk. "When you say, *people who do what we do*, are you suggesting that *you* are like *me?*"

"Let's just say the people you and I work for have similar interests. Same playground, different sandboxes."

"So we're competitors?" he mused.

"No. We share acquaintances, which sort of makes us *friends*."

"I don't have any *friends*."

"I'm not talking those friends." She clarified. "I'm talking *friends*, as in we have the same enemies."

Miss Parker reached into her briefcase and, one by one, dealt 8 by 10 hospital surveillance photos of O'Quinn, Kaj and Jarod onto the desk.

He shot her a threatening gaze. "If we truly have mutual acquaintances, then you know better than to tangle with me."

Miss Parker grinned and walked up close, invading his space close and using her pointer finger, tapped O'Quinn's eye patch three times. "Listen, one-eyed-jack. I don't give a shit what you're up to," she pointed at Jarod's picture, "but he does. And he'll stop you."

O'Quinn found himself intimidated, and turned on, by her close proximity. He caught himself, stepped back and refocused. "Different sandboxes or not, you have no idea who you are playing with here."

"Neither do you. This clown in the doctor's garb is a certifiable genius. I guarantee that whatever your operation is, he's ten steps ahead of you." Miss Parker then poked his chest. "I can see you're half blind, but don't be deaf and dumb too. He's all I want. Help me find him and I'll get him out of your way." Miss Parker glanced at the O'Quinn family photo. "Then we can all go on with our happy little lives."

O'Quinn decided it was time to shut this down. "Sorry, *Lady*, but I have no idea what you're talking about."

"There you go with the stupid look again."

O'Quinn watched as the sultry siren reached under her sweater, into her bra, and pulled out a business card. "You ever get smart, call me." She grabbed her briefcase and strolled toward the exit. The door opened before she got there, courtesy of the Dog and the Indian Dr. Dojame. Miss Parker looked from Dog's broken paw, then to O'Quinn's eye patch and shrugged. "Dangerous business you're in." And with that, she walked out.

Dog and Dojame eyed Miss Parker's rear as she marched down the hall and disappeared into the elevator. Dog then closed the door and panted. "What was that?"

"A living nightmare." O'Quinn rubbed his temples as he looked at the photos on his desk. "Tell me you have good news."

Dojame placed a medical satchel onto the desk.

"The anti-comatose drug is ready for the Libyan," Dojame chimed in. O'Quinn actually smiled and revised his current status one last time, *shitty day just got better.*

Only after the elevator doors closed did Miss Parker allow herself to smile. She had been certain O'Quinn wouldn't cooperate in finding Jarod and was now equally confident that he would take her right to him. The cocky bald man had been too focused on his bruised ego to realize the tapping of his eye patch wasn't just to be a bitch; it was to attach a nano-GPS device that would allow her to track his every move.

Sooner or later she knew his path would cross with Jarod's, putting the Pretender in her crosshairs.

Chapter 53

JAROD'S SCREAM WAS deafening. He could taste the electricity coursing through his body on his tongue. The jolt caused Jarod's abs to spasm with such force his spine cracked. Thirty seconds later his muscles relaxed as the voltage ceased, the weight of his body only adding to his pain.

Jarod was suspended from a chain, one end of which was wrapped around an overhead beam, the other to the handcuffs that were slicing into his wrists. He twitched as the bucket of cold water was splashed over his naked body. The water served to shock his senses back into line, and to increase the electrical conductivity when Montoya's men touched the picana to his ribcage.

The wand was designed specifically for human torture. Its high voltage, low current shocks enabled longer sessions of suffering for its victim. That, coupled with portability and ease of use, made the picana the *go to* torture tool on the market.

Jarod had been hanging for three hours, the whole while listening to Eydie Gormé's version of *Piel Canela*. The Spanish lyrics about the love and singular devotion between man and woman had always moved him. Many a night growing up, Jarod wondered what it was like to love a woman that deeply, the same way he was certain Sydney had been connected to his beloved before the incident. *Piel Canela* was the term of endearment Sydney had used to refer to the woman whom he longed for, even after so many years.

Jarod remembered the tears Sydney had running down his cheeks when he had said those words to him. It was the only time he had ever seen Sydney cry, though on many occasions he'd heard him weeping. Jarod had similar tears on his cheeks as he thought about the late nights when Sydney played the song over and over and over until he fell asleep in the recliner in his office. On those nights, Jarod would sing along in his mind just as he was now.

Or was he?

The truth was Jarod didn't know if the song was playing on the radio or on a recording in his memory. He was no longer sure where reality stopped and the fantasy he was employing to get through the torture began. All he knew for certain was that he'd made it through one more minute of this test. A minute at a time was the best he could hope for with the picana.

Minaya, the man incapable of smiling, was in charge of the rheostat control, changing the voltage as he saw fit. Ramirez, the bucktooth Neanderthal, wielded the wand and seemed to connect with his more primitive self when he applied its tip to the Pretender's body. Jarod was certain these men were well versed in the picana's operating manual and suspected they may have, in fact, made a YouTube video on how to use it for maximum pain.

Concentrating on the words to the song and their meaning, that the one you love was all that was important in life—gave Jarod a momentary reprieve, but only momentary—he knew the picana would be recharged again in seconds.

As he concentrated on the meaning of this love song, the faces of two women came to Jarod's mind. One with violet eyes who he had only known for a short time, the other with steely eyes of depth and pain he had known more than half his lifetime.

Chapter 54

A THOUSAND THINGS swirled around Miss Parker's mind as she stepped out of the Centre elevator. Top three among them were that she was starving, exhausted and pissed. Hot on Jarod's trail again she had neglected to eat during her 12-hour round trip to El Paso—a trip upon which she had not only been forced to fly commercial, but *coach*. She made a mental note to add that to her list of things Jarod would pay for upon his return.

As she made her way, Centre personnel who were in the hall scattered like gazelles in the crosshairs of a lioness. She was used to people scrambling out of her way, but what wasn't normal was the creature left alone in the hall once they had all vanished.

It looked up at her and, nonchalantly, licked its front paw.

Miss Parker stopped and stared at Spike. The scrawny tomcat had been an unwanted fixture in the Centre as long as anyone could remember, but an elusive one that demanded—*and received*—respect. The two predators stood their ground, eyeing each other.

As a child, Miss Parker had loved the *Poussy Cat* storybooks that her mother would read to her but after her mother's death she found herself repelled by the species. Cats were strong, independent forces of nature that only accepted human affection on *their* terms. In that way they were way too much like her to be tolerated.

Spike, seemingly reading her mind and sharing the same sentiment in reverse, showed Miss Parker his hindquarters, looked over his shoulder and hissed at her.

Nonplussed, Parker raised an eyebrow and hissed in return. Spike's ears went back and he bolted off into the darkness. Parker grinned for the first time since she'd returned from Texas, then burst through the doors into the tech theatre.

The various surveillance screens were alive with maps of the world. Sweating profusely, a frantic Cornelius was pounding on multiple keyboards as Parker entered.

"So, Cornball," Parker said, startling the tech nerd, "What was the range of the thing you had me put on O'Quinn's eye patch?"

"The ah, the monitoring device? That would be the planet Earth," he remarked snidely.

"That should narrow things down."

"I'll say. We have been tracking O'Quinn and he's been traveling across it all afternoon."

Cornelius was about to speak when another voice beat him to the answer. "He took off in a private jet minutes after you left his office."

Miss Parker didn't have to turn to the voice. She knew it readily now. It was Daphne, walking in behind her, holding two large Styrofoam cups with straws.

Miss Parker continued. "Can you tell me where the bald bastard is headed?"

"I can *tell* you with certainty the Emtrex jet is on final approach to a small island off of Venezuela."

Daphne shrugged. "Mr. Cornelius is just having trouble *showing* you."

Cornelius shot daggers at Daphne. He'd reached the end of his rope with her and all that was left was noose.

Miss Parker raised an eyebrow to Cornelius that had the same neutering effect it had had on Spike. His eyes dropped to his keyboard as hers scanned the flat screens that showed a progressive dotted line from West Texas to a speck off the coast of South America. "I risked my ass placing a tracking device on that psycho Cyclops and you can't show me where he is?"

Cornelius began to unravel. "It's not my fault! I mean ... well ... see, the thing is, I'm trying to tap into an NSA bird so we can see him, but every time it passes over that island, they block me out."

Daphne smiled at her boss. "I'm sure I could help you, Mr. Cornelius."

Cornelius gritted his teeth. "No need to worry your blonde bonnet."

Miss Parker turned on Cornelius. "*She's* not the one who needs to worry." Cornelius' left nostril let out a sharp, fearful whistle.

Daphne handed Miss Parker one of the cups. Parker raised an eyebrow for the third time in as many minutes, this one out of curiosity.

"Centre jet missing, brutal round trip. Your notorious blood sugar must be plummeting, so I had Dani make this especially for you."

Miss Parker took a tentative sip. It was a blueberry protein shake, a recipe concocted exclusively for her by Dani, the Centre's North Tower Executive Chef, that contained designer herbal power boosts that got Miss Parker through her roughest days. She swallowed and smiled. "How'd you know?"

Daphne raised an eyebrow of her own, one that Miss Parker noticed was now over an eyelid with the shadow perfectly blended. "I've always been a quick study."

Turning away from Cornelius, Miss Parker indicated for Daphne to come closer. "Tell me you solved Jarod's unsolvable problem and I'll be a very happy woman." Miss Parker took another sip. She could already feel the much needed nutrients restoring her energy.

"No, but you will be soon. The supercomputer is halfway to the solution, Miss Parker—or should I call you Minerve?" Miss Parker let the straw slip from her mouth. A drop of lavender clung to her bottom lip as she stared at the blonde. Pronounced in French with Daphne's lilting voice, the name *Minerve* sounded like the taste of clover honey, crisp, clean and sweet.

Licking the droplet Miss Parker asked, "You think my mother named me *Minerve?*"

"Makes logical sense. *Minerve* is a beautiful village close to you mother's heart. She spent time there as a child, made her first communion in the Church of Saint Étienne, which is where her brother—of the same name—is buried."

"You know a great deal about my mother," Miss Parker replied, a forced casualness in her voice.

"Curiosity has drawn me to study the history of the Centre, in my spare time of course."

"Of course."

"It's a history full of intrigue and fascination, much like the hamlet of your mother's youth," she explained, coyly. "As I have been drawn to the Centre's history, I assume someone as intelligent as yourself would have been drawn to your mother's, especially during your years of CIT training in France."

Miss Parker's look made it clear that she was impressed. "You thumbed through her photo albums. I'd forgotten they were still in the Centre's Library."

"When it comes to discovering things about you, Miss Parker, I use more than my thumbs. Your mother was an amazing photographer. Her pictures reveal amazing truths," she smiled confidently. "Minerve."

Miss Parker saluted Daphne with her cup. "I have to hand it to you. You're good Daphne, very good." Miss Parker took a long pull, enjoying the sweetness of the berries. "But you're still wrong."

Blondie's smile faded, but only a little. "*This* time," she replied, undeterred.

They were interrupted by the sound of an exasperated honk coming from Cornelius's right nostril courtesy of his deviated septum. He stared at the screens as the satellite image of a tropical island went to black. The words *Access Denied* took its place. "I can't comprehend this!"

Miss Parker sank her nails into Cornelius' hairless cranium and physically twirled him face to face with her.

"See if you can comprehend this. You've got five minutes to show me what's happening on that island or I'm going to find out what you'd look like with a sucking chest wound." She increased her talon's grip. "Is what I'm saying sinking in?"

Cornelius nodded and whimpered.

"Good boy." She twirled him back to face his keyboard.

Chapter 55

JAROD HUNG, SLACKEN and pale, concentrating on the Spanish lyrics. After the latest round of shocks, it had taken much longer for the song to return, and when it did it was so faint he had to struggle to hear. He believed she was saying *black eyes* and something about *cinnamon skin* but was no longer sure of the true meaning of Eydie's despair; he was in a struggle to remain conscious.

Bucktooth grabbed a handful of Jarod's hair and placed the sparking prod so close to Jarod's eye that the Pretender could feel the heat through his cornea. "You can't take much more, my friend, and I am running out of sensitive places." He shrugged, as if to say *help me out here.*

Minaya looked up from his controls. "I ask you again who are you? What is it that you *really* want here?"

Jarod tried to answer but couldn't form words.

The smile-less one continued. "Do you work for a foreign power? They must be powerful to have such a nice jet without serial numbers anywhere. Is it someone who wants to know about our island and its arrangements?"

The Pretender dug down into his final reserves and repeated the same story he'd said over and over, claiming to be a drug dealer who wanted to take over Harlem from small time operators, and was willing to spend money to get it. He was spitting out a Swiss Bank account number when Bucky shocked him over his heart. This time, Jarod's eyes rolled back in his head and he went limp.

Minaya looked at Ramirez. "Check out his story." The men left Jarod hanging like a side of beef.

Chapter 56

THE SATELLITE'S VIEW of the island was still blind, Cornelius' nostrils still whistled and honked, and Miss Parker and Daphne still waited as the doors burst open and Sydney rushed in.

"Good thing it's a double feature, Syd," Miss Parker drawled, "looks like you slept through the first show."

During his reckless drive and subsequent sprint to the tech theatre, Sydney had anticipated Miss Parker's sarcasm and prepared to face it as neutrally as possible but upon hearing the barbed remark he found himself suddenly forceful. "At least you were granted the courtesy of a ticket, I had to hear about this performance through the grapevine. Did you really think I wouldn't find out about what you are doing here to find Jarod?"

"I really didn't care. Besides, this isn't about Jarod *directly*, it's about the bald man with the eye patch."

Miss Parker's statement caught Sydney off guard. "You uncovered his identity?"

"Even better. Found Patchy Pete himself. Name's O'Quinn." She indicated the dark screen. "We've been tracking him all day. He's currently about to land on an island off the coast of Venezuela."

"And you think there is something there of interest to Jarod?"

"That's what we should be finding out right now if it wasn't for Cornelius and his, oh, what's the word I'm looking for?" Cornelius stole a look out of the corner of his eye as she finished, "Incompetence."

Cornelius banged his head on the keys so hard that the space bar left an indentation. "It's impossible!" he moaned.

Miss Parker drummed her fingers on the table. "Nothing's impossible, Corncakes—as you're about to discover."

Cornelius' right nostril moaned like a terrified kazoo.

Daphne looked at Parker, then down to her desperate boss with a look that almost contained sympathy. *Almost.* "I can help you with this, Mr. Cornelius."

Cornelius wiped sweat from his brow and sent an indecisive glance to Miss Parker. Parker shrugged. "It's your succotash."

Though wondering how Daphne had snuck her way into Parker's good graces and aware that the power dynamics were shifting in her favor, Cornelius nodded for Daphne to sit.

Sydney turned to Miss Parker. "Whether the information you gained was about Jarod or O'Quinn, I still should have been informed."

"I thought we might try a *new* relationship," Parker said. "Ignore each other and see what happens."

"I'm still every bit a part of this pursuit as you are," Sydney pointed out indignantly.

"And therein lies the rub. Call me cynical, Syd, but the big parade's about to come down Fifth Avenue and I'm not sure what side of the street you're on."

Miss Parker gave the psychiatrist a visual inspection and he didn't like the feelings it conjured. "So," she began casually, "is there anything you want to tell me about last night's *escapades?*"

Sydney's insides turned frigid. He stammered, trying to sound as unconcerned as possible. "I ... I did nothing ... last night."

"*Nothing?*" Miss Parker raised her sculpted eyebrow for the fifth time in as many minutes. Sydney didn't answer. Daphne looked up, engaged in the conversation. Cornelius clamped his nose to silence his nostrils, thankful for the momentary reprieve of not being the target of Miss Parker's ire.

Sydney's mind spun but he fought for composure. "Nothing of any note," he calmly amended.

Miss Parker bore in. "I think you're lying, Sydney; I think something happened last night in SL-13. Something that *changed* you."

Sydney found himself engulfed in a whirlwind. Parker picked up on the shift and decided to exploit the opening. She shared a knowing look with Daphne. "I'm sure it's as obvious to everyone here that you are *not* the same man that you were yesterday." Daphne nodded in agreement. "No doubt about it, Sydney, you're definitely projecting the vibe of a man with something to hide."

Sydney struggled for something disarming to say, but what came out was a little off pitch. "What would—give you that idea?"

Miss Parker gave Sydney a coy smile. "Maybe I'm a little like Dara, or *maybe* it's because you're wearing the same rumpled threads you were yesterday?"

As he realized his clothes were, in fact, yesterday's, the vortex Sydney had been sucked into began whirling. After the heart-palpitating exploits in the Ice Cube, Sydney had driven around Blue Cove in a daze until the sky began to purple with the dawn. He'd then gone home to shower and shave, planning on coming to work as he would on any other day, but collapsed into his Lazy Boy to rest his eyes for a planned five minutes and instead had been unconscious for the intervening hours. It wasn't until he was alerted to what was going on in the tech theatre by one of his own spies in the Centre that he had woken up. Desperate for news he thought may lead to Jarod, he had rushed over without even so much as a thought about changing. "So what if this is the same outfit?"

"As a woman who's shown up many a morning sporting a hangover and the remnants of the previous night's *antics* wrinkled on her clothes, it makes me wonder what a man who didn't change his two days in a row was doing the night in between."

Sydney flew out of the tornado and sailed through the air. *My God, she knows. But, if that's true, why is she toying with me? Why am I even still alive?*

Parker glanced at Daphne. "Something tells me Sydney was up to something naughty. Maybe even with a member of the opposite sex." Miss Parker looked back at Sydney and zeroed in. "If that's still physically possible."

A short high-pitched chirp sounded from Cornelius' left nostril, the one that he often laughed with.

"Like his little Belgian truffle in the Archives warehouse, perhaps?"

Sydney's eyelid twitched, but not because of the reason Miss Parker thought. "You're not the *only* one wired into the Centre grapevine."

Sydney landed on *terra firma*. Miss Parker didn't know about what he'd done in the Archives warehouse. To his relief, he was saved from further inquisition by five words from Daphne. "I think I've got it."

She hit the *enter* key and looked up at the main screen to where the eye of the NSA satellite blinked to life. They watched in fascination as a white private jet began its final approach to Isla Raton.

Chapter 57

THE LAST TIME O'Quinn had brought the Hawker 850XP in for a landing he'd been angry, which was never a smart way to pilot a jet, especially with only one eye. His wrath then had been focused on the Libyan terrorist who was the cause of *all* of his current troubles.

O'Quinn wasn't angry, though; he was annoyed.

His irritation began midway over the Gulf of Mexico when he got his first waft of a funk that had turned his stomach. At first, he thought it was a fart. A fart so rancid your dog would leave the room. He immediately turned to the co-pilot seat where his deputy, the man with the face like a butcher's dog, was shoving a pencil into his arm cast between skin and plaster to service an itch inside. With every scratch, the sweaty cotton was prairie dogging in and out. O'Quinn was about to punch him in the paw, when he noticed the malodorous scent wasn't coming from the direction of Dog but from behind O'Quinn's chair and cascading down over his bald head.

Disgusted, he put the Hawker on final approach glide, then stole a glimpse over his right shoulder to the only other passenger on board. Dojame was in the first seat in the fuselage, asleep, mouth agape and gurgling.

O'Quinn scowled. He'd always been blown away with the kinds of cuisine the man from Mumbai, or whatever third world armpit he came from, would slap Indian spices on and shove in his pie hole. The curry-muncher's breath could usually stop an 8-day clock. At this moment it had O'Quinn's good eye watering as he strained to focus on a landing point mid-runway. If he missed it, they would end up as a fireball in the jungle; still he wasn't about to give the controls to anyone else, ever.

He wiped the tears on his sleeve and felt a sharp pain. It wasn't in his eye; it was in his gut *because* of his eye. O'Quinn realized the disgusting, rotting smell wasn't coming from the little brown doctor with chronic halitosis, or the one armed, dog-faced idiot next to him.

It was coming from behind the patch on his face.

And yet ironically, that was the least of his worries. If he did not find Luke and finish the project on time, his employers had made it clear that the rest of his body would be decomposing as well, all because of the Libyan he had flown a thousand miles to talk to.

O'Quinn radioed in. "Air Control, this is O'Q. Have Montoya meet me on the strip. Now!"

Chapter 58

THREE MINUTES BEFORE O'Quinn's midair revelation, an astonished Cornelius saw the image of the descending Emtrex jet appearing on his tech screen. He swiveled his hairless head toward Daphne, past a stoic Sydney, and Miss Parker's glare. "How did you do that?"

"I noticed every time the satellite passes over Isla Raton, the NSA shuts down its cameras. So I retraced the original command signals to the satellite and discovered it's been programmed to go black like this for the last three years."

Cornelius could no longer avoid Miss Parker's stare and his eyebrow started to quiver. Daphne smirked, confirming the shift in the power dynamic of their relationship, indicated the screen and tapped some keys. "Sensors also just picked up a radio signal from O'Quinn's jet."

"Air Control, this is O'Q. Have Montoya meet me on the strip. Now!"

Miss Parker shook her head, "That *turd* in the middle of the ocean sports a control tower?"

"Among other interesting things, look."

Miss Parker looked up at the main screen, her trained eyes absorbing the island's topography instantly. "A mansion, an airstrip ..." She narrowed her eyes. "Aircraft hangars?"

"Yep." Daphne tilted her head, "And is it me or do they seem small?"

Miss Parker knew immediately, "They're for drones." Her attention moved to the building surrounded with barbed wire. "Hey, Freud," she called, getting Sydney's attention. "What do you make of the Hotel California?"

Sydney glared at the ominous structure. It triggered an unpleasant memory from an unspoken part of his heritage. "It appears as if it were *designed* to evoke emotional distress."

Miss Parker grinned, "That's because it *was*." Miss Parker stood close to the screen, focusing on the building. "It's a smaller scale, but the specs are identical to the rendition facility at Bagram. The one that *doesn't exist*." Miss Parker turned and faced the group, surprised to see identical deadpans on their faces. "What? I'm the only one who's been there?" she asked incredulously.

Cornelius blinked, but his eyelids were out of sync and he looked like a broken doll. "Are you saying you think this island is a secret internment facility—like a black site?"

"I'm saying it *is* a black site, just like the ones the Triumvirate built and run in East Africa that also *don't exist*."

Parker squeezed the shoulders of her blonde protégé. "Good work." While Daphne fought to remain composed, Miss Parker returned her attention to the screen as O'Quinn's jet touched down. "Things just got really interesting."

Sydney gestured to the big screen. "And they're about to get more so." The psychiatrist was pointing at a sleek image Miss Parker recognized as the Centre jet.

Cornelius' eyelids fluttered, this time in unison. "What the hell is Jarod doing there?"

"He wants what O'Quinn stole out from under him." Miss Parker slapped the back of the hairless wonder's skull. "Kill the lights and heat some kernels, Popcorn, the second feature's gonna be a doozy."

Chapter 59

AS THE HAWKER taxied to a stop, a Land Cruiser sped toward it. Inside, Montoya questioned Minaya about Jarod. "50 thousand volts and he never wavered?"

The man without a smile shook his head. "Ramirez is checking his story now."

Minaya stopped next to the jet just as O'Quinn and the other two men descended. "Do we tell the gringo?"

Montoya, while plastering on a toothy smile for O'Quinn, thought out loud. "No. If the buyer is real, the arrogant prick will want a cut."

Montoya exited the car and opened his arms in greeting. "Señor, what a pleasant surprise. How is the lovely Louise and your little Katrina?"

"One's still fat and the other one's still a bitch. Now, where's the fucking Libyan?"

Montoya signaled the rendition building. "Where he has been this whole time."

O'Quinn and his men headed that way, leaving Montoya to stew in disrespect.

Dangling in silence, Jarod was now certain the music playing was only in his mind, but that was good. He knew that if he could determine hallucination from reality, he was thinking clearly enough, and ultimately, that his plan was working.

Jarod swung his legs back and forth, propelling himself higher and higher until he reached an apex that allowed him to wrap his legs around the beam. Hanging upside down, a burning pain rushed throughout his body as circulation returned and awoke nerve endings. His hands felt on fire as he brought them to his mouth and regurgitated the paper clip he had swallowed on the plane.

Thirty seconds later, the handcuffs slipped from his wrists and he was free.

The setting sun turned blood orange as the Land Cruiser pulled up in front of Montoya's mansion. Before the humiliated drug lord could get out, Rodriguez rushed out holding an iPad. He had a look of amazement in his eyes and a tale of riches on his tongue. "One hundred nineteen million dollars." He shoved the device in through the passenger window. It showed several Swiss bank accounts belonging to Jarod that contained a fortune.

Ninety seconds later, the door to the Pretender's torture room flung open and Montoya and his minions entered, shocked at what they found. Empty handcuffs hanging on the wall next to an infinity sign and the words *Jarod was here*—written in his own blood.

Just as he had when navigating the Centre's air vents, Jarod crawled as silently as possible through the metal tunnels to his destination. The second Jarod had hacked into the Emtrex Construction files of the rendition building, he had burned into his mind the exact twists and turns that would take him to the infirmary cell—the only place with the technological wiring for the equipment needed to keep Kaj, the coma victim, alive.

According to the countdown in Jarod's mental clock he would reach his destination two levels below in 3 minutes and 39 seconds on the ground floor wing known as the *quiet rooms*.

Chapter 60

THE HALLWAY MANUEL guarded unnerved him. It was not because of what he heard that made him feel so isolated, but rather what he *couldn't* hear: the everyday noises of life from the din of the outside world, to the sounds of a match igniting, to the leaves of the tobacco crisping as the flame he sucked into his cigar was swallowed by the thick padded tomb-like walls.

Manuel had no idea what happened behind the doors he guarded, nor did he want to. The spaces were built to keep the sounds the prisoners made *inside*, whether they were whispers or screams. Adding to his discomfort was the standing order to never sit during his shift. The hallway had no furniture and the Venezuelan native was supposed to pace. But walking in hollow silence made him ulcer-wracked, so he had managed to sneak an old wheelchair from the infirmary. Puffing on his cigar, he sat rolling back and forth in it, when the unnatural quiet of the environment shattered and O'Quinn and his entourage entered.

Manuel bolted to stand, but his foot got caught on the footrest and fell back and dropped the cigar onto his chest. Before he could react, Dog and Dojame had grabbed him under the arms and raised him face to face with the one-eyed bad man. Manuel's sense of hearing may not have been getting much practice, but his sense of smell was working overtime and the foulness coming from behind the bald man's patch caused his stomach to flip. "Hola, Jefe."

The terrified guard flinched as the bald man reached out to him. He needn't have. O'Quinn's action wasn't in malice. It was to brush ashes off Manuel's uniform. "Hola, Manuel."

O'Quinn pulled a fresh cigar from the terrified man's pocket and gestured, *May I?*

Manuel's head bobbed. "Si, Jefe!"

O'Quinn dug for a wooden match, struck and placed it at the tip. Manuel and the others watched the ember glow as he sucked in the flame. O'Quinn enjoyed a long pull and release of smoke. "Cubano?"

Manuel's head had not stopped bobbing. "Si, Jefe!"

The bald man tilted his head to the quiet room in the middle. "Open it."

Manny broke free from the grasp of the other men, his shaky hands rattling keys as he unlocked the door.

Chapter 61

THE ONLY ILLUMINATION within the room came from the glow of the machines surrounding a hospital bed. By monitoring Kaj's heartbeat, breathing rates and, most importantly, brain wave activity, his captors kept constant track of just how *alive* the comatose Libyan terrorist was.

O'Quinn's breathing became shallow and excited. He turned to face Dojame. "Time for sleeping beauty to get his kiss."

Dojame reached into his satchel and hesitantly removed two very large syringes with 20 gauge razor sharp needles. The liquid inside, an experimental nanodrug, was designed to form an artificial synapse connection between Kaj's cerebral cortex and brainstem, creating a transcranial stimulation to shock the coma patient awake. The Doctor's angst stemmed from uncertainty about the exact dosage to use. This apprehension was only exacerbated when his boss thrust his hand out and said, "I'll do it."

The man with the fetid breath looked at his employer. "It needs to be administered directly into his heart. It is a very *delicate* procedure."

O'Quinn clenched the cigar in his teeth and, with smoke curling up in front of his good eye, lasered a hole into Dojame's skull. The Indian doctor instantly offered one of the syringes to his boss, but one wasn't enough for O'Quinn. "I want both."

"An overdose could cause permanent brain damage ... or worse."

O'Quinn scowled. "After he tells me what he knows, *worse* is what he'll be praying for."

The hair on the back of Jarod's neck stood up and he stopped crawling. Alone in the dark tunnel, he concentrated on collecting what little information he could from his environment to determine the cause. He could hear a slight beeping noise. Tilting his head, he also discerned other electronic tones and voices. *Arguing voices?* He wasn't sure. The sound in the air vent was faint and hollow. He raised his nose to the air, closed his eyes and inhaled. Unlike the vents of the Centre, in the warm updraft that flowed here, he didn't perceive smells from a far off kitchen full of spices he dreamed of one day tasting, or colognes of distant strangers. What he detected was a uniquely sweet, yet putrid odor he had first encountered as a little boy during a simulation about murder investigation forensics. The scent of rotting human flesh.

The smell of *death*.

The bald man ripped open the Libyan's gown. "Make sure the frog doesn't jump out of the frying pan." His compatriots moved in to hold the terrorist in place. Dojame pressed down firmly on Kaj's ankles while Dog, a tinge of revenge in his eyes, twisted the arm of the man who had broken his.

O'Quinn wrapped his fingers around the shafts of both syringes, his thumb on their plungers.

"This needs to be done very carefully," Dojame cautioned.

"Whatever you say, Doc." O'Quinn hammered his fist downward, plunging the needles through the Libyan's sternum and injected half of the meds into his heart.

Lightning bolts erupted in Kaj's brain. He sucked in an enormous breath through a phlegmy throat, as his face twisted into a grimace, followed by spasms that contorted his body.

Then his lids flew open.

While the reflection of his flashing vital monitors danced wickedly in the glass eye, his working one darted back and forth searching for refuge. When Kaj found O'Quinn's face, his body stopped and his eye stared—his memory probing for a name to go with the clouded recognition of the face. As quickly as he had regained consciousness, Kaj's eye began rolling back up into his head.

O'Quinn brutally slapped his face. "You've had enough shut eye, ass-hole." The bald mercenary depressed the plunger, sending another quarter of the nanomeds straight into Kaj's bloodstream. Instantly, the EEG and heart monitors surrounding the bed exploded into the danger zone, Kaj's body jolting as he gasped for breath. His eye opened as wide as a saucer. He again fought to place the elusive face that floated through his memory.

"Don't recognize me with the new look?" O'Quinn asked with a frigid tone. "Maybe this will help." O'Quinn leaned face to face with Kaj and pulled the patch away.

Recognition swept his face. All he could manage was a whispery whimper. "Oh *shit*."

"That is the understatement of your lifetime."

Unable to swallow, Kaj pleaded. "Wa ... wa ... water."

"I have none of that, old friend." With his right hand O'Quinn twirled his cigar while puffing till the tip was bright orange. "But I do have this." O'Quinn blew the excess ashes off the tip, then with his left hand he reached down and held Kaj's eyelids open. Terrified, Kaj fought against the restraint of Dog and the equally frightened Dojame. O'Quinn slowly brought the ember to within a millimeter of Kaj's eyeball. "Unless you want your glass ball to have a twin, you will tell me where the fat man in the Adidas suit is holding the boy."

Kaj was suddenly drenched in a sweat that stank of fear. O'Quinn moved the ember closer—so close that the terrorist's eyelashes began to curl.

Jarod was only 20 seconds away from his destination, when he heard the blood-curdling scream. Knowing the walls were soundproofed, he could only imagine what kind of pain had caused the horrible shriek. He sped through the remaining distance, not stopping until his face was pressed against the air grate.

The smell of burning flesh hit him before he saw O'Quinn pull his ci-gar out of the burn mark on Kaj's cheek.

"You were saying?" O'Quinn asked conversationally.

Kaj continued to whimper more, then spoke. "The boy … is in … a farmhouse off Lansil Road … near Point View Reservoir … New Jersey."

O'Quinn looked at his men and took a step toward the door. "That's all we need."

Dojame stopped him. "You can't just leave him like this …" he trailed off.

"As before, whatever you say, Doc." O'Quinn turned back and plunged the remaining meds into Kaj's heart. The former goat herder let out a silent scream and began flip-flopping like a fish on a pier. O'Quinn looked back at the terrified Indian, then calmly regarded the scene. "Let's roll."

Chapter 62

THE DOOR HAD barely closed behind the three men when Jarod's feet hit the ground. In less than a second, he was by Kaj's bedside as the terrorist went from shuddering spasms to rock hard rigidity. The Libyan's EKG flatlined and his EEG showed that his brain was experiencing a psychotic explosion. Jarod knew that if he didn't do something quickly, Kaj would die.

Jarod yanked the empty syringes out of his chest and stabbed both into the hanging I.V. bag. He filled and plunged them back into Kaj's sternum, flooding his heart with saline. Done, he pulled them out and slammed his palms onto the man's chest, forcefully pumping the solution through Kaj's brain and body in hopes of diluting the drugs. After several strong thrusts, Jarod placed his mouth over Kaj's and blew breath after breath of life back into the man responsible for taking it out of so many others.

After three cycles the heart monitor returned to normal rhythms but not his brain. Jarod raised Kaj's eyelid to see a dilated pupil indicating he'd slipped back into a coma. Jarod knew if he didn't find Luke before O'Quinn did he would still need Kaj's knowledge or thousands were going to die. He rushed to the door, cracked it open, peeked out, and saw a man in a guard's uniform out in the hall.

Manuel's ulcer was on fire. The surprise visit by O'Quinn had caused the security guard's gut to fill with nervous acid. He plopped into the wheelchair, but neither a suckling pull from his cigar, nor the motion, as he roll-rocked himself, calmed his nerves. Lost in his torment, Manuel did not notice Jarod as he exited the quiet room, which was just as well. Realizing the Pretender was about to knock him out would have only added to his distress.

Jarod opened the door to the building and sucked in a breath as he saw the Emtrex jet taxiing down the runway. More worrisome, however, were the 30 armed men between him and the Centre's Gulfstream. Surmising there was only one way he could catch O'Quinn, Jarod picked up Manuel's smoldering cigar and puffed it back to life.

In Blue Cove, Miss Parker stared at the satellite image. Though obscured by approaching nightfall, she could still make out a commotion near the Isla Raton airfield. She slapped Cornelius on the back of the head. "This home theatre have night vision?"

The hairless wonder could only wonder. "Uh …" He nervously looked to Daphne to throw him a lifeline. She bent down and hit a few keys and the screen turned a green monochrome that made clear what was happening in the growing shadows.

"People running, jeeps rolling," Miss Parker pointed to a large object moving down the runway. "What's that?"

Daphne concentrated her focus. "I think it's a fire truck."

Miss Parker was left to wonder. "What's happening?"

Sydney smiled knowingly. "*Jarod* is happening."

Blaring alarms cut through the silence of the quiet rooms hallway. The smoldering Cuban cigar was jammed, ember first, into the ceiling-mounted smoke detector and the sprinkler system showered down on Manuel, who was lying naked below.

Outside, wearing the guard's uniform, Jarod rushed through the reactionary melee, pushing Kaj in the wheelchair through the compound, yelling in Spanish to the guards rushing in with fire hoses to save the people inside the infirmary. Jarod dashed out of the gate and onto the tarmac, just as the Emtrex jet accelerated down the airstrip for takeoff. The instant the Hawker went nose up, Jarod met eyes with O'Quinn and Dog in the cockpit.

Dog looked to his master and growled. "Who *is* that guy?"

O'Quinn grabbed the radio and, with a new sense of urgency in his voice, issued a set of orders to his associate on the ground.

Thirty-four seconds earlier in his 8 by 16 shithole workspace, Wang was seated at his command center, staring at the boring blips on his boring radar screen, multitasking.

With one hand he was applying medicated powder onto his raspberry-chafed crotch, while the other was writing out his top 8-to-hate list for the next day.

The self-described *master of his airspace* was on his #3 most hated topic: *Being Unappreciated.*

He had figured out how Jarod had avoided the radar and snuck onto the island, yet was still snickered at by El Jefe's morons. Fantasizing about how he'd one day show all these assholes what he was all about, he heard the commotion outside. He stood and opened the door to see the utter chaos at the same time O'Quinn's voice crackled on the radio.

"Tower. Find Montoya and tell that little jungle savage that if the man causing all the trouble on his island lives, *he* won't."

Chapter 63

THOUGH IT ALL suddenly made sense, Wang was shocked when he spotted Jarod lifting an unconscious Haji from a wheelchair onto his shoulder, carrying him up the steps and into the black jet. But the hater was blown away when, seconds later, the G650 *started taxiing. Did those machete-swinging morons actually refuel it? Of course they did—because they were fucking morons.*

As the G650 rolled down the runway toward takeoff, a vengeful grin slowly curled up the sides of Wang's mouth.

The hater wasn't hatin' now.

He was loving him some opportunity.

This was his chance to prove himself once and for all to his screwed up parents, the Air Force and all the other PTBs who'd bitch-slapped him in life and thought his drone plan foolish.

Wang returned to his seat at his command center. With steady focus, he removed a thumb drive from a lanyard around his neck and slipped it into his computer.

"Copy that, O'Q—consider the intruder splashed."

He pressed *send* on his keyboard and looked at the radar signals of his drones. Their signatures all turned red. Just as he had in Kandahar, Wang had taken it upon himself to modify several drones with onboard computers and other specialized weaponry.

For the first time in as long as he could remember, Wang grinned *happily.* He had six birds prowling the sky. Four small ones with machine guns and two big ones packing guns and Sidewinder AIM-9 air to air missiles. Once he had his drones in position, their weapons hot, his grin turned evil.

Jarod was plotting a course to the New Jersey airport closest to the safe house where Luke was being held, when out of the blackness above, a stream of red tracers began raining down and past his left wing.

He jerked his stick away from the line of fire when just as quickly, two other streams appeared, one up from below his right rear, another from behind his tail. In less than two seconds, he was bobbing and weaving his way through a half-dozen streams of machine gun fire from six unseen bandits attacking him from as many directions.

Miss Parker stared at a screen that looked like a video game, a sense of urgency in her voice. "Daphne—talk to me."

"Upon takeoff I switched the satellite image to 3-D radar." Daphne referred to the six red drone avatars that were closing in on a blue one representing the Centre jet in the middle of the swarm. "It appears the drone operator on the island is attempting to shoot Jarod down."

Cornelius smiled cryptically as he cast a triumphant look at Sydney. "Unarmed, I'm afraid your boy is a sitting duck."

Sydney took in a concerned breath for his longtime charge.

At Mach one the six drones crisscrossed over, in front of, below and behind the Gulfstream. The resulting sonic booms rocked the G650, causing Jarod to momentarily spin out. As he fought to right the roll, all of his warning systems began screaming.

Jarod leveled off and remained calm in the eye of the storm. The instant the first tracers appeared, he realized what was happening. They hadn't elicited fear in him; instead, they brought a memory of a tale Sydney had once shared with him about the *Simorgh*, a creature of Iranian fable, that performed wonders in mid-flight. As he searched the dark heavens the drones had disappeared into, Jarod suspected he would need to draw upon his own version of *Simorgh* if he were to survive the next few minutes.

Chapter 64

GAME ON, SMARTASS mofo. If your pants aren't wet already, they soon will be.

Wang sent the commands that reassembled his predators into a heavy right V formation. He ordered them all to take a left turn to intersect with Jarod's flight path. They were at ten o'clock streaking in, right on Jarod's rear, when they unleashed a torrent of lead from their GAU-22 four-barrel cannons.

Finding himself in another hail of tracer fire, some of which was chewing up his back end, the Pretender remembered reading that *great fighter pilots all share one outstanding trait -aggressiveness.* So at 550 knots, he ruddered hard and throttled down, which caused two things to happen: the formation of Bandits to slingshot past him, and his own jet to slide just behind the tail of the last two drones on the end of the heavy right formation.

If the Centre's G-650 had been armed with guns or missiles, these last drones would have been toast, but with no offensive weaponry, Jarod instantly devised another method for self preservation.

He pushed the thrusters and jetted through the gap between the second and last drones.

He dipped and clipped the leading bird's wing, sending it spinning out of control and into the following bandit. Jarod lost sight of both as gravity pulled them downward in a fiery death spiral.

Sydney beamed like a proud papa, as two of the drone avatars dissolved into nothing.

Miss Parker had to admit it was a pretty good show. "When did you teach him how to fly like that, Sydney?"

"I didn't. He's teaching himself now. Survival is the best instructor."

Sydney cast a glare at Cornelius. "Jarod is playing three-dimensional chess. He just removed two pawns from the board. Only four more to go. So much for a sitting duck."

Cornelius grumbled at this development.

Wang was astounded by Jarod's tactics as well. Instead of being angry, the hater was in love. "Oh and I thought the Radio Shack shit was epic." Wang hit on his next approach. "Let's see just how clever you are."

Jarod slipped into the darkness to lick his wounds and gather his wits. He shut down his warning systems and did a visual damage assessment. His vertical stabilizer and rudder had taken several hits and were no longer completely responsive. Before he could factor a solution, he caught a glint of moonlight reflecting off the wing of one of his predators.

This time, they were lined up in a string formation—the large birds up front, the smaller two in the rear—and they were diving directly at his tail.

Most pilots in Jarod's position would cut and run as far north as possible. Jarod was not most pilots. Instead, he went full *Simorgh*: yanked hard on his stick, curved into a barrel roll and at its apex, twisted around, looping down, so he was now facing the string of drones head on.

Jarod leveled out, took a bead on the lead bandit and slammed his throttle forward.

Wang was impressed with Jarod's choice of tactic. A game of aerial chicken. "You audacious bastard." Determined not to blink first, the Hater increased speed, thumbed his trigger and fired.

Jarod didn't juke away or swerve. Instead, he corkscrewed through the machine gun stream as he continued to scream headlong at the drone's nose. Wang didn't flinch; he'd happily sacrifice all of his birds in Kamikaze fashion if it meant victory, which was the exact move Jarod had expected from his foe.

In the last instant before impact, Jarod locked himself upside-down, yanked on the yoke and dove, sending his jet wash directly into the path of the first two drones.

The good news was that both bandits began to pitch up hard and stall in the wake of Jarod's turbulence, but before they did, the second drone placed several shots directly into Jarod's left engine and fuselage, ripping gaping holes in both.

Chapter 65

A MAELSTROM ERUPTED around Jarod as his jet lost compression. Everything not bolted down was being sucked out of the holes as the interior and exterior air pressures fought for equalization.

The alarms shrieked and Jarod thought he heard Kaj moan. One engine flaming out and two Hellfire armed bandits in hot pursuit, Jarod could think of only one thing to do to survive.

He rolled and headed back to Isla Raton.

Wang was proud of the man in the black jet. He had proved himself beyond a worthy adversary and the recordings of this dogfight would not only be witness to that, but total vindication of his original thesis. Wang almost felt bad that the ending was so close and that his competitor would soon perish. He would have loved to share a coffee, even if it *had* to be iced, with the man who had tested him and his skills so thoroughly.

As he lined his predators up side-by-side, Wang knew that latte's would no longer be in the cards for Jarod. His birds were quickly closing the distance between themselves and the Gulfstream and soon, Jarod would be a crispy critter.

Wang flipped a latch over a red button on his joystick.

Miss Parker cringed at a high-pitched tone coming from the remaining drones. "What is that?"

"It's called the Hellfire squeal," Daphne stated knowingly. "It's the sound the seeking systems within the missiles make when attempting to gain radar lock on a target."

Sydney tightened. It wasn't just a *target* they were locking onto, it was the one living person he cared for more than any other on the planet.

Spotting Sydney's discomfort, Cornelius's demeanor buoyed. He turned to Daphne. In his nasally know-it-all intonation, he asked, "Are you saying the man on the island is programming missiles to zero in on Jarod's exhaust and blowing him out of the sky?"

"That's exactly what I'm saying," she answered.

Miss Parker noticed Jarod's airspeed. "Jarod has to know that as well. So why is he slowing down?"

A weight suddenly lifted off of Sydney's shoulders. He turned to her and smiled. "He wants to make sure the missiles lock in on him."

Cornelius shrugged. "I knew your boy was insane, but I didn't know he was *suicidal.*"

"On the contrary," it was Sydney's turn to bask. "His move is neither insane nor suicidal."

The other three raised curious eyebrows.

"Jarod has changed the competition. This is no longer 3 dimensional chess," Sydney sat and stared at the screen in anticipation of what Jarod had in store. "It's Judo."

As Jarod approached Isla Raton, the predators were closing within range. Jarod pulled back on the yoke and sent the G-650 into a radical climb. Wang's bandits followed suit. With both Newton's Law and his injured bird working against Jarod, Wang's drones made up nearly all the distance they needed to lock onto their target. As Jarod reached the top he pulled back and started plunging downward. After the drones reached their upper apogee, they followed in his path and accelerated. Combined with the power of gravity, they were soon approaching Mach speed, closing the gap between themselves and Jarod. As his drones reached the speed of sound, Wang received the indicator alarm that his missiles were locked on.

Cornelius cringed as an ear-piercing tone emitted from the console. He shot a smug look at the psychiatrist. "Looks like you were wrong, Sydster."

Miss Parker had to agree, though she was surprised with her solemn response. *Is this really how the pursuit of Jarod ends?* The thought of it triggered a chain reaction of emotions inside her.

Daphne read something in Miss Parker's demeanor that surprised her, but before she could determine what, Sydney startled everyone. He snatched Miss Parker's protein shake out of her hand, took a sip and as if channeling the confidence of his Pretender, announced, "This chase is far from over."

In the same split second Wang unleashed the Hellfires, Jarod throttled up, pulled the yoke to a hard right and his tail flaps down. The G650 began to shake, rattle and roll far outside the performance standards. Jarod thought she might break apart, but right before she did, she began to nose up. The Hellfires, going much too fast to self-correct as quickly, zoomed past his exhaust ports and continued straight downward. It was when they began slamming into the command center itself that Wang realized what was happening.

By then it was too late. The last thought Wang had before two drones turned his world into an enormous fireball was how much he loved Jarod's brain.

Everyone stared at the tech theatre screen in hushed amazement. The only avatar left alive was Jarod's blue blip, heading north. The silence was shattered as Miss Parker slapped the back of Cornelius' head for the third time. "Onyssius may have bent wings, but he's *still* flying."

Daphne looked up from her monitor. "He'll be out of satellite range in 30 seconds."

Miss Parker spun to face Cornelius. Terrified, he raised his hands to ward off a fourth blow to the back of his skull. Instead, Miss Parker flicked his forehead. "Lose him and you'll be sorry you ever met me."

Cornelius cradled his brow with his palm. He already was.

Miss Parker snatched her protein shake back from Sydney, and bolted out.

Four hours later, flames licking his engine cowling, sputtering on fumes, Jarod glided the Centre jet to a landing at an abandoned airstrip fifteen minutes south of Hoboken where Chaz and Skylar were waiting. Jarod secured Kaj on the stretcher inside the van he'd asked them to acquire, then hopped into the other rental sedan and sped off.

He had a boy to save.

Chapter 66

LUKE WAS SURE he had not slept for even one second since the outburst that had raged above him, Adidas Man's incessant ranting then chaotic destruction, finally ended. It had been replaced with a haunting silence.

Silence, save for the monotonous thumping.

Luke was unable to shake the feeling that the sudden lull was just the quiet before yet another storm, a killer storm that would manifest itself as an even more deranged Adidas Man.

It had grown so cold that Luke was shivering and could see the steam of his own breath. He didn't dare wonder if this could get worse, because he knew it could. Luke closed his eyes, trying to wish the thought away. His painfully empty stomach rumbled. There had been no meals for what seemed like days. He parceled his water, which was nearly dried up, too, and when he had to pee, he did so in the fireplace, unable to bear the stink that came with opening his overflowing chemical toilet.

The muffled thumping upstairs droned on. Luke sat up, felt himself succumbing to the despair that he would never leave this room alive. He stared into the darkness surrounding him, and just—cried. He didn't even try to prevent the tears from forming. The trickle of moisture at the corner of his eyes began to flow.

He imagined the warmth of his mother's hug, her soft voice whispering after she'd awakened him from the nightmare he had about the man
with a knife. *Crying is God's way of cleansing your heart, so when the tears arrive, you
do service to His will by letting them flow.* And so they did. As his eyes drifted up
toward the ceiling, he lay back down, the thumping droned on. Luke pulled
the covers up to his chin as if to ward off the demon above.

Adidas Man absently stabbed the gleaming blade of the knife into the bottom of the overturned kitchen table, oak chunks spitting out onto his naked
belly. His position was virtually fetal now, sitting on the floor in a crush of
shattered glass, ripped up carpet and splintered window blinds twisted in
heaps around him like a tornado's wake. That's just what it had been—a
righteously vehement tornado—and the tornado was him.

He had smashed windows, ripped out drywall, yanked off cabinets and
kicked holes in every other surface that he hadn't already violated in a desperate onslaught against his withdrawals. No rock star could have done a
more thorough job of trashing the place.

Ironically, like the boy in the basement whose life this out of control
lunatic controlled, Adidas Man was crying too. Reaching that easy oasis
Kaj's plan had promised was, after all, nothing but a mirage, and Adidas
Man could go on no longer.

He pulled the knife blade out of the table and stared at it. *What's left to
do when there's nothing left to do,* his brain screamed. Kaj was likely dead and the
longer Adidas Man remained loyal to their plan, the likelier it was that he
would end up dead as well. He knew Kaj's clients were evil and powerful
people. Maybe Kaj had tried some kind of fast play on them and failed.
Maybe Kaj had scored the payoff with a sleight of hand and absconded
with Adidas Man's share of the money? Or had Kaj just totally fucked up
with no way of getting word to him that the deal was off?

Adidas Man's fried brain settled on the notion that the *why* didn't really
matter. What *did* matter was that he was now left with baggage that, in no
likely scenario, would fit into the overhead bin of his newfound hell. Now it
was time for self-preservation, to flee the scene and disappear and that
meant, *leaving no trace behind.*

The man in the blue warm-up suit struggled to his feet, clutching the knife like it was his only friend. He wiped the drool from his chin and eyed the basement door. It was time to get rid of the person who could identify him.

A rooster tail of dust spun in Jarod's wake as he sped down the dirt road near Point View Reservoir in the New Jersey countryside in his quest to get to Luke's location.

He spotted the lone, wooden farmhouse on its barren acreage about a quarter mile up.

Without warning, he jerked the steering wheel and spun the back end dead left into the thicket of tall, dying corn stalks and killed the engine. He leapt out and plowed through the dried corn, racing towards the rear of the farmhouse that backed up to the forgotten field. As he ran, he silently called on his angels with a plea that he was not too late.

Luke's tears had stopped when he heard the sound of the basement door deadbolt being thrown, replaced by the immediacy of the worst kind of danger. He wrapped his blanket around himself defensively, sprang from his cot ready to face whatever came down those stairs.

Adidas Man appeared at the top of the steps. Luke caught a glimpse of a shiny carbon steel blade in the hand of his captor and thought to himself that his nightmare had become real. Adidas Man trudged toward Luke, who retreated until the brick wall stung his back, Luke's eyes never leaving the knife. Only steps away, his captor said the second thing he ever uttered to Luke in all this time. "Sometimes—sometimes it just doesn't work out, kid."

He raised the knife to kill Luke, but midway on its downward plunge Adidas Man's head exploded, spraying the petrified boy with mealy pieces of skin, bloody brain matter, and bone. The fat man's lifeless body bounced off the wall and hit the floor at Luke's feet like a rotting sack of meat. Terrified shock obliterated any sense of Luke's relief and by the time he wiped Adidas Man's blood from his eyes, everything was a chaotic flash.

Pushing himself toward the farmhouse, Jarod's heart sunk at the sound of the gunshot from inside the house, but it amped his momentum for the final 100 yards to his destination.

Luke only caught a glimpse of his rescuers as they walked toward him. One had a cast on his arm and stayed respectfully behind the other, who was lean and muscular with a shaved head and an eye patch. The boy smelled an intense odor from the approaching bald man and the feeling of dread he'd felt earlier did not dissipate. Instinctually Luke knew whomever these men were, they were not the rescuing heroes he'd wished for. He turned to run, but before he could, the bald man grabbed him and then everything went black as a hood engulfed his head.

Luke's precarious stay in the *frying pan* had just been relocated *into the fire.*

He heard O'Quinn bark the order to Dog. "Do it." Luke's mind raced. Did *do it* mean kill him? His heart pounded with heinous suspense until his nostrils told him that *do it* was something else entirely. Luke knew it wasn't gasoline by its smell but knew it was something akin to it.

Dog quickly sprayed the floor, walls and ceiling with the liquid combustible. O'Quinn pulled the boy to the stairs and paused but a second. "Make it fast," was all O'Quinn muttered as he jerked Luke up the stairs.

The bald man's smell was getting worse as he dragged the boy across musty shag carpeting. Moments later a door crashed open and Luke felt the blast of cold autumn air on his body. The sounds of the outdoor world and the sense of freedom it brought to Luke were welcome, despite knowing the feelings were misplaced.

Almost simultaneously came the sound of a van's double rear doors opening and the feel of his body being tossed onto the cold steel of its interior. Before the doors slammed shut, he felt the blast of heat at his back and the tumultuous rumble from the explosion. Wherever he'd been held all this time had just burst into flames.

Jarod emerged from the cornfield past a headless scarecrow and through the tangle of chains on a rusted swing set when the first explosion rocked him backward and off his feet. "Luuuuuuuke!" Jarod screamed in despair as he dragged up his body and struggled forward. A second smaller explosion was his only reply. The speed of the wooden farmhouse's burn was matched only by Jarod's heartbeat.

He heard a motor from the front of the structure cranking to life and with everything he had, the Pretender made a mad dash toward it. With flaming embers and inferno debris showering down around him, Jarod turned the corner as the van was peeling out.

O'Quinn, at the wheel, caught sight of Jarod chasing after them.

"Luuuuke!" Jarod yelled, pushing his body beyond its limits.

Luke sat up when he heard his name called by a voice he didn't recognize. He turned to get a better listen and the back of his head bumped against a hook mounted on the van's wall. He moved his head up and down, finally snagging the seam of the hood onto it, freeing his face from the darkness.

On his back, legs cocked and raised, Luke rocked back and launched his feet against one of the van's rear windows, smashing it out. He flipped to his knees, looked out and called to the running man shrinking in the distance. "It's Luke! I'm here!"

Jarod knew he was running a race he could not win. His eyes locked with Luke's, he could feel the anguish in the boy's gaze.

Luke's hope sagged as the running man became but a speck. Not even Dog's paw pulling him away from the broken window by his throat could take *that* resurgent hope away from him.

Chapter 67

FLASHING BLUE LIGHTS illuminated the insides of Sydney's eyelids. He sat up from the Lazy Boy recliner he slept in on the nights he *could* sleep and oriented himself enough to tighten the belt on his robe and make his way to the front door. Opening it, he found two men in suits—one fat, one skinny—both holding police badges.

The fat one took the lead. "I'm Detective Knott." He jutted his beefy chin toward the lean one. "This is Diestel. You live here?"

Sydney, still trying to clear his head, nodded *yes.*

Diestel craned his skinny neck and looked past Sydney into the house, seeing that all of the furniture in the massive home was covered in white sheets. The choice of decor registered on his face. "Doesn't look like anyone *lives* here."

Truer words were rarely spoken. Since the *incident* so many years ago that had ripped his wife and infant child from Sydney's world, *living* was not what happened within these walls.

Sydney nonetheless answered calmly, "I assure you, I do."

Diestel shrugged. "Your decorator has quite the sense of humor."

"So that would make you, Sydney ..." Knott brought his cell phone up to his face and squinted at a photograph on screen and attempted to read the words that had been captured on it. Frustrated, he tilted the screen in Diestel's direction. "What's that say?"

Diestel gave it his best shot. "Shit, that last name's a tongue-twister. I think it says ..." His face began a twisting jujitsu as he tried to pronounce

Sydney's very European surname. "Sydney *Goo-net-lady*—or maybe it's *Goon-earl-ay*."

Rarely irritated with anyone but Miss Parker, the Belgian flared. "I'm *Sydney!*"

Diestel, trying for the Deputy Fife award asked, "Can you pronounce your last name?"

"Since the day I learned to speak," Sydney patronized. Over the years, he had often been peeved as people twisted themselves into facial pretzels while trying to pronounce his family name. Of course, it never happened in Europe. Only Americans panicked when they saw an umlaut.

Diestel and Knott looked at the cell screen. Both of the cops made faces of surrender.

Sydney had been fighting a migraine since his failure in the Ice Cube. He *needed* to talk to Jarod, and had been desperately trying to think of some way to communicate with his protégé, when the intensity of the last few days finally caught up to him and he'd fallen asleep. Waking up to the intrusion of these two Neanderthals sent him over the edge.

"The two dots above the letter 'U' is an umlaut. It instructs the vowel to be pronounced as 'Oh.'"

Diestel and Knott shared a bemused look. "No shit?" the fat one said disinterestedly. He angled the cell so Sydney could see the photograph. It was Sydney's full name and address spray-painted on an interior wall. "What's the dots above the other letters tell you to say?"

"This is my house." Sydney pointed to the photo, "And that's my name. Now do you mind telling me what it's doing spray-painted on that wall?"

"We were hoping you could tell us that, Mr. *Gownt-ray-adye* ..." The skinny cop tried his best to follow the laws of pronunciation but unable to wrap his tongue around Sydney's last name, gave up. "Sir."

"We found it freshly tagged on the wall of a ..." Hardy looked to Laurel for help. "Ah, well, how would you put it?"

"How 'bout a bizarre-ass crime scene?" Knott looked down his bulbous nose to Diestel who though realizing his faux pas, added defensively, "Well, that's how I'd put it."

Knott silenced his thin partner with a scowl, then locked eyes again with Sydney. "It's less than a mile from here. You mind taking a ride?"

Sydney *did* mind taking a ride with these two, but knowing that his name had been painted on a wall in Jarod's hand made the decision easy.

Chapter 68

CONSTRUCTED IN 1771, the Public Hospital in Virginia was the first facility built for those with psychiatric disorders in North America. Though experts still argued the point, the second was the Greysmore Asylum for the Mentally Insane outside Blue Cove, Delaware.

Starting as a wooden structure on the promontory bluff overlooking the famous azure waters, Greysmore grew into a seven-story stone monolith that housed 367 patients too dangerous for civilian institutions. With the ascent of psychiatric neurology in the 20th century, Greysmore fell out of favor. Abandoned and long tarnished by decades of neglect, it was now little more than a hulking monstrosity and eyesore.

But boy did it have a view.

From its top floor, prominent landmarks could be seen for miles around. Facing south it was impossible to miss the highrises of downtown Blue Cove. Ninety degrees to the west was the majestic Ceon Forest where at its furthest edge, stood the gentleman's plantation three generations of Parkers had called home. To the north was a cold, art deco structure standing sentry on the upper shore of Blue Cove known simply as the Centre.

Sydney was still wearing his rumpled robe as Knott and Diestel walked him into the room that formerly held Greysmore's most serious patients. The first thing Sydney saw was Miss Parker staring out the window, angrily blowing a stream of smoke, stewing from the fact that Jarod had been right under their noses the whole time. When they met eyes, her disdainful look shifted from him to his name and address spray-painted on the wall above the same hospital bed where Jarod had kept Dr. Bilson. "Tell me something, Syd, just how the hell do you pronounce that last name of yours?"

Sydney wasn't surprised to see Miss Parker there but the cops were, especially Knott. "This is a crime scene. I'm afraid I'm going to have to ask you to leave, ma'am."

Miss Parker dropped her Pall Mall and ground it out with her toe. It was bad enough that she had been awakened once more in the middle of the night, courtesy of Jarod, but this *'Ma'am' shit again* really got her goat. In lieu of cold-blooded murder, she said in frosty tones, "I know what this is and don't call me 'ma'am'. I'm Mr. 'Umlaut's' lawyer. Now, you mind telling me why the hell you dragged my client here?"

The cops shared a bewildered look, "How'd you know where we brought him?"

Sydney raised an inquisitive eyebrow as well. "Yes. How?"

Miss Parker looked pointedly at Sydney while answering the cop's question. "I have friends in high places and they're not very happy with you right now." Parker snapped her attention back to Knott. "And unless you have something to charge him with, he's leaving with me, now."

Diestel began to answer, "Truth is, we just wanted to see if he could help us out—ma'a ..."

"It's *Miss!* Not Ms., and *damn sure* not Mrs." She smiled at them both—with her mouth but not her eyes. "Exactly how do you think my client could *help you out?*"

"The writing's on the wall, lady." Knott said, then turned to Sydney— "Any idea why your name would have been left behind here? Or more importantly, by whom?"

"Not off the top of my head," Sydney said, feigning puzzlement. As he walked over to the hospital bed he took note of the I.V. pump, the pile of used ringer bags, the empty box of adult diapers and a large manila envelope on the soiled pillow that had the words *evidence* stenciled across it. Sydney swallowed, wondering what it all meant, adding, "Perhaps if you can explain what happened, I might be able to lend some insight."

Diestel winked at Miss Parker as he pointed a thumb toward Sydney. "*That's* what we were hoping for. You're a psychiatrist from the think tank?"

"I'm in the psychiatric field at the Centre." Sydney confirmed, his focus now on the shackles on the bed. "So can you tell me what happened here?"

"I can do better than that—I can show you." Knott scrolled through photos on his phone. "Few hours ago we got an anonymous tip about a missing Manhattan doctor. He'd been heavily drugged and shackled there for days." Knott flashed crime scene photos of Bilson, a crazed look on his face, his diaper overflowing, eyes staring into space.

Sydney was stunned. "This man looks catatonic."

Diestel nodded. "That's what the paramedics said."

Parker pursed her lips with mock curiosity. "Wow. I wonder what kind of person would do something like that to a fellow human being."

Sydney met her sarcastic look but didn't take the bait.

"We were wondering the same thing," Knott said, nodding to Diestel, "That and why whoever it was would leave this behind." Diestel opened the *evidence* envelope and removed a red-skinned iPad. He turned it 'on' and handed it to Sydney. "Whattya make of this, Doc?"

On the first screen there was a headline from the New York Times online: *PHARMACEUTICAL RESEARCH HOSPITAL RAIDED IN FRAUD CASE.* In a separate window was a news video of Dr. Hiro Su being perp-walked out of Guardian General in handcuffs, the reporter telling the world—'Doctor arrested—missing partner found—both facing hundreds of years in prison.'

Sydney looked up and into Knott's eyes that seemed to contain a bit more intelligence than before. "This iPad. Your name on the wall, well, we figured maybe our perp might be a patient of yours."

Sydney looked to Miss Parker, who snickered at that description, and then back to the cops. "I don't treat patients any longer—I'm in research."

Miss Parker decided it was time to pull rank. "Gentlemen, may I have a private word with my client?"

Knott motioned to Diestel to follow him, leaving Parker and Sydney alone.

In lieu of a bullet, Miss Parker focused her harsh gaze between Sydney's eyes. "First the jet, now this. Your boy's getting cocky and I'm PMSing—not a good combo for you."

Sydney looked to Miss Parker and spoke with a clipped harshness of his own. "How did you know I'd be here?"

"I know everything, Sydney. Except what Jarod was doing here, playing scramble-the-grey-matter with Dr. Drools-A-Lot." Miss Parker looked over Sydney's shoulder and shared a smile with the detectives. She then looked back to face Sydney. "Now I'm gonna go have a chat with tweedle-dumb and tweedle-dumber and then you and I are going to have a chat about what Jarod is up to here."

"I'm afraid it won't be a long one," he informed her absently, already ruminating to himself on what it all meant. "I have no idea what he's up to."

"Don't lie," Parker sneered. "It only makes you look more ignorant than usual."

Sydney wasn't lying, though. As he watched Miss Parker walk over to the detectives and then out into the hallway with them, he had the same question running through his mind. *What the hell was Jarod up to here?*

He knew that Jarod left his address on the wall so the police would eventually bring him to this room, but why? As Miss Parker's reaction proved, Jarod would enjoy flaunting how close he had been, but Sydney suspected it was more than just that. Sydney felt that somewhere in this room was a breadcrumb Jarod left for him to follow.

He also recognized that Miss Parker, whose voice he could hear from the hallway, would suspect the same thing so if he wanted the message to remain private, he didn't have much time to find it. Sydney scanned the room for what it could be. There were no clues like those he had previously seen on Jarod's trail.

That was when he saw it. Jarod had hidden the message in plain sight, right above the doorjamb Miss Parker had just exited beneath. To the untrained eye the words in Latin appeared to be just another of the many layers of graffiti painted on these walls but to Sydney they held a special meaning.

Filii inlacrimat.

The son weeps.

Sydney knew that was only half the communication, a clue telling him *where* to go. Which, ironically, was right back to where he had gone searching for Jarod in the days immediately after his escape. Still, it didn't tell Sydney *how* being there would help him contact his protégé.

Sydney looked around the floor for the second part of Jarod's message. When Jarod was younger and angry with Sydney—angry enough to cry—Jarod would leave notes on small pieces of paper tucked between the top of the door of his living dome and the frame above it. These notes would fall onto Sydney's head when he walked in and the psychiatrist would know that his charge was upset.

Knowing Jarod was angrier now than he had ever been before, Sydney correctly surmised the same thing here. After a quick inspection, Sydney saw a rolled up piece of paper which must have fallen when Dr. Bilson had been found, swept to the side of the threshold amidst cobwebs and dust from years gone by.

To deter prying eyes, he nonchalantly knelt down next to it, pretending to tie his shoe, only to realize he was still wearing slippers.

Sydney plucked the paper from the crack with his left hand as he adjusted the back of his night shoe with his right. He felt as though he had gotten away with it all until the heel of a Jimmy Choo attached to a very long, very lithe leg landed next to his fingers.

He looked up and had Miss Parker not brushed her hand down her miniskirt would've caught a close-up of something he was thankful he hadn't. Her neutral expression didn't give away whether she had witnessed him palm the paper or not. He searched for the first indication of where his immediate fate rested.

She smiled. "Syd, you remind me of the pathetic old broad on that panic button commercial—'I've fallen and can't get up,'" she mocked.

Sydney acutely felt his own inadequacies as he rose. "You have no idea."

"Andy and Barney say you're free to go now—or should I say, *we* are free to go." Before Sydney could respond Parker received a text and eyed the screen. It was from Daphne, requesting a phone call ASAP.

Miss Parker looked to Sydney. "We'll finish our chat later."

As she walked away, Sydney released a sigh of relief, but when he unfurled the paper in his palm, his anxiety returned.

Jarod had written five more words for him in Latin—*eius in patris mei manus.*

It's in my father's hands.

Chapter 69

NINETY-THREE SECONDS LATER, Miss Parker was in her Porsche torching a cig and speed dialing. Daphne answered on the first ring. "Good evening, Miss Parker."

"The freak of nature find the Chameleon?"

"No, but the supercomputer solved the unsolvable. I just texted to you."

Miss Parker exhaled a celebratory smoke cloud and checked her texts to find two lines of information. One began with the letter W the other with N, each followed by an equals sign and a sequence of numerals.

Parker frowned. "That W equals N shit never made sense to me."

"In the world of Euclidian Geometry the answer didn't compute for me either—at first. Then I started to think about Jarod's mind and how it might work and, well, I assumed his brain was too multi-faceted to be working in just *one* discipline. That's when it all clicked into place."

Getting frustrated, Miss Parker flicked away her cancer stick. "Click it for me, Mensa—I'm still back at Euclidean G."

"While the problem is mathematical, the answer is geographical. The W and N stand for West and North, and their corresponding numerical values are GPS coordinates that pinpoint a spot a few miles from the Centre. I'm there now."

"Where—exactly?"

Daphne hesitated, then plunged ahead. "On your father's farm near the place where an old church once stood."

Miss Parker, a flood of dread drowning her soul, whispered, "That son of a bitch."

Chapter 70

SYDNEY'S COMMUTER PLANE out of Wilmington regional had taken off 30 minutes late. Dashing through the concourse in Philadelphia, Sydney came to the conclusion that if he missed his connecting flight he'd be more screwed than he could imagine.

Convinced that both mentally and physically, he couldn't take much more screwing, he actually ran down the gangway. He arrived as the stewardess was closing the door of the Boeing 737–300 barely able to hear over his pounding heart as she said a perfunctory 'good morning.'

Good? What's so good about it? Sydney thought, finding that his day had become worse as he discovered his economy class middle seat. He was sardined between an injured war vet and an chattering overweight big-momma who reminded him of the mother of some southern child on a reality show he had stumbled across one night while channel surfing in an insomniac stupor. Buckling himself in as the jet began to taxi, Sydney let out a deep sigh. It wasn't of relief, but apprehension and exhaustion.

The lies were stacking up ever higher and he feared he would break under the strain before he'd accomplished his mission. He was AWOL from the Centre today and prayed he wouldn't be missed, or worse, spotted on his journey. Not for a second had Sydney considered not going. Jarod had gone to a great deal of trouble to leave him a private message, and Sydney was determined to keep it that way. He had covered the tracks of his excursion as best he knew how, but lately his best was often insufficient.

Before 9/11 he would have traveled under an assumed name, but those days were gone forever. Sydney even toyed with the idea of traveling under his twin Jacob's identity, but if caught—explaining an unauthorized trip would be bad enough, but one in the guise of his *distant* brother would be impossible to justify. So Sydney purchased his ticket in cash, hoping somehow that would prevent a red flag going up if the Centre was monitoring his credit cards. He knew it wasn't much to bank on, but it was all he had.

He made the sign of the cross three times as the jet thundered down the runway. It was a takeoff ritual the man of science practiced religiously, even after he had lost his faith, a prayer to Saint Christopher placing his destiny in God's hands.

He knew in that moment, the prayer had more than one meaning.

Chapter 71

BILLOWING RED CLOUDS foretold of a coming storm as Miss Parker's gelding thundered across the field of heather. She caught a glimpse of the Grumpy Old Man and, for the first time, she thought the old growth oak looked like a man on his deathbed reaching upward for a loving embrace he would never feel again. She had felt that empty longing for years and knew Jarod understood that as well. Maybe too well.

I know the truth about what makes you sad.

With Jarod's words ringing in her mind, Miss Parker reined in her steed with such force his head twisted around facing hers. Both were full of rage. They came to an abrupt stop in what was once the courtyard of the old abandoned church. Dismounting, she heard, "In here."

Miss Parker spun in the direction of the voice. It had come from within the wall surrounding her family gravesite. Heart pounding, she made her way through the gate and into the solemn grounds where Daphne was kneeling next to a specific granite headstone. The name chiseled into it was *Catherine Parker.*

Through gentle eyes, Daphne gazed at Miss Parker. As the blonde stood, Parker could see that atop her mother's resting place was a present, a package wrapped in lavender paper with a royal purple ribbon, left for her by Jarod. Parker couldn't feel her feet as she walked toward the grave. Never once had she set foot here, not since the day she dropped a handful of soil onto her mother's coffin. Miss Parker had turned her back on her mother, the way she felt her mother had turned her back on her, and when she had walked away that day, she intended never to return.

On that day, from deep inside her soul, Little Miss had summoned a stern look she'd locked upon her face to stop crying, from feeling the pain. It was a look that had remained on her face for far too many years. A defense mechanism to shield her from the emotion surrounding the death of the one person she truly loved and *needed* in her life. A suit of armor she had built the day her father told her that grieving made her weak. Refusing to be weak, she summoned it again now as she knelt down and reached for the present. Daphne placed a gentle hand on Miss Parker's shoulder. Miss Parker didn't like being touched unless she had instigated it, but for some reason, she didn't flinch from this caring gesture.

The last time Jarod had left something for her it had been the Etch A Sketch of her crying on the day of her mother's death. She feared what was beneath the gift-wrap. Gathering her courage, she ripped it open and found a black folder with the words *Confidential Level 1, For Centre Use Only* printed across it in bold red ink.

A thought found its way into Miss Parker's jumbled mind. A quote she'd seen her mother write once in her diary from the poet Anna Akhmatova, *You will hear thunder and remember me, and think: she wanted storms.* As she opened the file and realized what she was seeing, Miss Parker felt a storm begin swirling in her mind.

Daphne asked, "What is it?"

Parker put her manicured hand to her mouth in surprise. "A draft file of the official Centre report … for the day my mother died."

Miss Parker saw that it had been drafted from her Uncle Zane's office and was later sent to her father for revisions and also included a psych evaluation section.

Reading over Miss Parker's shoulder, Daphne's eyes went wide. "Sydney did psychiatric sessions with your mother?"

Miss Parker hadn't known about the medical relationship her mother had shared with Sydney, nor that, according to the report, he had worked psychiatrically with Catherine for many years.

That revelation wasn't the one that affected Miss Parker the most. As she turned to the very last page, Miss Parker found a handwritten note.

Looking closely, she could see that the official cause of her mother's death had been redacted, blacked out so no one could read what had been written there originally, and replaced by a single word: *Suicide*. That word, and all of the redactions had been made and initialed in familiar writing: her father's. Confused, Parker found herself again summoning the stern look she depended upon to stop herself from crying. She wasn't sure if this document about her mother's death was real and, if so, what Jarod was trying to tell her with it, but more than anything, she was committed to finding the truth.

Chapter 72

TICK TOCK, TICK *tock, tick tock.* Time was running out and everyone knew it. Oscar looked at Skylar, who looked at Jarod, who looked at Kaj laying comatose on a gurney. Anxious concern was etched on all of their faces. The next step had to be taken with extreme care. The terrorist had survived his journey from Isla Raton, but he was far too unstable for what Jarod had in mind.

"I got what you wanted," an out-of-breath voice struggled to say.

Jarod turned and looked at Chaz, who hurriedly entered the loft lugging an antique barber chair that had to weigh several hundred pounds. "Now where you want it?"

Jarod pointed to a place in the far corner. "Over there. I'll need the best light possible."

"Whatever you say, Big Boss." As she struggled across the hardwood, Chaz stole a glance at Kaj and shook her head in disbelief. "I done trying to figure out how your big brain works, but it look to me that what Bad Boy here needs is more than a new 'do." The chair landed with a thump.

"You're right, Chaz." Jarod turned back to Kaj. "Give him a shave as well."

Chapter 73

THE GLOW OF the full moon barely pierced through the fog blanketing the hallowed ground and hallowed ground it was, as were the casualties of battles it had known. At 733 acres, Cincinnati's Spring Grove was the second largest cemetery in the United States. Founded during the Civil War, it was an idyllic final resting place for their country's fallen sons, both blue and grey.

Within its rolling hills, towering trees, winding pathways and soothing fountains, there was one deified parcel that stood out: 333 graves, the souls of 999 soldiers surrounding an officer's body that lay in the center of them all, as if silently commanding an army of the dead.

With great trepidation, Sydney made his way through these ranks, his leather valise in one hand, a flashlight in the other. Sydney continued to glance over his shoulder to ensure he hadn't been followed.

Turning right, he opened the ornate wrought iron gate that guarded the pathway to the bronze statue known as the Weeping Angel. The sorrowful guardian kept silent watch over the legions of the departed through eyes of perpetual grief. Grief was something Sydney had long understood. It was something that he had thought he had long ago come to terms with. Now, as he finally laid eyes on his destination, he wasn't so sure.

Shaded by the branches of a towering buckeye was an aged, two-person vestibule mausoleum. Sydney approached the marble structure, feeling an implacable pull from within and great foreboding. His world was suddenly deafeningly silent, save for his heart pounding in his chest.

The Belgian flashed his torch on two words carved above the bronze door: *filii inlacrimat.* Feeling a downward tug on his soul, Sydney thought the words prophetic: *the son weeps,* indeed.

He lowered his light, illuminating the roses left behind by Jarod, who had placed them on the very structure in which he had been told his 'parents' had been laid to rest. The blooms were long dried and brittle, yet Sydney still picked them up and breathed in the last of their essence.

Sydney examined the rusted padlock on the door of the tomb with great care. The Watchers from the Centre all knew Jarod had come here in the days after he had escaped. They had only just missed him, as did his mentor. Yet no one, including Sydney, had noticed the shiny hairline scratch on the patina of the lock's first tumbler. Until now. He stared intently at it, realizing it must have been made by Jarod on the day he left the roses.

Sydney chastised himself for not realizing until now that Jarod would have entered the tomb to *see* the 'truth' for himself. He knew Jarod wanted him to go inside as well. Sydney removed a pair of bolt cutters, then cringed when the metal teeth sliced through the lock. He then opened the door of the vestibule and, after a moment of cognitive dissonance, stepped inside.

The interior was eight feet by ten. Its marble walls so cold that, as he painted the sacred space with his beam, he could see his breath. He could also see the two caskets atop stone catafalques. Sydney had been hoping for another simple clue, but Jarod was anything but simple.

Sydney pulled out and read the paper clue from Jarod: *eius in patris mei manus*—*It's in my father's hands.* Fearing it's meaning, Sydney lifted the flashlight beam onto the caskets. Jarod's 'father' was inside of one of them. On the base of the catafalques on the left was the name *Evelyn. On the other,* the name *Joe.* Feeling a second downward tug on his soul, Sydney made the sign of the cross, prayed for forgiveness, and then opened the lid.

What Jarod wanted Sydney to find was nestled in the folded hands atop the chest of Jarod's pseudo-father's corpse. It was impossible that Jarod's father had been buried with a 4G cell phone. They wouldn't be invented for 20 years after his death. No, this phone was left for Sydney by Jarod and, when he turned it on, he saw its battery charge was strong. He also discovered that the phone had one—and only one—number preprogrammed into its contact list.

Sydney sat on the mourner's bench, looked at the preprogrammed number, closed his eyes and made the call.

Jarod was sitting alone in the dark when he answered. "What did I tell you, Sydney? He doesn't even look like me."

Sydney shone light on the face of the well-preserved corpse. "No, he doesn't," Sydney said thoughtfully, then switched gears. "I assume you didn't arrange such a creative way for me to be able to contact you so that you could tell me where you are?"

"No, Sydney, I didn't." Jarod, too exhausted from his ordeals to be sarcastic, intoned flatly, "Truth is, I could be anywhere."

"As I have seen. I can hardly keep up with you, Jarod. Aerial dog fights. Kidnapping a terrorist. Torturing a physician into catatonia? This isn't like you."

"Just giving the doc a taste of his own medicine. We all need that kind of psychological reckoning once in a while."

"Is that what you are doing with me? Is that the kind of retributive justice Onyssius dispensed?"

Jarod didn't respond to either of Sydney's questions. As a child, he was often quiet when he was in a reflective or angry mood, and this silence reminded Sydney of that fact. "You don't have to answer, Jarod. I know you have reasons for what you are doing." Still, Jarod didn't—or *wouldn't*—respond. In the past, Sydney had learned that the only way to break through one of Jarod's silent treatments was to change the subject. "It's good to see you have a friend, that young woman from the hospital."

"Yes," Jarod replied, cautiously. "She's very nice."

"I'm glad."

"Are you really, Sydney?"

"I truly am." The mentor's words were truthful, yet while speaking them he felt the tug on his soul for the third time. "I'm truly sorry, Jarod."

The Pretender struggled to contain his emotions of a lifetime of betrayal that threatened to overwhelm him. After a long silence so heavy Sydney could feel its weight, Jarod finally asked, "For what?"

"Everything." Sydney whispered, his voice barely audible.

Uncomfortable with Sydney's reactions, Jarod changed the subject. "Tell me what you found."

Relieved to be back on a safer ground, Sydney replied. "Nothing, I'm afraid. I did get into the archives but, as I searched for your intake files, I was locked out."

"You didn't find *nothing*, Sydney, you found *everything*. The Centre is covering their tracks." Jarod said bitterly.

"They've *covered* their tracks."

"No," Jarod said with adamancy. "The truth still exists. For three generations the Parkers have kept *everything* on paper in a personal file room in the mansion."

Sydney was astonished. "Jarod, how ... how could you possibly know that?"

"Because I *do*. I know lots of things about the Centre and the people within it I never told anyone. I would have stolen Mr. Parker's files along with the DSA's, but I didn't have enough time to break into his house the night I left."

"And you think *I* can?" Sydney spluttered in shock.

"My life is in there!" Jarod blurted out before he caught himself. He struggled to regain his composure. "The truth about who I am. Please, Sydney."

"Okay, Jarod. I'll try." Sydney promised him, knowing that's the least he owed his protégé.

"One last thing. If I don't make it ... if my real parents are out there ..." Jarod fell silent.

Even over the phone line, Sydney could feel Jarod's pain. "I'll find them, Jarod."

As the phone went dead, a tsunami of emotions overtook Sydney and washed him out to sea. He looked at the corpse in the coffin and wondered just who the hell the dead man really was, who the hell was Jarod and, most troubling, Sydney wondered who the hell he had allowed himself to become.

Minutes later, while walking back through the cemetery, preoccupied and treading water in his soul, he didn't see the man spying on him from behind the Weeping Angel.

The man had one eyebrow undulating with excitement and a wicked plan.

For several minutes after Sydney's call, Jarod remained sitting in the darkness. He only looked up when a hand fell on his shoulder. He raised his eyes to meet Skylar's, but her eyes were focused on the phone in his hand. "A friend?"

"An old one. My only one—until now."

A voice shot out from afar. "And what the hell am I, just the Flying Nun?"

Jarod looked to the far corner. He had transformed the space into a surgical theatre, with one strange addition. Instead of the operating table, Kaj was sitting upright in the barber chair, hooked up to monitors and I.V.s. His face and head were freshly shaved and Chaz, dressed as a nursing-nun, was securing thick leather restraints that held Kaj in place.

Jarod thought for a moment. "I'm not sure what you are, Chaz."

Chaz put one hand on her hip and pointed the other toward the ceiling, wiggling it as she declared, "I tell'ya one thing I'm *not*." She tilted the wiggle finger down so it now pointed toward Kaj. "And that's messed up in the head like this boy. His brains'a'been scrambled but *Lord* have mercy!"

"Jarod?" Skylar asked.

He returned his gaze upon her with tenderness. "Yes?"

She was confused, looking at Kaj. "If that man can't tell you what is inside his mind, what good is he to you?"

Jarod reached down to the Libyan terrorist and opened his eyelid. He gazed deeply into his one good eye, as if peering straight through his dilated pupil and directly into his brain itself. "If the answers I need are in there, I'll get them out." The resolve in his voice was unmistakable.

Chapter 74

NEITHER KNEW IT at the time, but to both the inquisitive Oscar and the anxiety-riddled Chaz the rivulets of blood cascading down either side of Kaj's face and meeting under his jaw looked like stampede strings holding a cowboy hat in place atop his cranium. Or they would have, but Kaj was not a cowboy, nor was he sporting a Stetson. Not to mention the fact that the top half of his skull, which would have been supporting the western headgear, was currently being removed by Jarod.

Standing behind the barber chair, the Pretender placed the concave bone on a table next to him. Without taking his eyes from the pinky-grey dome of the Libyan's exposed brain, he extended his gloved hand toward Skylar, who was standing beside a tray of surgical tools.

"Tunneling rod."

Skylar didn't respond. She had not heard him nor seen his outstretched palm. The loft was cold and her focus was ensnared by the unnatural sight of steam rising from the gelatinous material inside Kaj's head. As she thought that his brain reminded her of the inside of a walnut, the world around Skylar began spinning out of control. Jarod's soothing voice steadied her. "I need you, Skylar. You can do this."

She let out a sharp breath she hadn't known she had been holding and regained her equilibrium. Jarod nodded toward a slender, hollow stainless steel rod with a rounded tip and a T-shaped handle. She picked it up and placed it gently into his gloved fingers, but did not let go. He met her concerned eyes. "Jarod, I know he's an evil man, but …"

His reassuring gaze stopped her. Skylar was a good person, but she hadn't honed the compartmentalizing skills necessary to wall away the natural human response to something as psychologically and physically complex as what they were doing. He did his best to alleviate her guilt, as well as that of the other two uneasy bystanders. "While the brain is the tool we use to detect discomfort in other parts of the body, it contains no pain receptors itself. Technically, he won't feel anything."

Skylar allowed an unsteady smile of relief to escape. It pierced Jarod's heart. The truth was Jarod wasn't sure Kaj wouldn't feel pain or that the ultimate outcome of this procedure wouldn't lead to serious adverse effects on the Libyan's long-term health, and he didn't really care. The ultimate fate the one-time goat herder deserved would be decided by a power beyond his control.

Skylar released the tunneling rod into Jarod's care. Focusing his attention onto the millions of neurons making up Kaj's brain, Jarod delicately placed it into a crevice of the twisted mass. An aberrant sucking sound echoed through the room as the rod slowly disappeared deep inside the terrorist's grey matter. As it did, a sudden gasp escaped through Chaz's high glossed lips.

With the rod placed midbrain, Jarod tilted the handle back, then indicated to Skylar an electronic device on the surgical tray. She handed the pulse generator to Jarod.

Chaz nervously chewed her thumbnail as she watched Jarod guide the activated wire down through the hollow rod and into Kaj's brain. When the terrorist suddenly began jerking, Chaz snatched Oscar to her bosom and looked to Jarod. "What kinda *Green Mile*, dry sponge, 'lectric chair kinda shit chew doin' to that coma-boy?!" Chaz exclaimed in horror.

Jarod shared a look with Chaz. "Deep brain stimulation to modulate neurophysiological activity in certain pathological circuits." Jarod slightly retracted the electrode and Kaj immediately slipped back into his vegetative state.

As he readjusted the probe position, Jarod explained that he was searching in the ocean of grey matter for an island of cells called the fornix. "It's a C-shaped bundle of nerve fibers that serves as the main highway connecting the entorhinal cortex and the hippocampus, the brain areas that compose the brain's memory circuit."

Chaz shared a puzzled look with Skylar, then raised a perplexed eyebrow to Jarod.

Jarod rephrased his explanation. "I'm shocking him awake with the memory stick."

Skylar was confused. "I thought you said his mind was fried from the O.D. O'Quinn gave him."

"There's only one way to find out," Jarod said.

Jarod reinserted the electrode, this time guiding it into a nearby brain zone. Kaj's face began animating. Like a long unused ventriloquist dummy, his jaw muscles loosened and his mouth started flapping up and down. Encouraged, Jarod cranked the juice up a notch and, suddenly, Kaj's eyes flashed open like high-beam headlights. His good one searched the room all crazy daisy until it found and locked onto the face of Chaz.

The startled nursing-nun gasped and made the sign of the cross. "Jesus, Mary, and Joseph ... and all the waiters at the last supper, this sinner done seen it all."

Kaj tried moving, then focused on the restraints holding him in place. "Am I tied to this chair for a reason?"

Jarod leaned down to Kaj's ear. "Yes. It's so you don't fall over and spill your brain onto the floor." He said, playfully serious.

Alarmed, Kaj's good eye looked up to see what was going on. "Who is that?"

Jarod leaned over so the Libyan could see a glimpse of him. "My name is Jarod." Kaj's face scrunched as he searched his mind. "Do ... I ... know you?"

"We have spoken once before. I need answers about a boy named Luke."

The man strained for recognition, but genuinely came up empty. "I am sorry, but I don't remember." He tried to swallow, but his throat was full of dust. "May I trouble you for a cup of tea?"

"We have no tea," said Jarod, straining to keep the hostility out of his voice.

"What do you have?"

Jarod slightly maneuvered the tunneling rod. "Hopefully a way to help you remember." He sent a pulse surge to a new part of Kaj's brain and an eruption went off.

Kaj thought death was coming for him as his entire history began flashing before his eyes but actually, it was Jarod methodically running his fingers down the piano keys of his life. The terrorist's face contorted in rapid fashion as he experienced a gambit of emotions, as Jarod fast-forwarded through the freeze frames of his existence.

To Oscar, it appeared like he was witnessing absurdist mime theatre. Still, what was happening to the open-headed terrorist wasn't the weirdest thing happening in the room. For the rat the strangest was being cuddled tightly to the breasts of the once broom-wielding maniac who, only days earlier, had tried to kill him.

A thousand things coursed through the rodent's tiny head, but it was nothing compared to what was going on inside the exposed brain of the terrorist. Memory sensations began flooding through Kaj's clouded mind. The feeling of immense pride accompanied by a flash of a seven-year-old Kaj kicking a football goal on the dusty streets of Benghazi; the pang of hunger as the smell of grilled lamb filled his mind along with the image of a woman—*his mother*—as she handed him a kabob. *"Served warm—never hot."* A blast of heat, as a teen watching flames engulf an effigy of George W. Bush. He relived the sexual stirring he enjoyed as a young Islamic radical fantasizing about his promised "seventy-two virgins" and the horrible breath of the toothless old whore who gave him his first taste of that kind of pleasure.

In computer terms, Jarod was exploring Kaj's lifetime browser history, looking for one particular incident. "Tell me about the boy."

"Which boy?"

"Luke."

At the mention of this name, Jarod gave Kaj a jolt. The Libyan's memory flashed to the door of a van opening outside a school where Luke stood waiting to be picked up. Kaj yanked the boy into the van and closed the door, his actions obscured by a fat man in a blue Adidas suit who was limping by. Kaj felt a sensation of satisfaction as he remembered the child looking at him with terrified eyes.

He smiled. "We took him in the van."

Kaj's memory was just where Jarod wanted it to be. "You realized he was very valuable, so you double-crossed O'Quinn, holding the boy ransom from the man who hired you to steal him in the first place. The same man who caught and tortured you, trying to discover where you were holding him."

Kaj gritted his teeth as he felt the sting of O'Quinn's backhand, the blow that had sent his glass eye flying out of his head. Kaj envisioned watching it spin slowly atop the rusty table, then stop. It was staring at him, reflecting the horrible beating O'Quinn had inflicted upon him. A cold chill gripped him. "The bald man is a heartless narcissist."

A rush of satisfaction washed over Kaj as he remembered grabbing O'Quinn's head with one hand and shoving his cigarette into the asshole's eyeball with the other. A smirk formed on Kaj's face. "I bet he's not so pretty now."

"He's not pretty but he does have the boy." Jarod added soberly. "When we last talked, you told me Luke was the key to what O'Quinn intends to do on the 28th of October. What is O'Quinn planning?" There was no mistaking the urgency in Jarod's voice now.

Kaj squinted his eyes, slowly realizing that he did know this man after all. "I remember you—the doctor. I told you then all I know, thousands will die; after that O'Quinn will no longer need the child."

The final straw of the pressure he'd contained for so long finally snapped the camel's back and Jarod erupted, with an unmatched sense of desperation. "Why! Why does he need the boy? Did Luke see something he wasn't supposed to? Know something he shouldn't? What can a ten-year-old boy possess that would be so important to a man like O'Quinn?"

Kaj made an unembellished smile. "The boy has the love of a father who would do anything, anything at all to get him back."

Jarod froze.

It suddenly all made sense. He stared into Skylar's eyes. "We're almost out of time."

Chapter 75

NOTHING MISS PARKER encountered in the tech theatre was as anticipated.

"The economic yo-yo must be spinning back up its string if the Centre's hiring doormen now." Miss Parker greeted Cornelius, whom she found just inside, leaning on the door.

Miss Parker took a step toward Sydney and Daphne, who were seated across the room, but Cornelius halted her with a light grip on her arm. His sweaty touch felt like fingers made of oysters, but he was ready for her quick glare. He was overconfident. "What if I told you I was waiting here for you, specifically to shower you with riches."

"I'd say that you have exactly two seconds," she shot back.

"I found Jarod's hideout." Cornelius grinned. "Our Belgian friend took an off-the-books trip, to Cincinnati, to a grave, and the stealth master, *moi*, followed his wool-blended rumpled ass there." With his excitement bubbling, Cornelius's eyebrow involuntarily rippled. "There was a cell phone waiting there. He used it to call Jarod, I triangulated the call ... and *voila!*" He handed her a map of New York City, a red dot marking Jarod's location.

Parker's scowl panned over to Sydney now and, once again, her momentum to head that way got her another half-shell grab. Miss Parker did *not* like being grabbed and her look from his hand to his face told a scary tale. "If you want to keep that clammy claw, I suggest you un-grip it *now*." Cornelius swallowed, then released her.

She glared. "So you went out in the field—unauthorized?"

Cornelius felt a chill when he had been expecting warmth. "Well, yes, but I came back with the goods."

"And what if you *had* screwed the pooch?"

"But, but, but—I didn't," he stammered as he felt his victory slipping away from him, *again.*

"As far as *you* know."

Miss Parker double slapped Cornelius's cheek hard enough to make him wince. "Cornelius, have you ever *heard* the term bat-shit crazy?"

"Y-y-es."

"If you're wrong about this," she raised the map, "you're going to get an up close and personal of what it *looks* like."

Miss Parker blew around him and joined the others, landing her perfect buttocks on the edge of the table next to Daphne's laptop so she could face Sydney.

Daphne greeted her with a smile. She was comforted to again be in Miss Parker's orbit, but the gravity pulling her this time was mixed. Daphne had always been compelled toward Miss Parker's *physical* beauty, but since their shared moment at her mother's grave, she felt attracted by a different force. She saw Miss Parker in a different way now, as a perfect doll with a broken heart, a sorrowful beauty encased in an armor of strength and guile that was currently on full display.

Miss Parker grinned and smoothed Sydney's tie for him. "Got to hand it to you, Syd. Sometimes you're particularly impressive with your idiocy." Sydney didn't react—at least not in the manner Miss Parker had anticipated. He beat Parker to the punch, threw a knowing glare at Cornelius, and made her intentionally uncomfortable by putting his hand on her knee to help push himself to his feet. "It's true, I spoke with Jarod."

Parker hated the hand on her knee, but even more so, she hated when Sydney robbed her of her rage-gasms. Though she would rather die than admit it, Sydney's hopping over the turnstiles of her surprise attack flustered her. She hadn't seen it coming any more than she had seen his secret Cincinnati road trip. Hating being trumped in any fashion, she briefly wondered if a reassessment of him might be in order.

"As I have repeatedly explained, I knew Jarod would eventually reach out to me and *only* me. I've been waiting for you to arrive to tell you all about it." Sydney smiled.

She quirked an eyebrow at him. "And *why* would I believe that?"

Sydney didn't speak. He just locked his calm eyes onto her and flashed his elusive European grin. Miss Parker *hated* that grin.

It made her do stupid things. Say stupid things. After a night of reading and rereading the file about her mother's demise, she was so enraged she spoke before thinking. "Bet that's the same stupid smirk you flashed to comfort my mother when she was vulnerable on your shrink sofa, eh, Syd? When you *lied* to her?" The moment she said it, she knew she had revealed too much.

Corn and Daphne felt like stoned concertgoers rushing to the front row from their cheap seats after someone cleared the place by setting a mattress on fire.

Sydney would've loved to give the stage crashers an encore, but took the high road. "The sessions I conducted with your mother will always remain confidential, Miss Parker but I assure you I didn't lie to her then, nor am I lying to you now."

He shifted his gaze to Daphne, who nervously cleared her throat. "Sydney gave me the cell phone from Cincinnati and asked me to triangulate the call to locate Jarod."

This information caused a caution flare to explode in Parker's mind. Sydney was obviously telling the truth, but the question was *why*. Seeing this concern, Daphne spun her laptop to face Miss Parker. On it was a map of the Eastern seaboard. "I've narrowed Jarod's location down to New York. I believe he's somewhere in Manhattan."

"Let me help you *all* out. I'm *certain* Jarod is in Harlem." Cornelius flashed an overconfident smile that triggered a second warning flare in Miss Parker. She carefully, but quickly, studied Sydney. She knew never to trust anyone in the Centre; people who had sudden changes of heart had often acquired them courtesy of a transfusion of tainted blood.

Deciding Sydney wouldn't be the only one to zig when they normally zagged, Miss Parker just—laughed. "Feels like it's time we took a road trip together, Syd. Bury the hatchet in Jarod instead of each other for a change."

As she said that, she smiled at Cornelius and Daphne. "Aw what the hell, let's bring *the kids* along on this one." Daphne tingled at the unexpected invite.

And then Parker finished, "And may the fittest survive."

Chapter 76

SURVEILLANCE SUCKS.

It was miserable on the rooftop of the decrepit building. The freezing wind chilled Sweeper Pedro to the bone and caused his injured head to ache almost as badly as the other region of the frustrated newlywed's body. Both made focusing on his task increasingly difficult. He missed his Vania. With all the travel and overtime he was putting in on Jarod's pursuit, they had only shared their marital bed three times. Yet when you were a Sweeper for the man-eater in the miniskirt you learned to compartmentalize your pain—lest you wanted to receive a whole lot more. Staring through binoculars at an upper-story window of the converted warehouse across the street, he could see Jarod pacing back and forth. Each time the Pretender looked up and spoke to another unseen person in the room, Pedro felt confident his nightmare was almost over.

His boss's voice chirped in his ear. "Request visual confirmation." Sam had been Miss Parker's number one Sweeper for as long as Pedro had been at the Centre. Pedro was not a fan of his immediate superior. "Positive I.D. plus at least one other."

Sam looked to Miss Parker and the others on the assault team positioned outside the door to Jarod's loft. He nodded in the affirmative. Eyes sparkling, Miss Parker touched her Bluetooth.

"Go!"

Watching the assault team appear on the opposing rooftop made Pedro forget his various pains. In fact, as they swung down in one perfectly timed repel and crashed through Jarod's windows, Pedro smiled at a thought: *when the Pretender is captured I'll take my Vania on a real honeymoon.*

A half second after she heard the glass shattering, Miss Parker led her group into Jarod's loft. It was organized madness as the assault team and sweepers all aimed their weapons directly at the Pretender.

Jarod showed no concern whatsoever. He kept pacing, then looked up with a calm yet mischievous smile and said directly at his pursuer, "What took you so long?"

Miss Parker tasted the bile in her throat as Jarod took a few more steps, looked up again and repeated, "What took you so long?"

Sydney entered behind Miss Parker and lowered her weapon. "I don't think he can hear you." He then walked *through* Jarod, or more accurately, the hologram the Pretender had left of himself projected in the room.

Miss Parker wanted to stab kittens. "Great, your boy is now a performance artist. Soon he'll be rapping with Tupac."

Sydney caught sight of something on the ceiling and a large expressive smile formed on his face. "Not performance art—more like the work of the master."

Daphne and Cornelius entered the room and, along with Miss Parker, strained their necks to look up at what the psychiatrist was analyzing.

Spanning the entire ceiling was Jarod's vivid, color-exploding rendition of Michelangelo's *The Creation of Adam* panel from the Sistine Chapel.

In the original, Adam was depicted lying naked on his back reaching out across a chasm to the image of God, whose extended finger was nearly touching Adam's. The image of God is surrounded by many bodies and faces with one in particular, a sensual female most believe to be Eve, eyeing Adam from under God's protective arm.

Miss Parker clearly did not see it through Sydney's pride-filled glasses. In Jarod's *chef-d'oeuvre*, he had painted himself as Adam, arm extended out to God, but rather than lying on a bed of green, Jarod's Adam was lying atop the hood of a Centre Town Car with a Delaware license plate reading, *LIARS,INC.* Instead of being naked, he was dressed in a tee shirt emblazoned with; *PROPERTY OF THE CENTRE ATHLETIC DEPARTMENT,* spinning his Challenger Sim orb on the tip of his finger like a would-be LeBron James. Jarod's Adam was also wearing vivid red boxers with a repeating pattern of gold infinity symbols.

On the other side, Jarod depicted Sydney as the God figure, a rumpled houndstooth blazer instead of a flowing white garment, a long tie dangling from his neck with The Centre logo on it and the words, *The Shrink is In.* Jarod's final editorial touch was adding dangling handcuffs on Sydney's outstretched wrist.

As for Miss Parker, she was the face of Eve, who in this version, had three lit cigarettes protruding from her lips and was wearing a Centre logo baseball cap. Next to Parker, resting on Sydney's hip, was a bottle of Maker's Mark with a straw sticking out of it, mere inches from Parker/Eve's occupied mouth.

Jarod saved his most pointed comment for the remaining faces of the children surrounding God and Eve—each with the same word emblazoned across their eyes: *Stolen.*

Miss Parker looked disdainfully at her amused counterpart. "Wipe the grin, Sydney, I've scrawled wittier doodles sitting in a Centre stall."

She'd spotted something else and was already moving to the kitchen area. There the refrigerator door was covered in colorful children's magnets, made up of numbers, letters and symbols, several of which had been assembled into an elaborate math equation.

She snapped her fingers at her blonde protégé. "Daphne, slap your Euclidian super computer on this one."

Daphne joined her, studying the mathematical puzzle. "I'm afraid Euclid can't help this time. This isn't geometry—it's physics."

As Daphne began taking pictures with her iPhone, Cornelius muscled in his eyes on the magnets. "*Quantum* physics to be exact." Cornelius threw a grin over at Blondie that had *I got this one* spewed all over it. "Luckily, that was one of my several minors in college."

Miss Parker gave him a dubious look. "Is that right?"

Corn Man, never one to let something as insignificant as honesty get in the way of personal gain, gave his boss a cocky chuckle—"I assure you I'll have Jarod's little Rubik's Cube solved in no time."

Miss Parker wasn't chuckling. "You *assured* me the bastard would be here."

"Well, he obviously *was* here." Cornelius tossed a panicked look to Daphne. "Which means I've gotten you closer to him than anyone else."

"Close only counts in tiddlywinks and thermo-nuclear war. Now pack up your eyebrow pencil and get out of my life."

Cornelius's brow began to quiver. "But Miss Parker—wha … wha … what does that mean?"

"That when you get back to Blue Cove there'll be someone *new* in your chair." Miss Parker looked away from Cornelius, locked eyes with Daphne and pointed to the problem on the fridge. "I want answers."

"And answers you will have." Daphne replied with confidence.

Sydney's voice rang out from above. "Parker!"

Miss Parker looked up to where a deeply concerned Sydney was standing on the top step of the loft. "Jarod has left us another body."

Chapter 77

THE *BODY* WAS Kaj.

Sydney stood in front of the barber chair the sedated terrorist was lying in. The Libyan was fully covered to his shoulders with a blanket, on his head he wore a surgical cap and was connected to all necessary forms of life support.

While Sydney studied him, Miss Parker kept her distance. Though she would never admit it, Jarod's body drops—first with Bilson, and now Kaj—were starting to creep her out. Truth be told, she was far more comfortable finding dead ones than living. They didn't talk back.

Sydney mumbled his annoying "Um, hum." She hated his *Um, hum's*. They always meant he'd made a discovery. "What is it this time, Vespucci?"

"See for yourself." Her eyes followed his finger down a single line drawn with surgical pencil that originated under Kaj's cap, traveled behind his ear, down the side of his neck and then vanished again under Kaj's blanket. Sydney looked up and met her eyes.

"A hand, please."

Miss Parker reluctantly walked over as Sydney gingerly removed Kaj's surgical cap. Her eyes were drawn not only to the Libyan's completely shaved head, but also the stitches that now encircled it. "A picture may be worth a thousand words, but I'm a few conjunctions short of understanding this one." Miss Parker locked eyes with Sydney, hoping for explanation.

He examined the terrorist's scalp. "The incisions are neurosurgical, as are the tools on the tray. The long ones are deep brain probes."

Miss Parker looked at the blood drops on the floor under the head of the barber chair and then to Sydney. "You're saying Jarod opened this mope's hood and took a poke around inside?"

"It would appear so."

Miss Parker had finally seen it all. "I was wrong, Sydney, I thought *you* were Doctor Frankenstein, when all along it was *your little monster.*"

"Jarod is *not* a monster," he said protectively, even though his own mind was spinning now. "There must have been something he needed to find."

She smiled sarcastically. "Oh, and what do you think that was, Syd?"

As Sydney gently examined the back of Kaj's skull, his mouth dropped opened. "Apparently, he was searching for what we all are."

Miss Parker moved over so she could see. When she did, she shook her head, realizing she hadn't seen it all, after all.

The sutures on the patient's scalp spelled out the word *truth.*

Below them was the origin of the surgical pencil mark that they then followed down. Miss Parker tore back Kaj's covers to reveal the line ended in an arrow pointing at a broken heart hand-drawn over Kaj's real one. On one side of the heart was the name *Sydney;* on the other side, *Little Miss.*

They shared an unsettling look.

"Apparently, *truth* leads to a broken heart, for both of us," Sydney said without surprise to Jarod's crypticness.

Miss Parker waved off another round of psychoanalysis. Between *creation* on the ceiling, *equation* on the door of the refrigerator, and *truth* on Kaj's scalp, her ever simmering headache was starting to boil.

Chapter 78

THE GRIZZLED CONSTRUCTION worker stumbled out of Landsbury's Tavern on 52nd Street with a snoot full of Old Bushmill's and PBR chasers. Just like with every one of those after-shift outings, he squinted out across the Harbor at Ellis Island to say a silent prayer for his grandparents who came through those historic grounds from the old country. But no amount of spirits and nary a one of those prayers ever produced the vision he found himself staring at on this pre-dawn morning.

Hovering above a rake barge dry-docked at Pier 53, were three glowing disks. They were silently chasing each other round and round. He'd seen a lot in his days: a man cutting his own hand off with a wedge saw, a co-worker losing an eye with a nail gun, even a murder or two, but never one of them *goddamned UFOs*, let alone three. And, while a native Brooklynite like himself would never turn away from a good old-fashioned fight, a *goddamned UFO* was clearly another matter. In fact, it was just enough to get his ass fired should he so much as speak a word of it. So, he shortened his Ellis prayer and hustled the other way, leaving the wonders of the universe to greater minds.

Like Jarod's.

Technically, they were *unidentified* flying objects, they just weren't UFOs in the *traditional sense*. They were an experiment of Jarod's, a demonstration in Quantum Levitation that had him moving and shifting like some kind of a hi-tech plate spinner, commanding the disks to seemingly defying the laws of gravity.

Looking on through sleepy eyes, Chaz, Skylar and Oscar had no clue what Jarod was up to. They had been awoken by the commotion on the roof of their new hideout, only to find Jarod concentrating intently on his orbs. He hadn't had time to explain he was experimenting with liquid nitrogen-cooled surfaces to ensure the superconductivity necessary to create magnetic levitation.

So they just sat and watched, happily ignorant of and fascinated by the Pretender's process. Trouble was, Jarod wasn't smiling. He was seeing something far different in his light show, displeased by the response time of the orbs floating back down when the nitrogen shut down. Without a word, Jarod gathered up the orbs and headed back to the drawing board below deck.

The show suddenly over, Chaz, Skylar and Oscar found themselves alone in the dark as the sunrise began peeking up over Manhattan, too awake now to resume any kind of restful sleep.

Sleep for Jarod wasn't an option either. He was too busy beating himself up over his latest failure and listening to Sydney's words ringing in his ears. *Concentrate, Jarod, don't let your emotions get in the way of your reasoning.* Yet that was exactly what he had let happen.

The answer as to *why Luke* had been in front of his face the whole time, but he'd been too blind to realize it.

Jarod pulled out his iPad and, again, played the Christmas morning videotape Cassandra Hearns had posted on Facebook: Luke and his father sitting under the tree playing with his new present, a toy train zooming along over the tracks. Unlike every time he'd previously watched it, Jarod caught himself *before* he got swept up in the emotion of that family moment he so desperately wanted to feel for himself.

This time, he remained focused as Roger explained to Luke that it wasn't just any toy train, but an exact scale replica of a Maglev bullet train of the future. *Just like the ones Roger Hearns works with in real life,* Jarod thought.

Roger placed his thumb and forefinger onto the train's acceleration control, then looked at Luke with an anticipatory grin. "Now, watch the magic."

Luke watched intently as the train sped up, going faster and faster until the wheels lifted off the tracks, the Maglev now *floating above them.*

Luke turned and looked at his father with amazement. "It's flying!"

Jarod froze the frame and stared at the train. *Flying indeed.*

Chapter 79

ULCERATIVE COLITIS AFFECTS only the colon and rectum, and since Miss Parker had thrown him out of Jarod's lair in Harlem, all six feet of that twisted exclamation point inside of Cornelius was on fire.

Especially the period at the end.

The acute onset of the cramps, diarrhea and bleeding had erupted the instant Miss Parker left him in Jarod's kitchenette. As he made his way out of the bathroom stall and performed his 187-second hand-sanitization ritual, he could still feel the cold of Miss Parker's final look. It was incomprehensible to him that somehow his pathway to the Elysian Fields of intellectual superiority had been blocked by people with the collective brainpower of a basset hound. Now he had to figure out a way to get his first class ticket to his destiny reinstated, post haste.

Keeping his chin up, Cornelius returned to the—no, to *his* tech theatre. Along the way, he had convinced himself that he could salvage his career by getting the PTBs to realize he would be much more valuable in his position than anyone they could possibly replace him with. Upon entering, that fantasy was quickly shattered as well, when he saw a bald man sitting in *his* chair—at *his* command terminal—*typing on his computer!*

Had that piranha Parker already chewed him up and spit him out? *Replacing him with that little tech worm bastard from the past?* Though he was sure he had none left inside, Cornelius knew the shit was about to hit the fan, because he was going to throw it!

He hissed in shocked disbelief. "Of all the assholes in the world, I can't believe that bitch brought *you* back!"

The figure whose back was to the approaching Cornelius didn't react in the slightest, so when he could reach it, Cornelius grabbed the top of his rolling swivel chair and yanked it around, forcing the intruder to face him. "Hey, I'm talking to you, bitch boy!"

Cornelius's body jerked and his brain glitched when he computed the face he was staring into did not belong to the young man he expected. The ancient creature before him barely resembled a man at all. Certainly, not one who was *alive*. The aura was macabre: purple lips, a deathly white pallor and heterochromatic eyes—one iris blue, the other black.

"Mr. Zane?"

"Cornelius, we finally meet." Zane gave a reptilian smile. "I've been watching you ... from afar."

Cornman couldn't speak, was pretty sure he had nodded, but was definitely mute. He tried clearing his throat, but it wouldn't comply. So through phlegm, or was it bile, he said, "Mr. Z—holy shit, even Miss Parker is afraid of you." He said that to himself. What he mumbled in a hoarse whisper was "What are you doing here, sir?"

"Righting wrongs from the past." With that, Zane stood, glanced back at the computer and started slowly out of the room.

Cornelius stared at the screen, then sat like gravity had grabbed his ass. Before him was the official Mensa archive dating back to 1987. He couldn't believe his eyes. In full living color were the names of the top three Mensa awards for 1987. Cornelius was no longer listed as number 3; he was now officially number 2. Zane had somehow partially righted that most egregious wrong.

"One day, you may actually get the gold medal you rightfully deserve." Mr. Zane stopped at the doorway, looked back at Cornelius and, in his mesmerizing voice, added, "Yet, not all of us get to top podium the way we think we will."

Chapter 80

JAROD'S CELL PHONE clock read 4:00 p.m.

Cassie Hearns' face tugged at Jarod's heart as he watched her pull out of her driveway for her visit to the Tourne River, to the site of where her husband's car had plunged into the water, to where she placed flowers daily into the swirling water she feared had washed her son away forever.

It took every fiber in his body not to stop her, to tell her not to give up, that her son was still alive.

His cell alarm echoed in the empty kitchen of the vacant house next to the Hearns' residence. He'd noticed the *For Sale* sign when he checked in on Cassie a few weeks prior and immediately began using it for surveillance.

Jarod looked out the window onto the Hearns' patio where Roger paced around a table next to the pool stealing anxious stares at his cell phone laying on the glass top. Suddenly, Jarod's personalized ringtone, Johnny Boy Creed singing Robert Johnson's *Cross Road Blues,* sounded. At the same instant, Jarod watched Roger freeze and shoot a look at his own cell phone now vibrating on the table. He nervously picked it up. As Roger answered, Jarod did the same on his phone tapping into Roger's call, hoping it'd be the one he'd been waiting for. "Tomorrow," said the voice Jarod recognized as O'Quinn's.

"I want to talk to my son," Roger shouted.

"You'll see the boy there," O'Quinn countered.

"No! I'm not coming unless I get to talk to him *now*," Roger shot back. "That was the deal!"

Jarod watched Roger stop in his tracks, wondering in those seconds of silence on O'Quinn's end if his resolved stance had worked or not.

"Dad? Dad?"

Roger crumbled into the patio chair. "Luke—are you okay?"

Luke's sobs answered back. He was then replaced by O'Quinn. "Mr. Hearns. You know where to be and by when." The line went dead.

As Roger gunned his rental Ford Fusion out of his garage, the last thing he was expecting was Jarod's sedan blocking the driveway exit, but it did not deter him. Roger jerked his car hard left, through his wife's immaculate shrubs, across the neighbor's *For Sale* sign as he made his way back onto the pavement.

Jarod nimbly pulled a dead stop spin and gunned his ride in pursuit of Roger.

Before long they found themselves in the sparse Jersey countryside. Jarod thought he saw Roger glance to his right just as the Morristown Green Line Express edged into view running parallel to their two-lane frontage road. A split second later as Jarod closed the gap, Roger slammed on the brakes.

Jarod stood hard on his—tires smoking.

When the dust cleared, Roger was well in the distance nearing the rail crossing.

Jarod slammed his sedan into gear and peeled out. He watched the train, its angle to the road rapidly narrowing. They were both approaching the crossing on a collision course.

Roger hit the tracks and flew through the air as the gates started down.

Jarod gunned his motor—if he missed beating the train, Roger would be gone and virtually all hope of saving Luke would be lost.

His eyes shot around; train—crossing—road, train—crossing—road—his mind literally calculating and recalculating by the millisecond—speed—distance—angle, speed—distance angle. Fifty feet and closing—horn blaring—Jarod's eyes widened—foot mashing the gas pedal until . . .

Jarod lurched, obliterated the crossing gate and went airborne just as the train blared by behind him.

The sedan slammed back to earth, and Jarod gunned it toward his target.

Roger couldn't evade the hit when his Ford was slammed from behind, spinning it 180 degrees, forcing it to crash rear first into a ditch. Before he could climb out from behind the inflated airbag, Jarod was at his side, lifting him out of the seat.

"You son of a bitch!" Roger screamed as Jarod pressed him into the car hood. "What kind of a cop are you?"

"I'm not a cop, Roger. Not when I first came to your house all those weeks ago and certainly not now."

Roger began to unravel like a trapped animal. "Who the hell are you?" There was a void of resounding silence, until Roger Hearns began to cry.

"I'm someone who wants to save your son's life—and I'm going to need your help to do it." Roger looked blindsided, as Jarod's unexpected words sunk in. While his mind raced, Roger could see something in this man's eyes, in his tone of voice that disarmed him, that fostered an unexplainable feeling of trust toward Jarod.

The Pretender quietly continued, "I was stolen from my family as a child. All that matters right now is getting your son back, the one thing *my* parents were never able to do for me." Jarod felt Hearns relax and saw a glimmer of hope in his eyes. "Roger, I know O'Quinn has him and what you've been going through, and I know it's about a Maglev train whose safety protocols you designed. The only thing I don't know is which one. Shanghai? Munich? Aichi? Seoul?"

"It's not that simple." Roger wiped his tears on his sleeve. "O'Quinn said that if I don't carry out his plan, Luke *will* die." Roger spoke softly, as if whispering the words would make them less devastating. "Still, a two thousand ton train moving in excess of 400 mph? The kinetic energy released when it crashes ..."

"... Would be like a nuclear weapon," Jarod finished, knowingly.

"I'd do anything to bring my boy home." Jarod wondered if *his* father had uttered those same words. And, in that moment, he loved this man.

Jarod gazed firmly into Roger's eyes. "If the only way to save Luke is to crash a train—then we'll crash a train."

Chapter 81

SKYLAR, CHAZ AND Oscar were all shivering from the chill within the barge lair, but Jarod was oblivious to it. Using an industrial sewing machine, surrounded by yards of colorful carbon fiber Mylar, Kevlar and Nomex thread, Jarod was in one of his hyper-focused states.

Having nearly bested O'Quinn at Guardian General and again on Isla Raton, Jarod was certain O'Quinn would be prepared for him. This problem had been vexing Jarod since he'd been with Roger. Knowing he couldn't take the risk of being stopped at the train station, how was he to get aboard a bullet train going hundreds of miles per hour without being spotted?

The answer came to him while he napped. Jarod had learned much about the power of the mind in dream states. Throughout his youth, Sydney often repeated a quote from Jung on the subject, "Your vision will become clear when you look into your heart. Who looks outside, dreams. Who looks inside, awakens."

Jarod had dreamed of Onyssius.

Chapter 82

DAPHNE LEANED DOWN next to Miss Parker and adjusted the image on her laptop of the refrigerator magnets Jarod had left in the Harlem loft. "The formula, $F = qE + qv \times B$, is a law of physics that says the force on a charge moving through a field is a product of velocity, charge and magnetic strength."

Miss Parker looked up at Daphne like she was speaking Swahili. Daphne felt faint. Being in Miss Parker's executive suite for the first time, not to mention the North Tower of the Centre, was intense. It didn't matter to her that Sydney was there, too. With Cornelius now out of the picture, Daphne had Miss Parker's full attention and growing trust.

Miss Parker stopped her scientific ramblings with a raised hand. "I don't need to know how Big Ben was built, I just want to know what time it is."

Daphne liked that Miss Parker wanted control. "The formula is considered the root understanding of electromagnetic levitation."

Miss Parker pointed at the magnets and stared at Sydney. "What the hell's he saying, leaving that?"

Sydney shrugged, genuinely baffled. "I have no idea."

"Neither did I," added Daphne. "Until I realized that wasn't Jarod's entire message." Daphne magnified the lower half of the screen. "I studied the other letters Jarod left and discovered that, when unscrambled, they formed these words." She hit a few keys. On the screen, the jumbled letters arranged themselves into a sentence in Latin: '*Rotarum sunt in ultimo saeculo.*'

Miss Parker gazed at Sydney. "Seeing as you're the puppeteer who taught Pinocchio the ancient tongue, how 'bout you cough up the translation for us mere mortals?"

Sydney tilted his head at the letters, "It says, *Wheels are so … last century.*"

Annoyed, Miss Parker just shook her head, "Greeeeeat, so his message is about a magic carpet ride?"

"Actually, sort of, yes." Daphne hit a few more keys. "I think he is talking about one of these." Images of Maglev trains from around the world sprang up on several split screens. "There are only four trains on the planet currently operating on magnetic levitation systems. Three in Asia and one in Germany."

Miss Parker saw Sydney's silent agreement with Daphne's assessment, then looked back to the increasingly impressive blonde.

"I don't suspect boy wonder left us a bread trail to lead us to which one?"

"*He* didn't—but someone else just may have." Miss Parker looked confused, just as Daphne had anticipated. Her hands flew over the keyboard. "Assuming Jarod is still after what O'Quinn has and that your GPS beacon is still on his eye-patch …" She pressed *enter* and smiled. "I thought I'd let the bald man himself lead us where we need to be."

Miss Parker and Sydney stared at a blip on the screen indicating O'Quinn's location was currently in the Garden State itself.

"Jersey? You said there were only four of these trains on the planet. All overseas."

"I said *currently operating*. The fifth is an American prototype, supposedly the fastest in the world, that has its inaugural run from Atlantic City to Newark, *tomorrow morning*. It will be full of dignitaries from around the world."

Chapter 83

AS HE WALKED, O'Quinn mopped up the ooze dripping from under his eye patch with a handkerchief and looked around the gathering crowd filled with dignitaries and officials, a cool look covering the intensity he was feeling. It wasn't the impending death of hundreds of innocent people O'Quinn was thinking about as he led Roger Hearns down the steps of the Maglev train platform. The blood of thousands had dried under his fingernails far too long ago to keep him up at night now. No, he was thinking about getting the job done and done right.

This job had been fraught with obstacles and screw-ups, so much, O'Quinn felt obligated to finish the job under the adage of—*if you want something done right, you do it yourself.*

Kaj had screwed him.

Bilson had screwed him.

That woman, Parker, was a wild card.

And this Jarod son of a bitch was starting to unnerve him. He was an element outside of O'Quinn's control and experience; and for O'Quinn, whether he was killing one or a thousand, *control* meant everything.

Roger couldn't allow himself to think about the lives hanging in the balance or how he had placed his trust in the hands of this stranger named Jarod. Roger's solace in all this was that he trusted his own instincts, and his instincts had told him Jarod was a man of his word and yet …

"I want to see Luke, now. You said …"

"I said, *I would let you see the boy when I let you see the boy,*" O'Quinn's tone, calm, quiet but intense. Roger knew O'Quinn's demeanor all too well by this point and did not issue a rebuttal. He just stared at the disgusting man pulling his eye patch from his face and wiping away something horrible Roger wished he had not seen.

The bald warrior snapped the patch back in place as they stepped up to the metal detector at the check-in security area. As one of the lead men on the OmniCorp Maglev project, Roger Hearns knew his security access was no problem and wasn't wasting a single brain cell about O'Quinn's clearance.

All that mattered to Roger at this juncture was getting onboard, getting the job done, then waiting at the front door to see the smile on his wife's face when she opened it and saw her son on the other side.

Daphne typed frantically, but her frustrated expression showed it was to no avail. She looked at a motionless red blip on the laptop as she voiced her confusion into a speakerphone. "It doesn't make sense, Miss Parker. According to this, O'Quinn is 30 feet southwest of you."

Miss Parker peered from around a large column at the top of the platform stairway to where Daphne indicated the bald man should be: a metal detector where a female TSA guard was wanding a short fat woman. "Well, unless he's had his junk cut off and he's shrunk a foot, he's not there anymore."

"The nano-tracker must have fallen from his patch. It hasn't moved for the last 45 minutes."

Miss Parker hung up, then looked over to what she knew in her gut had been O'Quinn's destination all along; 20 yards beyond the security gate stood the ten-car Maglev test train, the Garden State Lighting Bolt.

With what appeared to be locomotive cars at each end and eight passenger carriages in between, the ultra-modern, aerodynamically sleek land rocket looked like a two-headed viper that could strike just as quickly in either direction.

But the locomotive heads were not what they appeared. Depending on the train's direction, they were merely electronic brains controlling the power source of the Maglev's magnetic propulsion. A source that, unlike in traditional trains, wasn't located in the lead vehicle, but underneath every car. The *Lightning Bolt's* aggressive look mirrored that of Miss Parker's as she calmly reassessed her strategy.

Beside her, an antsy Sydney shifted his weight from foot to foot. When a near silent whir of power began emanating from the train, followed by a purposely old fashioned, "All aboard," he took a step out and looked back at her saying, "We have to go now!"

Miss Parker snatched his arm and through clenched teeth hissed, "Not yet!"

Her eyes scoured the jam-packed throng. A pang in her gut was screaming that there were predators among the multitudes and that she was among their prey. She understood that if Emtrex was a competitor of the Centre, they had to be good and, if O'Quinn had survived long enough to lose his hair and an eye in service to it, he had to be damn fearless as well. He may not be as shrewd as she, but he was definitely a worthy adversary and as such Miss Parker was certain he'd have people watching his back while targeting Jarod's and *hers*.

She examined their faces and mannerisms, searching for any nuanced facet that would indicate that they were not who they appeared.

It was the young Jersey Transportation Department worker's thumb that gave him away. His jeans, muddy worn work boots, fleece-lined jacket and battered hardhat were straight out of the state's highway ditches but his manicured nails weren't, in particular, the thumb scrolling through images on his cell phone.

From her angle, Miss Parker couldn't see that they were surveillance photographs: of Jarod as a surgeon and an albino orderly at Guardian General Hospital, as a mercenary pilot on Isla Raton, or images of Parker herself on the hospital rooftop or entering the Emtrex complex. But her Sweeper, Pedro, could.

Two seconds after spotting *Transpo Guy's* metrosexual thumb, Miss Parker barked in Pedro's ear and the Portuguese sweeper shoved his .40 caliber into *Transpo Guy's* ribs and escorted him off the game board.

Miss Parker and Sydney were joined by Sam, reporting in on the results of the operation. "We think he was the last, Miss Parker, but we're not positive." Hearing this, Parker calculated her odds had just gone up. She knew she wouldn't be able to get anyone but herself and Sydney onboard but hoped this had at least stopped O'Quinn from being tipped off.

Sam handed her a small package. "Non-metallic. Won't set off the detector." She slipped Sam her Smith & Wesson and was tucking the packet into her waistband as *ooohs* and *ahhhs* suddenly arose from the crowd. Miss Parker and Sydney turned and watched as the two thousand ton train began levitating above the rails.

Parker nudged Sydney. "Step lively, Uncle Joe, we don't want to miss the Hooterville Cannonball." She lead him through the security checkpoint and onto the 9th car of the soon-to-be speeding bullet. To her left was a door with a sign on its window, reading: *Authorized Personnel Only*. Beyond it was a passageway compartment, inside of which a two-ton ape of a guard stood at the door at the rear locomotive car. He looked up and made eye contact with Miss Parker, just as the *Lightning Bolt* shook slightly and began to pull out of the station. She turned to her right, where eight compartments worth of teeming passengers let out cheers, then, chatting animatedly and reveling in the piece of history they were about to share, began snapping posterity selfies.

With Sydney trailing behind her like a lost puppy, Miss Parker strolled through the space-chic interior that Sir Richard Branson could have designed himself. Scanning every face on both sides of the aisle, she made her way through car #9 and into #8. In the class structure of the multinational corporation that had built this ride, the higher on the totem players were, the closer to the lead car they would be. Up there is where she suspected she'd find O'Quinn, and most importantly, Jarod.

Chapter 84

ROGER SAT AT the driver's keyboard, fighting to suppress the burning fuse that had his heart racing, his mind throbbing and his body seeping sweat. Just when he needed to be his coolest calmest self, Roger was collapsing under the emotional weight of the last several weeks with anxiety that had only been complicated by a stranger with a strange plan.

Where the hell is Jarod?! This mystery man who forced his way into my life, claiming to be Luke's savior? Promising to save my son by going through with O'Quinn's scheme?

Roger felt like he was sitting on broken glass. He looked over at the bald man talking into his cell, the sight of which took him back to the previous Halloween. Luke had dressed up as the eye-patched character from *The Avengers*, Nick Fury. Cassie had said no to *The Hulk*, Luke's first choice, for fear of head-to-toe green body paint all over the house, but Luke compromised and agreed that a patch and leather jacket constituted a 'cool enough' costume. Roger remembered Luke asking, 'Is Nick Fury a good guy or a bad guy, Dad?' Roger was wondering the same about himself, shocked by what he'd discovered he was capable of when those he loved most were threatened.

He realized it would be Halloween again in a few days, and allowed himself the thought that he and Cassie would have Luke back with them. If so, at what price? And could he live with himself for paying it? Roger stared out the windshield, watched the world rush by and prayed that good would somehow win out. His racing thoughts then shifted back to the man who had come up with this insane plan.

Jarod, where the hell are you?

Chapter 85

IT WASN'T THE rush of cold air swirling around his body, nor the jolt of hot adrenaline churning between his ears that alarmed Jarod's most basic instincts. No, as he slid the door open on the Cessna 182, it was a survival warning from a primal space deep within his mind. When he looked down to the earth from 9000 feet, his brain started screaming—*Get away from the door!* Instead he sat, legs dangling out.

His mental clock told him he had only ten seconds to go when he turned to a voice behind him. Skylar gave a shake of her head and shouted. "You know you're crazy, right?"

Securing his rubber-tipped gloves, Jarod grinned, "That's what they say about all high functioning sociopaths."

"*And* madmen," she countered.

In many ways, that's how Jarod appeared. Head to toe in a bizarre out-fit of blues and golds, Jarod looked like something concocted out of Stan Lee's noggin. Despite her anxieties, she kissed him. With the sun glowing on her face and the wind rushing through her hair, Jarod felt Skylar looked as beautiful as any woman could.

The last thing he saw as he jumped was Skylar's smile. A good omen he thought, though one that was delivering him into what could very well be his final minutes of life.

After all, Jarod wasn't wearing a parachute.

Chapter 86

THE MOMENT SHE stepped into car #7 Miss Parker felt a chill go up her spine. It wasn't from fear or anything bad happening to any of the oblivious people zooming along at 300 mph. It was more premonitory. She had the overwhelming feeling that, when this journey was over, not all those exiting would be doing so with smiles.

Throughout her lifetime, Miss Parker experienced these feelings. It was at age four when she first told her mother she *sensed* something might happen. Her mother had given these sensations within her a name—her *inner sense*—and encouraged her to listen to them. Stepping into car #6, one full of mid-level corporate types with smug grins on their faces, Parker's *inner sense* whispered that Jarod was near, or soon would be.

Chapter 87

SKYLAR WAS RIGHT, this was madness, *calculated madness,* and Jarod loved every second of it. Flying a plane had been liberating, but plunging head first toward the earth nearly two miles beneath him, arms tucked in tight to prevent drag, he was defying death, and never felt more alive.

But he had a job to do so he quelled the rush. He memory locked this joy for another day and got down to business.

It's serious time. Thinking, feeling, breathing.

Even though his landing target had yet to come into view below, he arched his muscled body against the wind, correcting his positioning with the slightest movement of his right hand to stay on course. It was all about glide ratio now, lift versus drag—and timing.

The timing had to be *perfect* or his landing would be *deadly*.

He was flying downwind with an average speed he could control with body pitch alone at somewhere between 100 and 160 miles per hour. With every second of this journey, his brain was in constant calculate/recalculate mode. His plan consisted of a steep approach and last minute flatten out above on his ultimate target; the surface of the Maglev train's roof. Jarod was nearly certain the train's forward motion would work to his advantage, that with the perfectly timed and executed plane-out, he could touch down atop the train at a not-too-variant speed as his landing target would be moving at more than *300 mph.*

Nearly certain.

Jarod's eyes scanned the New Jersey countryside rushing up to him with each passing second. As expected, he could not see the speeding bullet yet. It was still well behind him. *Just trust the math* he thought. And trusting in it he was.

Still, there had not been time for a test jump or much research. At 6000 feet the thought of those who died attempting similar chute-less landings pricked his mind, but he dismissed it. It was time to make his first big maneuver. If it didn't work, well, he'd be lucky to even be conscious for the fate awaiting him below.

Jarod spread his arms and legs. The pain in his shoulders and hips exploded as the nylon foils between his extremities popped full of air, arresting his acceleration, transforming Jarod from an incoming missile into a man with wings—an *Icarus* who hoped his flight was not too close to the sun, an *Onyssius* who had a mission to accomplish below.

Adjusting the foils to flatten out and slow his descent, Jarod became one with the wind. Soaring free, he understood how blessed eagles were to experience this magnificence every day, the silence majestic, the view endless. Jarod looked below and far behind him to his right. There, a glistening silver streak slicing across the farmland, was the Garden State Lightning Bolt.

Jarod felt confident now his plan and the math were working until a tear suddenly ripped in the wing pocket under his left arm and all hell broke loose.

Jarod's body flipped upside-down and jerked sideways. He tumbled violently end over end, lost sight of the horizon and became buried in a spatial disorientation he was desperate to correct.

4000 feet and dropping ...

Kicking his legs as wide as he could and lifting his head, Jarod righted the end over end, but not the side-roll.

3000 feet and swirling in a whirlpool of air, he told himself to *think! What did it say in the Complete Idiots Guide To Flying about arresting control?* A word cloud emerged in his photographic memory: *adverse yaw ... pitching to wings level ... coordinated aileron and rudder pressures ... same direction as roll.*

Jarod commanded himself—*do that with your body*, and reacted instanta-neously. He pulled the torn side of his left arm flap in tighter to his torso and thrust his right arm out to the maximum.

2500 feet. Not working ...

As quickly as one could write the symbol for Pi, the equation had changed—the math key erased—recalculate, literally on the fly ...

At 2000 feet, he was little more than an assassin's errant bullet tum-bling toward a disintegrating rendezvous with asphalt, so Jarod switched to physics to save him. With all his wearying might, Jarod pulled his extremi-ties in close and morphed from wayward projectile by curling himself into a cannonball flying straight through the air.

The Maglev loomed larger behind and below him. At 1500 feet, like a tacking sail, Jarod thrust his legs and arms back out to their full extent.

The wind took hold and flipped Jarod upright. He tucked in his knees for a second to hold the position, then flatten out. Flying right now, sensing the train closing in behind him, he dove straight down to pick up speed for his final descent plane-out. *Tray tables up, fasten your belts, it's got the makings of a bumpy landing.*

1000 feet. He kept his dive steep, intuited that with the tumbling above he needed to make up time. Arrive at the landing site too late, or too soon, he'd be dead. In the midst of this high speed madness, Jarod's brain flashed to a children's story he once read, and the random thought, *this Goldilocks desperately needs a landing that is just right.* Jarod aligned his body with the tracks below.

At 600 feet he could hear the whispering whir of the train behind him. At 400 feet, he made a quick glance back and down, careful not to veer himself out of alignment. He saw the train. 300 feet, it was all or nothing. *Math, don't fail me now.*

200 feet. He planed out, flattened his arch, and slowed his air speed drastically. *Too quick? Too slow?* This was it—and with the ground racing up at him, he stretched out with every fiber—planed out—100 feet—where's the train? ...

The Maglev raced below him and, in that instant, Jarod's body slid belly first right onto the train surface.

Jarod lifted his head against the G-forces to get his bearings, seeing that he had landed on the crease between the 5th and 6th train car, some 410 feet from his intended target, the roof of the locomotive control car. He would have to crawl to his destination without being blown off and he had less than three minutes to get there.

With his free fall behind him, Jarod breathed a sigh of relief and had an ironic thought: *Now things are about to get dangerous.*

Jarod was right.

He began to slide off.

Chapter 88

MISS PARKER FROZE. She sensed that her prey was near, but little did she imagine that Jarod was only *30 inches* away on the roof above her. She was far too preoccupied fighting to banish from her mind the feelings he'd awakened in her soul. *Goddamn Jarod, his Etch A Sketches, his riddles and his games!* She had come to believe that Jarod, just as her father had warned, had earwigged her by stirring her emotions. Her rational mind and emotional heart were in a cage match that was crumbling the outer protective shell that held in her inner sense.

Screw Jarod and his manipulative bullshit! I will not let that bastard win. Deep down, she felt the only way she'd ever exorcise herself of this demon was to kill Jarod before whatever he was doing *killed* her. Resolved to doing just that, she flung open the door to car #5 and resumed her hunt.

Trailing behind, Sydney felt goose bumps as well, but his were not caused by some ill-defined foresight. He was terrified. The science of fear was one Sydney had studied his entire life. He wished he had brought a paper bag in case he started hyperventilating. Yet, for the first time he knew what triggered his nervous reaction and it was not about preservation of self. The *fight or flight* response was not personal—if it had been, Sydney would have chosen *flight*. Today's goose bumps were about Jarod and, today, he would *fight*.

Jarod clawed frantically for grip atop the speeding Maglev, thinking two things: This was a battle he couldn't win for long and he was in this predicament because he had let feelings get in the way of his plan. Jarod had prepared for all contingencies, but had been so lost in the joy of Skylar's smile as he jumped from the Cessna that he had neglected to execute one of them.

The Lightning Bolt's skin was covered in an ultra-thin, hi-tech coating, 100 times thinner than a human hair, making it much more aerodynamic and, as a result, damn slippery.

With stop and start jerks, the rubber of his gloved fingertips and boots caught and released, each time inching him toward the edge. If he released one of his hands, he was sure he would be swept off. He computed he had one way to do what he needed to and one way only.

Slipping further, Jarod turned his head, tilted his chin down to his chest and with his mouth strained to catch the tip of the flapping wing-suit collar. As he maneuvered to grasp it, the purple strip smacked his cheeks and lips in rapid-fire bullwhip fashion. Heading over the edge, he made a final grasp at the collar, this time catching it between his teeth. He bit down hard onto the switch sewn into it and the electro-magnets in his gloves and boots he was supposed to have activated during free fall came to life, locking his hands and feet onto the train roof.

He didn't have time to breathe a sigh of relief. He was way behind schedule, and it was time to crawl.

Chapter 89

STARING OUT OF the windshield, watching the countryside blur past, O'Quinn had a pleasant realization: His rotten eye had stopped throbbing. In fact, he wasn't feeling any of the typical aches and pains of a man his age or stress levels. He smiled knowing his endorphins were finally kicking in. These highs—danger, intrigue and victory—were what got him out of bed every morning. O'Quinn was already cranking, and the exciting shit hadn't even started yet. Enjoying the rush, he leaned back and raised his feet onto the dash. Looking out, he thought he saw a glint in the sky. He couldn't tell how far off it was and, while realizing that, he had another epiphany: He would never again have the depth perception to tell and he didn't care. *It's all going to work now. It was all worth it. I can retire off of this one, get the eye fixed, take the chubby wife and kid on a vacation—or better yet, the girlfriend.* He stood and turned to Roger, who was seated at the computer controls, his hands hovering above the keys but his focus at the door to the locomotive's rear compartment. Hearns expected it would have flown open before now and he was getting anxious.

Roger hadn't heard O'Quinn walk up behind him, but he felt the bald bastard's Kung Fu grip as it clamped onto the back of his neck and twisted his face toward that stinking eye-patch. "Showtime."

He jerked out of his hold. "Don't touch me!" Roger caught himself and, realizing that relative civility to O'Quinn was one of the only things between his son's life or death, changed his tone. "I miss one keystroke and it's all over."

"Miss a stroke and you and your son will not leave this train when I do."

"Why should I believe you?" Roger questioned. "How do I know that everything you've said about me and Luke getting off this train hasn't been a lie?"

O'Quinn looked back out of the windshield and pointed. "Because of *that*." Roger turned to look. The glint in the sky was closer now and even a terrified father could tell it was a helicopter coming their way. And not just any helicopter, but a Eurocopter X3, modified to be the fastest in the world. *This lunatic O'Quinn's got it all figured out, I'll give him that,* Roger thought.

He then turned back to the keyboard, his fingers still twitching as they hovered over the keys. Roger took a deep breath and began typing the codes that would put ultimate control of the train in O'Quinn's hands.

Chapter 90

WITH THREE MORE cars to crawl over, Jarod could smell the adrenaline in his sweat. The only other roller coaster he had ridden had ups and downs and twists and turns, but most importantly a safe and happy ending. Unfortunately, on this Cyclone he was riding, nothing was guaranteed. Especially now.

Not only was he behind schedule but, according to plan, he had needed to be *inside* the locomotive 30 seconds ago.

He could only hope that Roger would remain levelheaded enough to improvise until he arrived, and if he didn't, to do whatever was necessary to limit the loss of life.

Roger looked at the second hand on his watch. He'd never felt so alone. Not even after the first threatening phone call from O'Quinn informing him that if he did not cooperate, his son would be killed. Roger had let hope slip into his heart, allowed this stranger, Jarod, to make him believe he would be able to win. The stranger hadn't shown up and now it was all up to him. Roger was not a brave man.

In spite of all that, he decided to do a brave thing. He raised his hands and stopped typing.

The silence drew O'Quinn's attention. "Why aren't you coding?"

"'Cause I'm a fool and have been since day one. My boy's not even onboard, and no one is going to escape with you after I've turned this train into a runaway. If I'm going to die anyway, I'm not going to let you kill everyone else."

"Brave words for a weak man," O'Quinn sneered.

O'Quinn pulled out what looked like a toy gun. Roger recognized that it was made of plastic but knew it was no toy. The weapon, a 4th generation improvement of the original Lulz Liberator, was a crude, but effective 3D printed, automatic handgun, perfect for skating through metal detectors that was starting to stir the shit in the halls of the ATF. O'Quinn aimed his at Roger's head. "And I think you're bluffing."

For one of the first times in his life, Roger Hearns acted contrary to the fear controlling him. "Then push in your chips, O'Quinn—'cause I'm all in."

The man with the eye-patch cocked his weapon.

Chapter 91

MISS PARKER MOVED through car #3 and into #2 with renewed purpose. She absorbed the faces of the powerbrokers of business
and politics toasting each other with Cristal, unaware of what was happening in their midst. When she passed the last row of seats she turned and
gave Sydney a vexed look. "Perhaps we were wrong, Miss Parker, it appears
neither Jarod nor O'Quinn are on this train."

"Though I'm sure that would get you all tingly inside, we weren't
wrong. At least *I* wasn't." She read his confusion. "For fuck's sake, Sydney,
you're the one who taught him to play 3D chess, did you really expect him
to be the pawn?"

Miss Parker closed her eyes, pinched the bridge of her nose and replayed the nightmare of the last weeks. "Your avenging angel pulls off an
elaborate pretend in a hospital and then another on a Caribbean island, all
to suck the truth out of a terrorist's head. *The truth* about what is happening
on this train." She opened her eyes and faced forward, consternation on her
wrinkled brow. "And what's happening on this train is happening in ..."
Her voice trailed off as she stared into the compartment connecting to the
lead locomotive.

That was where she had to go, but there was an obstacle in her way.
Within the compartment, standing guard in front of the entrance to the locomotive was another two-ton ape who she could swear was the identical
twin to the one she saw when she first boarded the Lightning Bolt.

Miss Parker reached into her waistband and pulled out the packet Sam had given her. Inside were two thumb plunger syringes with carbon fiber needles. She turned to Sydney with quiet intensity, "You taught Jarod how to pretend; now it's your turn."

Jarod arrived at a hinged emergency access panel on the locomotive's roof. With one hand he reached into an inner pocket and pulled out a palm-sized drill with a specialized bit used to remove the first of eight aviation screws holding the panel in place. He was now 60 seconds late.

As Roger continued to stare down the barrel of O'Quinn's weapon without flinching, the man with the patch allowed a small curl to escape the edge of his lips. He reached into his jacket, pulled out a communicator and pressed a button. After another two seconds, the door to the rear of the locomotive compartment opened. Dog and Dojame entered. Between them was Luke.

"Dad!" Luke broke free and rushed toward his father's outstretched arms.

Before Roger could feel the warmth of his son in his arms, O'Quinn swooped the boy up into his own.

Roger sprung to his feet enraged. "Let him go!" O'Quinn's gun halted Roger's actions but not those of the boy squirming in his arm. In the midst of his punches and clawing, the boy got hold of O'Quinn's patch, which went flying off his face. The sight and smell of the rotten hole froze every-one in the room—except Luke, who kept struggling.

O'Quinn tilted the gun away from Roger and onto the back of Luke's head.

"Luke, stop!" Hearns screamed. Luke looked at his father. "We'll be going home soon." The boy stopped struggling.

O'Quinn handed the boy off to Dog. He retrieved his patch and while replacing it, calmly moved in, face to face with Roger. "I am a man of my word. Once you have locked in the sequence, the five of us will climb up the ladder of that chopper and go back to our lives. But ..." He turned to

Dojame and Dog. "If I haven't summoned you in 90 seconds, return with a memento of this special occasion Mr. Hearns can bring to his wife. May I suggest the boy's head?" O'Quinn waved the others back into the rear compartment, then turned to the defeated father.

"The choice is yours, Roger."

Roger sat down at the keyboard and stared at it. Jarod was a no-show. The choice indeed was his.

The two-ton guard was startled when the door to the passenger car whipped open, courtesy of Miss Parker. "I'm sorry, but this compartment is off limits," he said in a practiced monotone.

The alarm that Miss Parker was feeling inside was also noticeable on her face, half carrying a delirious Sydney clinging onto her. "Something is wrong with my father!" Miss Parker let Sydney drop to the floor inside the compartment. Sydney was grabbing his chest. The big man kneeled next to him. "Ma'am, it looks like he's having a heart attack."

"Actually, he's faking it—and *don't* call me ma'am." Before the ape had fully registered what she had said, Miss Parker plunged the syringe into his carotid artery. His *two tons* went down hard and instantly. Before Sydney could get to his feet, Miss Parker had checked to ensure their actions had not been seen by any of the passengers, removed the guard's 9mm, and checked the door, preventing access to the locomotive. It was secured by a biometric lock.

Miss Parker got beneath the big man's shoulders. "Give me a hand here, grandpa." She indicated the door. "It's a palm print reader. We either lift King Louie's fat ass or cut his arm off. Your choice."

As Sydney joined her in the heavy lift, catecholamines flooded his system, leaving him both lightheaded and with an overwhelming sense of impending doom.

Dog tossed Luke against the staff lockers that lined the walls of the compartment. The employee break room would not be utilized for the 20 minute test run which made it the perfect hiding place for a kidnapped child.

Luke rubbed the back of his head. He was scared and knew his father was as well, but he hadn't given in to the twisted man in the Adidas suit and was determined not to give in to either of these pricks. That was until the ugly man with the broken arm slid two fingers into his cast and pulled out a hardened plastic blade and looked at him.

As he approached the boy, an alarmed Dojame grabbed Dog's denim sleeve. "O'Quinn said *if he didn't* buzz us!"

Dog rolled his eyes and yanked his arm free. "Read between the lines, shit breath. There's only enough time for three of us to get up the chopper ladder. The kid's value as an insurance policy just ran out."

The boy backpedaled until he was cornered. Luke had felt every emotion possible over the last few weeks and had never given up, but as Dog's shadow fell upon him and he felt the man grip his hair and yank his head back, all hope died. The bad man was about to kill him and all he could think of was how he would never see his parents again. He would never play trains with his dad, never taste his mother's Saturday morning pancakes. As tears started to flow from his eyes, a blast of sunlight blinded him from above. A tornado seemed to have ripped a hole in the ceiling and the Hulk fell from the sky.

Jarod dropped directly atop Dog's broken arm. Before Dog could howl, he slashed at Jarod with the blade in his other. The razor edge sliced through Jarod's clothing across his chest. Dog kicked Jarod, who went down. Dog flipped the knife hilt up, blade down and dove atop the Pretender, plunging it toward Jarod's eye. Instinctively, Jarod grabbed Dog's wrist, but not before what seemed like fire erupted in his left eyebrow as the tip penetrated skin. Dog applied all his weight, intending to force the point through Jarod's eye and into his brain. As it sank deeper Jarod did the only logical thing. He stopped resisting against Dog's force, while in the same instant turning his head abruptly to the right. The blade sliced his eyebrow open as it plunged into the floor. Jarod countered Dog's downward momentum and in one motion grabbed his good arm, twisted it with all his might and spun in the opposite direction. Dog's other paw broke with a sickening snap.

As Dog let out a plaintive wail, Jarod stood, turned and focused his bloody, frigid ire onto Dojame. The terrified Indian stumbled backwards as

Jarod approached. "I'm just a doctor. I never wanted to hurt anyone! I don't even know how I got here." Before Jarod could lay a hand on him, Dojame's eyes rolled back into his head and he fainted.

Jarod turned to Luke. The boy looked at him through saucer-sized eyes. "You okay?" Jarod asked, as he tore off the wing suit.

Luke nodded, "You were at the farm, trying to save me. Who are you?"

Jarod knelt down to face him. "I'm a friend of your mom and dad's. They asked me to give you this." Jarod reached into his pocket and pulled out Luke's Hulk PEZ dispenser. Luke eagerly took it. Having something in his hand that was from home, from his real life, gave him renewed hope and trust in this strange man.

The young boy smiled at his savior. "You're bleeding."

Jarod put pressure on the cut to slow the blood flow and gave Luke a reassuring smile. "I'll be okay, and so will you." He opened one of the wall lockers. "Now, hide in here until your dad and I come get you."

Luke motioned his head toward the bad guys on the floor. "What about them?"

"They won't hurt you again. I promise."

The light bar cycled over the ape-guard's palm and the door to the locomotive unlocked before his two-ton bum hit the floor.

Miss Parker nodded to Sydney and whipped into the compartment, sweeping the room with the guard's Glock. The lights were on inside the employee's break room, but no one seemed to be home. Miss Parker moved through, gun at the ready, eyes taking in everything: the lockers, the special carpet on the pristine floor, the emergency access panel in the ceiling. *Nothing.*

They moved into position next to the door leading to the driver's compartment. Miss Parker did a silent count and when she reached three, burst inward into utter chaos. Not the one she expected.

Jarod wasn't here.

Nor was O'Quinn.

Inside the driver's compartment several corporate executives and technicians were in the midst of a panicked meltdown. Pounding at computers and staring at screens, screaming at each other, trying to understand the crisis they suddenly found themselves in. It didn't take long for Miss Parker and Sydney to untangle the madness and grasp what was happening.

"Somebody tell me what the hell is wrong?!"

"We're accelerating past our parameters ..."

"She's a runaway ..."

"Seven minutes to Newark!"

"Alert the station!"

"We've lost *all* communication—even cell signals have been cut off!"

"Hit the brakes."

"We have no brakes! We have no control!"

"It's been taken by someone else."

"Who?!"

A terrified tech looked up from her screen. "Someone in the rear locomotive control car."

Sydney and Miss Parker shared an ashen look. They were in the wrong locomotive on the wrong end of the train. She nearly knocked Sydney over as she blasted out and sprinted to the rear.

Through the windshield O'Quinn saw the chopper now 100 meters behind and closing quickly. He stood on the driver's seat, popped open the emergency escape ceiling panel, then looked back at Roger seated at the control computer. "You sure no one can override what you did?"

Roger's face had little color left in it. "This operates on a random rolling hop code." His eyes now glazed with a haunting sorrowful thousand-yard stare. "Not even I can override it now."

"Well, just to make sure ..." O'Quinn put a bullet into the computer screen at the same time the chopper appeared above the opening. Roger didn't even flinch. He simply raised his eyes to O'Quinn and said, "Tell them to bring my boy and let's go."

O'Quinn ignored him and instead signaled a thumbs up to the chopper. A rescue ladder descended and bulls-eyed into the hatch. O'Quinn scampered up the rungs, wrapped his arms in tight and finally answered Roger. "Sorry, but I can't do that."

O'Quinn raised the weapon toward Roger and pulled the trigger. A bullet ripped into Roger's leg, blowing him out of his chair. Writhing, holding his thigh he looked up, distraught.

"We had a deal!" Roger cried out with both physical and emotional agony at the betrayal.

"I lied." O'Quinn signaled the pilot to take them up. "I'm the only one leaving." As he ascended toward the hatch, he took careful aim at Roger again. Squeezing the trigger, he barely heard the words, "You're not going anywhere," as Jarod dove and slammed his shoulder into O'Quinn. The errant round shattered the chair leg just behind Roger's skull. Jarod wrapped his arms around O'Quinn's waist as the man's body was exiting through the ceiling.

The Pretender thought he heard O'Quinn's spine crack as the round peg of their bodies jammed into the square hole of the hatch, preventing the chopper's rise. The chopper bucked wildly, trying to free itself, each time painfully stretching O'Quinn more and more. Trapped halfway to safety and unable to see below to get a shot off, the bald man pressed the nose of the gun against the thin metal roof of the train and started firing wildly. Bullets rained down around Jarod, the third skimming his shoulder painfully, causing him to lose his grip on O'Quinn's thighs and drop to the floor. O'Quinn immediately began to rise, but before he could clear the hatch, Jarod grabbed the end of the ladder and wrapped it around the legs of the swivel chair. O'Quinn disappeared from the Locomotive but the metal legs lodged in the hatch.

At 400 miles an hour, the chopper above him trying frantically to fly free, O'Quinn was stuck halfway up the ladder. In the torrent of wind O'Quinn's eye patch flew off. The demented cyclops then looked down through the hatch and saw Jarod staring up at him. "Who the fuck are you!?"

Jarod looked up at him calmly and yelled, "Someone who knows there are bridges on this track—and we're about to reach one."

O'Quinn slowly turned, facing forward. As he did, the rush of wind grabbed his rotten eyeball and whisked it out of his skull and away. In that instant he wished it had taken his good one as well. That way he would not have had the visual confirmation that Karma was, in fact, a bitch. The payback for all he had done in life was the crossbeam support between the towers of the train trestle his face was now inevitably rushing toward.

Miss Parker dashed into the last passenger compartment when she and the other passengers felt the explosion rock the train and caught sight of the helicopter fireball that rained down upon the bridge that they were crossing. She knew this could mean only one thing: Jarod.

Even the two-ton ape guarding the entrance to the rear locomotive was staring out the window, wondering what the hell was happening. He wondered it again when Miss Parker whipped open the door. His fingers had just wrapped around the handle of his holstered Glock when the barrel of the one Miss Parker had taken from his twin brother kissed the spot between his eyes.

Sydney spotted several executives rushing their way. "Miss Parker, we won't be alone for long."

Parker silently acknowledged Sydney. With a nod to the guard, she snarled, "Put your palm on the reader or I'll splash your brains on the wall." The guard did as he was told. As soon as the door unlocked, she and Sydney entered, slamming the door behind them. Miss Parker smashed the handle of the Glock into the inner panel lock, shorting it out to ensure no one would be able to enter behind them. She then swept the room for movement.

It was identical to the rear compartment of the other front locomotive with two distinctions: There were blood droplets on the floor and the emergency hatch above was slightly ajar, a torn piece of material hanging from a screw. She and Sydney shared a concerned look and moved toward the door to the driver's compartment.

Jarod used his belt as a tourniquet to quell the bleeding from Roger's leg. "Forget me. Help Luke."

He finished the tie-off and lifted Roger into a new chair. "Your son is safe and needs his father." He lowered his eyes in shame.

"It won't matter now. I did what O'Quinn asked. You weren't here and ..." He looked up in anguish. "I just wanted to save my son."

"The only way to do that now is by stopping this train."

"That's impossible!" Roger offered, defeated.

"I was raised to believe that nothing is impossible."

Roger read the data. "Five minutes to impact."

"Where's the undercarriage access?"

"Below your feet, but why?"

Jarod dropped to his knees, found a loose corner of carpet and pulled it back, revealing a floor hatch. "We're in New Jersey. What if we recreated what happened at Lakehurst, but in a more ... *controlled* manner?"

Roger thought about this, his eyes going wide. "Jarod that's—insane!"

"True, but it's possible." Jarod twisted the hatch handle.

"Not at this speed, we won't be able to outrun the reaction."

Jarod looked up, dead serious. "Then make us go faster."

As Jarod said this, one could see the wheels turning in Roger's mind. "Theoretically that could work, but it would be a one in a million chance."

"Better than what we have now."

Jarod pulled open the hatch and was greeted by a pressurized whoosh from the maintenance compartment below.

"What's our best option?"

"The out-facing side of car eight."

Jarod nodded in grim determination. "Eight's my lucky number."

"Your luck just ran out." Roger and Jarod turned to see Sydney and Miss Parker. The brunette leveled the Glock on them.

Jarod looked at her, smiled broadly with genuine affection and said something she would have never imagined. "Miss Parker. I'm *so* glad you're here."

Chapter 92

MISS PARKER POPPED her signature eyebrow, perplexed. "What the hell is that supposed to mean?"

"I need your help." Jarod reached for the weapon. "Specifically, your gun." She took a step back and aimed right between his eyes. "Very funny, Jarod. Time to stop Mr. Toad's wild ride and return to the second happiest place on earth."

"That's what I am trying to do."

"Give him the gun, lady!" Roger blurted. "It's the only chance we have."

Reading the sincerity in Jarod's eyes, Sydney finally spoke. "Give it to him, Parker."

She shot an incredulous glare at Sydney. "Has the whole fucking world gone insane?"

"This part of it has," Jarod said again, offering his open hand. "Now do the right thing. Like your mother tried to."

"*Tried to*, clever Jarod, but not clever enough. You played that Mommy card with me before—fool me once shame on me, fool me twice …" Before she could finish, a chair crashed down on her arm. The Glock went skittering, stopping under the toe of Luke's Converse All-Star high-top. Luke dropped the chair he was holding and picked up the gun.

"He *said* he needed the gun, lady!"

Miss Parker shot the kid a *who-the-fuck-are-you* look.

Jarod smiled. "Say hello to Luke."

Luke tossed the gun to Jarod, then rushed to his father's waiting arms. There was no time for Jarod to relish this moment of reunion, one he had risked everything for. He still had a job to do. As he moved toward the hatch, Sydney stepped around Parker and eyed the blood dripping from his protégé's eyebrow and shoulder. "Jarod, you're hurt."

"These are wounds that will heal, Sydney." He turned to Roger. "Give me everything you have."

Roger let go of Luke and typed in commands on an auxiliary keyboard.

The Lightning Bolt lurched forward. Sydney grabbed a railing just in time, but Miss Parker didn't, and the acceleration pitched her back straight into Jarod's arms. Their faces were inches apart and their bodies were suddenly clutching each other. Their eyes locked.

In that split second, time stood still.

He smelled of blood and sweat and she felt an urge to touch his face.

He was surprised at the softness of her skin. Took in the warmth of her breath against his neck and the fresh scent from her hair—one he recalled from earlier days. All at once she was that young girl who used to sneak into the Sim lab just to watch him—*being*. Jarod's mind drifted to seeing her in the shadows watching him, wanting so badly just to touch her, but scared that doing so might chase her away.

She felt consumed by the feel of him against her, the gentle strength of his touch she'd always been denied. And now, she never wanted him to let go.

This unrequited connection that now bound them was something both felt but never spoke of. It was stronger than their human forms and in the silence of each other's eyes at that moment flashed the powerful intensity of it, the miracle of it, the seeming impossibility of it. It was a *look* the world could never see—but a moment shared that neither would ever forget.

"Jarod—we're four minutes out," Roger shouted.

Parker pulled away, Jarod knelt beside the floor hatch, was sliding in until a hand on his shoulder stopped him. Jarod turned, finding himself face to face with Sydney. "Jarod, if we don't make it, I just want you to know ..." Eyes welling, Sydney's words stuck in his throat.

Jarod nodded. "The tragedy of life is not death, but what we let die inside of us while we live." Jarod turned to Miss Parker. "Your mother knew that truth—and *many* others."

Roger looked up from his computer. "Three minutes, forty-five seconds." Jarod synched his mental clock with Roger's, then smiled and winked at Luke. "Take care of your mom and dad, okay?"

Luke nodded.

Jarod disappeared head first down into the compartment.

Chapter 93

HAVING SECRETLY NAVIGATED the Centre air vents many times, the Pretender was used to small spaces like the claustrophobic Maglev underbelly, but not the extreme cold. The massive canisters of liquid nitrogen necessary for the superconductivity that made the Maglev propulsion system possible had to be kept at extreme temperatures of -452.2 degrees Fahrenheit. The canisters were so cold that, even through Jarod's clothing, they burnt his skin. But he had to keep moving. He'd gone through Dante's nine circles of hell to save Luke and he wasn't going to give up now.

Jarod continued forward with two and a half minutes left before impact, which was really only 90 seconds since it would require a minimum of one minute for friction to stop the train before a catastrophic arrival at Newark Station.

2:10 to impact.

Miss Parker, being a control freak, yanked open the floor latch and called down, "Jarod?"

"He can't hear you." Miss Parker looked up to see Roger tucking seat cushions around Luke, who was sitting in a secure spot behind the driver's seat. "By now, he should be at least under the ninth passenger car." Finished with securing his son, he turned her way with a stern expression. "Now lock the hatch and brace yourself. There is going to be an explosion."

"An explosion? The Lakehurst thing you two were talking about?"

He answered her question with one of his own. "Remember the Hindenburg?" She gave him a look of confusion.

Sydney, positioning his body under the legs of a table, answered. "He's referring to the infamous Nazi dirigible."

"The blimp that blew?"

"Yes. Jarod is going to recreate that under the train."

"Are you fucking kidding me?" Parker asked.

"The train is a runaway. When it reaches Newark Station, it will be little more than an incoming missile. Think of it as a kinetic energy bomb with the destructive power of a little Hiroshima. Blowing it is our only hope," Roger informed.

An emotional chain reaction blindsided Miss Parker: *Shock* of the situation's reality, *confusion* surrounding Jarod's sacrifice, and the primal *fear* of dying. "Are you saying Jarod's going to put himself in the middle of a Hindenburg? Why would he do that?"

Sydney answered before Roger could. "So *we* can survive."

1:50 to impact.

Onlookers crowded around the arrival platform. Officials, dignitaries and corporate brass anxiously waiting finally caught their first glimpse of the magnificent tech beast on the horizon. Smiles grew and applause began to build, but so did the sense that something wasn't right. *The train was moving too fast.*

1:20 to impact.

Jarod reached the connection passage between cars nine and eight, but instead of continuing forward, the Pretender turned and crawled left until he reached a dead-end at a maintenance access hatch. With no time to fool with locks, he used the gun to blow it off its hinges. The equalization of air pressure nearly sucked him out of the streaking Lightning Bolt. Battered by the wind and disoriented, he moved on, inching his upper body out the opening while bracing his legs against the inner wall. Eighteen inches below, the ground streaked by at over 400 miles per hour. With the Glock gripped in both hands, he focused on the base of the eighth passenger car at his specific target: a black triangle with a white snowflake inside, the international symbol for liquid nitrogen.

Buffeted by the turbulence, knowing he had *only* one shot, Jarod calmed himself by concentrating on the single memory of his parents, the very technique he had used to conquer his apprehension so many times as a child. A diffused image of a woman with red hair rocking him in her arms danced in the back of his mind as a male voice sang a nonsense nursery rhyme, '*Kri Kraw Toads Foot, Geese Walk, Bare Foot.*'

He sharpened his gaze onto his target.

One minute to impact.

His last thought, as he squeezed the trigger, was *where are my mom and dad?*

Then all was silent.

Chapter 94

THE EXPLOSION ROCKED Parker into Sydney's arms.

Roger rolled protectively on top of Luke, shielding him as the second canister blew. They could hear the panicked cries of the other passengers as the chain reaction of explosions moved methodically up the outer left side of each train car like a choreographed Fourth of July fireworks show.

30 seconds to impact.

The joy and applause from those on the arrival platform stopped cold at the sound of the first detonation. The flames exploding out from under The Lightning Bolt reflected in the terrified eyes of the onlookers. For an instant, they watched the now out of control Maglev on a straight trajectory for the platform where they stood. Calm was not in the cards as bodies scattered, running haphazardly like ants from their crushed hill. Gasps and screams reached a fever pitch as the train lost levitation and collapsed down onto the track. Sparks from the scraping of metal on metal flew everywhere, the fury of the friction emitted a high-pitched scream amid the crunching cacophony, yet the beast miraculously remained in its tracks as it roared toward its eminent demise.

10 seconds … smoke everywhere. 5 … bodies diving for cover. 3 … the steel on steel a deafening roar. 1 … passenger faces pressed against glass, silently screaming from their front row seats to a grizzly death. And then—silence.

The train hissed and moaned in its stillness, stopping only ten feet from the platform. Given a sudden re-gift of life, of being spared, those still atop the would-be ground zero gazed out with stunned silence at the slayed dragon.

Chapter 95

WHAT WAS LEFT of the derailed Lightning Bolt hissed and moaned like a wounded sidewinder on hot asphalt. Smoke, fear and panic enveloped the post-relief euphoria on the arrival platform. Officials scurried around on their phones feverishly spinning the event and pointing fingers. Rescue teams used the Jaws of Life to pry open doors, allowing shocked passengers to spill out. Although it was clearly a disaster, it was nothing like it could have been.

No one had died—at least, *onboard.*

Miss Parker was the last of the four in the rear locomotive to pick herself up off the floor. Rubbing her eyes, she gazed over to Roger, who was already shouldering the locomotive door, yelling at rescuers on the other side, desperate to get him and his son to freedom. Sydney on the other hand was sitting silently in the driver's seat, staring solemnly out the window at the Jersey countryside. *As usual,* she thought, *he was in his own world.*

She knelt and opened the hatch into which Jarod had vanished. Savior of hundreds of lives or not, he was her quarry, and she still had a job to do.

Miss Parker peered into the darkness thick with vapor and smoke. She could feel fresh cool air coming from somewhere and slithered her frame inside.

Through the tunnel of twisted metal and blown tanks she slid under the locomotive to the passenger car connected to it. At the junction with the subsequent compartment, darkness gave way to sunlight and crisp air reached in from her left. She crawled toward the icy breeze and climbed out of a huge gash blown through the train skin and to the outside.

Miss Parker walked back on the tracks, senses alert, looking for any trace of Jarod. She feared finding the mangled remains of his body, almost as much as not finding him at all.

Then she saw it.

Crumpled on the rails, one sleeve flapping in the breeze, was the tattered remnants of the jacket Jarod had worn. There was nothing else of him she could find.

Miss Parker picked it up and, following her first impulse, brought it to her nose and took in a deep breath. At that moment she couldn't have said why she did it, but she did. The smell of Jarod was still there, the same scent she had smelled on his neck not five minutes before.

With tragedy's smoke wafting back at her, wind tussling her hair as sporadically as the memories swirling in her mind, Miss Parker stood in the Jersey sunshine, just ... *holding* Jarod.

Stumbling down the tracks, a thousand-yard stare in his eyes, Sydney swiped the wild strands of hair off his forehead. He searched the multitudes of people wondering, hoping, *praying* that one of them was Jarod. When he spotted Miss Parker and what she was holding, tears slipped down his cheeks.

A woman's cry of "Oh my God!" startled both of them out of their moments.

Sydney and Miss Parker turned to look at the woman now running straight for them. But she ran right past, instead sweeping up into her arms the young boy named Luke, hugging him like she would never let him go.

Miss Parker gazed evenly at Sydney. For the first time since she'd been called in to search for the Pretender, she spoke to him without an ounce of malice.

"Let's go home, Syd."

Sydney looked at her, surprised by her genuineness—and his sense of *disgust*.

Ignoring her, he turned and walked away.

Chapter 96

EIGHT HOURS LATER, Sydney's flashlight's beam was swallowed by the utter blackness. He had forgotten how dark it was inside the shaft. What had it been, 20, 30 years since he'd last traversed it?

Nearing the end of the mile-long tunnel that originated behind the Ceon Forest waterfall, on Delphine Creek, Sydney's eyes still hadn't adjusted to the darkness. Directly above him was some of the most fertile land in eastern Delaware, soil from which grew incredibly rich grasses that fed unbelievably expensive horses on farms of people of wealth and privilege like Mr. Parker and his forbearers. It was in the basement of the historical mansion that three Parker generations called home that the passageway ended.

At the hidden doorway an ice-cold droplet of water splashed onto Sydney's forehead. Catherine Parker had once told him that she thought the droplets that fell from the brick ceiling were the tears of the slaves whose hands had originally dug the tunnel and later, those who escaped through it as an underground railroad to freedom in the north.

Long before the miscarriages, long before Catherine was finally blessed with her Little Miss, she had discovered the forgotten tunnel while overseeing the restoration of the mansion's wine cellar. It was the night of the Parkers' first major fight, the first time Catherine questioned her husband about the Genius Project and other Centre studies involving children. It was also the first time she questioned her physical safety—frightened by a look in his eyes, one she had never experienced before. As the confrontation escalated, she felt the need to flee and had ended up hiding in the basement behind a forgotten rack of Pinot's. While leaning against the wall she felt a wisp of cool air leaching in through a crack in the plaster. Curious, she picked at the decaying lime and sand until the crack became a small hole through which she caught her first glimpse of the slave tunnel beyond.

Fueled by a growing fear of her husband's volatility, Catherine kept the tunnel secret. Over the years she used it for both refuge and safe passage in and out of the mansion. Sydney secretly met Catherine in the tunnel on several occasions—for reasons he did not want to recall. As he reached for the hinged panel with which Catherine had replaced the plaster wall, he thought about how he had failed her. In the aftermath of the Maglev crash he had decided not to fail any longer. Even if his Pretender had not survived to discover his true identity, the least he could do, in Jarod's memory, was to discover that truth for him.

Sydney doused the flashlight, reached into his pocket, donned night vision goggles and, for the second time in a week, entered into yet another world of secrets and lies.

The wine cellar was vast and green and silent. River rock walls surrounded rows upon rows of wine racks. Venturing in, Sydney passed a wooden staircase that rose up to the kitchen door. Heart pounding, he stopped, looked and listened. There was no light coming from beneath the door, no footsteps that he could detect, all of which he took as a good sign.

He kept moving to his destination, a door at the front edge of the fourteenth rack of wine, and found the hand-carved door just where he remembered seeing it so long ago.

On that night, Catherine had told him many, many things. One of which was that Mr. Parker stored important papers in the file room his father had installed in early 1950, a room in which it was rumored Grandfather Parker brought his numerous paramours for trysts during Triumvirate dinner parties.

One twist of the knob and Sydney was inside. The furnishings were sparse: one large wooden desk and two high-backed leather chairs surrounded, floor to ceiling, by wooden oak file drawers. There had to be 300 to 400 drawers. None were labeled by name, only number. Everything was dusty and appeared little used, which would complicate Sydney's work. While he desperately wanted to find Jarod's secrets, if the intrusion here was discovered, self preservation demanded he not leave a trail leading back to him. Careful to slip his gloved fingers behind the brass drawer handles, he slowly began opening and closing file drawers searching the contents inside. He was shocked at some of what he saw: yellowing files in German with mentions of Nazi atrocities, others regarding kidnappings by the OSS, an array of Cold War projects, a whole drawer given over to the *Argentine Problem*, an entire cabinet of files code-named *Dealey Plaza* and several more filled with distinct red files.

A creak on the floor above caused Sydney's heart to skip a beat. He wasn't alone in the house and yet he had just begun his search. *Think, Sydney. What would Jarod do?*

Sydney methodically scanned each drawer in the room. They all looked exactly the same—except for one. The dust on drawer #318 showed fresh handprints left by someone who had recently opened and closed it.

He quietly pulled it open. The two-foot deep drawer contained a hanging folder rack exclusively belonging to a massive file labeled: *Jarod*.

But the file was empty.

Someone had beaten him here. In frustration Sydney shoved the empty file folders and noticed something lodged in the bottom of the drawer. Fallen or overlooked when the contents were removed, there was a small manila envelope that had to be at least 30 years old.

He reached in and picked it up. As he opened it and eyed the photograph inside, he heard the cellar door from the kitchen above open. Someone was coming.

Pocketing the envelope, Sydney closed the drawer. As he exited the file room, he heard people coming down the wooden stairs; four feet, two voices; one dominant, that he recognized as Mr. Parker, the other wheezing and gravely. "The Jarod situation has gone goddamned nuclear!" he heard Mr. Parker bark.

Sydney pondered if he could make it back to the door he came in through, unobserved, when a visual explosion went off. Mr. Parker turned the lights on, temporarily blinding the Belgian shrink who was still wearing the night vision goggles. Sydney lifted the device from his eyes and, as he spun to glue his back against a rack of Cabernets, he nearly fell.

While rubbing his searing retinas, he listened, trying to determine down which row of wine racks the men were approaching.

Mr. Parker continued, "And with that fucking Zane stirring the cauldron, those ignorant Swahilis are slapping on their loin cloths and sharpening their spears for me!"

Sydney thought he heard shoes pivoting one rack over, the squeaking sound telling him they turned up the row to his right and were headed directly his way.

The psychiatrist felt his sight slowly returning, as he slipped left into the parallel row, catching blurred movements and realizing if he could see them, they could see him. He dropped on all fours and peered through the bottles at their feet passing inches away. The first set belonged to Mr. Parker. The person following then spoke up, "The situation is bad but not unsolvable. Don't worry, Mr. Parker. I will always have your back."

Sydney held his breath for what seemed like a lifetime until the two men entered the file room. Sydney turned and sprinted the opposite way through Catherine's tunnel.

His eyes still stinging, Sydney was not positive about the identity of the person with Mr. Parker, but he could have sworn they were pulling a wheeled oxygen tank that squeaked.

Chapter 97

MISS PARKER RODE in silence as the North Tower elevator ascended. The only reason she had returned to the Centre and not straight into a bath of Maker's Mark was the realization that she was going to face the music one way or the other. Might as well face it head-on tonight. Write up and send her report to her father about the day's debacle.

When the doors opened on the second to the top floor, she was greeted by the nasty tomcat, Spike.

The defiant feline stopped scratching the back of his ear and stared at her with his penetrating glare. Then, as if sensing her anguish, he softened his aggressive stance and, for the first time in his life, moved aside.

Miss Parker moved on through the lonely hallway. She normally loved the noise her stilettos made on the marble, the sound of power, of presence, but tonight it just rang hollow. When she rounded the corner to her office door she found Daphne there to greet her. The blonde offered her a protein shake.

"Thought you might need this."

"Not hungry tonight."

Daphne nodded knowingly. "Then a heads-up—word around the campfire is Cornelius didn't take his dismissal lightly."

"Too bad I didn't shoot the prick when I had the chance. I might feel better right now." Miss Parker reached for the doorknob, stopping when Daphne gently touched her arm.

"I'm sorry, Miss Parker—about what happened today. If you need anything …"

"Appreciate it." Miss Parker moved past Daphne's sympathetic eyes, and entered her office.

As soon as she opened the door, Miss Parker spotted someone sitting on her chair, facing away, typing at her computer.

The top of her head almost exploded because of the back of the head she was staring at.

The little bald bastard's chrome dome was peeking up from behind her office chair. His little monkey hands were typing on her computer keyboard. Miss Parker had survived a train wreck—but damned if she was going to let Cornelius be so lucky.

It took her three strides to reach the chair, two stifled F-bombs to rear back, one kick to spin him around and a split second to press the barrel of her Smith & Wesson against his forehead. Miss Parker was about to blow his *single eyebrow* out the back of his bald head when she realized the terrified man in her chair actually had *two*.

She leaned back for a better look, and realized much to her shock that the *him* sitting before her was not Cornelius but a face she didn't realize to this moment she had missed. "*Broots*?!"

In the flesh. Face scrunching, lip quivering, eyes darting, nads shrinking, finger twitching Broots. "What the hell are you doing here?" Parker glared.

"Whaddya mean? I ca-ca-came from where you banished me as soon as I got your message. I'm back to help you catch Jarod."

She re-holstered her gun.

"Afraid you're too late."

"Are you sure?"

She gave him the evil eye. "What do you know?!"

"N-Nothing!" Broots instinctively stood and started backpedaling. "You know I've never known anything. Well, except for …"

She stalked him step for step. "Except for what?"

Out of real estate, Broots' back slammed against the handmade bar from which he grabbed a package. "This was just delivered for you a few minutes ago. And, well—"

Miss Parker snatched it out of his hands. He flinched and continued. "That's Jarod's handwriting, isn't it?"

She stared at the address, then ripped the package open. Inside was a shoebox diorama of the old abandoned church where her mother was buried.

Chapter 98

THE VOLVO WAS idling.

So was Sydney.

He watched his breath as he sat outside the French Colonial. Even after today's ordeal, although a goblet of *Vin de pays des Jardins de Wallonie* was calling to him, he was in no rush to enter the lonely cavern in which he lived—or was it where he hid? The truth was, hiding was what he'd really been doing for as long as he could remember.

Bucket of bolts as it was, the Volvo had a great heater and, sitting there with his windows down, eyeing the photograph he found at Mr. Parker's, the rush of hot air onto his loafers was the only warmth he was feeling at the moment.

Only your heart is cold. Isn't that why your sorry ass is sitting out here? Because of the chill that comes with going inside that house—the chill of your own voice echoing back to you over and over—a chill that grows with each passing day like freezer burn on your soul?

Sydney couldn't get out of his mind the images Jarod had left on Kaj's body for them to find: a broken heart and the word *truth*.

Why do things break your heart? What was the truth anyway? About anything? It's just a seemingly endless tangled chain, isn't it? The Centre's lies, your own misplaced loyalties, lack of courage, self-delusion about what really was best for Jarod all those years?

Sydney turned the ignition off. *Mental masturbation can just as easily be done inside* as he knew all too well but as he started to roll his window up, he heard something familiar. He paused to listen, the sound was music—the song *Piel Canela.*

It was coming from inside the house.

Sydney nudged open the front door. He listened, then followed the source.

The music was coming from his son's nursery.

Sydney walked toward it, trepidation building. He peeked into the crack of the ajar door and spotted a 60's-style portable turntable, Eydie Gorme on vinyl spinning, crackling.

The song, usually soothing, now had his stomach roiling. He nudged the door open all the way and his world seemed to brighten. Though battered and bruised, standing there staring into his son's empty crib, holding a baby pillow with the name Patrick Sydney Günterläde II embroidered onto it, was Jarod.

"My God—I thought you'd been killed?" Sydney breathed, surprise and relief flooding through his veins.

"Not hardly. But it has been quite a day." Jarod smiled wryly. "But even the most difficult ones aren't so bad when you're free."

As Jarod replaced the pillow into the crib, Sydney felt the urge to run and hug his Pretender, but fearing a very possible rejection, instead blurted out, "I did what you asked! At Mr. Parker's." Sydney reached into his jacket and handed Jarod the manila envelope. Jarod looked inside, eyes scanning the photograph contained within.

"It's not everything you wanted but it is all there was. Hopefully it's a first step."

"Then we're even." Jarod gazed into the crib.

Sydney followed his eyes. Next to the pillow where Sydney's infant son had once rested his head, was a box. Jarod's mentor hesitantly walked over. "What is it?"

"A first step."

"To what?"

"The truth," he answered. "The truth as to why this room is empty."

Sydney slowly reached in and lifted the box lid. Inside he found a police file. He picked it up and began to go through it. Confusion formed on his face. "I don't understand—this is from a crime that happened years before my Amalia and Patrick vanished. How can *this* tell me the truth about what happened to them?"

Sydney looked up and over, but the Pretender was gone.

Chapter 99

SCREW JAROD'S FOURTH grade diorama. Screw Jarod's immature folly to manipulate her. Dead or not, *screw Jarod!*

Following her shocking but predictably frustrating encounter with Broots, Miss Parker jettisoned any thought of writing her report to Daddy.

She vowed to get in her Porsche and go straight home for her overdue meeting with three cubes and four fingers of Maker's Mark.

She vowed to climb into one of her excruciating ice baths, the glorious agony which always served her soul a summons to numb the pain.

She was convinced she had sealed the deal with herself, but as she reached for her open briefcase on the floor, Jarod's diorama tumbled off her desk, bounced off her left foot and landed right inside.

Parker hated so-called *omens,* but not even her overused denial gene could doubt that this was likely one. Probably a monumental one. It was as if her angels—no, make that her demons, were screaming—*try ignoring this one, bitch.*

She glared at the diorama—*You wanna fuck with me, God or whomever you are? Bring it. You wanna give me the facial from hell after the day, weeks, months I've just had? Game on.*

Which is how she ended up wobbling past her car in the Centre parking lot with the neck of her half empty office bottle of Maker's wrapped in her fist. How she ended up trudging into the blackness of the Blue Cove night toward her mother's grave.

What she found there were freshly cut daffodils, piled in an orderly fashion, atop Catherine's grave. *Daffodils, mother's favorite.*

Parker sat down, Catherine's headstone as her backrest. She swigged from the bottle and looked around, checking her morbid surroundings for eyes from the night that should not see. Satisfied, her body slackened, she lowered her guard and allowed her mind to drift without stopping it. Two overarching thoughts echoed inside. *How the fuck did I end up here and why did you leave me?*

Miss Parker angrily grabbed a handful of the flowers and tossed them as far as she could. The action did not change her mood, but seeing something beneath where they had been, did.

A tinge of red plastic.

She swept the remaining daffodils away, revealing another Etch A Sketch. Miss Parker's eyes filled with fury. *Okay, Jarod, you wanna do this at my personal ground zero, then do it. At least my blood-letting will stay in the gene pool.*

On the toy's screen a picture began to appear—this time it was the face of Catherine Parker, tears welling in her eyes, followed by words that sprang up one by one: *I know the truth about what makes you sad.*

There wasn't the slightest bit of doubt in Miss Parker's mind that Jarod *did* know. *The son of a bitch.*

Miss Parker began to weep. She took another long pull from her bottle until a stallion's whinny startled her.

She looked up, squinted through the darkness and found Jarod on horseback watching her from a clearing in the trees. "I knew you being dead was too good to be true," she growled. She pulled her gun but was too drunk to aim it. *Perfect,* she thought. She lowered it, took another swig, trying to wash the bitterness away, then looked back over to him, tears now painting her face. "Why the hell are you doing this to me?"

"A long time ago your mother helped me try to escape the Centre. I want to do the same thing for you." Jarod replied.

"By making me watch her die?"

"No, Little Miss. By letting you see the truth—for once."

Their eyes locked, but there were no more words. With a gentle kick, Jarod's horse reared and turned on its hind legs, then galloped into the night.

Parker's now spinning head drooped down, staring once again at the Etch A Sketch. The drawing of her mother began to move. Springing to life, the screen image morphed into live action surveillance video with time code. The image widened along with Miss Parker's eyes.

Catherine hurried down the dark Sim level corridor, anxiously pressing the call button for the elevator. She dabbed her tears, tried to calm her harsh breathing and tore open an envelope she pulled from her pocket.

Inside was a single cocktail napkin.

Jarod had employed some kind of digital magic to zoom in on the square of paper itself on which were printed the words: *The Snake Eyes Lounge* with the logo of *a hissing rattler with dice for eyes.* Handwritten just below that: *4 p.m. —W.S.*

Catherine looked over her shoulder then anxiously folded the cocktail napkin and carefully slid it into her bra.

She then heard a sound and looked down to the end of the corridor where a figure in the shadows was watching her as the elevator tolled its arrival.

As Catherine boarded the empty lift, the Etch A Sketch's image shifted to a surveillance angle inside the elevator and above her.

Miss Parker's head started shaking as more tears streamed down her face. Did she really want to see her mother's suicide? She pawed at the Etch A Sketch knobs to kill the image, but it wouldn't stop playing. She then regathered the daffodils and tossed them back onto the toy to cover the screen.

As she did, a glint of moonlight flickered off her mother's square platinum ring. She froze, remembering the last time she had seen her mother wearing it.

Catherine had just tucked her in and kissed her good night. While closing her bedroom door, she looked back at her daughter and pointedly said, "I love you, Little Miss." As she clung onto her Etch A Sketch, Little Miss didn't know that would be the last kiss her mother would ever give her—or the last time she would see her alive.

As Miss Parker wiped her tears, she heard the audio playing from beneath the daffodils. Two raised voices, her mother's and a man's she didn't recognize. She couldn't tell what they were saying but they were followed by a woman's scream—her mother's scream. Miss Parker closed her eyes tightly, shuddering when a gunshot rang out.

Listening to the sounds of building chaos that erupted from under the flowers—people running, shouting, doors crashing open—Miss Parker felt like she would throw up. She had heard enough—*more than enough.* While she stumbled to her feet, another familiar voice screamed out from below the daffodils. It was hers.

"Momma, no! Momma! No!!!"

A man yelled, "Get her out of here!"

Little Miss Parker's voice cried in anguish. "No! Let me go to my mother! Let me go!"

The man yelled again. "Get everyone out of here!"

Unable to bare witness to her past any longer, Miss Parker turned to walk away, but as she did, the sounds from the hallway where her mother had died, the haunting echoes from her past, suddenly went quiet.

She stared down at the pile of daffodils. There was nothing but a peaceful silence coming from beneath them now—a silence then shattered as a series of gunshots rang out from the video playing at her feet. The one she could not bear to watch.

Chapter 100

INSIDE THE RAKE barge, Oscar suddenly raised up on his hind legs and began sniffing the air.

Outside, a cab deposited Jarod at Pier 53. He carried two large duffle bags that he set down on the deck as he boarded, a pacing Chaz waited there to greet him with a hug and a scowl.

"We saw it all on the news, 'Nilla boy, but the deats was sketchy and we didn't hear back." She playfully slapped his chest, then mock glared— "What? None of those 100 cell phones of yours workin' these days?"

Jarod laughed and then Chaz hugged him even harder.

"Sky's inside waitin' for ya. I got my cute little bag packed already."

Jarod looked away with a hint of sadness. He knew that he couldn't stay with his three new friends. His presence in their lives placed them in as much danger from the Centre as he was—only they were expendable. Painful though it was, it was time to move on.

"S'okay J-Rod, a girl can sense when it's time to find a new street corner."

Chaz used one of her French tipped nails to lift Jarod's chin up. "Like Bob Marley once said—*In this bright future you cannot forget your past*. You, my incredible friend, have made mine bright and I will *never* forget our past together."

This made Jarod smile. "Where will you go?"

"Here, there, wherever." Chaz laughed—"Harlem's home, so likely the same place you first met me."

Jarod opened one of the two canvas bags. Chaz peered inside, seeing bundles of hundred dollar bills, so many she almost fainted.

"For you to start a new life, even if it's still in the old neighborhood but it does come with one stipulation."

Chaz felt tears forming in the corners of her eyes. "For all this, you can have two."

Jarod opened the top of the other bag. It was filled with every cookie imaginable. Jarod tossed a thumb toward Oscar, who had crawled out onto the barge roof, raising and wiggling his tail in a happy dance. "Promise you'll keep my buddy supplied with the good stuff."

"Anything you say big boss." Chaz began to cry and slapped Jarod's chest once more. "Now get on in there so this girl can have a good cry to herself, okay?"

As Jarod smiled and disappeared below, Chaz and Oscar both looked over at the Pretender and shook their heads.

"I'm gonna miss that crazy man, too." Chaz then began her good cry, tears lasting long after Jarod was out of sight.

The single sheet of paper Jarod had handed to Skylar not a minute earlier nearly slipped from her fingers under disbelieving eyes. It was heavier now, stained with her tears. "How—how did you find this?"

Jarod sat gently next to her. "It doesn't matter. All that does is you have it now."

On the paper was a photo and a Maryland address of a man Jarod believed was Skylar's natural father. The most telling familial trait was that the man was staring back with deep violet eyes.

Skylar wrapped her arms around Jarod's neck, her emotions flowing uncontrollably against his warmth.

They stayed that way, in their silent embrace, neither wanting to let go. Two people changed forever by their brief union, two souls crossing the cosmos at intersecting lines drawn by a higher power.

Skylar cupped his cheek in her hand. "Where will you go?"

Jarod pulled the small envelope Sydney gave him from his pocket and removed the photo inside. "To search for someone."

Skylar peered over his shoulder. "Who is she?"

"Someone who was waiting for my train to come in many years ago." A wistful look crossed Jarod's features. "Someone who loves me." Jarod gazed at the photo, then lightly touched the face of the striking woman in it, a woman with auburn hair.

And in that instant, Jarod allowed himself to become lost in the hopeful possibilities of her.

His new journey was about to begin.

IT'S ALL ABOUT THE FANS

The Pretender fandom is the most amazing, interactive fan base in the world … so much so that The Pretender is not only created for them, but *by* them.

The cover of this book was designed by a fan.

The cover of this book was chosen by the fans.

The covers of all future Pretender books will be created by the fans.

Dozens of fans have become characters *within* the novels and *within* the continuing storylines on our website. They have become part of The Pretender, forever.

Our website, http://www.thepretenderlives.com was not only created by three very special fans, but it was designed as a community and playground for likeminded fans to come and explore and *be a part* of everything in The Pretender Universe.

Within the site, there are fans building interactive maps that show everywhere Jarod has been and what he did there. There are fans building out the Centre sublevels as a place we can explore to learn more about Centre secrets. There are fans writing fiction, some of which will become canon of The Pretender mythology and be published within either a future novel or on the website. And much, much more.

The opportunities with The Pretender Universe are only limited by your imagination.

The Pretender Universe and its incredible stories will always be expanding.

Come be a part of it at http://www.thepretenderlives.com.

<u>Next in the Pretender Universe…</u>

The Shattered Doll

Ever wondered how Miss Parker *became* Miss Parker? What happened to the nice young girl between the 'suicide' of her mother and when she became the acerbic wünderkind operative in search of the Centre's escaped Pretender? Book One of the Young Miss Parker Series, *The Shattered Doll*, will show you.

Sexy, funny, and deeply personal, young Miss Parker's formative journey to adulthood begins in *the Shattered Doll*, an edge-of-your-seat thrill ride set in her freshman year at CIT, the Centre's Indoctrination Training, a university known for producing ruthless agents. There, she is taught to kill, infiltrate, connive, and succeed at any cost, molding her into a bitter, unforgiving ball breaker.

In the world of *The Shattered Doll*, growing up can be a real bitch.

Patterns

Book One of the investigative psychological crime thriller series *Patterns,* is a pulse-racing page-turner that shadows the exploits of a brilliant, one-of-a-kind investigator traversing the world's underbelly, stalking the psychological fingerprints of his prey in pursuit of the world's most notorious serial killers, while struggling with his own troubled soul.

As his mentor, an enigma known only as Jarod, once told him, "Sometimes, to catch a sociopathic killer, you have to *become* one."

A Personal Thank You From Steven Long Mitchell and Craig W Van Sickle:

We loved writing the Second Pretender Novel *Saving Luke* and we hope you enjoyed reading it! We really want to hear from you about the book, and it would really be great you'd send us an email to introduce yourself and share your thoughts. We respond personally to all of our readers.

Be sure to get on our mailing list so you don't miss out on notifications about future books, Pretender related news, updates and contests.

Please send an email to us at **centreinsider@thepretenderlives.com** and introduce yourself, so we can personally thank you for trying our books.